AD LUMEN PRESS

American River College

LET THE WATER HOLD ME DOWN

A NOVEL

MICHAEL SPURGEON

AD LUMEN PRESS

Sacramento

For information address Ad Lumen Press
American River College | 4700 College Oak Drive, Sacramento, CA 95841
www.adlumenpress.com
Part of the Los Rios Community College District

LIBRARY OF CONGRESS CATALOGING-IN-PUBLICATION DATA

Spurgeon, Michael, 1970-
    Let the water hold me down / Michael Spurgeon.
        pages cm
    ISBN 978-0-9860374-4-3 (hard cover) — ISBN 978-0-9860374-5-0 (pbk.) — ISBN
978-0-9860374-6-7 (kindle) —
    ISBN 978-0-9860374-7-4 (epub) — ISBN 978-0-9860374-8-1 (pdf)
    1. Americans — Mexico — Fiction. 2. Chiapas (Mexico) — History — Peasant Uprising,
1994 — Fiction. I. Title.
    PS3619.P87L48 2013
    813'.6 — dc23

THIRD US EDITION 2014

This book is for Elizabeth.

And you may ask yourself—well … how did I get here?
Letting the days go by / let the water hold me down
—Talking Heads

No te fíes del mexicano que fuma puro
ni del gringo que te dice compadre.
—Chicano Proverb

I

1

I first met César Lobos de Madrid in our junior year of college. I went to one of those small, interchangeable liberal arts schools that dot the New England countryside and it always seemed an unlikely place to meet someone like César. Even though the college made a big deal of diversity, the student body was mostly upper-middle-class WASPs like me. As far as I know, César was the only person of Latino descent in my entire class. Of course, César didn't look much like most Latinos because he was white, not mestizo. He could trace both sides of his family all the way back to fifteenth-century Spain and he looked every bit like his European forefathers. He looked like the Mexicans you see on Spanish-language TV. Watch it sometime and you'll know what I mean. More fair skin than a Swedish ski team. Also, César didn't come from the average Mexican socioeconomic class. His family was one of the oldest, wealthiest, and most politically connected in Chiapas, if not in all of Mexico. They'd made their money in mahogany and coffee and land and cattle and oil and politics and who knows what else. There's no doubt that if César had wanted to go to any of the Ivy Leagues, he could have. He was smart and studious enough, or if he wasn't, his father could have built a dorm or library or hospital or something to get him admitted. But as it was, César ended up at my little second-tier college for overprivileged white kids. His father, it turned out, had a great admiration for a particular economics professor who'd made a big stir in Reagan's first administration. Señor Lobos de Madrid wanted his son to study with this conservative economist, so he pulled some strings to postpone César's enlistment in Mexico's compulsory military service and shipped him off to Vermont, where César became the darling of a certain faction of the econ department.

Of course when Coach first introduced us, I didn't care about the Lobos de Madrid family's interest in supply-side economics. What I cared about was César's talent as a striker. He was an absolute soccer phenom. In my freshman and sophomore years we'd been playoff contenders thanks entirely to a defense anchored by Billy Jones in goal, Chris Thompson at sweeper, and me at left back. Our problem was scoring. We just didn't have any offensive weapons. If we fell behind, that was it. Hit the showers boys and we'll get 'em next time. But all that changed with César's arrival. In his first season he shattered the league's single-season scoring record. Senior year it was like we were playing with three extra guys. We went undefeated and won the division championship by a score of six to one. César scored four goals and was unanimously voted the league's MVP. He was so good that after he went back to Mexico and completed his stint in the military, he played three seasons with Cruz Azul in Mexico's professional league. He got passed over for the 1990 World Cup, but just barely, and there was talk that he would probably be called up to the national team the next time around. He was that good. Then, in an improbable accident, he shattered his femur on a goalpost during a corner kick and was forced to end his career. More than one analyst described it as a sad day for Mexican soccer.

But it wasn't just his soccer skill that I liked. I liked him. Almost everyone did. He had unusual charm. Sure it didn't hurt that he was a rich, good-looking star athlete with just enough

Latin lilt in his voice to, in the words of a female classmate, "make a lady cross her legs," but he had something more to his personality, something less tangible, something magnetic.

He could be in a crowd of fifty people and he'd make every one of them feel like the most interesting person in the room. He hadn't been on campus more than forty-eight hours when he showed up at a party and left with Lesley Brandtforth Covington, universally recognized as the most attractive and unapproachable woman on campus.

The funny thing is that for all his popularity, very few people actually knew César. You could have a conversation with him and, because he listened and made you feel important, you'd think you'd made some profoundly intimate connection, but more likely than not, you would have learned next to nothing about him. Just about everyone who met him would refer to César as a friend, even a close friend, but I'd bet only a handful of us knew anything about him besides that he was a soccer star and came from someplace in Mexico that nobody had heard of.

Part of it was César's natural personality. Some people are simply born with more charisma than others and he was one of those people. But his family cultivated that quality too. César grew up with what I can only call old-world values. Being a good listener and making other people feel comfortable was, for César, a question of good manners, a matter of grace. Of course, it's easier to be a polite listener if people aren't always telling you about their problems and faults. In César's world, people, particularly men, didn't talk about their private lives or personal problems. He was horrified by the whole touchy-feely American thing about expressing yourself and sharing your feelings. As far as he was concerned, that was what the confessional was for, and although César was Catholic by culture, he wasn't someone to spend Sundays in church. Really, he was a caballero in the classical sense of the word. If something bad happened that he couldn't control, César picked it up and carried it, chalking it up to *mala fortuna*. If something bad happened that he could control, he took his licks and then took action. What he didn't do was go sob his guts out to someone else. And he didn't appreciate men who did.

One night in college Johnny Gilbride got drunk and came crying about his girlfriend cheating on him. César had been on campus only a month or so, but because César was César, Johnny went to him with his problem. César listened and ultimately sent Johnny away feeling better. But from that moment on, César lost all respect for Johnny. For César, a man simply didn't break down and blubber over an unfaithful girlfriend. To behave that way showed a certain flaw in character—a lack of moral toughness and a degree of bad manners. He never said another word about it, but he also never looked at Johnny the same way again.

I felt bad for Johnny because he never did realize that César wouldn't be caught alone with him. To tell the truth, though, the incident didn't make me like César any less. If one of my American friends had thought the way he had, I'd have thought the guy was being a narrow-minded jackass, but because César's reaction was cultural, it seemed somehow acceptable, even appropriate. Plus it was pretty amusing to see the lengths to which he would go to avoid poor Johnny. I don't think César ever did find a balance at school between being polite and avoiding people who wanted to tell him their woes. Of course, as I'd later learn, there came a point at which social etiquette mattered less. There came a point when such trivialities as manners mattered not at all. But I didn't know that then.

So just about everybody liked César and liked him a lot, even if they didn't really know him. I don't hold that against anyone. We were best friends, and it turns out I didn't know him all that well either.

Now before someone says maybe I just thought we were best

friends and maybe he was duping me the way he did Johnny, save it. César and I hit it off from the start.

One reason we became such fast friends was that I could speak Spanish. Growing up in the West, I'd studied Spanish in high school and found I had a natural knack for the language. Also, a high school job as a short-order cook where most of the other guys in the kitchen were Mexican and spoke limited English gave me lots of chances to practice. Once in college, I breezed through the course sequence for the foreign language requirement and then ended up taking an extra semester of advanced conversational Spanish as an independent study to make up units from a dropped Humanities class. It was the easiest A I ever earned.

My fluent Spanish might not sound like such a big deal given that César's English was flawless, but it was. César was proud to be Mexican and he didn't appreciate that some of our classmates seemed to think of Mexico as little more than a spring-break beach resort. He even became rankled when people asked him what he thought of America and Americans, like Mexico isn't in America. So the fact that I could speak Spanish showed a certain respect for his identity, or at least an awareness, and as a result I earned César's trust as few others could. Our conversations in Spanish provided us with an intimacy and they definitely improved my command of the language.

The other instant connection we had was soccer or, more specifically, Mexican fútbol. One of the ways my high school Spanish teacher had us practice the language was by reading newspapers and whatnot, so I'd taken to reading Mexican fúbol magazines and had become a fan. I followed teams like Chivas de Guadalajara and America and Pumas de la UNAM, and César and I spent countless hours talking about the merits of certain players and teams. Even then César knew he would go pro, and he was constantly revising an imaginary roster of guys with whom and against whom he'd like to play. That I actually knew the names of the players he was talking about served as something of a homesickness salve for him during the cold Vermont winters.

It's not like we ever sat around talking about our friendship, but I knew it was important to him. For a while, I didn't understand how important. Because he was such a force of personality, I couldn't help but feel like I was sort of following him around, like I was getting all the advantages of his company. There's no doubt things were more fun when he was around. And then one day César and I walked into the locker room after practice and Billy Jones referred to us as "Batman and Robin."

"I'm nobody's Robin," César said, his index finger jabbed into Billy's chest. César was pissed.

Of course Billy hadn't meant that I was the Batman of our duo, but César's response made me think differently about our friendship and myself. He wasn't anyone's sidekick, but it turned out he didn't think I was either. That was something of a revelation for me. It was a huge ego boost, and from that point on, César could do no wrong.

Don't misunderstand, not every side of him was so easy to like. César was a jumble of contradictions. He was a playboy with an insane work ethic, both on and off the field. He was an athlete and a serious intellectual. A gentleman and a womanizer. A traditionalist who loved all things modern. Someone easy to like and almost impossible to know. A man enormously generous who could be ridiculously self-centered and self-righteous. Even back then he had an incredible temper that would come out of nowhere. It was rare, but volcanic. He could be petty and cruel. But just when you'd decided to tell him he was being a prick, he'd turn on whatever that quality was that he had to turn on, and no matter how unreasonable he'd been, he'd make you feel like it was you who'd been at fault and he'd forgive you for it. Like the time he asked to borrow my old Buick station wagon. I said yes, but then we had an argument. It wasn't any big deal, but I didn't expect him to take the car in light of our spat. He did, though, and he accidentally wrapped it around a tree. Totaled it. I'd spent most of my high school weekends and two summers flipping burgers to buy that car, so you can imagine how I was more than a little furious. Technically he hadn't stolen it, but in the heat of the moment I kind of felt like he had and I had visions of punching him in the nose. But a single look from César at the hospital where he was getting his ribs taped and the only thing I wanted to know was if he would be ready for our next game. Never mind that he'd wrecked my car. What difference could an old beat-up station wagon make? That's the kind of power he had. No matter how angry I might be with something he would do, I could never be angry with him. Besides, he matched what my insurance gave me for the car and I bought a newer model Subaru with the proceeds.

So when César asked if I wanted to room with him senior year, he didn't have to ask twice. We were the best players on the best team in the league. We were the big men on campus. He was Mr. Offense and I was Mr. Defense. We were Batman and Batman. That's what I told myself. It all seems pretty childish now, but back then I thought our friendship made us both more cool and important. I suppose in some ways it did. Our friendship definitely made me feel like I was owed more attention and respect. He gave me the self-confidence to be myself. I thought I did the same for him. Of course, that kind of self-confidence isn't really any kind of self-confidence at all, but that's what I thought.

César was an undeniable force, like gravity, and I was drawn in.

2

CÉSAR AND I ONLY saw each other once between graduation and the day I moved down to live with him in Chiapas seven years later. We'd been great college friends and we stayed in fairly close touch by phone, but when college ends, friends part, so we went on to live our lives. For César that meant compulsory service in the Mexican military and then professional fútbol and a certain measure of fame. For me it meant meeting Jenn.

I'd moved back to Denver, was living above my parents' garage, and had taken a job in the human resources department of a subpoena and copy service. After the good times of college, I was stupefied by the boredom and monotony that can be adulthood. Like me, my two best friends from high school had moved away after graduation, but they had not returned since college, so I didn't have much of a social life. And my job was fantastically dull. Then winter arrived. Having skied in Vermont the previous winters, I was excited to get back to Rocky Mountain powder. We'd had good early snow, so the first weekend the resorts opened, I loaded my skis on the roof rack of the Subaru and headed for Breckenridge. It was a perfect ski day: fresh snow on a thick base, clear skies, no wind, and only moderate crowds. I'd completed a couple of runs and was standing in one of the singles lines, just waiting my turn and people-watching, when I noticed the weather gal from one of the local TV news stations. I couldn't remember her name, but she was really attractive and it was pretty clear that she had the attention of most of the men in the lines. It was also pretty clear that she knew it. I watched the order the chair operator was using to load the lift and match singles and it was my lucky day because in another five chairs I was going to be paired with her. Then a man standing outside the ropes told a boy to get out of the line. The boy complained, and when I saw that his exit meant the chair pairings would change, I almost spoke up on the kid's behalf. But I didn't. The weather beauty went up the mountain with some other guy and I got matched with another single—Jenn.

I'll never forget the way she turned to me once we were on the lift. She moved her goggles from eyes to her forehead, smiled that goofy guffawing smile she had, and said, "I just took the biggest digger ever."

After all this time, the image that has always remained most clear from that moment is the moving of her goggles, her white gloves grasping the white frame with magenta lens and pulling it from her face and setting it over the purple ski cap. It's not her eyes or the way she looked at me. It's just the way she moved the goggles. That and the smile. Even now, when I think of our first meeting, this is what I see.

We fell into a conversation about the snow conditions and skiing and which slopes we liked best. At some point it came out that her family had a house in Breckenridge and they were up for a long weekend, but she was the only one who had decided to ski that day. I don't know what else our conversation was about or who suggested it, but by the time we'd reached the top of the mountain we'd agreed to go down a particular black diamond run together. It turned out we were good skiing partners. She was a much better technical skier than I was because she'd been skiing since she could walk and I'd only picked it up my junior year of high school when my family moved to Denver. But soccer had made my legs strong and I liked going fast and tended to bully my way down the mountain. We ended up pounding the slopes all day together.

On the lifts we talked about all kinds of stuff, the conversation natural and easy. I told her about soccer and Vermont and my stupid job and not being sure what I wanted to do in the long term. She told me about the sorority she'd been in at UC Boulder and growing up in Denver—we'd gone to rival high schools—and her horses and working in her dad's company and taking night classes to get her MBA. Somehow it came out that we both spoke Spanish, and we conversed some until she decided my fluency made her self-conscious about her grammar. We talked about food, and she told me she had a soft spot for ice cream, a fact that I later learned was a gross understatement. Ice cream was an obsession. She'd cross state lines if it meant trying a new ice cream place. We talked about music and all the bands we'd seen at Red Rocks Amphitheater. We'd been to a lot of the same shows and we'd both gone to the Bob Dylan and Tom Petty concert that past July. We even figured out that we'd had seats practically right next to each other.

We laughed a lot too. Jenn was blonde and she liked to tell "stupid blonde" jokes. She had a seemingly endless repertoire: "Why'd the blonde climb the chain link fence? To see what's on the other side. How do you make a blonde laugh on Saturday? Tell her a joke on Wednesday. How do you get a one-armed blonde out of a tree? Wave."

"Those are terrible," I'd said, laughing.

"I know, right? Why do blondes always smile during lightning storms?"

"Why?"

"They think their picture's being taken."

We had such a good time that we skied until the lifts closed and the afternoon sunlight cast long shadows of the ridgeline across the mountain.

The following July we were married. In the lead-up to the wedding, I asked César to be my best man, but he'd just signed his contract with Cruz Azul and it turned out that the first game of the season was scheduled the same day as the wedding. He halfheartedly offered to ditch the game despite the contract's strict rules about what constituted a "personal matter," but I told him it wasn't worth it. In the end he would have come to the same conclusion on his own. There was no way he was going to miss the first game of his professional career. We were sorry he couldn't attend the wedding until César scored the winning goal and dedicated it to us in English during the postgame interview. "That goal was for Hank and his new bride, Jenn," he said. "Congratulations, guys."

Jenn thought that was quite the wedding present. She must have shown the video to fifty people. Even though they hadn't met at that point, they'd spoken several times on the phone and Jenn had been taken in by his charm as much as anyone. Also, Jenn could be easily starstruck, which was funny because it wasn't a quality you'd expect in her. I think she was impressed that my friend was on TV all the time, like his relative fame somehow rubbed off on us.

As cool as the dedication was, it was the day I finally did see César again that cemented our connection forever. It was the day of Susan's baptism. The week Suzy was due, César was playing in an exhibition tournament in Brazil. Even so, he called every day to see if the baby had arrived. We'd just come home from the hospital after Suzy was born when the phone rang. It was César.

"So?"

"Seven pounds, six ounces."

"Felicidades!" he cheered through the phone. I could picture him jumping up and down. "¿Como se llama?"

"Susan Anne Singer."

"Que lindo. How is she?"

"Beautiful."

"And Jenn?"

"Fine. Tired, but fine. Better than fine."

"That's good. I'm glad."

"César," I said. "We're going to baptize her at the Episcopal church. It's where Jenn's folks go."

"Uh-huh."

"Jenn and I have talked about it a lot and, well, she wants me to ask you if you'll be Susan's godfather."

There was a long silence on the other end of the line.

"Are you there?" I asked. I thought maybe we'd been cut off.

"You tell Jenn it would be my very great honor." His voice was as solemn as I'd ever heard it. "Do you know what this means?"

"What?"

"It means we're going to be compadres."

In Mexico, you'll hear men call each other "compadre" a lot. Even before I asked César to become godfather to my daughter, we called each other "compadre" just like we might call each other "buddy" or "pal." The word is used loosely between friends all the time. In Mexico, you can even hear virtual strangers call one another "compadre." As a colloquial form of address, the word can be applied in all sorts of situations. But in its formal or traditional use, men can only earn the title when one man becomes godfather to the other's child by taking an oath as a part of the religious ceremony during a baptism or first communion. It's a sacred trust. Once a man's your compadre, no matter what happens, he's always your compadre. You're family, brothers for life. The bond

15

can't be broken. While I knew what the word meant, I didn't fully comprehend its significance.

"You're not going to cry, are you?" I asked.

"I mean it. Don't make jokes. Es algo sagrado. You've asked me to be your daughter's second father, to watch out for her in case you die."

"Let's hope that's not necessary."

"No, compadre. Do you understand?"

"I do," I said. And suddenly I did. I had at least one friend in the world who would look out for my little girl no matter what.

"When is it?"

"We haven't decided. I'll let you know."

"I'll be there. It doesn't matter when. I'll be there."

True to his word, he flew in for the baptism on the family jet and flew out the same day to get back for a game. Even though he was in town for less than five hours, it was five hours that changed us. From that time on it wasn't a question of *if* we'd see each other again. It was a question of *when*. But before Jenn and Suzy died, never in a million years would I have pictured myself living in César's house in southern Mexico. Never. Of course, before the accident I thought my whole life was going to turn out different than it has.

As soon as he heard, César started calling almost every day. I rarely had anything to say, so after some long periods of silence when César would be waiting for me to talk, he'd tell me about his physical therapy or his getting involved in the family business or whatever. It didn't matter what he talked about. It was just his way of letting me know I wasn't alone. I knew he was hurt and more than a little angry that I hadn't called him after the accident. I hadn't even told him about the funeral. He hadn't seen Suzy after the baptism, but he'd sent her presents for Christmas and her birthdays and the anniversary of her baptism and he'd developed a phone friendship with Jenn. So I knew he was upset with me. He had a right to be, but the truth was I hadn't called anyone and he never again brought up this lapse of courtesy once he knew that. He just called to remind me that he had my back. Even now, as angry as I can get about what happened later, I have to admit those phone calls meant as much to me as anything anyone has ever done. They were one of the few things that kept me sane that whole year.

It was about six months after the funeral that he started suggesting I come down. The phone would ring and I'd answer it.

"Hey, compadre, que estás haciendo?" he'd ask.

"Sitting."

"And doing what?"

"Drinking scotch. Watching tapes of Suzy at swim class."

"Puta madre, compadre. What are you doing to yourself? Turn that shit off and get out of there. Come down here. We'll drink scotch together."

"I've got a job."

"¿Como? You still think you're going to take over the company from Jenn's dad? What's the matter with you? Get down here."

César had a point. I'd gone to work for Jenn's dad. He'd offered me the job the day we got back from our honeymoon. He had a big construction company, Talbert Construction, and with Jenn being his only child, the plan had been for us to take it over when he retired. A week after the funeral, Jenn's folks had me over for dinner and her dad told me that what had happened wasn't my fault. Where else the blame could possibly lie he didn't say. He said that it wasn't my fault and they'd always think of me like a son and that the company was still mine if I wanted it. He meant it, too. At least I think he wanted to mean it. But he must have known I wouldn't stick. Call it age or wisdom or whatever. He knew in a way I didn't yet. Take it from me, when you're twenty-eight and you watch your wife and three-year-old daughter drown in a river because you were foolish and arrogant enough to take them down a rapid in a canoe that had no business being there, you have a tendency to feel like you watched your whole life end with them. You have a tendency to wish it had. Like it or not, it didn't. Not by a long shot.

So while it took me more than a year to try to start my life over, I think Jenn's dad saw it coming before dessert was on the table that night. He knew I had my whole life ahead of me and, once I got past the accident, I'd have to make that life, one way or another. Jenn's mom took it hard, though, particularly when I sold the house and most of our stuff. The sale of the house brought the final realization that the girls weren't coming back. I had to sell it, though. There were too many ghosts.

After the house was sold, I made the mistake of moving back into the room above my parents' garage. I'd simply known I had to get out of the house and I hadn't thought too much about what came next, but living above the garage was worse. It was like I'd slipped back rather than moving forward. And to compound my misery, I found myself trying to avoid my parents and all their efforts to be comforting and sympathetic. I'd get home from the office and park my car in front of the neighbor's house and try to slip into my room without being seen. I'd leave the lights off and just sit with my thoughts. In my mind I saw myself forever slipping into a hole of black water, my fingers digging desperately into the blackness to stop the perpetual slide. It was like I was watching myself watch myself sink into oblivion. It wasn't like drowning. Drowning ends in death. This was like drowning without dying. The whisky may or may not have made it worse.

This went on for almost three months and then one morning, sitting in my car in the parking lot before work, I noticed an airplane trail in the sky. Then I noticed the sky. It was astonishingly blue and I think that was the first time I'd really seen the color of the sky or the color of anything since the girls' deaths. Then I realized I was sitting beside myself and watching myself begin to recognize the world. I didn't feel any more inside or outside myself than I had before I saw that blue sky, but I was suddenly conscious of the separation, like I finally recognized what I had been experiencing for months. And in that moment I felt an absolute necessity to get as far away from Colorado as I could. I went into the office and called a travel agent. I watched myself push the buttons on the phone and listened to myself buy a plane ticket to Chiapas for the following Monday. I watched myself phone César and leave a message with my itinerary on his machine. Then I watched myself walk into my father-in-law's office and tell him I was leaving. He made a halfhearted effort to convince me to stay, but like I said, he'd seen it coming, so he gave me a hug and told me he understood. And that was it. I walked out of the office, drove home to that damned room above the garage, and packed. That night, I watched myself tell my parents I was leaving. My mom cried the whole time, but my dad thought it was a good idea to get away and get a fresh perspective. I watched myself listen to him say the words *fresh perspective*. I went to see Jenn's mom the next day and there were more tears. Three days after that, I got on the plane. I hadn't even heard back from César. It didn't matter. I was going. In a lot of respects, I was already gone.

3

HE LOOKED THE SAME. Maybe a couple of pounds heavier and half an inch taller than I remembered, but otherwise unchanged in the four years since Suzy's baptism. Same short haircut. Same classical features and smooth skin. Same tumbling-kaleidoscope blue eyes, the Castilian trademark of generations of Lobos de Madrid men. Same mischievous grin that spread into that famous smile of his as he looked me over.

"Compadre, I can't believe you're here," he said in Spanish as we shook hands. I'd been standing on a dark, empty sidewalk in San Cristóbal de las Casas and knocking with the heavy brass knocker on the wooden gate of César's house and then he answered and there he was and he looked the same. I watched myself shake his hand. There was never any of that male awkwardness about whether we should hug or not. "I only got your message a few hours ago. I was out of town."

"Yeah. Sorry," I said. And then: "I hope it's okay. It was kind of an impulse thing."

"Of course it's okay. Hell, I've been telling you to come down. I just wish I could have picked you up from the airport. It's good to see you."

"Thanks. You too." I didn't know what to say. I hadn't known what to expect, but this felt wrong. "You look the same."

21

"Yeah?" he asked and glanced down at his body as if to see what I saw. He turned his gaze back on me. "Not you. Me gusta la barba," he said, rubbing his fingers over his clean-shaven chin. "How long have you had it?"

"A couple of months."

"It suits you. Come on in," he said as he shouldered my backpack.

I stepped through the doorway—the door had been cut in a larger wooden gate that could be opened for vehicles, the thickness of the wood suggesting it had been built to withstand a battering ram—and into the expansive and fully enclosed courtyard of the colonial-era compound. Despite the darkness of the night, various lamps lit the cobblestones and the walls and buildings of white stucco and terra-cotta tiles. It looked like the architecture at the Alamo. Jenn and I had taken a detour there on our way back from our honeymoon in Corpus Christi. I pictured Jenn on the beach at Corpus Christi.

A fountain stood in the middle of the broad space and an ornamental garden occupied a far corner. A black pickup truck was parked in the shadows of an open garage bay. I watched myself taking it in.

"That's the main house," he said, pointing to the two-story house that ran the whole length of the far side of the yard. "You'll be over here." He led me over to the bungalow on the right side of the courtyard. The bungalow had its own covered patio. "Your message didn't say how long you planned on staying, so I thought I'd put you up in the guesthouse. Is that okay?"

"Sure."

He looked at me. "How long do you plan on staying?"

"I don't know."

"Well, stay as long as you like."

"Are you sure?" In that moment I almost wished I was back in the room above my parents' garage. "I don't want to put you out."

"Of course I'm sure."

"Thanks."

"Mi casa es tu casa," he said, smiling as he opened the door.

The room was dark and cool in the night. César flicked a switch, illuminating wooden furniture and a leather sofa. I looked at the candelabra chandelier that provided the light. He put my bag down in the bedroom and, in the bathroom, showed me how to jiggle the handle of the toilet.

"There's hot water, but you have to let it run for a few minutes."

"Okay."

He led me into the kitchen, opened the refrigerator, and pulled out a six-pack of beer. "I had the maid stock the fridge with a few things, but if you need something, just give her some money and she'll get it. Only on the weekdays, though. She goes home on the weekends."

"All right."

"Her name's Pascuala. She's slow on the uptake, so you'll have to tell her more than once if you want what you ask for. Don't bother making a list. She can't read. Also, make sure you get a receipt and count your change."

I nodded.

"Here's a key to the house and front gate."

I took it.

"I'll show you around town, but I left a map of the city on the table in case you want to go out and I'm at work or something."

"Okay."

"I know how you are with directions." He was referring to a road trip we'd taken in college. I had gotten us lost for three hours in the middle of a Vermont winter night and César became convinced we were going to die in the snowy wilderness.

I wasn't sure exactly what I was supposed to say. "Well, I did finally get us there."

César smiled and lifted his beer. "Salud, compadre."

"Salud," I said and touched my bottle to his. I felt I should say something more. "And thanks."

"For what?" he asked and grinned. "I'm just glad you're here so I can kick your ass in foosball." He laughed.

There'd been a foosball table in the rec hall in college and between the two of us we'd probably dumped three thousand dollars' worth of quarters into it. You don't become an athlete of César's caliber without being naturally competitive and I think that secretly it irritated him that he could never beat me at foosball. Probably it was the only thing I was better at than he was and in college I'd gloated about it every chance I got.

"So," he said, "have you eaten? We could get tacos or something and then go to a bar. There won't be much going on at this hour on a Monday, but we can probably stir up a good time."

"I'm kind of worn out," I said. Then I added, "I ate during the layover in Mexico City."

"Are you sure? I have a meeting in the morning, but I'm not afraid to party down."

"I think I'd rather just stay in."

"Really?" He looked disappointed. "Sure, compadre. You're the boss. Let's go over to the main house."

César led me across the courtyard and through the big front door. The house seemed even larger on the inside than it did from the outside, a broad staircase rising straight back from the middle of the tiled foyer with the two-story ceiling.

"Ramón's down at my parents' house," he said, checking his watch and stopping to take a key from atop the grandfather clock and open the cabinet face. I watched him crank the weights up and into place. "So it will just be the two of us for a few days."

I'd briefly forgotten he lived with Ramón. Ramón and César

had known each other since childhood and Ramón's family had worked for César's family for generations. As I understood it, besides being César's surrogate brother, Ramón was sort of César's personal assistant and one of the managers of the Lobos de Madrid family holdings. I'd not met him.

We made our way through several large rooms filled with leather sofas and chairs and antique wooden furniture and art and intricately woven rugs. A library with wall-to-wall bookshelves was crammed with books. The game room was off the library and came complete with big-screen TV, pool table, pinball machines, and the original *Space Invaders* and *Asteroids* video games. There was a foosball table, too.

"You're sure you're not hungry?" he asked.

"No. I mean yes. I mean I'm sure."

"Want to play a game of foos, then?"

I didn't.

He looked at me.

"I haven't played much since school," I said. That wasn't totally accurate. Before the accident, I'd played just about every week down at McGreeley's Bar & Grill. My photo hung on the wall of McGreeley Foosball Tournament Grand Champions. But I hadn't played since the accident.

"Come on." He stepped around to the far side of the table and looked at me.

"Yeah," I said. "Okay, I guess."

I watched my hands grasp the handles and we played. Actually, there was something about the mechanical nature of playing, something about my automatic body taking over, that was relieving. I kept the first two games close, only winning by a goal or two.

"Want to make it interesting? ¿Diez pesos?" he asked.

"Nah."

César started to cluck like a chicken.

"All right," I said. "Make it a hundred."

"A hundred it is."

The game took about ten minutes. He had three goals when my left wing slammed home the winning shot.

"You hustled me."

I looked at him. "You're the one who wanted to bet."

He shook his head in mock disgust, pulled out a fold of pesos, snapped a bill off the top, and stuffed it in my shirt pocket. "So," he said, collapsing into an oversize armchair. "I got a letter from Amanda Schelling last week."

"Amanda Schelling," I said. "There's someone I haven't thought of in a while."

"She keeps trying to get me to go to a class reunion."

A class reunion. I couldn't fathom what that would be like.

"I don't know," he continued. "Maybe I'll go to the ten-year. That all kind of seems like another lifetime."

I looked at him again. What was I doing here? "That's the truth."

César nodded and gave a knowing smile, but he didn't say anything. I watched him pick at his beer label. It was clear he was offering me a shoulder to cry on if I wanted it just as he had done with all those phone calls. He didn't have to worry. I wasn't Johnny Gilbride. There was nothing to say. Jenn and Suzy were dead. Just that.

"What time is it?" I asked. I was ready to be alone in the guesthouse.

"Close to midnight."

"I'm fried. I think I'm going to go to bed."

"¿Como? You just got here."

"I know. Sorry."

"Weak."

"It was a long trip."

"Come on."

"Really, I'm done."

He looked at me like he was trying to figure me out. Then he said, "Well, if you say so, compadre. Let me know if you need anything."

"Sure," I said, rising to my feet. He stood too.

"I'm glad you came."

"Me too." That wasn't true, but in that moment I determined to try to act like it was. "And César, thanks."

"For what?"

"The hundred pesos."

He laughed and punched me in the shoulder. "Don't spend them. I'll be winning those back."

"That's what I like about you, César," I said, watching myself say it. "Always the optimist."

"Optimize this," he said and gave me the finger.

He opened the front door and I went down the steps into the courtyard.

"So I have to leave pretty early for that business thing," he said. He must have seen some expression on my face because he added, "Hey, I'm not the one going to bed. I'm ready to disco down, but I have to be at this thing tomorrow morning. Business is business."

"That's fine."

"Really, I can't get out of it, but I'm canceling everything in the afternoon."

"I said it's fine."

He grinned. "Buenas noches."

"Yeah," I said. "Buenas noches."

Back in the guesthouse I unpacked my bags and drank two more beers from the six-pack. There was a pint of Hornitos tequila as well and I downed most of that. Then I watched my reflection in the mirror as I brushed my teeth. I stripped down to my boxer shorts, switched off the light, and climbed into bed. The room was so quiet I imagined I could almost hear the moonlight reflecting off the tiles in the courtyard outside the window. I thought about how strange it was to see César and to be speaking Spanish. It made me feel both more and less removed. I lay in bed. Then I looked at the shadowed photographs of Jenn and Suzy that I'd put on the nightstand. Besides those few seconds right before I'd wake gasping at three in the morning, bedtime was always the worst. But it must have been true that I was tired from traveling because I only lay there for a couple of hours or so before finally drifting off.

4

I AWOKE LATE IN the morning to sunlight streaming through the windows, the sky outside clear and blue. The room was cold and quiet as I took my bearings from beneath the warmth of the wool blankets. My head felt slightly clouded from the tequila, but otherwise I felt rested and it occurred to me that I hadn't awakened even once in the night. I couldn't even remember dreaming. That was unusual. The photos of the girls were on the bedside table, the same eternal expressions on their faces as always. I looked at them.

"Well," I said finally. "We're in Mexico."

I went to the kitchen and got the coffee brewing. The pint of tequila was on the counter. I unscrewed the cap and held the bottle up to the light, a finger of pale, translucent yellow in the bottom of the bottle. Then I screwed the cap back on and put the bottle atop the refrigerator. From the kitchen I could see out the windows of the front room and across the courtyard. César's pickup was gone. After I'd showered and dressed, I took a cup of coffee out to the patio table in front of the bungalow, where I lit a cigarette and unfolded the map César had left. He'd marked the location of the compound for me. We were only six or seven blocks from the city center. I told myself that I should have another cup of coffee and then go see the city. Then I told myself what I should really do was find a travel agent and buy a ticket home. I had been a fool to think coming here would change something. Take it easy, I told myself. I was still pretending to study the map when César pushed open the heavy wooden gate and drove the pickup into the courtyard, parking it in the garage bay where it had been the night before. He'd already closed the gate when he saw me sitting at the table.

"Hey, compadre," he said. He was grinning. "How'd you sleep?"

"Fine." I thought I should say something more. I didn't know what.

"Have you had anything to eat?"

"I haven't been up that long."

He looked at his watch. "It's early for lunch, but we could walk around town for a bit and then grab a bite."

"Yeah. Okay."

"Let me just grab something from the house and we'll go."

"All right."

Outside the compound, the words I had spoken to the photographs of Jenn and Suzy in the morning became true for the first time. I was in Mexico. Everything had seemed muted when I'd come from the airport the night before, the countryside dark, everything beyond the windows of the taxi a black void. Even once I was in the city, the streets had been quiet, dim, empty. But now the world outside the compound's heavy door was bright and loud and moving. The sidewalk was busy with pedestrians making their way along the flagstones, men and women and children, young and old, moving this way and that. Cars rolled down the narrow streets and a line of Indian men in sheepskin ponchos, enormous loads of charcoal heaped on their backs, hustled past barefoot, weaving between people.

"It's almost like another country," César said, smiling at my apparent expression of surprise.

"Almost," I agreed. It was not Colorado, that was for sure.

"Vámonos."

He seemed to cleave his way through the waves of people, like they were parting the way before him, and I followed, more than once bumping into someone and mumbling, "Perdón."

"I have to make a stop," César said as we crossed the street and he waved a VHS tape in his hand as though that would explain the reason. I hadn't even noticed he'd been carrying it. We walked through a crowd and I bumped into another person and excused myself. César paused at a storefront. "This is where Pascuala buys our tortillas." Inside was a room empty save for a rickety metal contraption, a man loading corn masa into one end of the machine, and a woman peeling tortillas off the conveyor belt at the other. "They're the best in the city."

I tried to think of a response, but he'd already resumed walking.

We came to a church with elaborate carvings of saints and columns and geometric patterns in the stone façade. People milled about. "The Templo de Santo Domingo," César said. He seemed to think I would find this important, so I admired the church for what I thought was an appropriate number of moments. Then I nodded to César to indicate that yes, it was indeed of note, but he had already begun moving on. I followed into the tree-shaded park next to the church where rows of Indian merchants hawked dolls and knickknacks and handmade clothing and brightly colored blankets all piled up on tarps spread out on the ground. César didn't pay any of it any mind.

A man at a large metal kettle was selling steamed cobs of corn on a stick. He slathered something on them and then dusted them with a powder. "¡Elotes!" he called.

In one part of the park, several long-haired, hippie-like young men were selling rough jewelry. As we passed, an artisan with hoop earrings held up a silver bracelet of birds for me to see. It reminded me of one Jenn used to wear. I looked at myself looking at it.

"A hundred and fifty pesos," he said, but I shook my head and moved to catch up with César. Along with the rings and bangles were jade and amber pieces and marijuana pipes hand-carved in wood.

"¡Elotes!" the corn seller called again.

Two young foreign women were talking with an artisan with a bony face, the backs of both his hands bearing henna designs. A blonde guy with a backpack haggled over the price of a leather belt with an Indian girl who didn't look old enough to be the mother of the baby strapped to her back. Two boys ran by.

"¡Elotes!"

The whole scene was some weird time warp. I caught up to César at the edge of it all, and he said, "It's just Indians and losers selling junk, but I thought you should see it."

We crossed the street and a shopkeeper standing in front of his business encouraged us to come in. "Buen precios," he said.

César ignored him, and when the man gestured at me, I shook my head. He gestured again, but I went on and he turned his attention to someone else.

At a stoplight, a group of teenage girls in the knee-high stockings and plaid uniform skirts of Catholic school waited to cross the street. César winked at one of the girls as the light changed, and she and her friends burst into a fit of giggles. Their old crone chaperone glared at both of us and César smiled broadly in return.

"This is the zócalo," he announced when we came to a square plaza the size of a city block. Eight evenly placed cobblestone footpaths between well-groomed beds of trees and flowers led from the center of the park like spokes from a wheel. "That's the Kiosco Café," he said, pointing toward an octagonal white building in the middle of the park. "It's a good place to sit and read the paper if the house gets too quiet for you." People sat at umbrella-covered tables on the raised patio encircling the building. An ornate gazebo covered seating on the rooftop terrace. "This is the main cathedral," he said. It ran the whole length of the north side of the square. "And that's the municipal building," he added, pointing now to the west. Lots of people were going about their business or sitting on park benches or getting their shoes shined in a row of chairs.

"You getting hungry?"

"I guess so." I tried to force a smile. "It's a good thing you gave me that map."

"Don't worry," he said. "It's not that complicated." He flashed that famous smile and for a moment everything seemed just as it should be. I was with my compadre and we were in Mexico. It felt, for a brief instant, as if Jenn and Suzy were waiting at home back in Colorado and I was simply visiting César on some improbable vacation.

"Let's go this way," he said and I followed him along an arcade of shops and businesses. "If you need to change money, use the bank on the corner and not one of the casas de cambio. You'll get a better rate."

"Okay."

He looked at me. "Do you need to change money?"

"I changed some in the airport."

He smiled. "Good."

We walked a few more blocks, César pointing out various buildings or points of interest as we went, and then he stopped and nodded at an open gate. "I have to stop in here for a minute. You might want to wait outside."

I looked at the gateway and at the series of blue-and-white buildings beyond the fence. People, some in white lab coats, moved between them. It was a hospital. I turned back to César. I thought he might do more than wave the VHS tape to explain why we were here or why I wouldn't want to join him.

"Or come in if you want," he said.

He led us through the gate and past a line of people waiting to speak with the receptionist at the window of the building. We crossed to a second building and moved aside while a nurse pushed a man in a wheelchair out through the doorway. Then we went in. I couldn't tell if it was an office or an examination room. It may have been both. The man standing in a lab coat smiled at César's arrival.

"Buenos dias, Doctor," César said as the man stood up. They shook hands.

"Señor Lobos de Madrid, what a pleasant surprise. What can I do for you?"

"May I introduce my friend, Mr. Hank Singer."

"Hola," I said from the doorway.

"Mucho gusto, señor," the doctor said, bowing slightly in my direction.

"Here's my highlight reel as promised," César said, handing over the VHS cartridge. "You might show it to them a day or two before the visit. I'll bring a box of jerseys, a dozen or so balls, and some photos that I can personalize for them when I come. Can you think of anything else?"

"No, that's more than enough. The hospital and the community owe your family a real debt of gratitude."

César smiled and shook his head. "It's our pleasure. So I'll see you next week."

They shook hands again and the doctor nodded at me and we went out. When we were back on the street, César said, "Cruz Azul had us visit kids in the hospital as part of our community outreach. Now it's just good PR for my family. I try to go at least twice a year." He looked at me. "It can be kind of hard, though," he said.

I nodded. Then I understood why César had suggested I stay on the street. He'd been trying to protect me from seeing sick kids. I didn't bother to tell him sick kids weren't any worse than healthy kids when it came to reminding me of Suzy.

"This is it," César said, interrupting my thoughts. "Let's eat."

It was an unremarkable taco place with red plastic tables and chairs and a white linoleum counter that ran the length of the building. Despite the ambience, there was a sizable and noisy crowd of locals. César shook hands with two men who were on their way out as we went in, and the three men working behind the counter all called greetings to him by name as we took seats at a table. The three men looked like brothers. I read the hand-lettered menu board affixed to one of the walls, but when one of them asked what we wanted to eat, César ordered the combination plate.

"Trust me," he said. "You want the combination plate."

A few minutes later the man who had taken our order came around the counter with our tacos. "Who do you like this year?" he asked as he set the plates on the table and then shook César's hand.

"Tecos," César said. "They've got the whole package."

"That's what I say too." Then the man called to the men behind the counter: "You see, Paco. I told you. César likes Tecos just like me."

I tried to recall what I knew about the current Tecos squad. I hadn't been paying much attention this season.

"You said you like Monterrey," the man named Paco said.

"Yes, you said Monterrey," confirmed the other man behind the counter.

"I did not. I said Tecos. I only said Monterrey would be difficult to beat." Then to César: "I only said Monterrey would be difficult to beat. I'm like you. Tecos is the best team this year."

"Monterrey doesn't have a defense this year," said César.

I'd seen a recent Monterrey game. They didn't have a defense. They didn't have an offense, either.

The man at our table seemed to consider what César had said. "That's true." And then wagging his finger in the air and speaking so Paco and the other man behind the counter could hear: "But Tecos, Tecos will be good this year. That is what I've said." And then to us: "It is good to see you. Enjoy your tacos."

"Gracias," César said.

"Gracias," I said.

"Monterrey," César said once the man had moved out of earshot, "sucks this year." He grinned and held up one of his tacos. "They may not know fútbol, but they know tacos al pastor."

He was right. I tried to remember when I'd had tacos this good and I suddenly realized that I couldn't remember having tasted food in months. While I ate, César told me about his meeting earlier in the morning. It had something to do with mobile phones and some business friend of his family who was looking to corner the market. I only half listened. My attention was on the tacos.

After I'd finished a third order, César paid and the three brothers all wished him well and told us to return soon and we went out to the street. He continued talking about the meeting as we walked along the sidewalk and about how the business-man's representatives had basically convinced César that mobile phones were going to be much bigger than most people realized. "You'll see, Compadre. A couple of years from now, like '96 or '97, everyone will have a cellular phone."

I watched him as he spoke and I realized again that it really was him, that I really was walking on a sidewalk in Mexico with my compadre. There was something astonishing about that. I felt simultaneously hyperaware and utterly confused.

"Hey," he said all of a sudden, stopping on the sidewalk and peering through an open doorway as if to see who or what was inside.

I looked at the sign above the doorway. It read "El Acuario" and included a small painted octopus. A menu board beside the entrance indicated it was an Italian restaurant specializing in seafood.

César turned back to me as if satisfied with whatever he'd been looking for or at. "Let's pop in here for a minute."

I looked at him. It was César. I followed him in.

The interior decoration was overwhelming. The walls had been painted aqua blue with green trim and the chairs had been painted to match the walls and the tablecloths to match the trim. Bright modernist paintings of fish and other sea creatures hung on the walls and several potted plants that I took to represent a kelp garden framed the stage. Swaths of blue and green fabric diffused the sunlight streaming through the glass pyramidal ceiling. The patterns on the fabrics cast shadows of starfish and sea horses all around the restaurant. I felt like the whole room was in Technicolor. Two guys sat on stools at the bar. One of them was wearing a cowboy hat. The other got up to greet us when we came in.

"César," the man hollered. He threw his arms open wide and then clapped his hands together and pumped them up and down at us. "This is a surprise." He looked to be in his midthirties and the way he wore his belt cinched high up on his waist said he was European.

Blue and yellow tangs traversed a reef in a long aquarium behind the bar.

César and the man did one of those handshakes that have three or four different grips to it. Then César introduced me to Antonio, and Antonio led me through a slower version of the same handshake. I muddled through it.

"¿Americano?" Antonio said, more like a statement of the obvious than a question. "I know America. New York, Chicago, Los Angeles, Miami. Ooh Miami," he said. He pinched his fingers together and kissed them. "Que bella ciudad."

"Hank is from Colorado."

"Sí, Colorado. Denver. Mile High City. Go Broncos," he said.

"Right," I said. "Go Broncos."

"So," César said, glancing at the man at the bar and then turning back to Antonio. "I wondered if we could talk business."

Antonio looked from César to me and back to César. "Your friend will wait at the bar?"

César winked at me. "Sure," he said. "Hank, have a beer. I'll just be a minute."

"Félix," Antonio called through the doorway to the kitchen. "Come watch the bar for a minute."

A small Mexican man in an apron and chef's skullcap came out from the kitchen and Antonio led César into an office, the door closing behind them.

I leaned against the bar. It felt good to steady myself and I wondered if I was having a panic attack or something. It felt like wave after wave of stimuli—the blue walls, the abstract paintings, the bright furniture, the aquarium behind the bar, Antonio's cinched belt, César's wink, the cowboy hat, everything—was washing over me.

The cook asked me what I wanted to drink.

"A Sol and a tequila."

He opened the beer and poured a caballito.

I drank the shot. I felt like I knew what every molecule in the room was doing. The air was a mill of equations. The blue and yellow fish swam in their tank. The man in the cowboy hat was two stools over. He wore round spectacles and a full and bushy beard. He was watching me. It wasn't a cowboy hat. It was the hat of a Confederate Cavalry officer. Confederate Cavalry gloves sheathed his hands and forearms. I ordered another shot and drank it. The decibel level of the visual world eased.

The cook was pouring a third shot when she came through the front door.

I noticed her. We all noticed her. We all would have even if the place had been full. Women like that don't go unnoticed.

A man was with her. He sat on a far stool while she went around the end of the bar, gave the cook a peck on the cheek, and put on an apron. The cook exchanged some pleasantries with the man who had sat at the bar and then disappeared into the kitchen. The woman came over to see if either the tourist in the hat or I needed anything. I felt confused to be looking at her. I thought she might have been the most beautiful woman I'd ever seen. The tourist in the hat said he was fine. I said I was fine.

"Some nice sights in Mexico," the tourist said as we watched her move. His English had a slight German accent.

I looked at him.

"My name's Bern," he said. He touched a riding-gloved hand to the brim of his hat as if he were a cowboy in a John Wayne movie.

"Hank," I said.

"You're American?"

"That's right."

"The South?"

"No."

"The American Civil War's a hobby of mine."

"I can see that."

"Oh," he said, taking the hat off to admire before returning it to his head. "I forget sometimes I'm wearing it. I have the whole uniform back in Germany. Sword and everything."

"It's not something I see everyday."

"No. It's not," he said. "I had it special ordered from the Virginian Daughters of the Confederacy," he added, just in case I might want to order one for myself.

He said something else, but I missed it because the woman had pulled her dark hair off her neck and was tying it up in a loose knot.

"Sorry, what was that?"

"I said I bought a horse today."

"You bought a horse?" I was confused. Had I missed part of the conversation? "What for?"

"For riding," he said, as if the answer was self-evident.

But before he could say more, César and Antonio came out of the office.

"¿Listo?" César asked.

"Yeah," I said, downing the third shot and chasing it with a long pull from the beer.

"Let's go," César said.

"I'm coming," I said. I took one more hit from the beer and I pulled out my wallet. I was feeling the tequila, but it had chased most of the weirdness away. As I left pesos on the bar to cover the drinks and tip, I thought I saw César exchange an unpleasant look with the woman and the guy she'd come in with.

Antonio walked us to the door. "So I'll let you know," he said to César.

"Bueno," César said and he led me out to the street.

We stopped at the corner pharmacy so I could buy cigarettes. I was still thinking about how odd everything had been—the colors and patterns, the handshake, the way I'd felt, that guy Bern and his hat, the woman. I looked at the cashier. She rang me up. I looked at César as he flipped through a fútbol magazine.

"Hey," I said, "do you know that woman?"

"What woman?" César asked, only half listening.

"The woman at the bar. The bartender."

The cashier counted out my change.

"Maria?" César put the magazine back on the rack and looked at me. "Yeah, I know her. Stay away from her. She's a puta."

"Really?"

"Really."

I didn't say anything more, but I thought about the woman and Bern and the bar. I looked around at the cars in the street and the pedestrians walking past us on the sidewalk. I looked at César. It was him. We were in Mexico. I was in Mexico.

"Hey, compadre," he said, smiling, after we'd walked a block or two. "That's the first time I've heard you talk about women in a long time. You want to meet some ladies? I know a bunch of señoritas."

"No," I said, "I didn't mean it like that." And I hadn't, but as we walked I wondered if I could have. That was the first time I could remember that I'd looked at a woman since Jenn, and the realization filled me with an overwhelming surge of guilt.

5

WE SPENT THE REST of the afternoon and evening drinking beers and talking about the college days. César did most of the talking. I listened and thought about things. I thought about Jenn. I thought about everything I'd seen on the streets and the hospital and the flavor of the tacos and the hyperawareness I'd felt in the restaurant and that in some ways I continued to feel. I thought about the female bartender and then I thought about Jenn some more.

I don't know what time we went to bed, but I only woke once in the night. I thought about the fact I was in Mexico. I thought about walking next to César.

I was rinsing my cereal bowl in the sink the next morning when I saw César crossing the courtyard. He rapped on the door and then entered before I could even say "Come in."

"You feel like playing some fútbol?"

I didn't. "Who with?" I asked.

"Whoever shows up. There's always a game."

"I haven't played in years."

"That can be your reason for sucking. Come on."

I tried to think of another excuse. "Okay," I said finally.

"That's the spirit."

"Anybody any good?"

"No," he said and then grinned his César grin. "Not unless I play."

He drove us through the old part of town and out past a new housing development. The new houses were cookie-cutter, just like all the wretched urban-sprawl tract housing springing up across the western United States, except these houses were unfinished and made from concrete cinder blocks and small, like they could fit in the garages of their US counterparts. Maybe it was simply their unassuming size, or maybe it was their juxtaposition to the rickety wooden shacks dotting the hills beyond, but something about them was less keeping-up-with-the-Joneses-soul-destroying than the developments back home. Still, there was something shameful about them in comparison to the old part of the city. Why build these when you had the example of the colonial architecture?

We pulled into a gravel lot next to an open field where a game was under way. The pitch looked reasonably flat, but the grass was patchy at best. Goalposts stood at both ends of the field. Only one had a net. They did have chalk lines and there was someone with a whistle as referee, so that was something. Actually, it looked like a serious game.

"Just like the pros," I said and César grinned and nodded.

We got out of the truck and laced up our cleats. César had given me a pair from the dozens of unopened boxes he'd received from various sponsors from his pro days. He even had my size. The ref blew the whistle to end the game. The players were drinking from water bottles and forming new teams on the sidelines when someone recognized César and people on both teams started shouting dibs. Five or six guys even jogged over to greet him and persuade him he should play with them. One guy in particular, with a square face, kept tugging on César's sleeve. César acted very nonchalant about all the attention, but I could tell he enjoyed it.

After several players were shuffled from one group to another to compensate for César, I found myself on the sideline without a team. Nobody wanted to take a chance with the unknown gringo. But then César said he wouldn't play unless I did too. To vouch for my ability, he made up a ridiculous story about me once having been a defensive star in the British Premier League. He really laid it on thick and it was decided that I should play opposite him.

"Thanks," I told him. "Now I'm really going to look bad."

César laughed. "Think of it as payback for foosball."

My team huddled up and everyone agreed our strategy should be to keep the ball away from César as much as possible. The strategy worked for the first ten minutes or so. Despite what César had said, there were some guys who could play. Our midfielder did a good job of controlling the tempo and distributing the ball and our left wing had a hammer for a foot. He blasted a shot from a good twenty yards outside the goalie box. The ball ricocheted off the crossbar.

Then César got the ball. I tried to stay with him, but one of the earmarks of a great offensive player is his ability to move without the ball, not just to anticipate where the opening will be, but to create the opening by drawing the defense out of position. He creates his own opportunities. And with a player as good and fast as César, you can know he is drawing you out of position and there is nothing you can do about it because if you don't go to meet him he will burn you for not following. To my credit, I saw the play unfolding and I knew right where César was going to get the ball two passes before he got it, but knowing something is going to happen and being able to prevent it are two different things. All things being equal, an offensive player should always beat a defensive player anyway because ball possession dictates the conditions of the game. In this case all things definitely were not equal. Even in peak shape I'd never been able to keep up with César. And I was five or six years from peak shape while he seemed to have just gotten faster. There's no doubt he was better. I did manage to hang him up just long enough to get another defender back to help, but then César did this stutter-step move that left both of us standing upright and he was gone. A third man tried to slide-tackle him, but César burned him too and then bent the ball into the upper right corner of the goal.

The rest of the game was a whole lot more of the same. I managed to take the ball from him a couple of times, but for the most part he had his way with me. We double-teamed him. We triple-teamed him. It didn't matter. It was all the more irritating when I realized he was mostly playing with his left foot. Then in the second half he did this absolutely amazing reverse double-touch move I'd never seen before.

"I want to see that again," I said after he'd passed the ball away.

"Sure." And sure enough he tangled me up with the same move the next time he got the ball.

"Want to see it again?" he asked, trotting back from having scored his fifth or sixth goal.

"What's that called?"

"I don't know. I just invented it. Maybe I'll call it 'The Hank.'"

"Swell."

By the end of the game I don't know if everyone else had stopped keeping score, but I had.

César and I were sitting on the grass, passing a jug of water between us when the midfielder from my team, who was just a kid, brought a pen over and asked César to sign his ball.

"Ah, fame," I said in English.

César frowned at me and took the ball and pen. He asked the kid's name and the boy told him.

"You're good," César said.

The kid blushed.

"De verdad," César said. "Keep playing. You see the field. That's a talent most people don't have."

"Gracias," the kid said and carried his ball away. He stood about six inches taller.

"He really is pretty good," I said.

César shrugged. "He's fair."

Some guys had started a juggling circle and one of them called to César.

César looked at me. "You in?"

"I'm good right here."

"I'll just be a few minutes." Then he grinned. "I can't disappoint my fans."

He joined the circle and I watched the group pass the ball back and forth through the air. Across the field, a group was playing three-on-three within the confines of the goalie box. I looked at the housing development and the shacks on the mountain beyond. The mountain was forested and green. The sky was that deep blue hue you can only find at higher altitudes. It was like the color of the sky I'd seen in the parking lot in Colorado. That blue.

"Eso!" someone cheered from the group and I saw that César had the ball trapped on his forehead, his head moving ever so slightly from side to side to keep it frozen there. Then he made the ball roll into the crook of his neck. He held it there a moment before letting it drop behind his back so he could strike it with his heel, sending the ball rainbowing over his head and across the circle to another man who trapped it with his chest. Several members of the group clapped or hollered or whistled and César looked at me and smiled broadly and it was in that moment that I thought for the first time that maybe, just maybe, coming to Mexico might have been the right choice.

...

I FELT THAT WAY more and more as the week progressed. I won't pretend that I understood what was happening or that I'd yet found any answers. I didn't even believe there were answers. I still don't. But as the days unfolded I began to think that maybe the move to San Cristóbal might begin to help me understand the questions. And I attributed that possibility mostly to César, to being in his presence and his world. It was that same quality, that magnetism, he'd had in college.

Then on Friday word came from César's father that he needed him to pick two business associates up from the airport in Tuxtla late that afternoon and to drive them to the family ranch, where they would be guests of Señor and Señora Lobos de Madrid. César explained that usually they would helicopter the guests from the airport or send a hired hand to drive, but in this case the associates were being inflexible about some aspect of a deal and his father wanted César to use the extended drive to play the business equivalent of good cop on the road to his father's bad cop at the ranch. "I soften them up," César said. "Then my father drops the hammer." Apparently it was a tactic he and Señor Lobos de Madrid had employed on previous occasions.

César said he was sorry he had to leave me alone for the night, but there wouldn't be room for me in the pickup truck. "Besides," he said, "we'll be talking business the whole time. You'd find it boring."

"Okay," I said.

"But I'll be back late morning or early afternoon tomorrow, and then you'll get to meet Rámon."

"All right."

"I promise we'll go to the ranch soon," he added. "My parents really want to see you."

I could tell he felt bad about leaving me for the night. Frankly, I felt bad about it too. Bad and a little nervous to be alone again.

César left for the airport just after four. I read some, tried to write a postcard to my parents, and then decided to go out for a coffee. At the zócalo a man with a small Canadian flag patched to his jacket was passing out xeroxed handbills to tourists. He handed me one. It advertised "yummy pizza, cheap beer, and good live music" at some place called La Taberna.

I sat on the terrace of the Kiosco Café in the shade of a tree, ordered a coffee, and smoked a cigarette. A flock of starlings, moving like a single animal, swooped through the twilight sky before returning to roost atop the cathedral. Several young couples milled around the park or held hands on the wrought iron park benches. Three well-dressed middle-aged men sipped espresso and held an animated political discussion at the next table. Although I tried to eavesdrop, only the gentleman with the neatly trimmed mustache spoke loudly enough for me to hear. He objected to some new property tax and deliberately counted on his fingers as he articulated each of the four ways property owners were already overburdened with taxes. The jeweled ring on his pinkie caught the light when he made his final point. It was quite a ring.

The waiter brought my coffee and then seated two women at another table. One of them removed her sunglasses and propped them on her forehead and something about the gesture reminded me of Jenn on the ski lift and that got me thinking about Jenn and how interested she would have been in this city. Why hadn't we come down to visit César when she'd been alive? She had loved traveling and exploring. There were so many things I regretted not having done with her.

I was still thinking about Jenn when a small boy of six or seven came up and tried to sell me a shine. "They're very dirty," he said, pointing at the boots I'd had shined while waiting for my connection in Mexico City. "Muy sucio." He wouldn't take no for an answer, so when he dropped the price by a peso, I relented. He made a big production with his tins, brushes, and rags, but he was too small to rub very hard and I was fairly sure I was going to end up with polish on my pant cuffs. I tipped him five pesos anyway. It's what Jenn would have done.

After a second coffee, I paid the bill and strolled the streets. I couldn't help but feel again as I had several times over the week that there was a certain magical otherworldliness to the place, that the city seemed to avoid all the machinations of time's progression. I felt a million miles and a million years from my life back in the States.

It was dark and the street lights had come on and most stores and business had closed for the night by the time I decided to go looking for La Taberna and "yummy pizza." All the streets and buildings in the old part of San Cristóbal look kind of the same and I'd forgotten my map at the house, so I got lost, but once I found the right street, it wasn't hard to find the restaurant. A small group from the international backpacking set was crowded around a doorway out of which very loud and very bad music spilled onto the street. The music was bad enough that if I hadn't had so much trouble finding the place, I probably wouldn't have gone in.

Despite the wailing of the Mexican hippie band, complete with three sets of bongo drums and a chick with a rain stick, the tables were crowded with a mixture of foreigners and long-haired Mexican men, a couple of whom I'd seen selling jewelry outside Santo Domingo. I recognized the guy who had come in with the bartender at El Acuario. He was with some of the artisans. He was subdued, but several of his friends were loaded and putting the moves on a couple of foreign women.

I elbowed my way to the bar for a beer and a slice of pizza, which was indeed cheap, so at least the flyer hadn't been a total come-on.

"We meet again," a voice said.

I turned to see the man with the Civil War hat standing next to me. Bern. "I see you're still defending the land of cotton."

"Yes, yes. Dixie forever. Come with me. I have a table." He took my arm and led me through the crowd to a group of people at a table before I could decline the invitation. "Everyone, this is Hank. Hank, everyone."

The people at the table offered me a chair and introduced themselves. There was a couple from England whose names I didn't catch because the band had started wringing the neck of another song. They said they were architects and that they'd been in San Cristóbal for three months.

"We hadn't planned on staying," the woman said, "but we got caught up in a project for Na Bolom."

"Na Ba-what?"

"It's a museum and cultural center dedicated to the Lacandón Indians," the man explained.

The other two girls at the table were college students from Canada who were taking the semester off from school. They'd been in San Cristóbal for two days and were traveling by a bus to Guatemala in the morning. After Guatemala they were headed for Costa Rica, where they hoped to find jobs. The reference to Costa Rica got the architect couple started on their trip to Costa Rica and before long the four of them were absorbed in their own conversation, which left me to talk with Bern.

Actually, once you got past the Civil War thing—or perhaps I should say in addition to the Civil War thing—Bern turned out to be a pretty interesting guy. He'd been a medic in the Gulf War as a part of a Danish detachment, which he said was too complicated to explain, and he had been wounded himself. He opened the collar of his shirt to show me the raised pink quarter-sized scar on his shoulder. He said there was a larger scar on his back where the bullet had exited. Recently engaged to a local Indian girl from some rural village to the south where he'd bought a small ranch, Bern was only in San Cristóbal to pick up some money that was being wired from Germany. As soon as the money came, he planned to ride his new horse back to his ranch and get married. What a German Gulf War veteran with an abnormal fascination with the Civil War could have in common with an Indian girl from southern Chiapas, I didn't know or have the heart to ask. Whatever it was, he seemed excited about his prospects.

Bern and I matched beers for a couple of hours. The architects had left and the Canadian girls had moved to another table where they were talking with some Australian surfer types. Thankfully, the band had wrapped up. Bern had gone to take a leak and I was getting up to buy the next round when it happened. I stood up and, being drunker than I'd thought, accidentally knocked my chair into the chair back of one of the Mexican artisans.

The guy in the chair jumped up and started poking me in the chest and yelling in my face. If I was intoxicated, he was absolutely hammered. His speech was so slurred I couldn't make out most of what he said. I kind of understood something about gringo tourists and I totally got the "hijo de su puta madre" part, but most of what he said seemed nonsensical at the time: "Chigada neoliberalismo" this and "pinche güeros y el banco mundial" that and a whole bunch of other stuff that I thought was equally unrelated to anything, like him being a Palestinian and me being an Israeli. I get it now, but at the time the specific meaning of the words was lost on me. The general tone, however, was perfectly clear.

Now I don't want to give the wrong impression about me because what happened next might make me sound like someone prone to violence and I've never thought of myself that way. I still don't. Even after what I did later, it's not like I'm one of those incarcerated, wild-eyed monsters you see on TV. I'm not a willfully bad person. I'm not. But there in the bar and squared off with the Mexican hippie, I didn't have any idea as to what I would later prove capable of. So trust me when I say I was as surprised as anyone when this guy punched me in the side of the head and something like a wire of instantaneous white-hot rage shot through me. I picked him up, slammed him to the floor, and put my boot on his throat. Fortunately that was as far as I went because the jolt of fury disappeared as quickly as it had come and I immediately realized I'd done something colossally stupid as the whole place became instantly silent and all his friends were on their feet. I pictured the four of them taking me outside and kicking my head in.

"Oye," I said, raising my hands and backing away. "No quiero problemas."

They must have decided their friend had deserved it because after a couple of moments of hard glares, they helped him up instead of jumping me. By then the Canadian who had been passing out the flyers in the zócalo had rushed over to break things up. In my defense, a couple of backpackers explained what had happened and the Canadian told the artisans to take their friend home. On their way out, I distinctly heard the skinny guy I'd seen with Maria at El Acuario call his drunk friend a "pendejo" and say, "El es amigo de Lobos de Madrid."

6

THE NEXT MORNING I sat in the shade of the covered terrace in front of the guesthouse, sipped hot coffee, and listened to the water splashing in the fountain. The coffee was dark and strong and combined with the rhythmic sound of the water to help clear the fuzz in my head. I was on my third cup when César came through the door from the street. I was a little surprised at how happy I was to see him. It had been a long time since I was happy to see anyone. He unlocked the front gate and the black pickup drove through and parked in the garage. César was closing the gate when he noticed me.

"Compadre, come meet Ramón," he said, waving me over as he walked toward the truck.

I hauled myself out of the chair and waded across the great expanse of sun-filled courtyard. Even with sunglasses I must have looked hungover because César started chuckling as soon as I reached them.

"Wow, compadre," he said and pushed my glasses up so he could see my eyes. "¿Estás enfermo?"

"I had a few beers last night," I said, pushing the sunglasses back down.

"A few? You're green."

"A few more than a few."

César laughed and Ramón grinned.

Ramón. I suppose because I never got to know Ramón all that well before it all went down, I have trouble divorcing my feelings for him now from my feelings those first few months I knew him. I do remember thinking that he didn't look the way I'd expected. Somehow I'd pictured him like another version of César. Good looking. Well proportioned. Fit. Graceful. But he didn't look anything like César. His head seemed small compared to the rest of his large-boned body. A long, deep scar cleaved the length of one side of his pudgy face. He had small eyes and tiny ears and he wore one of those neatly trimmed mustaches I tend to associate with highway patrol officers and Middle Eastern strongmen. A tattoo of La Virgen de Guadalupe was on his forearm.

"Mucho gusto, Ramón," I said. "I've heard a lot about you."

"Mucho gusto, Señor Singer," he replied. He tossed his keys onto the seat of the truck and shook my hand. He had quite a grip.

"Hank," César corrected him. "You can call him Hank."

"Mucho gusto, Hank," Ramón said, pumping my hand one last time before turning me loose and reaching into the bed of the pickup to hoist out an army-issued duffel bag. "Bienvenidos a Mexico."

"Thanks."

"Hank," César said. "Give us a hand, would you?"

There were two more duffel bags in the bed of the pickup, so César and I each took one and carried them to the house. The bag I carried looked half full but was heavy. Metal clanked on metal as I carried it.

"What do you have in there? Tire irons?" I joked when we reached the living room and César took the bag from me.

"Armas."

"Say what?"

"Armas," he repeated.

With keys from his pocket, he unlocked the padlocks securing the top of the bags and carefully slid the contents of each onto the rug. Sure enough, they were guns: six or seven pistols, mostly revolvers, five shotguns, a dozen or so hunting rifles, and two automatic rifles. César sat on the floor and picked up one of the automatic rifles. From the way he began breaking it down, it was clear he knew what he was doing.

"Wow," I said, gingerly picking up one of the revolvers. "They're not loaded, are they?"

"No," he said, putting the rifle down. "But never take somebody's word for it." He took the revolver from me and demonstrated how to open it and check.

"What are they for?" I asked as I practiced the steps he'd just shown me.

"I collect them. I started in the army."

I didn't know anything about guns or gun collecting, but a couple of the hunting rifles, worn and covered with rust, looked worthless. I put the revolver back on the rug and lifted one. I'd be afraid to fire it for fear it would blow up in my face.

"You collect this crap?" I said.

César laughed. "Some I collect. Some I sell. You'd be surprised what junk people will buy."

"Really?"

"Sí."

"Why on earth would somebody with your money want to sell used guns?"

"The first rule of business is, never turn down a chance to make a profit." The way he said it made him sound like he was repeating something of a family slogan.

"If you say so," I said.

He laughed. "I'm joking." He tested one of the rifles' mechanisms by pulling it open and letting it slide closed in rapid succession. "There's no real money in it. We do it for fun."

Ramón came back from wherever he'd taken the third bag and sat on the sofa. He picked up the automatic rifle that César had just reassembled. Like César, Ramón handled the rifle in a way that indicated it was not his first time.

"Hey," I said, suddenly remembering something I'd either heard or read when going through airport customs, "aren't guns illegal in Mexico?"

Ramón smirked and I suddenly felt like I'd embarrassed myself. I suppose the question did sound a little naive.

"I mean it's not like the States, where you can buy a machine gun at the Kmart or swap meet or wherever, is it?"

"No. Technically they're illegal unless you're a soldier or police officer or you have a special license."

"Do you have a license?"

"Of course, but it's not like I need it. This is Mexico."

"Oh," I said. "So where do you get them?"

"Get what, the licenses?"

"The guns."

"I have friends in the police."

"You get them from the police?"

"Federales."

"Really?"

"Sí. They confiscate them from narcotraficantes. They're supposed to destroy them, but my friends don't make very much, so it is a good way for them to make a few extra pesos. They destroy some—you know, for the TV and newspapers—and then sell the rest."

"And you said you sell some. Who the hell buys them?"

"Whoever wants. Los narcos, mostly."

"What? You buy guns that federales take from drug smugglers and sell them back to drug smugglers? What if the federales find out?"

"They know."

"What?"

"Sure. Los narcos are going to get the guns one way or another, so the police figure they might as well get a cut. Besides, this way they limit the guns in circulation."

"Oh, that makes sense."

"No. De verdad," César said, laughing at my reaction. "You see that shotgun?" He nodded at the shotgun in Ramón's hands. "I've bought and sold that same shotgun two other times."

"You're kidding."

"No," Ramón said and racked the pump action. "It's a very profitable gun."

I wish I could say that I saw, right then and there, the sheer stupidity and danger of hanging out with two guys who bought illegal guns from crooked federal police before selling them to drug smugglers. I didn't. I blame the fact that I was in a foreign country, in César's world, and that he was so nonchalant about the whole thing. I bought into that whole "when in Rome" syndrome. But really, how much of a brain does it take to figure out that the combination of gun smugglers, drug traffickers, and Mexican police is a bad one? Of course, the great irony is that if César had really sold the guns exclusively to drug traffickers, at least four people wouldn't be dead.

"Do you want one, compadre?" César asked me. "Take your pick."

I looked over the guns spread before me. "No," I said. There had been a time not long after the girls had died when I'd been perpetually aware of the garden hose in the backyard and my car in the garage. While I'd gotten past those thoughts, a gun seemed like a bad idea. "Thanks though."

"Suit yourself."

We made quesadillas for lunch and they spent the rest of the afternoon trying to win the foosball table from me. They didn't have much luck and by the time I'd taken two hundred pesos off each of them, I didn't give the guns another thought.

The three of us hung out some those first few weeks—playing foosball, grilling food, and surfing three hundred channels of satellite TV—and a few nights we went out for tacos and too many shots of tequila. But I confess that I was a bit disappointed that Ramón was always around. It kind of felt like having a third wheel. Maybe that's not fair, but César and I didn't really get a chance to talk, though I don't know what I would have wanted to talk about if it had just been the two of us. César had to work a lot too. It's not like he had a regular nine-to-five job, but three times a week a courier would arrive with documents related to the various Lobos de Madrid business holdings and investments and César worked diligently for four or five hours each morning doing things related to the management of the family empire. Plus he had to go out for a lot of meetings, often to Tuxtla for the better part of the day. On top of everything, César's father recently had bought a hotel in San Cristóbal, so César went to the hotel in the afternoons to supervise the remodeling work. Ramón either drove César to his meetings or ran errands related to Lobos de Madrid businesses or went to the hotel in César's place. If he wasn't doing any of those things, he wrenched on the truck.

Because they were so busy working, I spent a fair amount of time by myself. César's personality sucked me in when we were together, particularly if Ramón was elsewhere, and Colorado and the girls slipped to the back of my mind. But when César and Ramón were off doing something and I was alone with nothing to do, I watched myself think. It definitely was better than it had been when I was still in Colorado, where I couldn't even go into the supermarket cereal aisle without regretting having refused

Suzy the Lucky Charms and Coco Puffs and all the other sugar varieties she'd pleaded for or where I couldn't go to the gas station without remembering how Jenn jokingly tried to make me jealous of the attendant who was so blatantly ogling her. That was always so funny. When I think about what I miss most about Jenn—and it's a long list—the first thing that always comes to mind is the way we used to play with one another, the way we shared our experiences by teasing one another. We never did it with anything that mattered, but we never made a pot of coffee in the morning without a fifteen-minute debate about why each thought the other should get up to make it. Whoever came up with the more ridiculous argument usually won, but it never mattered who actually rolled out of bed. We pretended it did, me grumbling about the unending duties of a husband or Jenn claiming she would be submitting a bill for services rendered, but it didn't matter. It was all just a game, a way for us to be together. If there was one thing I had learned more clearly since arriving in San Cristóbal, it was the dangers of being alone with my thoughts. By the time Saturday came, I was pretty down, so I was relieved when César said there was a well-known band performing at El Acuario that night. I needed some noise to drown myself out.

7

It turned out that César didn't really want to go to El Acuario. It was business. His father had given him instructions to entertain the son of a business associate who was in town from Mexico City. It was the business associate's son—Gilberto something was his name—who wanted to go to the party. César planned to collect Gilberto from his hotel and then meet Ramón and me at El Acuario. We were waiting in line when they showed up. Gilberto was dressed like a pirate. César introduced us. Ramón and I both said hello, but Gilberto barely acknowledged my presence. He didn't even look at Ramón. César whispered in my ear: "He's a prick, but his father's an important connection. It's business, compadre. Just ignore him."

"What's up with the pirate outfit?"

"Tomorrow's Halloween. It's a Halloween party."

"Ah," I said. I'd forgotten about Halloween. I thought about taking Suzy trick-or-treating. We'd dressed her as a pumpkin the first two years, but the last time she'd insisted on going as a princess.

The band was called Los Reyes and, according to César, was well known in the area. Judging from the blend of reggae and salsa that washed over us, the band's popularity was well deserved.

Antonio had plastic devil horns on his head and was sitting at a table and collecting a cover charge as people came through the door. The tables were all full and a mob of people, about half in costumes, danced in front of the stage. The vocalist sang a line of the chorus and the crowd called it back to him. I recognized several people from my night at La Taberna. Everyone was clearly having a good time.

Antonio asked Gilberto for his money and Gilberto pointed at César before pushing his way into the crowd. César and I exchanged a look at Gilberto's expense. Then he said to Antonio: "He's my guest."

"Okay," Antonio said as he did the three-grip handshake with each of us.

"It's quite the party," I said.

"My doorman didn't show up," Antonio explained as he took our money. "That's the third time."

"You should fire him and get somebody else," César said.

"I know. You want a job?"

César cocked an eyebrow and smirked as he took his change.

"No, I didn't think so," Antonio said. "Oye," he said, suddenly snapping his fingers as if he'd just had a revelation. "How about you?"

"Me?" I asked, pointing at myself and checking over my shoulder to make sure he wasn't talking to someone else.

"Claro. I heard what you did to Víctor at La Taberna. He's an idiot. Every time he shows up here he gets hammered and makes problems with all the tourists. Que bueno que le rompiste la madre."

"You were in a fight?" César asked, surprised.

"It wasn't a fight." I was embarrassed that word of the scuffle at La Taberna had preceded me.

"That's not what I heard," Antonio said.

"It wasn't a fight."

"With who?" César asked.

"I don't know him. It was nothing."

"You know him," Antonio said to César. "Víctor. He's part of that artisan gang. I like those guys. Most of them are good friends of mine. Even Víctor is okay when he's not drinking. The problem is he's always drinking. When he gets more than one shot of tequila in him, he goes ..." and Antonio whistled and circled his index finger next to his head.

"What's he look like?"

"Long, stringy hair. He always wears the same vest, one of those embroidered ones from Guatemala. You must have seen him around."

"With a mole on his cheek?"

"Eso," Antonio said, indicating César had the right guy. "He's a pendejo."

César gave Ramón a look and Ramón nodded as if to say he knew who Víctor was.

"Why didn't you tell me?" César asked me.

"There was nothing to tell. He was drunk. I'd had a bunch of beers. He said some things and smacked me, so I kind of pushed him onto the floor."

"I heard you dropped him on his head," Antonio said.

"He hit you?" César asked and glanced at Ramón again.

"Yeah, I guess. It wasn't much of a punch. Forget about it. It was nothing. Really. No fue nada."

César studied my face for a moment. "Sure," he said, kind of quietly. "Whatever you want."

"So, you want the job?" Antonio asked, taking some money from some people who came in behind us. "Fifty pesos a night and all the free cerveza you can drink."

When I didn't immediately respond, he said, "Come on. You'll be helping me out. Look at the bar. Maria can't serve all those people."

People were standing three or four deep in front of the bar, waving money in the air, trying to get drinks. I couldn't even see Maria beyond the crowd.

"And what? I just sit here and take the money?"

"That's it."

"They drink for free too?" I asked, pointing my thumb at César and Ramón.

He thought about it for a moment.

"Está bién. But only tonight," he said.

"Yeah … okay."

"Gracias," Antonio said and handed me the cigar box. "I'll go get your cervezas."

"What?" I asked when I saw the way César and Ramón were looking at me.

"You don't want to work here," César said.

"Why not?"

"You just don't."

"There aren't any other empty tables or chairs and it's not like we were ever going to get a drink standing at the bar."

Looking around the restaurant, they saw I had a point.

"I mean he's paying me to drink beer," I added as we sat down. "How am I going to pass that up? I only have to do it tonight."

While the free beer was the obvious incentive, the real reason I think I took the job was because I thought it would give me something to do that didn't rely on César or Ramón to keep my mind occupied. Plus, I figured the money I'd made on the sale of the house in Colorado wouldn't last forever. Fifty pesos wasn't exactly going to make up for my lost Talbert salary, but it was something.

It was a good party. I don't know if there are fire codes that set occupancy limits in Mexico, but if there are, we had to be way over. I collected so much cash at the door that I twice had to give a big wad of bills to Antonio just to make more space in the cigar box.

The architect couple from La Taberna paid the cover charge.

"I didn't know you worked here," she said as I handed back her change.

"Started tonight."

"I see."

"It's a fun place," the man said.

"I like it so far. How goes the building project?"

"We made reasonable progress this week. Next week, who can say."

At first César seemed to be annoyed that we'd come. I caught him checking his watch more than once, but after a while a European woman asked him to dance and in no time he had four other foreign gals rubbing up against him as well. Between songs he'd rush to our table, chug his beer, flash me his sly grin, and rush back to the ladies for the next dance. It bummed me out a bit that he left me sitting at the table with Ramón to collect money, but I had done it to myself by agreeing to the job. Plus I'd forgotten how much César liked dancing. At college parties he'd always gotten women to dance with him. It didn't matter if they were the only ones out on the floor or not.

A couple of the women with César saw that Ramón and I were his friends and tried to get us to join them. I explained that I had to watch the door, but Ramón lumbered onto the floor once César grabbed him by the collar and dragged him out of his chair. After a song or two he sat back down and mopped his forehead with a handkerchief.

Gilberto had wedged his way up to the bar and he wasn't moving. César checked in with him a couple of times, but he didn't seem like he particularly wanted César's company either and I certainly didn't regret that he hadn't sat with us.

César apparently knew some of the guys in the band because at one point they tried to get him to come up onstage to sing a song. He refused until the lead singer got the audience chanting César's name. I joined the chant and he cocked an eyebrow at me and rubbed the corner of his eye with his middle finger. Ramón saw it too and we laughed. Then César winked at us and bounded onto the stage while Ramón and I led the catcalls and whistles.

In Mexico, telenovelas, prime-time soap operas that only run for a season or two, are a national pastime. Everybody watches them. At that time, a telenovela called *Dos Mujeres, Un Camino,* or *Two Women, One Road,* was all the rage. Ramón was hooked and I'd watched it a few times because it starred Erik Estrada. I'd liked *CHiPs* as a kid and it was a sort of odd nostalgic fun to see him getting a second crack at his career via Mexican primetime. Not only was the show a hit, but also its theme song was all over the radio. You couldn't go anywhere without hearing it. Well, when the band started into the first chords of the song, everyone started cheering, but rather than sing the original lyrics, César improvised his own. I was laughing too hard to remember exactly what he said, but the chorus started, "Dos mujeres, un pepino." A pepino is a cucumber, and the rest of the song went in that general vein. He had all these gestures and facial expressions to go with the song, and when he finished, the whole place roared with approval. It was vintage César. I couldn't help but think of how funny Jenn would have thought it was. I could almost see her standing next to me, laughing as only she could, mouth agape, her whole body rocking with it, and then the way she would look at me, her eyes atwinkle, as if to make sure I was sharing the joy. But she wasn't there. It was just me and the crowd. Then César pointed at me and said, "That was for my compadre, Hank." The gesture wasn't equal to Jenn's look, but I smiled and pointed back at him and he jumped off the stage. About half the bar bought him drinks.

A couple of guys came through the door. They were sharply dressed and smiling and pointing out various people they recognized on the dance floor as I counted out their change. They thanked me and Ramón leaned over and said, his hot breath in my ear, "Maricones." I looked at him and he grinned and nodded toward the two guys who'd just gone past. I watched the guys go onto the dance floor and then shrugged at Ramón. The shrug was supposed to mean, "What's your point?" but Ramón was still grinning and nodded again like he'd understood my shrug to be disbelief. "Sí, son maricones."

Around midnight César came over with Gilberto and one of the foreign ladies in tow. She had the black nose and whiskers of a cat painted on her face. César introduced us. Her name was Monique something. She was Swiss.

"Gilberto's ready to go," César said. "So I'm going to walk him back to his hotel. Are you ready to split?"

"Given the beer we drank, I think I'd better finish out the shift."

"I'll just pay for the beer."

"It's okay. I like the music."

"Do you want me to come back for you?"

I looked at Monique and then back at César. "I suspect there are more productive things you can do with your time."

César smiled. So did Monique. "Okay, compadre," he said. Then to Ramón: "Stay with Hank."

"I can take care of myself," I said. Ramón hadn't been much company.

"Are you sure?" César asked.

"Absolutely," I said.

César looked at Ramón and shrugged.

"Then I think I'll go," Ramón said, rising again, "if you don't mind walking home by yourself."

"No problem."

"You're sure?" César asked again.

"Yep."

Antonio came over with another round.

"The lightweights are leaving," I said. "But I'll take their beers."

"Muy bien," Antonio said. He'd noticed the Swiss woman on César's arm.

They did their handshake ritual.

"Can I come to the house tomorrow?" Antonio asked. "I have something for you."

"Good," César said. "I have something for you too."

"Por la mañana, entonces," Antonio said.

"Hasta mañana, compadre," César said and slapped me on the shoulder.

After they'd gone, Antonio said he was going to cover the bar while Maria went on a break so this would be the last delivery of beers for a while. I took a look at the bar. The crowd was still three or four people deep, as it had been all night, and I hadn't seen Maria even once behind the wall of peso-waving humanity. A short while later, though, she was dancing with the men Ramón identified as maricones. The guys might have been gay, but they definitely were dancing with Maria.

The band played their last song shortly after one o'clock. The crowd called "Otra! Otra!" hoping for another tune, but the lead guitarist unplugged his guitar and said they'd have to wait until next time. The party started breaking up fairly quickly after that.

Antonio called me over to the bar. I sat on a stool and nursed a bottle of mineral water while he counted the cash from the cigar box and bar register. His lips moved as he thumbed through the bills. Then he went over to pay the band.

Maria, who had been talking to the drummer, went back

behind the bar and poured herself a shot of tequila. She drank half the shot and sucked on a wedge of lime. Just when I'd decided to introduce myself, she spoke: "Antonio says you are going to work here."

"Tonight anyway."

"You're American?"

"Yes."

"Your Spanish is very good."

"Thanks."

"Where did you learn?"

"School, mostly."

She nodded and sipped her tequila.

"My name is Hank."

"I know. Antonio told me."

"Oh. Right."

"Tell me, Hank. Are you one of those American boys who likes to fight in bars?" Her tone was pleasant but the use of the Spanish word for "boy" was deliberate.

"I'm not sure I understand the question."

"I heard you were drunk in La Taberna and you got in a fight."

"You heard that?"

"Are you angry? Do you want to fight with me?" Her tone couldn't have been more patronizing.

Antonio came back to the bar before I could tell her to step off.

"Fifty pesos," he said, handing me the bill. "So you have met Maria."

"Thanks. Yes, we've met."

She looked at me and sipped her tequila.

"Good. Then you will come tomorrow? Say, seven thirty?"

"Sure. Seven thirty." I was so preoccupied with Maria that I barely realized I had just agreed to take the job.

8

IT WAS THE RAPPING of the brass knocker on the front gate that woke me up, but I felt too lazy to get out of bed to answer. Whoever was knocking, they weren't coming to see me.

I lay in bed for a few minutes, wishing the coffee would brew itself. It didn't, so when my coffee jones finally eclipsed the comfort of the bed, I got up.

I brewed a big pot and took my mug and cigarettes out onto the patio. I like good coffee. For a while, before Jenn showed me the basic math, I'd been one of those idiots who goes to Starbucks every day for a three-dollar latte. But nothing was like the coffee in Chiapas. César's family grew it on their ranch, had their own roasting company, and exported it to the most exclusive markets in the world. César told me it went for more than twenty dollars per pound in Europe. The dark roast was my favorite.

I was on my third cup when César and Antonio crossed the courtyard. César was shirtless. Antonio carried two of the green duffel bags. They disappeared out the door to the street and then César came back in. He started toward the main house but veered my way when he saw me sitting on the patio. He still had the six-pack abs he'd had in college. I needed to get back to the gym one of these days. Jenn and I had gone religiously. She would climb the StairMaster for hours and then joke, "I climbed the Republic

Plaza twice today," or "I just summited a fourteener."

"Coffee?" I asked him.

"Thanks. Lots of milk and sugar."

I went into the house, poured his cup, added the milk and sugar, and topped off my own. César was smoking one of my cigarettes and blowing smoke rings when I sat back down.

"Did Antonio buy those guns?"

"Traded for them," César said, blowing into his cup.

"Traded what?"

César put his cup on the table and pulled two film canisters from his pocket. "Damn near the best coke I've ever had. You want to do a line?"

"It's like ten in the morning."

César shrugged and put the canisters back in his pocket.

"So Antonio deals coke?" I asked.

"Not exactly. He knows someone. I think it's one of the Italians, but he won't tell me. Says he's sworn to secrecy. It must be one of the Italians, though. Probably Rinaldo or Silvestro."

Because I didn't know Rinaldo or Silvestro, I tried to picture which of the Italians I'd seen the night before might fit the image of a gun-toting coke dealer. None did. Of course, that probably had to do with the fact I kept picturing Ray Liotta in *Goodfellas*.

"And why do they need guns?"

"I think they trade them. This is the fifth time Antonio's done a deal with me and it's not like the Italians need all those guns."

"So Antonio is just a connection."

"Yeah. That's why we stopped in there the other day. I was hoping he was holding so we could party." César blew a smoke ring and we both watched it drift in the morning air. "To tell the truth, I don't particularly like him or his restaurant. Before the other day, I'd only been there one other time. He usually comes to me. I wouldn't have gone yesterday but for Gilberto."

"What a jackass that guy was."

César rolled his eyes in agreement.

"Still, that was a good party. That band can play."

"Yeah, and it's obviously one of the best places in town to meet fresh fish."

"Do you mean eat fresh fish?" I asked, thinking I'd missed some sort of Spanish colloquialism.

César laughed. "Fresh fish is what Ramón calls the tourist girls. They're good for the first two days, but after that they start to stink. Most of the tourists are here a couple of days and then they head off to Palenque or Guatemala and a whole new batch comes in. You get it? The place is called El Acuario and—"

"I get it. It's stupid and shallow, but I get it."

"Shallow? Way to stick with the metaphor," he said and grinned as I groaned.

"That's as bad as one of Jenn's jokes."

"No way. Hers were the worst. What did the blonde say when she opened a box of Cheerios?"

"Look! Doughnut seeds! Believe me, I heard them all at least a dozen times."

He smiled. "I bet. Is there more coffee?"

"In the kitchen."

"Do you want a refill?"

"I'm good."

César crushed his cigarette butt in the ashtray and went in to fill his cup and I thought about Jenn's jokes: "What do you call a blonde with a high IQ? A golden retriever." "What do call a blonde with half a brain? Gifted." "Why are all blonde jokes one-liners? So men can remember them." She'd thought that last one was hysterically funny.

"What are you grinning about?" he asked when he came back.

"Nothing," I said. "So you really don't like Antonio?"

"It pisses me off that he lets Maria work there."

"She is kind of a bitch."

"You have no idea."

"She gave me a bunch of grief last night about that fight I was in. What's her story?"

"Her story is that she would sleep with a dog if it rubbed against her leg."

"If I didn't know you better, I'd say you were jealous." I'd meant it as a joke, but César seemed to flinch and he gave me a look I'd never seen before, like his whole insides turned over. Then he picked up my Zippo from the table and turned it over in his hand.

"Without going into it," he said, "let's just say our families used to be close. We did a lot of business together. Her father was a pretty good guy. He and I convinced my dad to invest in this big project, but then all her sleeping around twisted everything. The two families had a big falling-out. A big falling-out." César shook his head in disgust at the memory of it. "The project went all sideways and my father got burned for tens of millions of pesos." He took another cigarette from the pack, lit it, and exhaled a long plume of smoke. "Because I was the one who had talked my father into investing, I ended up looking like a total ass. He still doesn't trust me with big decisions because of that. He says he does, but he doesn't." César returned the lighter to the table. "It was even worse for her father. It killed him. He lost almost as much as my father and he had a heart attack. It served him right, too, given how he screwed us over, but imagine what kind of heartless whore would kill her own father." He looked at me. "Just stay away from her." I could see he meant it. Then the look was gone as quickly as it had come and César smiled. "And don't worry about that fight. You won't have any more problems with those guys."

"How's that?"

"They know who I am. I'll straighten them out. Remember,

compadre, in Mexico it's all about who you know."

"Isn't that true everywhere?"

"Sure. It's just more true in Mexico."

"If you say so."

We drank our coffee.

"Antonio said you're working tonight," César said after a time.

"At seven thirty."

"Why? I can't believe you're going to work there."

"It's something to do."

"Are you bored?"

"I'm not bored. I just hadn't expected you to be working so much."

"What did you expect? I mean, I have to work."

"I know, but I hadn't thought about it before I came down. To be honest, the whole trip was an impulse. I don't know what I was expecting. You kept saying to come down and then one day I said fuck it and that was that."

"I'm sorry if I misled you."

"There's nothing to be sorry about. You have to work. You have a life. You can't drop everything. I get it. I just need something to do that doesn't rely on you being around twenty-four/seven. I don't need a whole lot of time alone."

"But do you really want to work there? You could come work for me."

"Compadre, I'm not going to be your employee."

César nodded and pursed his lips and I thought he might say something. He had that expression he would get when he had something important on his mind. At the time I thought he was just sympathetic to my not wanting a lot of time for navel gazing, but looking back on it I think he wanted to say something more about me not working at El Acuario. He didn't. Then the expression went away. "You want to play some fútbol?"

"Do I have to play opposite you?"

"Do you think your teammates will let you?"

"Very funny."

"Come on," he said and gave me a brotherly shove. "I'll name another move after you."

"That's what I'm afraid of. Ramón coming too?"

"Nah. Ramón doesn't play." He grinned. "Come on."

"All right. Let me get changed."

I HAD EVEN MORE fun than the first time. I played quite a bit better too. Not that it mattered—César still dominated. But it felt good to be playing and to play well. We stayed at the fields for several hours and my legs were stiff by the time we climbed out of the truck back at the compound, so I took a long, hot shower, ate a banana, and took a nap. I dreamed about a game in college. Then I had the dream about the river. I woke gasping at the usual spot.

The sun was casting late afternoon shadows across the room. I took another hot shower, got dressed, and went to see what César and Ramón wanted to do for dinner. Ramón wasn't home, but César suggested steaks and salad. Because fresh produce had to be cooked or disinfected against food-borne illnesses, I'd found myself eating fewer vegetables than I had back home. I wasn't exactly a leafy green vegetable kind of guy, but a salad sounded unusually appealing.

César got the grill going and marinated some fillets while I washed the lettuce and tomatoes, placed them in a bowl filled with purified water, and squirted in a few drops of Microdyn. I peeled and sliced cucumbers and waited for the lettuce and tomatoes to soak. César told me to keep an eye on the steaks while he went to get some wine from the bar in the game room. I was setting the table and César was just forking the meat off the grill when Ramón pulled into the courtyard and parked in the garage.

"How did it go?" César asked. Ramón apparently was back from some errand César had sent him on.

"They got the message."

"Good."

The exercise must have made us hungry because there was a ton of food and we ate our plates clean and washed the food down with two bottles of French wine.

We cleared the dishes and then, around quarter after seven, I decided I'd better be on my way to El Acuario.

César pulled one of the film canisters of cocaine from his pocket. "Do you want to do a rail before you go?" he asked me.

"Maybe later."

"You sure?"

"I'm good," I said and went into the guesthouse for my jacket.

They were drinking cognac and smoking cigars when I came out. The film canister was on the table next to a razor blade and mirror. So was the pistol Ramón had kept.

"That looks like a recipe for a bad headline."

César grinned. "Our own little Halloween party. We'll save you some for when you get back."

"You'll still be up?"

"Oh," César said. "Don't worry, compadre. We'll be up."

"Okay," I said. And I left for work.

9

THE KITCHEN AT El Acuario was open until eleven thirty, but the drinking crowd usually started showing up around nine o'clock when the live music got started. As with many restaurants, the bar was the real moneymaker. When I got there, a solo musician was playing acoustic guitar onstage. Antonio was taking dinner orders and wore a pair of Groucho Marx glasses with the nose, mustache, and eyebrows. Maria was behind the bar. She was wearing all black and a matching black Zorro mask and looked as good as ever and for a moment I forgot our conversation from the night before.

I caught Antonio on his way into the kitchen. "How much are we charging at the door?"

"No cover charge tonight," he said as he returned two menus to the shelf behind the bar. "I only charge at the door when I have a big name playing."

"So what do you want me to do?"

"Greet people at the door and show them to a table."

"That's it?"

"That's it. Mostly I need you to help me if there is a problem with a borracho."

"Okay," I said, nonplussed by the idea of basically playing maître d' unless some drunk started trouble.

Despite a good-sized dinner crowd, the job was about as dull as I expected and by ten o'clock I'd decided that free beer or no free beer, tonight would be my last night. In fact, I was just about to tell Antonio I'd changed my mind when a skinny guy with glasses came in. He was the same guy who'd been with Maria the first time I'd seen her. He'd also been among the artisans when I'd gotten into the altercation at La Taberna.

"Welcome to El Acuario. Would you like a table or do you want to sit at the bar?"

He gave me a cold look, frowned, and walked past me to the bar. I watched him, thinking he might start trouble, almost hoping he would. He started talking with Maria and whatever he was saying clearly wasn't making her happy. When Antonio got in the conversation and started with his Italian gesturing, I took that as my cue and walked up behind the guy.

"¿Todo está bien?" I asked.

"Maria's daughter is sick, but if she leaves I don't have a bartender," Antonio explained. "Just stay until the kitchen closes," he pleaded. "Por favor."

"Okay," she said, although the concerned look on her face made it obvious that she wanted to go. "Salvador," she said to the skinny guy, "she'll be okay."

"She's really scared," Salvador said. "You know how she gets after an episode."

"Can't you take care of this? I'll be there in an hour."

"She wants you. You're her mother."

"How is Doña Asunta?" Maria asked.

"She's as upset as Luz is. You should come now."

Maria bit her lip and looked at Antonio.

"I'll cover the bar for you," I said.

Antonio looked doubtful. Maria looked at me like she thought maybe I was trying to take her job.

"Really. It's no problem. It's mostly just opening bottles of beer and pouring shots, right?"

"Sí," Antonio said, still somewhat reluctant.

"The prices are listed, and if I have a question, I'll ask."

Antonio and Maria exchanged a brief, silent conversation.

"So what's the problem?" I asked, looking from one to the other.

After a moment, Antonio shrugged.

"Okay," he said. "Maria, I'll see you Tuesday."

"I can stay. Luz can wait an hour," Maria objected.

"No. Go home. Take care of Luz," Antonio said.

She was obviously reluctant to leave with me in her job, but she put on her jacket, took her handbag from under the bar, and started to leave with Salvador. She stopped and came back. For a moment I thought she was going to thank me, but instead she came around the bar and emptied her tips from the tip jar. I got the impression she was waiting for me to make a claim.

"That's okay. They're yours."

She snapped her eyes at me. "I know."

I watched as she left with skinny Salvador. She really was remarkably beautiful. And what a charming disposition.

As I expected, the job was easy. Most people ordered beer, shots, or simple drinks like screwdrivers or rum and Coke. A couple of French women asked for daiquiris and I had Antonio walk me through the house recipe.

One thing about bartending is that everyone wants to be your friend, if only to get faster service, and the impersonal but constant interaction kept my mind distracted from itself. Besides the French women, who spoke little English and less Spanish, there was a Mexican biologist, who was doing research in the Lacandón jungle; three Italians, two of whom turned out to be Rinaldo and Silvestro; and several German, Australian, and

Canadian backpackers who were in San Cristóbal for a few nights on their way to or from Guatemala. A couple of the female backpackers had some local artisans with them. I'd seen two of the artisans at La Taberna. They seemed to be using the women to pay for their drinks and the women were clearly using the guys for a night or two of "Latin romance." The whole scenario reminded me of César's fresh fish joke.

An older American couple finished dinner and moved from their table to the bar. He ordered a beer. The woman had brought her coffee cup from the table.

"More coffee?" I asked.

"Decaf, please."

"What kind of beer?" I asked him as I topped off her cup.

"What's good?"

"I like Victoria."

"Let me try one of those, then."

I set a chilled glass on the napkin in front of him, opened the beer, and poured half the bottle before setting it next to the glass.

He lifted the glass to the light.

"It's dark," he said.

"A little," I agreed.

He tasted the beer and set the glass on the napkin.

"Is it okay?"

"It's fine. It's not Budweiser, but it's fine."

"You all on vacation?"

"Mr. Thompson is retired," the woman said.

"Thirty-six years in the construction business," the man added.

"Congratulations."

"Don't miss it at all. Mrs. Thompson and I, we bought an RV. We did the continental forty-eight and now we're in a caravan doing Mexico."

"Sounds like fun."

"It's the only way to travel. I wouldn't do it any other way."

"Mr. Thompson doesn't like hotels."

"I just like to have the comforts of home. When you get older, you get stuck in your ways. How about yourself? I take it you live here."

"I've only been here a few weeks."

"Plan on staying?"

"I don't know. For a while, anyway."

"What do you do back in the States, if you don't mind my asking?"

"I was in the construction game too."

"Is that so? Labor?" he asked and sipped his beer.

"I was the assistant manager in the concrete division of a company called Talbert."

"I know about Talbert. Out of Colorado. That's a big operation."

"Yes, it is."

"Pardon me for saying it, but going from management in Talbert's concrete division to bartending in Mexico strikes me as a bit of a step down."

"It's certainly less money," I agreed. "John Talbert was my father-in-law."

"I see," he said. "*Was* your father-in-law."

"You'll have to forgive Mr. Thompson," his wife said. "We have some old-fashioned ideas about marriage. Our son back in Omaha just went through a divorce."

"Fine gal too. I don't know what the boy is thinking."

"I wasn't divorced," I watched myself say. "My wife and daughter were killed in an accident."

"Oh, how awful," Mrs. Thompson said and touched my arm.

"Darn, son. I'm sorry to hear that." Mr. Thompson shook his head. "That's a darn shame."

"Thank you."

"That's just awful," she repeated.

"It's okay," I said, reassuring them. I couldn't quite believe I had told them. "I don't like to talk about it very much."

"Understood," Mr. Thompson said, but I could tell they were both looking for something to say. Thankfully, the Mexican biologist called for another Cuba Libre.

"Excuse me," I said and went to make the drink.

A while later Mr. Thompson waved me back over. Mrs. Thompson was still looking at me as she might a lost puppy.

"Can I offer you another beer?" I asked.

"No thank you, son. It's getting late and Mrs. Thompson only lets me have one." He put exact change on the bar.

"You're lucky I let you have the one," she said. They stood and he helped her with her jacket.

"Well," he said, extending his hand. "It was nice to meet you—"

"Henry," I said. "Henry Singer. It was nice to meet you as well, Mr. Thompson. And you, Mrs. Thompson," I said, shaking her hand as well.

"I really am sorry for your loss," she said.

"Thank you."

"We'll be in again, Henry," he said. "They've got good food here."

"I'm glad you like it. I'll tell the cook."

They waved from the doorway and she took his arm as they went out.

The backpackers ordered another round of beers for themselves and their artisan friends and then Antonio announced last call. A half hour later, only Antonio and I remained in the building. Félix had already closed the kitchen and left for home. Antonio came behind the bar and counted the till while I started washing glasses.

"Leave it," he said. "I have a muchacha who comes in the

morning to clean."

"Okay," I said, drying my hands on a towel.

"Oye Hank, dame una cerveza."

I opened a beer for each of us and went around the bar to sit on a stool. Antonio lit a cigarette and offered me the pack. I smoked and drank my beer while Antonio counted the money.

"So," I said when he'd finished counting, "you think I can work behind the bar? You don't really need a doorman."

"The thing is," he said, gesturing with the cigarette in his hand, "Maria lives off her tips. If you work behind the bar, she'll have to split the tips."

"She can have the tips."

Antonio drank from his beer and took a drag from his cigarette. He looked at me and seemed to consider the proposal. "Okay," he said finally. "If you let Maria have the tips, that's good enough for me."

"Are you sure?"

"Sí," he said.

"Good. Thanks."

We sat in silence for a few minutes, drinking our beer and smoking our cigarettes. The fish swam in the tank.

"That guy who came in to get Maria—"

"Salvador?"

"Sí ... Salvador. ... Is he her husband?"

"No. He's her daughter's father."

"But they're not married?"

"Salvador would like to be, but they're not married. They're friends and they have Luz."

I waited for Antonio to say something more, but he didn't.

"So ... ," I said, trying to sound as casual as possible, "Does she have a boyfriend?"

Antonio smiled at the question. He opened two more beers

and slid one across the bar. "She is a real beauty, no? Che bel viso," he said. He looked up and rocked the pinched fingers of both hands toward heaven. "And what a body." Then, looking at me conspiratorially, he said, "She really brings in the customers."

"I bet."

"But no," he said, as if suddenly remembering my question. "She doesn't have a boyfriend. She hasn't dated anyone in all the time I've known her. And it's not like she hasn't been asked. She just works and takes care of her daughter." He looked at me with a touch of sadness or sympathy in his expression. "Her daughter has epilepsy."

"That sucks," I said. What I didn't say was at least she wasn't in a coffin in the ground.

He wore the expression for another moment and then shrugged and made a little splurting sound by blowing through pursed lips, an odd gesture I later came to understand was an Italian way of saying "That's that" or "That's life."

Antonio went back to his accounting and made some notations in a ledger and I drank my beer.

"Where are you from in Italy?" I asked finally.

Antonio looked up from his book and smiled. "Milano," he said, his affection for his hometown evident in his face. "It's the most beautiful city on earth."

"So what're you doing here? In Chiapas, I mean."

His expression clouded and he turned back to his ledger and gave a little shrug. "The fascists are back in power. I won't live in Italia with the fascists in control."

I nodded but didn't say anything. It's not like I could discuss Italian politics. I'd thought the fascist movement in Italy had died with Mussolini.

"Ready?" he asked, closing the book and putting it in the drawer beneath the register.

"Same time tomorrow?" I asked, climbing off my stool.

He put a fold of pesos in his pocket and switched off the lights to the aquarium. "We don't open on Monday. Same time on Tuesday, okay?"

"Okay."

10

ONCE I OPENED THE outer door of the compound, the tranquil and contemplative quality of the walk home ended abruptly. The main house was lit up like a chandelier and the Rolling Stones pumped out of the open windows and echoed off the walls of the courtyard. The music was loud enough that I was surprised I hadn't heard a single note from the street. The compound, with its three-foot-thick walls and anti-battering-ram gate, really was its own little world. The Stones could have been playing live inside and no one outside would have known.

I could hear César and Ramón shouting the lyrics to the song and occasionally bursting into laughter. The Swiss woman that César had picked up at El Acuario danced past one of the windows. For a couple of moments I considered going up to the house to see what they were up to, but the two times I'd hung out with coked-up friends in the past hadn't been all that entertaining. I'd smoked pot some in college, but I'd never done cocaine. I'd just never had an urge to go down that road. And once I got the job with Jenn's dad, my limited pot use came to an end because the company had a drug test policy. So I decided to skip César's party and went to bed.

Their noise kept me awake for quite a while, and as I lay there listening to them I kind of felt left out. I'd come all this way to

Mexico and here he was partying without me. Of course, I was being stupid. He'd told me to come hang out after work and I'd been the one who decided to go to bed. I guess a cocaine-fueled rage-a-thon wasn't the kind of hanging out I'd had in mind when I'd bought the plane ticket. Then I reminded myself that I hadn't had anything in mind besides getting out of Colorado and away from my life. César's voice rose above the music and I listened as he shouted the lyrics to "Sympathy for the Devil" into the night. It made me smile in the darkness of my room and I suddenly felt better. A short time later I fell asleep.

THE NEXT DAY THE lights of the main house were still on, and white curtains billowed out the open windows when I left after lunch. I figured César and Ramón would be crashed out well into the afternoon. I'd gotten up briefly in the night for a glass of water and the alarm clock had read five o'clock and they'd still been going strong.

Once out on the street, I walked toward the center of town. The air was crisp. A faint and pleasant scent of smoke from someone's chimney wafted up the street. Even though it was Monday, the automobile traffic was subdued and many stores were closed. I had to step into a doorway so three guys muscling an armoire up the sidewalk could pass. On the next block two Chamulan women tried to get me to buy some dolls. They were persistent, but I finally waved them off and they crossed the street to intercept a group of backpackers. But other than the furniture movers, Indian saleswomen, and backpackers, there seemed to be fewer pedestrians than usual. Then I turned onto Calle Cinco de Mayo and was surprised to find a column of maybe three hundred marching protesters. They were dressed in white and carried large white signs with slogans like "Tierra y Libertad" and "Recuerda los Inocentes" and "Comida y Justicia." Several of them carried photographs of children. What was disconcerting was their silence: no chanting or yelling or even moving with any aggressive purpose. They just quietly filed down the street, holding their signs and walking in their white outfits.

I followed them to the zócalo and watched while they circled the park several times before going silently down another street. I considered having a coffee at the Kiosco, but instead I decided to hike up to the tall cross next to the Templo del Cerrito San Cristóbal atop a hill. It looked as though it provided a good vista of the city. I'd been meaning to climb up there since I'd arrived in San Cristóbal but hadn't gotten around to it. Actually, I'd seen very few "sights" since I'd arrived.

It's funny how when people live someplace they never visit any of the places that are always first on the list for tourists. I lived in San Francisco for my first two years of high school because my dad got transferred there. In those two years I never went to Alcatraz. Not one time. I never went down Lombard Street or up to Coit Tower. I have a friend who has lived her entire life in New York City and she's never been to the top of the Empire State Building or to the Statue of Liberty. I guess when you live someplace you figure you'll get around to it.

The hill was steep and the climb up the zigzagging staircase was longer than it looked. My legs ached from the fútbol game, but it was a good ache. About halfway up I took a break and swore to myself that one of these days I would quit smoking. As I stood sucking oxygen, I wondered how many stairs I'd climbed. Jenn would have run up them, making some crack about the stronger sex as she left me behind. Suzy would have counted them. I smiled to think how Suzy liked to count things. She'd learned her numbers really early. Don't ask me where she got it because neither Jenn nor I was particularly mathematically inclined, but we would talk about how Suzy was going to grow up to be a physicist or an engineer or an astronaut. Jenn said maybe she would be all of them. But Suzy didn't grow up to be anything. She didn't even grow up. She'd be three years old forever.

I was sweaty and winded when I got to the top where the hill flattened out, but I was glad I'd made the trip. The view was worth it. The red tiled roofs of the entire city spread out below. To the northeast, the sun-washed pink cathedral towers rose above the other buildings, marking the location of the zócalo. Using the cathedral as the reference point, I saw what I thought was the skylight of El Acuario. I looked for César's house too, but it was farther to the north and trees blocked my view. Pine-timbered mountains encircled the city and valley. The dark green ridges contrasted sharply against the blue sky.

The only other people atop the hill were a couple of back-packers. They were admiring the cross that had originally attracted my attention. It stood about fifty feet high and now that I was closer I realized it had been constructed with discarded license plates. I wondered what fool had designed the monstrosity and what greater fool had approved the design for display atop the hill. It spoiled the otherwise idyllic scene.

"Ugly, huh?" I said to the couple.

"I do not think so," the man said. I couldn't tell if he was being curt or if that was just his accent. I think it was Austrian.

"I like it," the girl said. "I like the story behind it."

"What's that?"

"The license plates are donated by the truck driving and taxi unions," she said as if this fact suddenly would illuminate the rest of the story.

"So?"

"So," the man said, "this is the church of San Cristóbal, the patron saint of travelers. The truck drivers donate their license plates so San Cristóbal will protect them."

"Oh," I said.

The couple wandered off, leaving me to reconsider the cross. The patron saint of travelers. I was a traveler. I was looking at the cross and thinking about it when the blue sky against which the cross was framed caught my attention and I thought about that sky I'd seen in the parking lot outside work in Colorado when I had realized I had been outside my own body for so long without even recognizing it. It was as though my life had become a dream of a dream of a dream. Then, seeing the color of the sky in the parking lot had begun to make me realize that I was in fact in a dream—a terrible, terrible dream from which there was no awakening. But knowing that it was a dream somehow pierced the dream too and grounded it in reality. Reality was not any easier. In some very real ways it was much, much worse to be outside myself and to recognize I was outside myself. But now, standing in front of that ugly cross, I suddenly understood that in Mexico I'd been more and more inside myself without being lost in the labyrinth of my mind. It was as though the fragments of myself had come together somehow and I was aware there was a wholeness to me that had not been there since the accident. How had that happened?

I left the cross and went to look at the church. The Templo del Cerrito San Cristóbal was small and the outside had been painted white with blue trim and the doors were padlocked shut. I wandered around the hilltop and took in the view to the southwest. Far below I saw the same column of marchers I'd seen before. They were filing into a cemetery like a column of white ants. That's when I remembered it was November 1. Dia de los Inocentes. That's why they'd been marching. The day of dead children. I thought about Suzy. I thought about the river and I thought about Colorado and the sky. I thought about Mexico and

César. I thought about being inside myself. I thought about being inside myself and about Suzy and somehow it wasn't as bad as it usually was. I looked at the mourners in the cemetery one last time and then I crossed the hilltop and headed back down the stairs. I counted them as I went. Just like Suzy would have. There were 283.

Walking along Calle Miguel Hidalgo, I came upon an arts and crafts store that was open. A few months before the girls were killed, Jenn had roped me into taking a crafts class at the Community College of Denver. Jenn, who always had a particular talent for making things and who was trying to get me to share her passion for horses, made a pair of cowboy boots for me with all this elaborate leather work and intricate stitching. The boots are far and away the most comfortable and most durable shoes I've ever owned. They've hardly left my feet since she gave them to me.

Boots were beyond my ability, so I had been making a doll for Suzy's birthday. I'd taken a long time with it, but I have to admit that I'd been proud of the way it was turning out. I'd carved the head from cedar and glued on hair and stitched the body. I'd even hand-sewn a little dress using a fabric with little yellow flowers that matched one of Suzy's favorite dresses. When the accident happened, only the painting of the doll's face had remained unfinished—something the teacher had told me I should have done before gluing the hair. I hadn't touched it since then, but when I'd sold the house and was packing up all the stuff, I found I couldn't just box up the doll. Like my wedding ring, which I wore on a chain around my neck, I didn't know what to do with it, but I wasn't ready to let it go. So I'd brought it with me. Standing outside this art store on El Dia de los Inocentes, I decided I'd finish the doll. I went in and a friendly woman behind the counter helped me select some small jars of paint and a few brushes. As she was ringing up the bill, I looked over a counter rack of Saint Christopher medallions.

"He protects travelers like you," the woman said.

I looked at her and thought about my time on the hilltop. "How much?"

"Twelve pesos."

"I'll take one," I said, taking it from the rack and putting it on the counter with the paint and brushes.

Back at the compound, the curtains still billowed out the windows. I put my paints and brushes in my bedroom, threaded the medal on the chain with my wedding ring, and went over to the main house.

The game room looked and smelled not unlike our old fraternity house after a party. Empty and half-empty beer bottles were all over the place and the ashtrays were overflowing with butts. A couple of barstools were on their sides. The answering machine was smashed to bits and pieces on the floor and a pool cue had been snapped in half. They'd left the TV on, so when I finally found the remote under the couch, I switched from music videos to Monday Night Football. The Bills were beating up on the Redskins, with Jim Kelly ultimately completing eighteen of twenty-four passes. Washington's four turnovers didn't help their cause much either. The final score was twenty-four to ten, Buffalo. César never appeared, so after the postgame wrap-up, I went back to my place to make soup from a can.

While I ate, I thumbed through the personals in an old edition of San Francisco's free weekly paper, the *Guardian*—I mean San Francisco, California. The paper had been saved to start fires in the fireplace. How a copy of it had ended up in César's house in Chiapas was anybody's guess. In high school my friends and I had always gotten a big laugh from reading the personals. The qualities people sought in one another for a relationship went way beyond what our adolescent imaginations could dream up.

Single transvestite seeks single shemale. / Rasta man wants Rasta woman for reggae days and irie nights. / Married couple seeks other married friends for dinner parties and spouse swap. / Eclectic Wiccan circle looking for gender-balanced people to celebrate Esbats, Sabbats, etc. / You require punishment; I hold the whip / I'm a bull rider and you're a bull. Let's rodeo! / Young gentleman to serve older, wealthy woman's every whim.

On and on they went, to our pubescent disbelief and delight. But as I spooned my soup and glanced over the personals, the shock value I'd enjoyed as a teenager was gone and I was struck by how sad and lonely these people were. What does it mean when we live in crowded cities and still we need to advertise to find human companionship?

My husband passed. My children moved away. I can't stand the sound of the wind.

I closed the pages, tossed the paper back on the burn pile, and washed my soup bowl. In bed, I thought about how the *Guardian* was an old issue and I wondered if any of those people had found what they were looking for. I hoped they had. Then I rolled on my side and looked at the photos of my girls. I'd brought two of Suzy. One was a later picture taken not long before the accident. The other was from when she was about a year and a half. She was wearing nothing but diapers and standing in a refrigerator box in our living room. We'd cut a door and windows in the box so Suzy could have a little playhouse. It wasn't the best photograph of her, but I kept it to remind me of the first time she had gestured to me to come play with her. I don't remember if she actually spoke words at that point, but I remember the gesture she made and understanding that she was actually using her imagination and asking me to be a part of her imaginary world. To this day, when I think about that moment, my heart feels like crushed birds.

11

THE NEXT MORNING I'd just finished breakfast and was sitting at my patio table with a cigarette and cup of coffee when César and the Swiss woman came out of his house and crossed the courtyard to the gate. They kissed for a few moments and then César opened the door and ushered her through. Even from where I sat it was obvious she'd not wanted to leave.

"Hey," I called to him.

He looked in my direction, waved, and came over.

"You're alive," I said when he reached the table.

He grimaced and sat in the other chair. "Barely." He lit a cigarette and exhaled a plume of smoke before returning the lighter to the table. "You missed one hell of a party."

"So it would seem."

He rubbed his free hand through the close-crop of his hair and then looked at me and grinned. "Just because I spent the whole day in bed doesn't mean it was all about recovery."

"Ah," I said. "You and what's-her-name becoming an item?"

"Monique? Naw. We won't see her again. She's supposed to meet friends in Guatemala tomorrow. She was gonna blow them off to stay, but I convinced her that her friends would be worried if she didn't show up."

"Why'd you do that?"

He grinned again. "Fresh fish, compadre. Fresh fish."

"Oh, right. I get it."

He grinned even more broadly. "I had to throw her back."

I shook my head and he laughed.

"So," I asked, "do you want to play some fútbol?"

He glanced at his wristwatch. "Maybe for a little while. I've got to be in San Juan Chamula by noon."

"Business?"

He nodded and tapped his ash.

"How far is it?"

"Not far. Like ten kilometers. But it might as well be on Mars."

"How's that?"

"Crazy Indians doing their crazy Indian shit. I shouldn't be there that long. At least I hope not."

"Yeah?" I said. "Can I go?"

He seemed to think about this. "Better not. Chamulans can be pretty aggressive and they don't like outsiders. By outsiders I mean anyone who isn't an Indian from Chamula. It's sketchy enough when I go by myself. Tourists who are dumb enough to go up there get assaulted all the time."

"Really?"

"Oh yeah. Hell, they even expel members of their own tribe who leave the congregation," he said. "They expelled Pascuala's family," he added, referring to his maid. "And by expel I mean physically threw them out. Her family went Evangelical and they got the boot. They lost their house, their land, everything."

"And you do business with these people?"

César shook his head as though it barely made sense to him either. "You should see this man I'm gonna try to find today. He's a village elder. He has some sort of spiritual powers. He's a total Martian, but I'm going to see him because he's got the monopoly on Coca-Cola distribution in the community."

"So?"

"Chamulans have to be members of the religious congregation."

"What's that got to do with Coca-Cola?"

"So get this," he said. "Chamulans use Coca-Cola as part of their religious sacrament."

"Are you serious? I thought they were Catholic." I'd heard some tourists at El Acuario mention visiting the church there. Even the town was called "Saint John" Chamula.

"Well, they're Indian Catholics. Like I said, they're Indians doing their crazy Indian shit. They drink the Coke to help them burp out evil spirits or some such nonsense."

"Really?" I wondered how the Coca-Cola Company had gotten its hooks into some remote indigenous community in Chiapas, Mexico. Of course, if the Catholics and the Evangelicals could convert them, why not the Coca-Cola Corporation too? They'd gotten their hooks in everywhere else.

"Anyway, this village elder has the monopoly on Coca-Cola distribution in the municipality. So everyone has to buy Coke for the religious ceremony that they're required to participate in upon penalty of expulsion and he's got the whole market cornered."

"That's a pretty good business model."

"Hell yeah it is."

"So what's the meeting for?"

"Rumor has it this village elder has been approached by the statewide Pepsi distributor about making a switch. I'm supposed to find out if the rumor is true, find out the terms, and make it clear it would be a mistake for him to make the change."

I looked at him.

"I'm telling you," he said, laughing at my expression. "It's crazy Indian shit."

"So, do you think you'll be able to convince him to stay with Coca-Cola?"

César looked at me like I'd just asked a stupid question. "Trust me, Pepsi might be the choice of a new generation, but Chamulans will be drinking Coke until my family and our business partners say otherwise." He crushed his cigarette in the ashtray and checked his watch again. "If we're going to play, we'd better get changed and go."

We went to the park and played fútbol for about an hour and I had as much fun as the previous times, my mind focused on the game and nothing more. Then we came back to the compound and I told him I'd see him later and went inside to shower and make lunch and César got ready for his appointment and left for Chamula. I ate my sandwich and puttered around the house until the maid, Pascuala, showed up. Not more than nineteen or twenty years old, she was an attractive young woman with classical Mayan features. High cheekbones and forehead. Long, slightly hooked nose. Almond-shaped eyes. We had some difficulty communicating because her Spanish was limited and my Tzotzil was nonexistent. She was also quite shy, generally avoiding eye contact with me. Still, I could tell that she thought I was something of an oddity and that she was curious about me. I kind of liked her for that shy curiosity that came across as a sort of reverence. She seemed to think I was someone of importance, or at least that was the impression I got from her. I thought about what César had said about Chamulans being aggressive, but I didn't get that feeling from her at all and I wondered if that was because her family had been ejected from the community. I tried to ask her something about it, but the subject only seemed to make her feel more uncomfortable, so after a while, because I didn't want to be underfoot, I cleared out and left her to do her thing.

Not having any particular place to be, I wandered over to the zócalo and bought a newspaper and had a cup of coffee at the Kiosco. I read the fútbol scores. There wasn't much else of interest. But then on the editorial page I read an opinion piece by one Eduardo Gallegos that was critical of the privatization and subsequent monopolization of Telmex by someone named Carlos Slim Helú. He went on to argue that if Carlos Slim was permitted to expand his monopoly into the nascent cellular phone market, the problem would be exacerbated. I wondered if this was the cell phone guy César had talked about doing some work for. I imagined he was. Gallegos argued that such a monopoly would eliminate the potential for smaller companies to thrive, resulting in fewer good jobs for the Mexican worker. I folded the paper and made a mental note to show the article to César. The waiter came with the bill and I paid, left a tip, and decided to wander over to El Acuario to see what was going on.

The restaurant was empty except for Félix, who was cleaning up after the lunch rush, and Antonio, who was sitting in his office with the door open. I poked my head in the kitchen to say hola to Félix and he waved me in and dipped a spoon into a pan of simmering broth.

"Try this," he said, holding out the spoon toward me, the palm of his other hand opened underneath to catch any drippings.

"What is it?"

"Try it."

I took the spoon from him and tasted. "That's damn good."

Félix smiled. "It's my new cacciucco recipe."

"Whatever it is, it's great."

"I know," he said and turned back to his pots. "I'm a genius."

I smiled and went to knock on the doorframe of Antonio's office. He was sitting behind his desk writing some sort of list and looked up as I entered.

"Hank," he said. He checked his watch from habit. "You're early."

"I was bored. Have you tried Félix's soup?"

"It's good, isn't it? Do you want something to do?"

"Sure," I offered.

"I forgot to give Maria the money and shopping list when she left on Sunday. Will you take it to her?"

"Umm … I don't know where she lives," I said, hoping this would get me off the hook.

"It's easy. Her apartment is on the zócalo. I'll write it down for you." And he did before I could object.

"Here's the list," he said, handing me the list with Maria's address scrawled across the top. "And here is the money." He opened a desk drawer and took a small stack of bills from a metal box. One of the revolvers César had traded lay next to the box. "Why don't you go with her so she can show you how to do the shopping in case I need you to fill in sometime. Okay?"

"Sure … okay." I was already holding the money and the list, and I'd asked for something to do. What was I going to say?

Maria's apartment building wasn't hard to find. The only apartments on the zocalo were above the bank and shops, kitty-corner from the cathedral. I climbed the stairs to the third floor and found the door with the number Antonio had given me. Someone was playing classical music on a piano inside. I knocked and Salvador answered. He didn't seem pleased to see me.

"What?"

"Is Maria here?"

"Sí," he said, but he made no move to tell her I was at the door.

"Can I speak to her?"

"Maria," he called over his shoulder after a moment. The piano stopped. "The gringo wants to talk to you." He didn't take his eyes off me as he said it, nor did he move from blocking the doorway. Even when Maria came to the door, Salvador stood behind her as if expecting that at any second I might try to barge in.

"How do you know where I live?" She made it sound like I was stalking her.

"Antonio asked me to bring you the shopping list." I brought out the list for her to see.

"Oh," she said. She took the list and ran her eyes down it. "And the money?" she asked, her tone less sharp than before.

"Here," I said and handed her the cash. "He wants me to go with you so I can learn how to do it."

While she counted the money, a little girl squeezed between Maria's legs and made a face at me. She was wearing a foam helmet that looked like it was something from the wardrobe of a Star Wars movie but for the color—bubble-gum-princess pink. Then I realized it probably was an epilepsy helmet. The girl was about three years old and looked just like her mother.

Maria smiled at the girl. "Give me a minute," she said when she turned back to me.

"Sure. I'll wait."

She closed the door and I waited in the hall. Through the door I could hear Maria and Salvador arguing. I didn't catch everything, but the gist of it was Salvador didn't like the idea of Maria going with me. He said something about an arm breaker that I didn't understand. I heard Maria say something about her job and that Antonio had hired me whether either of them liked it or not. She told Salvador to mind his own business and then the door opened. Apparently Maria had carried the discussion because she had her purse and two large woven-plastic tote bags. She gave me the tote bags and bent down to kiss her daughter.

"Take Luz down to Doña Asunta when you leave," she said to Salvador.

"Where else would I take her?"

"Tell her I'll pick Luz up at the usual time."

"Okay."

"And don't forget to give her the medicine."

"I won't."

"You say that, but don't forget."

Maria kissed her daughter a second time and we started down the stairs. Salvador was frowning in the doorway. Something about him rubbed me the wrong way and I couldn't stop myself from waving good-bye just to antagonize him. He took it as I'd intended, but their little girl smiled and waved back. "Bye," the girl said.

Maria started up Calle Utrilla and I fell in step beside her. Neither of us spoke for the first couple of blocks and our silence was palpable.

"I take it that was your daughter," I said finally.

"Sí."

"Is she feeling better?"

"Yes, she is," she said. She came to halt and turned to face me. "Thank you for covering my shift."

"No problem."

"De verdad. Gracias."

"Really. It was nothing."

"Did you have any problems?"

"No. In fact Antonio's going to let me work behind the bar."

There was a flash of concern in her eyes.

"But you still get to keep all the tips," I added quickly.

She studied me for a minute like she was trying to decide if this was an acceptable arrangement. For a moment I thought she was going to say something, but finally she nodded, as if to herself, and continued walking.

"So how old is she?"

"¿Como?"

"Your daughter."

"Three."

"She's pretty."

"Thank you."

"She looks like you," I said and Maria gave me a funny look.

"I don't mean it like that," I said, trying to backtrack, but only drawing a more puzzled look from Maria. "I mean you're pretty, but that's not what I meant. What I meant was—"

"I understand," she said.

When we got to Santo Domingo, Maria paused to admire a handwoven blouse that caught her eye.

The Indian woman rose from her seat behind her pile of goods.

"La señorita recognizes quality," the woman said.

"It's nice," Maria said. "¿Cuanto?"

The woman told her.

"That much?" Maria fingered the material for a moment. "It is very nice." She sighed. "But too much."

"I can see la señorita appreciates fine embroidery. Para usted, twenty pesos less."

"Some other time."

"Perhaps the señor will buy it for you," the woman said, smiling at me. "Don't the colors become her?" She held the blouse up to Maria for me to admire. Maria and I made eye contact.

"They do," I agreed.

Maria fingered the fabric and stitching. I could see her calculating how the blouse would fit into her budget. She shook her head and handed it back to the woman.

"Some other time."

"Bueno," the woman said, resigned to the lost sale. "Some other time."

Maria smiled at the woman and then we walked on towards the mercado.

The mercado was an open-air market that stretched over several acres. It was crowded. Around the edges, brightly dressed Indian women sat on the ground in front of small pyramids of tomatoes and oranges and squash and radishes. Others sold roasted ears of corn flavored with lime and chili. Men sold sacks of wood charcoal or bundled sticks. A group of small, half-naked children shrieked by, knocking an older Indian woman off her feet. Without even thinking about it, I bent down to offer my hand and help the woman up.

"¿Estás bien?" I asked. The woman looked at me and I thought she seemed more startled by me offering to help than she was to have found herself knocked to the ground. "Let me help you," I said, taking her arm. We got her back to her feet, but she hadn't stopped looking at me as though I had three heads. Then I noticed Maria and a number of other people were giving me strange looks as well. "¿Estás bien?" I asked the old woman again, but she was already shuffling away from me, glancing back over her shoulder as she went. I looked at Maria. "What?" I asked.

"She thinks you're going to force her to work for you."

"What? Why?"

"Because coletos and güeros don't usually help indigenous people without expecting something in return."

"What? An old woman got knocked down and I just helped her up. Anyone would do that."

Maria looked at me like there was something about my Spanish she didn't understand. "Everyone should, but not everyone would. Come on."

I looked around and the same half-naked kids were chasing a half-starved, mangy dog. No one was paying them the least amount of attention, but a few people were still staring at me, so I moved to catch up with Maria.

"I still don't understand."

Maria stopped walking. "There's a joke," she said after a moment. "Have you ever noticed how many speed bumps there are on streets around the city?"

I hadn't, but I said, "Yes."

"Do you know why?"

"Why?"

"Because people walk in the street," she said. "Indians too."

"That's a joke?"

She studied me and then shrugged. "No importa. Let's do the shopping."

Farther into the mercado began the maze of wooden stalls and kiosks shielded from the sun by low-slung tarps. From these, people sold bright flowers and more fruit and vegetables. Being about a foot taller than the average Chiapanecan, I stooped beneath the low-slung blue and yellow tarps as I sidestepped people bustling through the narrow passages between the wooden booths. In one small, horribly dirty stall a man was practicing something akin to dentistry and in the next a man with a bad haircut was giving another man the same bad haircut. I followed Maria into the middle of the maze and a warehouse rose up and we went in. The sickly-sweet stench of all the fresh and putrid matter was strongest in the enclosed space where butchers swatted at the flies. Plucked chickens hung from hooks. Slabs of pork and beef settled in thickening pools of their own juices.

Maria deliberately chose a particular butcher, although on what basis I couldn't tell, and ordered the kilos of beef on the list. The butcher cleaved the meat, wrapped it in several sheets of newspaper, and passed it over. She paid the man and moved on to another stall for the chicken and then another for the longaniza sausage.

Once we had everything on Antonio's list, a taxi took us back to El Acuario. We carried the groceries into the kitchen, where Maria helped unpack the bags and put the food away.

"Find everything?"

"Yes," Maria said, handing Antonio the change.

"Did you have any trouble with my directions?" Antonio asked me.

"No. It was easy like you said."

"Good."

"I'm going to go," I said. "I'll be back at seven thirty."

"Okay."

"Hank," Maria said, "thanks for helping me with the shopping."

"Sure. Thanks for letting me tag along."

Rather than walk straight home, I took a more circuitous route to simply enjoy the walk. It really was a great city for walking. And then I found myself among the vendors at Santo Domingo and standing in front of the woman with the blouse Maria had admired. I have no idea what compelled me to hand over two hundred pesos, but I suddenly realized how idiotic I was being when the woman handed me the bag and said, "Your novia will be very happy." In Mexico they use the word novia like we use girlfriend, but a closer translation would be betrothed. If you have a novia, the assumption is you are going to marry her. At the very least, the word implies a serious commitment. To compound my self-disgust, I was too embarrassed to ask for my money back. It's not like the woman would have given it to me. The bills had been tucked away somewhere under her shawls and I was holding the bag with the blouse. But I still wished I'd tried. When I got to the house, I put the bag in the back of a drawer, where I hoped it would be forgotten.

To get away from myself and the blouse, I went to see if César was home. Ramón's truck was still gone, but the front door of the main house was open, so someone was home. I found César in the dining room. He was sitting in a chair pushed back from the table, the shards of a shattered crystal bowl on the table beside him.

"¿Que paso?" I said, more as a greeting than a question. My mind didn't quite register that Pascuala was in the room with her shirt open and off her shoulders until she drew it closed at my voice. In fact, the moment it passed I wasn't even certain it had happened at all, like it was something I wasn't sure I'd seen out of the corner of my eye.

"Compadre," César said breezily. "Where have you been?"

"The mercado," I said. The girl, still clutching her arms to her chest and staring at the floor, hadn't moved. "What's going on?"

"I was just explaining to Pascuala that the bowl she dropped was worth more than she makes in a year and she was promising me it wouldn't happen again. Isn't that right, Pascuala?" He spoke like a foster parent or school principal might to a delinquent child.

"Sí," the girl whispered without lifting her head.

"Bueno," he said. "You can go back to work."

"What was that?" I asked after she'd hurried out of the room.

"The pendeja broke my mother's crystal," he said, and then he laughed when he noticed my expression. "Relax, compadre. She's a simpleton. If I don't get her attention, she'll be breaking stuff all over the house." Clearly I didn't look convinced because his tone became less flippant and he switched to English. "Look, Hank, I know what you're thinking, but this isn't the States. Trust me. My family has been dealing with the Indians for centuries and there are only so many ways you can get them to understand."

"Do you hear the bullshit coming out of your mouth?"

For a split second, almost imperceptibly and just in the corner of his eyes, César winced, but then the famous smile spread across his face and he slapped me on the shoulder and switched back to Spanish. "Ah, compadre, you're a good man. When you're right, you're right. I went too far. I'll make it up to her. Now let's play a game of foosball. Maybe you'll show me a little of that American compassion."

"Don't count on it," I said, and I whipped him three straight games.

II

12

THE NEXT MONTH AND a half passed much like those first weeks. During the day, if César and Ramón weren't working, we'd hang out, playing foosball or shooting pool. César and I went to the park several times to play fútbol. When César wasn't around, I'd explore or read or work on Suzy's doll. Antonio and I went to race go-carts a few afternoons. In the evenings I'd work at El Acuario. On the nights we charged a cover, I worked the door, but otherwise I tended bar with Maria.

It turned out that Maria and I worked well together, but I wouldn't say we were friends. While we were cordial, ours was strictly a working relationship. She didn't ask me about my life outside work and, the few times I asked her about herself, she gave me pleasant—if not particularly personal—responses. We never saw each other outside the restaurant. There were a couple of times while working when we shared a look that I couldn't help but think could be open to interpretation and on more than one occasion we accidentally brushed against one another, but none of that added up to anything. I don't suppose I need to say I never mentioned the blouse or my lapse in sanity. We didn't even go to the market together again. In fact, I only did the shopping for the restaurant one more time because when I told Antonio what I'd paid for things, he realized I was getting charged gringo prices.

I think it is safe to say that Maria knew I found her attractive, but not more so than every other guy who laid eyes on her. I was just another man and we both left it at that. Besides, she didn't seem to put a whole lot of stock in whether men found her desirable or not, which of course made her all the more so. Mostly she seemed to concentrate on being a good mom to Luz.

Fairly often Luz would come to El Acuario with Maria at the start of her shift so she could do the parental handoff with Salvador. Probably because children are curious and because my height and light complexion made me something of a curiosity, Luz developed a certain attachment to me. She'd come running up, pumping her arms really fast like little kids do when they run, her pink helmet bobbing from side to side. She'd show me the latest toy Maria had bought her or some new scratch or bruise she'd gotten falling down. I'd taken to carrying butterscotch candies in my pocket in a meek effort to quit smoking and I'd slip her one on the sly when she came in with her mother, which naturally increased her fondness for me. If Luz's affection for me made Maria a little uncomfortable, it clearly drove Salvador crazy and he'd speak to Luz harshly when she started in my direction. I can't say I minded that Luz's affection for me bothered Salvador, but I didn't give her any candy when he was around. That seemed like a line I shouldn't cross.

It was a good month and a half, at least better than the many months that had come before. Life in the States seemed far away, as if I'd been gone for years, not months. I just stopped paying attention to the news from home. I don't mean I was totally oblivious to what was going on stateside. For instance, when I read that Toni Morrison had won the Nobel Prize for literature, I experienced a strange surge of patriotic pride. I hadn't read any of her books, but I still felt proud, like when some American you've never heard of wins Olympic gold in some gymnastics event you couldn't care less about. And of course I kept a steady lookout for the release of the new Nirvana CD. When *In Utero* finally reached the stores in San Cristóbal, I ended up paying about twice what I would have back in the States, but it was worth it. But for the most part, I felt as far removed from what was going on in the US as I did from what was going on anywhere else in the world. Even when I watched the TV as all those houses in Malibu burned, I felt like they could have been in Romania or Bangladesh or wherever.

I didn't miss anyone or anything from home. And this separation was a good thing. I'd carved out a life far enough removed from Colorado that the past year didn't overwhelm my days. Nights remained a somewhat different story, but the late shifts and free beer at El Acuario helped me crash when I got home. I wouldn't say I was dizzy with happiness, but for the first time in a long while I wasn't numb with unhappiness.

ABOUT A WEEK AND a half before Christmas, after promising Antonio I would be back in time for the New Year's Eve party, I went with César and Ramón to visit Señor and Señora Lobos de Madrid at Calvario, the family ranch about three and a half hours southeast of San Cristóbal. To get there we first traveled to Comitán. The elevation at Comitán is something like 1,300 meters lower than San Cristóbal, and between San Cristóbal and the village of Comitán, the steep and narrow mountain canyons open up and the pine forests give way to cornfields and expanses of lush green vegetation. From Comitán, which sits on the side of a mountain, a hilly plain rolls east like enormous waves on a green ocean for twenty kilometers to Las Margaritas and approximately another one hundred kilometers to what César called Sierra La Colmena, the mountains behind which lies *La Selva*

Lacandona, Mexico's one remaining true jungle. Las Margaritas is the last town before the rolling plain stretches out to the sierra, la selva, and finally, the southeastern border between Chiapas and Guatemala.

We drove through small, populated areas beyond Las Margaritas where the houses were nothing more than huts and hovels of sticks. Aside from these occasional clusters of sad little dwellings, it was pure wilderness. We were moving along a well-maintained gravel road when I asked how much farther we had to go.

"You remember where we turned off the main road?" César asked.

"You mean like twenty minutes ago?"

"Right. That's where the property starts. We'll be at the house in another fifteen minutes. Well … ten the way Ramón drives."

"Calvario," was all César said when Ramón stopped the truck on the crest of a hill and the buildings of the ranch, stretched over at least one hundred and fifty acres, lay spread in the valley below us. César and I got out of the truck to take in the view of buildings and cattle and men on horses and people working in the fields and trucks rolling down a dirt road. The main house was comprised of several large buildings on a single raised foundation. It was a big structure built of stone and great timbers of mahogany. César pointed out the gardens and a huge swimming pool that had been covered for the winter. Beyond the gardens there was a hangar and a helicopter pad. There were additional buildings for the house staff and guest quarters. Across a grass field where a group of children were playing fútbol was another series of long buildings that César explained were the garage, the machine shops, the workshops, the roasting room, the packing room, and storerooms. An industrial smokestack rose up from behind the roasting room. Farther back behind these buildings were the stables and corrals. And still farther back were the bunk-houses, laborers' quarters, school, infirmary, and store. It was like a small town. Actually, it was a small town.

"So, compadre, what do you think?"

I looked at him.

"Yeah," he said, turning back to the view. "It's something."

We looked on for a few more moments and then climbed back into the truck. Ramón drove down into the valley and under the arches of the main gate and a small pack of dogs came to greet the truck. Ramón dropped us in front of the house before heading off to the garage and César petted some of the dogs before shooing them away. An employee came down the front steps to greet us and carry our bags. He called César "Don César," which caused me to raise my eyebrows. Seeing I was making fun of him, César threw his head back, put a fist on his hip, and struck an affected pose. He offered a limp-wristed hand.

"You may kiss the hand of Don César," he said.

"And you can kiss my you-know-what."

Grinning, he slapped me on the back and we started up the stairs.

Someone must have announced us because César's mother came to greet us as we walked through the front door. I'd only met his parents when they'd come to graduation, but Señora Lobos de Madrid looked just like I remembered. She was a handsome woman and she clearly had been a great beauty in her day. She was still a great beauty. She also had a real warmth to her, and after she'd gotten a kiss from César she swept past him and embraced me.

"Henry, we are so happy you could visit us." Her English was without an accent. "We've been waiting so long to see you again and now here you are in our home." I remembered where César had gotten his smile.

"It's wonderful to see you again."

"We were so sorry to hear about the accident. What a tragedy. More than anyone should have to bear. Really, you have our deepest condolences."

"Thank you. I appreciate that. I also really appreciate you letting me stay in the house in San Cristóbal."

"Oh," she said. She smiled and dismissed any need for gratitude with a wave of her hand. "I'm glad you boys are there or it wouldn't get any use."

"My parents don't go to San Cristóbal very often," César said, smiling, clearly happy to see his mother.

"Have you eaten?" she asked, but before we could answer she turned to one of the house staff and told him to ask the cook to prepare us some food. "But don't spoil your appetites," she said, turning back to us. "We are going to have a special dinner in honor of Henry's arrival."

"Is my father home?" César asked.

"He had to fly to the coast this morning. He'll be back in time for dinner. Why don't you show Henry around and the cook will send you some botanas."

"And Alejandra?"

"You know Alejandra. She's off riding."

"By herself?"

"She's fine, dear."

"I don't know how many times I have to say it. I don't want Alejandra riding without a chaperone."

"Who would you like to have be her chaperone? I can't ride with her. Should I send her with one of the vaqueros?"

"That's not funny. If she doesn't have an acceptable chaperone, she shouldn't be riding."

"Well, you know your sister. I don't know how you're going to stop her."

"She's either going to listen or I'm going to shoot her horse."

At age seventeen, Alejandra was the younger of César's two sisters. Claudia was the middle child and she'd gotten married a couple of years before. Though we'd never met Claudia, Jenn and I had received her wedding announcement. I knew César was protective of his sisters to the point that he was kind of nuts because one time in college Billy Jones saw the picture of Claudia that César kept on his desk and, in a joking way, Billy had asked if César would hook him up with a date. César flew way off the handle, jumped on Billy, and threatened to beat him within an inch of his life if he so much as thought about either of his sisters. After that, César kept the pictures of his sisters in a desk drawer. I thought his behavior was so strange that I pretty much avoided any conversation about the Lobos de Madrid girls. Later, when I was working at Talbert, I had several Mexican employees and one of them ended up going to prison after he put his sister and her lover in the hospital. The other Mexicans explained to me that it wasn't so uncommon for a Mexican man to be almost insanely possessive of his sister. According to them, there is many an old maid in Mexico who would have married but for her brother. This information, combined with César's outburst with Billy, made me wonder how the guy who had married Claudia had managed the courtship.

"We're so happy you're here," Señora Lobos de Madrid said again, clasping both of my hands in hers and decidedly ignoring César's last comment.

"Gracias, señora. I'm happy to be here."

"Come on, compadre. Let me give you the tour," César said, leading me out of the room. But he stopped and spoke to his mother. "Mamá, you tell Alejandra that I want to see her when she gets back."

"Si, hijo. I'll tell her."

César walked me through the house, each room opening onto the next, sitting rooms and dining rooms and a bar and a library and a billiard room and a game room and offices and a second library and even a map room. One room was a chapel complete with altar, pews, and a place to kneel to take communion. Four generations of Lobos de Madrid men and women, including César's parents and Claudia, had been married there.

We sat at the bar and César got us a couple of sodas while we waited for the food.

"Bienvenidos a Calvario."

"Salud," I said and lifted my pop bottle.

A young Indian woman brought in finger sandwiches and several small plates of botana.

"So how many people work here?" I asked when the girl had left.

"At Calvario? It depends on the season. When we're harvesting coffee we have something like one hundred and fifty employees. Full-time, year-round, the number is closer to forty-five. Of course, a lot of the people who work for us have families that live on the property as well."

"And how many people work in the main house?"

He took a bite and calculated. "Anywhere between five and twelve, depending on how many guests we have. My parents have a lot of visitors."

While we'd been talking and eating, I'd gotten up and started to look at a number of photographs that hung on the walls of the room. Some were of prize horses or bulls. Others were of César's parents and sisters. Several were of César, including a formal portrait from his army days and one from when he was seven or eight. He didn't look much different except for a bowl haircut. His face also graced the framed cover of the Spanish-language fútbol magazine, *Gol*. I'd had a subscription to the magazine and had read the article.

"Remember this?" he asked, pointing at a frame on the table. It was a candid of the two of us taken the night we'd won the championship senior year. César had an arm around my shoulder and I was flashing the victory sign. We both were holding bottles of champagne and grinning through the cigars gnashed in our teeth.

"That was a good night."

"It was. Did you see this one?" he asked, turning my attention to a signed photograph on the wall. In the picture, César's father was at the stern of a yacht and holding up a large fish. Next to his father, frozen in laughter, there was a smaller, balding man who seemed familiar but whom I couldn't quite place until I read the inscription and signature.

"Your dad went fishing with Carlos Salinas de Gortari?"

"They used to go every once in a while. My dad is old friends with his brother, Raúl. Also, my father backed him in Chiapas in his bid for the presidency. A lot of politicians overlook Chiapas, but Salinas understands the wealth of natural resources in this state and he understands how those resources should be managed."

"Have you met him?"

"Sure. He's been to the house. Raúl comes all the time. We're going to the president's New Year's Eve party. I told you that you could come with."

"Yeah, but when you told me I didn't realize your father was fishing buddies with the president."

"So, do you want to go?"

"Umm … ," I said, remembering my promise to Antonio. "I'll think about it."

"Let's see," César said, reading my mind. "Should I tend bar at El Acuario or go to the New Year's Eve party with the president of Mexico? A real dilemma."

"Well, you're going. It won't be that great."

César gave me the finger and I blew him a little kiss in return.

From outside, the distant sound of a helicopter began to grow until it went right over the house.

"My father's home," César said. "Come on. Let me take you to your rooms."

I swallowed the last of my soda, grabbed an extra half a sandwich, and followed César out onto the terrace. We went around the third building that held the family's private rooms and down some steps. At the bottom of the stairs we paused long enough to watch Señor Lobos de Madrid's private helicopter pass back over Calvario, bank, and touch down on the helipad. Then César led me into the guesthouse and my suite of rooms. My clothes had been unpacked for me and hung in the armoire in the bedroom.

"We'll probably have cocktails in an hour or so, after my father has a chance to relax. I'll send someone to get you. If you want anything, just press this," he said, indicating a button on the wall. "Someone will come to see what you need. Okay?"

"Okay."

I took a long, hot shower and dressed in slacks and a button-down Oxford. I turned on the TV in the sitting room and sort of half watched a game show while I flipped through the pages of a guest registry I'd found on the desk. I didn't see any names I recognized, but there were people from several countries and every corner of Mexico. After a time, a man rapped on the door and said cocktails were being served and my presence was requested. I flicked off the TV and followed the man up to the main house.

The Lobos de Madrid family was sitting at a table on the terrace between the first and second building. César and his father rose from their chairs when they saw me. Señora Lobos de Madrid and Alejandra remained seated.

Señor Lobos de Madrid was much like I remembered, only more so. If César had gotten his smile from his mother, he'd gotten everything else from his father, most notably his blue eyes, his powerfully athletic frame, and his overwhelming charisma. But whereas César's personality sucked people in like some sort of gravitational force, Señor Lobos de Madrid's mere presence commanded attention.

"Henry, so good to see you. Welcome to Calvario," he said, shifting his cocktail glass to his left hand and offering me his right.

"Thank you," I said. He had a firm grip. "As I was telling la señora, I really appreciate the invitation and the use of the house in San Cristóbal. It's been a good move for me."

"Our pleasure. Have you met Alejandra?" he asked, indicating his daughter at the table. She was slender and attractive and wore a purple cocktail dress that became her. Even seated, she was clearly a tall girl. Like César, she had her mother's smile and her father's eyes and self-determination. If you asked me, she didn't look like the kind of girl who was going to be bossed around by her brother.

"It is a pleasure to meet you, señorita."

"Igualmente," she said.

They offered me a chair and the servant brought my drink. We made small talk for an hour or so. César's parents asked about my parents. I asked questions about Calvario and its history. Alejandra talked about her horses and César reiterated his disapproval of her riding without a chaperone. Somewhat to my surprise, Señor Lobos de Madrid sided with Alejandra on this issue so long as she stayed within certain limits of the property and told someone in the family where she would be riding. It grew dark and quite cool. Both women asked for shawls, which were brought to them, and a propane heater was lit. Shortly thereafter, dinner was announced and we adjourned to one of the formal dining rooms where the table had been set with fine china, silverware, and silver candlesticks. A fire burned in the large fireplace behind Señora Lobos de Madrid's chair.

It was during coffee and dessert that César brought up the idea of my going with the family to Cancún for Christmas and Mexico City for the president's New Year's Eve gala.

"What a marvelous idea. We'd love to have you join us," his mother said.

"Yes," Señor Lobos de Madrid added. "We'll be celebrating NAFTA. It's going to be the biggest party since the revolution."

"As you can tell," César said, grinning at his father's enthusiasm, "my father is more than excited about NAFTA."

"So should you be," Señor Lobos de Madrid reproached. "Think of it. We'll be in the largest free trading block in the world." He said it as though it was something he had said many times before yet could still not quite comprehend.

"I can't believe Clinton signed it," César said.

"Yes, I didn't think he really understood economics. He surprised me."

"Well, he did make those ridiculous concessions to the unions and the environmentalists," César said. He leaned forward as if to say something more but was interrupted.

"That is nothing," César's father said, dismissing the comment with the wave of his hand. "Nothing. With NAFTA Mexico has the opportunity to become a first-world country."

An expression I had not seen before crossed César's face. But then it was gone and he sat back in his chair and folded his hands in his lap as his father launched into a fairly arcane lecture on global economic theory. I knew that NAFTA was the Clinton administration's bid to eliminate tariffs and open bigger trade markets with Canada and Mexico, but much of the minutiae was lost on me. In any case, the lecture had been meant for César's benefit, not mine.

"You're right, of course," César said when his father had

finished explaining how NAFTA indeed promised great things for Mexico in general and for their various family enterprises in particular.

Señor Lobos de Madrid seemed puzzled by César's agreement, as though César were acknowledging the obvious. There was an odd silence. Señor Lobos de Madrid reached for a silver bowl and spooned sugar into his coffee. "In any case," he said, "you're welcome to join us, Henry."

"Thank you for the invitation," I said, "but I promised I'd work that night."

"Not again with the job," César groaned. "Hank has a job bartending," he explained to his parents. The way he said it made it sound like I was selling cologne in the men's room of a strip club.

"I'll admit," I said, "it's not much of a job, but I promised I'd be there."

César looked like he was going to launch into another tirade about the absurdity of my priorities when his father cut him off again.

"That," he said, rapping his index finger on the table, "that work ethic, that is what I am talking about. Los norteamericanos know what it means to work. Mexicans are lazy. Lazy, lazy, lazy." Each time he said "lazy" he brought the point of his finger down and our coffee cups quivered in their saucers.

César had that weird look again. I couldn't tell if he was irritated that his father had interrupted him or if he was embarrassed to have expressed an opinion Señor Lobos de Madrid did not share. Then I remembered what César had said about his father not fully trusting him about business since the failed deal with Maria's family.

"Please, mi amor," Señora Lobos de Madrid said. "Not at the table."

César's father looked at her and his jaw line softened and he

127

nodded. "Henry," he said, "the Lobos de Madrids and a handful of other families built this state. We carved it right out of the forests and jungle. But take my word for it, if we left today, the ground would go fallow tomorrow. Why? Because too many of my countrymen want to get paid without doing the work."

"My father is having some labor problems on the coast," César said.

"One day they will be your labor problems."

"I'll just do what they did in the old days."

"I had thought of that," Señor Lobos de Madrid said as if he had in fact considered whatever it was they did in the old days. "In any case, Henry," he continued, swinging the conversation back to its original topic, "if you promised to work, you are right to work. A man who fails to meet his commitments is not a man at all. He's—"

"One of our employees," César interjected.

Señor Lobos de Madrid looked at César, but then his expression softened. "Exactly," he said, amused and seemingly content to put his labor problems aside for a time.

"I do appreciate the invitation," I said. "It sounds like I'll be missing quite a party."

"We'll be sorry not to have you," Señora Lobos de Madrid said.

"No te preocupes," César said. He raised his coffee cup and grinned his grin. "I'll be sure to drink a toast to you with the president's champagne."

13

After dinner, I got my jacket and César went for the rest of the Johnnie Walker we'd been drinking before dinner. We took the bottle, an ice bucket, two glasses, and a flashlight and César led me down a stepping-stone path beyond the guesthouses. We hadn't gone more than thirty yards before we were outside the dome of electric light coming from the buildings and wading into a darkness that can only be found far from cities. When we finally reached the fire pit, César built a fire while I looked up at the stars. There were lots of stars. I found the Big Dipper and Little Dipper and Orion, which are the only constellations I know. If I ever got lost at sea, I'd be in trouble. César got the fire going, sat on one of the logs, and poured our drinks.

I held my palms out to the flame. "This is nice."

"It's one of my favorite spots on earth. Something about having a fire makes me feel more connected." He handed me my glass.

"Connected to what? You're not going to start chanting, are you?"

He laughed. "I might. No, I just mean connected to Calvario, its history. I don't know." Something in the fire popped and threw up a cloud of embers. We watched the fire. "Do you know how to ride horseback?" he asked. "We can go riding in the morning if you want."

"I'm no expert, but I can ride. Jenn's parents have a ranch with horses and Jenn did all that rodeo stuff in college."

"That's right. I forgot Jenn used to ride. So we'll go in the morning."

"Sounds good."

We sat sipping our scotches and staring into the crackling fire. I thought about Jenn, how sexy she looked in her Wranglers with her saddle slung over her shoulder and the brim of her hat pulled way down so she had to raise her chin just to see where she was going. God she was beautiful. How, I wondered for only the zillionth time, did I ever get a woman like that to love me? How was I supposed to ever get over her absence? "Man," I said, as much to myself as to César, "I just don't know what I'm gonna do."

"Do about what?" he asked, poking the fire with a stick.

"Well ... I don't know. Forget it."

"You mean like with life?" He looked at me.

"Yeah, I guess."

He nodded and then returned to poking the fire. "I always thought I'd play in the World Cup. It just wasn't meant to be."

"That's not what I mean."

He looked at me again. "I know exactly what you mean."

We fell silent for a time and watched the fire.

"You could have done the rehab," I said, finally.

He didn't say anything immediately in response. And then: "If I had been sure to make the team for the next Cup, I probably would have stuck with it. But they had to put a rod and five screws in my leg. There was some doubt I'd be able to walk normally. No one thought I'd fully recover."

"You never told me that."

"No," he said. "I guess not." Of course he hadn't. That was César. He wasn't going to burden anyone with his problems. He cleared his throat. "Well, that's what the doctors thought anyway, not what I believed. But let's face it, compadre, we're not getting any younger and every year there's a whole new crop of young talent. I couldn't stand the idea of doing all that physical therapy, playing another couple of years, and not making the national squad." He added another finger of scotch to his glass and offered me the bottle. "You want a dividend?"

"No, I'm good."

He slapped the cap back in with the palm of his hand and set the bottle on the ground between his feet. "I had to do enough physical therapy as it was."

"I don't know," I said and drank from my glass. "You seem to still have it when we play in the park. I think you're better now than you were in college."

"My game's better and I'm smarter, but I've lost a step."

"Not from what I saw."

"I have. One game is okay, but a full season would be a grind. I don't think my leg would hold up. Besides, the park isn't the World Cup."

"Yeah. I suppose that's true. Still ..."

"Listen, Hank," he said, his eyes alight with the reflection of the fire, his voice suddenly sharp. "The simple truth is things haven't turned out the way either of us hoped or expected. That's life. Sometimes it gives you a raw deal and there's nothing to be done about it. Do I miss playing? Damn right I do. I can't even watch a game without my blood boiling, but I can't give it up either. I could have been great." He looked at me hard. "I was going to be great. I knew it was true my whole life. I didn't think I was going to be great. I knew it. I knew it the way I know the sun rises in the East and sets in the West. It was a fact, a fixed star, and then it was gone." He let this hang there for a moment. "You lost your family. I can't imagine how hard that is. Sometimes I think that maybe I can, but I can't. But I lost something too. I lost my destiny. It's not the same as what you lost, but it's real and there's nothing to do about it but move forward. I have my family and our business and Calvario, but I don't have who I was meant to be. And I never will." He had not stopped looking at me the whole time he had spoken and he held my gaze a moment longer before turning to the fire and drinking from his glass.

I thought about what he had said. It was true. He had been on his way to greatness. It had seemed like a fixed star. Even in college we had all seen it and known it. I wondered what that must have been like. I had never really known where I was going in life or what I was supposed to be or do. Jenn and Suzy had given me what I was supposed to do. And I realized that he had lost something that I couldn't really understand just as I had lost something he couldn't comprehend. He was right. We just had to move forward. What other choice was there? What more was there to say?

In his tailor-made vaquero costume, César looked every bit like he'd just walked off a 1950s Mexican western movie set. It was a brown outfit with lots of shiny brass buttons running down the pant legs to his polished, knee-high riding boots. Intricate ornamental red stitching and more buttons adorned the jacket. The clothes fit him like a bullfighter's.

"You're only missing the sombrero," I said.

"Oh, I've got the sombrero," he said. "And if you think I look funny, wait until the vaqueros get a look at that Mickey Mouse."

"Okay, Pancho Villa."

As it turned out, he wasn't kidding about his matching sombrero or the looks I got from the hired hands down at the stable. Apparently Mickey Mouse T-shirts are not typical riding wear of Lobos de Madrid family visitors. In my T-shirt, blue jeans, and cowboy boots I looked more like one of the ranch hands than the average Calvario guest. The stable boy who had saddled the horses took one look at me and suggested to César that perhaps I should ride a less spirited horse than the big bay he'd saddled.

"It's a lot of horse," the stable boy said to César as if I wasn't present.

"He knows how to ride," César said, winking at me as he climbed aboard his stallion.

"Pues ..." The boy looked at me doubtfully.

"It's okay," I said, checking the cinch and dropping the stirrups two notches to accommodate my long legs.

"Bueno," the boy said, mildly offended that I would second-guess his saddling of a horse. "If the señor knows how to ride ... ," he said to César.

"You know how it is," César replied as I put my foot in the stirrup and swung my leg over. "Los gringos piensan que son los mas chingones del mundo."

The boy looked at me. He seemed confused by what César had said and it occurred to me that most Lobos de Madrid family guests probably didn't receive playful jibes from their hosts in the presence of the hired help, but César didn't seem to notice the boy's reaction. He turned his horse and started us away from the stable, but then he stopped.

"Oye!" he called to the boy. "There's a lot of sun. Give Mickey Mouse a hat."

The boy went into the stable and came out with a finely embroidered sombrero they must have kept for guests. The boy passed it up and I thanked him.

"De nada," he said and turned back to the stable.

"Thanks, you jerk," I said to a chuckling César as I put the hat on my head. Between the hacendado sombrero and my Mickey Mouse T-shirt, I looked like a total jackass.

"You're welcome, Pancho Gringo."

We trotted the horses away from the stable and corrals and up the road a quarter of a mile before cutting across the lush green pasture. The boy wasn't kidding. I had a lot of horse and it took all my attention to keep him under control. César's stallion was even more impressive, but he rode him like he'd been born in the saddle and, while it made perfect sense that someone born on a cattle ranch would know how to ride, I was surprised he'd never talked about horses.

We rode for another twenty minutes until we came to a barbed wire fence, which we traversed along until coming to a gate that divided two sides of a hoof-worn path. César took one boot out of a stirrup and leaned off his horse to unfasten the gate. He pushed it open and we rode through. We spurred the horses up a hill and stopped at the top to take in the view.

From the top of the hill, looking out across the acres upon acres of coffee fields and herds of cattle and vaqueros atop their horses and field hands at work, I marveled at what kind of men and women César's ancestors must have been to forge Calvario in such a place. But despite the active operations of the ranch, I had the impression that if Calvario were left unattended for a year or two, nature would swallow it back up as it had all those famous Mayan ruins from another age. Outside of Alaska, it's hard to find a place in the States that seems so far removed from civilization. Even the remoter regions of Montana and the Dakotas that I'd visited hadn't struck me as so ancient, isolated, and impenetrable. It was beautiful, but something about the vastness of the wilds and the impermanence of man that they signaled made me feel a certain emptiness.

We rode down the hill across the shallows of a stream. The water was clear and ran over a bed of pebbles. We let the horses drink and then walked them along the bank. After half a mile or so, the stream curved around a hill and we came upon a miserable collection of stick dwellings. A group of dirty, half-naked Indian children watched us ride up and then one of the older kids stepped through a doorway and reemerged with an elderly woman. She was gray and wrinkled. The children were all staring at me, but the old woman addressed César. "Patrón," she said.

"Where is Guillermo?" César asked from atop his horse.

"He's sick."

Someone inside started coughing. It didn't sound good.

César frowned and pushed up the brim of his hat. "Is he inside?"

"Sí, patrón."

He slid out of his saddle, handed me the reins to his horse, and stepped past the woman and into the hovel. I could hear César and another man talking. I couldn't make out what they were saying, but I could tell from César's tone that he wasn't happy. Then he was drowned out by another fit of coughing. After a minute or two, César came back out and reaffixed his hat. Then he turned and pointed through the doorway.

"I mean it, Guillermo. I want that fence fixed tomorrow, no excuses." César took up his reins and mounted his horse. "Señora, you get him to work. If you want to live here, he has to work."

"He's sick."

"Then he should go to the infirmary."

"He did."

"And what did they say?"

"They said there is nothing wrong with him."

"Then there's nothing wrong with him. Get him to work or get off my property."

The old woman looked at the ground. "Sí, patrón."

César turned his horse and we walked them out of the camp back the way we had come.

"Think he's really sick?" I asked when the last of the children who had been watching us slipped from view.

"Guillermo? He always says he's sick. It takes a cattle prod to get him to do an honest day's labor. Look at that dump they live in. I've told him I'd loan him the money to fix it up, but he'd rather live in that shack than work extra hours. You can see what my father means when he calls Indians lazy."

"That's a nasty cough."

"Then he'll die and we'll replace him. That's one good thing about the Indians. They're breeders. There's never a shortage in the work force."

César saw my expression. "Look, compadre. I'm not saying I want Guillermo to die or be sick. I'm saying that he's never worked a full day in his life and that he would have been treated at the infirmary if he was really sick. Either way the work has to be done. Calvario is a business, not a charity."

"Well, I just think you're a little harsh with the Indian talk."

César folded his hands across his saddle horn and cocked his head to the side, squinting at me against the glare of the sun. Then he shook his head and smiled. "Heaven help you, compadre. You're a gringo through and through."

"How's that?"

"You actually believe that bullshit about all people being created equal, like everyone is going to hold hands and sing 'It's a Small World.' But look at what your country did to the Indians."

"That was a long time ago."

César laughed. "Go tell that to one of your Indians and see what he has to say. Come on. I'm hungry. I'll race you back to the house." He kicked his horse and bounded across the stream.

...

I SPENT THE REST of the week enjoying the hospitality of César's family and Calvario. Most days César and I would go for a morning ride and be back in time for lunch. Twice Alejandra went with us and, besides being a skilled rider, she was clearly an intelligent and self-determined young woman who had her share of the Lobos de Madrid charm and allure. In her last year of boarding school in Switzerland, she was only home for the holidays. She had been accepted at the Sorbonne for the fall and I thought that if César hoped to keep French boys away from her, he was totally fooling himself.

One afternoon César and his dad took me on a tour of the coffee processing and roasting operation, but otherwise César helped his father take care of ranch business in the afternoons and I was free to lounge around or explore. In the evenings the family would meet for cocktails and then sit down to an elaborate dinner always served by a procession of help, rung for with a little gold bell on the table. After dinner, César and I would have a campfire or play billiards with his father, who from time to time would pause the game to receive a cable about various business matters. Phone lines didn't extend to Calvario and his father was constantly receiving and dispatching messages.

It was during these billiard games that I really began to see César in his father, not only in the way they talked with a kind of assumed authority, but also in the way they held themselves, every movement casual, graceful, and deliberate. And there was the way they interacted with the staff, or maybe I should say the way they didn't interact. The servants seemed invisible to them. With me, as I'm sure was true with all his guests, César's father was almost impossibly polite and gracious, but I never heard him say please or thank you to a single servant. Not once. He was master of his realm. Servants served and that was their purpose. César treated them the same way. And I could see that one day when all of Calvario and the rest of the Lobos de Madrid empire belonged to César, he would be the great patriarch that his father was—powerful, magnanimous, and decisive.

I only saw Ramón briefly a couple of times and César explained that Ramón was working and spending time with his own family. Even though they'd grown up more or less like brothers and shared the house in San Cristóbal, at Calvario I came more fully to understand the hierarchy of their friendship. It wasn't simply a natural hierarchy with César as leader and Ramón as follower, although it was that too. It was an imposed cultural hierarchy and they both bought into it. They might have grown up together, but they were never equals. They were employer and employee, master and servant. It changed the way I thought of Ramón, so I guess I kind of bought into it too.

None of this bothered me in the least. I liked having a chance to see César with his family—to see his respect for his father, his reverence for his mother, his love for his sister. In many ways that week at Calvario explained a lot about my compadre. His very identity, like the identity of his whole family, seemed to flow from that place. Calvario defined what it meant to be a Lobos de Madrid. I thought it was cool. The way I looked at it, if you are going to be defined by a place, you can do a lot worse than Calvario. It was big and beautiful and I got pampered the whole week. All in all, I had a great time.

Two days before Christmas I had breakfast with the family and then rode with César, Alejandra, and the luggage in the back of the pickup truck while his parents sat in the cab with Ramón behind the wheel. At the helicopter, the pilot had already gone through most of the preflight checks before we'd got there. César, Ramón, and I loaded the luggage into the chopper and then I said good bye to Señor and Señora Lobos de Madrid.

"You sure you don't want to come?" César asked. "Last chance."

"I'm sure. Have a good time."

"Okay. Your loss. You and Ramón are set about him driving you to Comitán for the bus, right?"

"Yes, Mother," I said. "We're big boys. We can manage."

César slugged me in the shoulder. "You're sure you don't want him to drive you to San Cristóbal? The bus really sucks."

"He's got better things to do than play chauffeur to me."

"No, he doesn't."

"Would you give it a rest, already?" He and his parents had appeared aghast when the issue of my getting back to San Cristóbal had come up and I'd suggested the bus. I don't know what their objection to the bus was. It wasn't a long ride and the first class buses in Mexico are nicer than first class in any commercial airplane.

César leaned in close so his parents wouldn't hear. "Sometimes I just don't understand you pinche gringos."

"It goes both ways, you wetback," I whispered in reply.

He grinned broadly. "Merry Christmas, compadre."

"Feliz Año Nuevo, César."

Ramón and I moved to the truck as the propeller whirred to life, the prop wash making us squint against the dust. The chopper lifted off the ground and César waved one last time and the helicopter banked left and headed west across the rolling hills and into the sky. We watched until it was a speck and then Ramón drove me to the bus station in Comitán.

14

BACK IN SAN CRISTÓBAL, I showed my claim ticket, collected my bag from beneath the bus, and went into the terminal. There was Bern, wearing his hat and gloves and looking at the departure board. Leather saddlebags were draped over his shoulder. He looked tired. We greeted each other and he told me he was waiting for a bus to Comitán, where he'd transfer to a bus to Las Margaritas. From there he'd ride his horse to his ranch. I'd forgotten about his ranch. He said he'd only come back to San Cristóbal to buy medicine for people in the nearby village.

"The poverty is terrible," he said.

"Mexico's definitely the third world."

"No. What I'm talking about is even worse than that." He seemed genuinely distressed by it.

I thought about some of the stick huts I'd seen along the road between Calvario and Las Margaritas and Comitán. I thought about the house of the old woman with the sick man inside who César had told to get to work. "Yeah, I'm just coming from a friend's ranch over in that direction. The poverty's bad."

"A ranch?" This brightened his mood. "Where? What do they grow?"

"Southeast of Las Margaritas. Coffee and cattle mostly. It's called Calvario."

Something in his expression changed. "I've heard of it."

"Oh yeah? Cool."

"Everyone in that part of the state knows about Calvario and the Lobos de Madrid family."

"Well, that's my friend, César Lobos de Madrid."

Bern nodded but didn't say anything. Then they announced the boarding of his bus and we said our good byes and I went out to find a taxi.

On the curb a small Indian girl tried to sell me a bag of oranges and one of the plastic keychains she had dangling from hooks on a stick. I told her I didn't need a bag of oranges, but then I thought about the stick huts and what Bern had said. The girl couldn't have been older than seven or eight. She should have been in school, not selling oranges. Like most of the Indians, particularly the women and children, she didn't even have shoes.

"Okay," I said. "Give me a bag."

The oranges were five pesos. I only had a ten-peso coin and the girl didn't have any change. She tried to get me to take a keychain or second bag of oranges, but I told her to just keep the change. I didn't want to carry a second bag of oranges and what did I need with an extra keychain?

No taxi had appeared in the time I'd been talking to the girl, so I took my oranges and decided to walk back to the house. It was another beautiful afternoon and people were out on the streets shopping and going about their daily business. As the bus had come out of the pine forest and into the outskirts of the city, something about my arrival after being away had made me feel for the first time that this was truly my home. Didn't someone once say, "You haven't been to a place unless you've gone back to it"? Maybe not, but that's just how I felt, like I finally had been to San Cristóbal and it belonged to me as much as it did anyone. Of course, I knew I was a foreigner, but I still felt like I was coming home. It was a nice feeling at first, but as I walked down Calle Insurgentes and saw the Christmas decorations, the wreaths on lampposts and the red and green tinsel strung above the streets, everything looking so joyful and festive, I began to wonder if I'd made a mistake by not going with César's family.

Since Jenn and Suzy's accident, I had tried to ignore the approach of holidays and birthdays, as if my ignoring them might prevent their arrival. In fact, the real reason I hadn't gone with César had little to do with my promise to Antonio. Who wouldn't blow off a bartending job for a party with the president of Mexico? The real reason I hadn't gone with his family was that I didn't want to be reminded that it was Christmas. You'd think that after more than a year I'd have learned that this strategy didn't work and holidays came anyway and I just ended up being alone and more miserable, but apparently I hadn't. The holiday spirit was all around and I had traded a great invitation for a chance to be alone and stew in my own juices.

My mood was pretty low when I dumped my bag at the house, so I decided to freshen up and go to El Acuario. Despite the Christmas decorations in the restaurant, which contrasted oddly with the underwater theme, I felt somewhat better just for walking through the door and seeing Antonio jump out of his seat at a table to meet me halfway across the restaurant for our ritual handshake.

"Welcome back," Antonio said.

"Gracias."

"Did you have a good time?"

"Sí. But I'm glad to be back."

"Lo vez. You can't live without me."

"I can't live without Félix's penne and shrimp. You're a different matter."

Maria was behind the bar. I'd almost forgotten how beautiful she was. She did a double take when I sat down on a stool at the bar.

"You shaved."

"Yeah," I said, touching my face where my beard had been. I'd shaved the morning César, Ramón, and I had left for Calvario. For some reason I'd convinced myself Señor and Señora Lobos de Madrid would expect me to be clean-shaven.

"It makes you look different."

"Better or worse?"

She studied me for a minute like she was making a genuine evaluation. "Younger."

"That's good, I guess. So how's business?"

Maria shrugged.

"Mas o menos," said Antonio, rocking one hand from side to side. "Christmastime is always slow, but we make it up on New Year's Eve. You'll see."

The man sitting at the far end of the bar called for another drink and Maria went to attend to him.

"We're not open for Christmas, are we?" I asked Antonio. I knew we weren't, but I was forcing myself to make conversation to keep from staring at the fit of Maria's jeans.

"No. Neither Christmas Eve nor Christmas Day, but we're open the day after."

"Do you and Francesca have plans for the holiday?"

"Yes. We're getting together with some friends," he said. I thought that maybe he'd invite me to join them, but as if reading my mind he said, "I'd ask you to come, but it's not my party." Then he added, "It's mostly an Italian thing."

"Sure," I said. "Have a good time."

A group of French tourists came in and Antonio grabbed menus and ushered the group to a table. Two German guys came in behind the French tourists and walked over to the bar. After poking my head into the kitchen to say hello to Félix, I went around the bar and took the Germans' drink order. It felt good to be back at work.

Business was steady at the bar all evening long, but the tables were almost empty and the kitchen was dead, so when Antonio's girlfriend, Francesca, came in and asked if Antonio would take her to see a movie, Maria told him she would cover the tables. He promised to be back in a few hours and they left.

Maria and I made small talk, about what I can't remember. A pair of Canadian backpackers told a harrowing story about getting robbed at gunpoint by some banditos who had stopped their bus on the road from Palenque. I didn't hear the rest of the story because Mr. and Mrs. Thompson came in and sat at one of the tables.

"I've got this table," I told Maria and took two menus from the rack at the end of the bar.

They greeted me warmly and said they'd missed me the last two times they'd been in and I explained that I'd been away at a ranch. They ordered the sautéed sea bass with polenta, the special. Mr. Thompson told me they were waiting for a member of their caravan to have his rig repaired before they headed to the Yucatán. He pronounced it Yickitan. Mrs. Thompson explained this was in fact a blessing because they'd been invited to the church services at the Tuxtla diocese on Christmas.

"I'm curious to see what a Christmas ceremony is like in Mexico," she said. "The regular services are quite different from what we're accustomed to back home." Then, half whispering as though not to be overheard, she confided, "The first time we went we weren't even sure it was a Methodist service for the first fifteen minutes. Can you imagine?"

I smiled and left them to their meal.

"And Henry," Mrs. Thompson asked when I brought them the

bill, "what do you have planned for the holidays?"

"New Year's Eve we'll have a big party here, so I'll be working."

"And Christmas?"

"I don't have any plans. I'll probably cook myself a big dinner and watch cable TV."

"By yourself?" Mrs. Thompson said, clearly appalled at such a notion.

"I'm afraid so."

"You'll do no such thing," she said. "Why don't you come with us to Tuxtla?"

I pictured myself trapped at a Mexican Methodist Christmas celebration with the Thompsons. It wasn't a pretty picture. "I have to work the next day."

"You could take a taxi back."

"I don't think so," I said, "but thank you for the invitation."

She looked disappointed. "Well, at least you'll join us for supper on Christmas Eve."

"That's right, son," Mr. Thompson added. "You come have supper with us."

"I don't want to put you out."

"Put us out?" Mrs. Thompson said. "Good heavens, Henry, you wouldn't be putting us out. It would be our pleasure. You know, we can't be with our own children this Christmas. It's nice to have young people in the home at Christmastime."

"Son, you can see she is not going to take no for an answer."

"I certainly am not." Then she laid her hand on mine and said more gently, "After what you've gone through, it's not healthy for you to be alone on holidays."

Of course, she was right. I suppose that's why I'd gone fishing for an invitation from Antonio. "Okay," I said. "If you're sure I won't be putting you to any trouble." And as the words came out of my mouth I thought how completely and totally and fantastically stupid it was that I had turned down Christmas with César to end up having it with the Thompsons.

15

THE TAXI DROPPED ME at the RV park and the attendant came out of the office and directed me to bay twenty-three. Several of the RVs were trimmed with Christmas lights and someone had set up and decorated a Christmas tree beside one of the trailers. A couple sitting in folding chairs under the awning of their Winnebago wished me happy holidays, as did a group of men, cocktails in hand, who stood around a Weber kettle loaded with burgers. They were all Americans and I felt like I might have been in any RV park in the States. The Thompson's rig was one of those big coach RVs that look like converted luxury buses. A pine wreath with a red bow adorned the side door. I knocked and Mrs. Thompson, wearing an apron and smiling brightly, opened the door.

"Merry Christmas, Henry. Come in. Come in," she said as she stepped aside.

"Merry Christmas," I replied, climbing aboard and handing over the bouquet of flowers I'd bought in the mercado.

"What lovely flowers. Let me find a vase for them," she said. "Have a seat. Supper's almost ready."

"Is that Henry?" Mr. Thompson called as he emerged from behind a door in the back of the coach. "Merry Christmas, Henry."

"Merry Christmas, Mr. Thompson."

"Dear, did you see the lovely flowers Henry brought?"

"Those are nice. Mother, are we ready for supper?"

"Almost."

"Sit down, Henry," Mr. Thompson said. He pointed toward two leather captain's chairs bolted to the floor. The table, which folded down from the wall, had been spread with a red tablecloth with a holly print. It was pure Middle America. He poured each of us a glass of rompope, a Mexican eggnog.

"I think I prefer it to our eggnog," Mrs. Thompson said. She sipped from her glass before turning back to the pots on the stove.

"Not me," Mr. Thompson said as he sat down in the other captain's chair. "So Henry, yesterday you said you visited a friend's ranch."

"That's right."

"What do they produce on the ranch?"

"Mostly coffee and cattle."

"Not corn like all the small farms I see around here. I wonder how they can survive on those little plots, although I have to say that from the looks of most of the houses I've seen outside the city, surviving seems to be all they're doing."

"My friend's ranch is a big operation. It's almost ten thousand hectares. I think he said they have something like six thousand acres of coffee and thirty-two hundred head of cattle."

"That is a big spread."

"Yeah. They've had it a long time. His family first came to Chiapas with Diego de Mazariegos."

"The conquistador? We heard about him on the tour, didn't we, Mother?"

"That's right. My friend's family has one of the oldest houses in San Cristóbal. The ranch goes back over a hundred years."

"That's interesting. How'd you meet this friend?"

"In college. He was an exchange student and we both played

on the soccer team."

"Soccer. Now there's a sport that escapes me. I just don't under-stand how the rest of the world can be so crazy for it. College football. Now that's a sport."

"Supper's ready," Mrs. Thompson said as she set several plat-ters and bowls on the table. "I hope you like leg of lamb, Henry."

"I do."

"Mrs. Thompson usually cooks a honey smoked ham for Christmas Eve, but we couldn't find one down here."

"Frankly, we're fortunate to have the lamb. I had a great deal of difficulty explaining to the butcher what I wanted," Mrs. Thompson said as she set a bowl of mashed yams on the table, untied her apron, and slid into her booth seat. She lit two candles with a match. "Henry," she said, "would you say grace?"

"Ahh … I'm afraid I'm out of practice. Maybe we should let Mr. Thompson do the honors."

"All right," Mr. Thompson said after a moment. Mrs. Thompson looked disappointed.

Mr. Thompson recited a simple prayer and closed with "Amen."

"Amen," Mrs. Thompson.

"Amen," I repeated. The word felt strange in my mouth.

Mr. Thompson started carving the lamb and Mrs. Thompson passed me the mashed potatoes and yams. I waited until everyone had been served and Mrs. Thompson had taken the first bite before I picked up my fork. The dinner was superb and I realized how long it had been since I'd had an old-fashioned American meal.

"You don't go to church, Henry?" Mrs. Thompson asked.

"No, not since I was little."

"But you did go? What church?"

"I was baptized Presbyterian, but the only church I ever attended was Congregational. I think my mother would have liked for us to keep going, but my father wasn't interested. My wife's family was Episcopalian. They went to church."

"I would think religion," Mrs. Thompson said gently, "would be a great comfort to you."

"I suppose it would. I just don't believe."

"You don't believe in God?" She said it the way all the devout speak to those of us who aren't, like we're kidding ourselves.

"I guess I believe there's a force greater than ourselves. Call it God or physics or dark matter or the majesty of the universe or whatever, but I don't think that force takes a particular interest in us. I don't think there's an afterlife. The only heaven or hell I believe in is right here on earth."

"But Jesus loves you. He died for your sins."

What do you say to that when you're the guest at someone's dinner table on Christmas Eve? I wanted to ask if he had died for my wife's sins. How about my daughter's sins? What sins had she committed? And if he'd died for their sins, why did my girls have to die? I'd been over this ground with Jenn's parents. There wasn't any comfort in it.

"Yes, ma'am," is what I said.

Mr. Thompson smiled at me and we ate.

"A man should belong to a church," he said. "I don't think it matters so much what church, so long as it isn't one of those wacko groups in California that I'm always reading about, mind you. But a good, upstanding Christian church provides one with a sense of community and civic responsibility. It keeps him on the straight and narrow."

"Can't someone be a good person without belonging to a particular religion?"

"Oh sure. I just say it's harder. Life's hard enough as it is. See, that's the problem with young folks today. They want to reinvent the wheel. If something has served people for thousands of years, why change it? Take our son, John Jr., for instance. He's divorced from a perfectly nice gal because he thinks he'll be happier, that life will be all roses. He won't be and it won't be. It's the grass is always greener syndrome. That's what's making a mess of America today. If you want greener grass, you've got to water it and fertilize it and take care of it. You can't throw up your hands and walk away. It takes work. Marriage, just like everything else that's worth a darn, takes lots of hard work."

"I'll agree with that."

"Take this friend of yours who has this ranch. You say his family has had it for generations."

"His great-great-grandfather started it."

"You see, now they've committed themselves to something, and I'd bet you a brand-new dollar bill it would take darn near an act of God to get him and his family to give it up."

"Please, dear, watch your language."

"I said 'near,' Mother."

"You're right," I said, thinking of César atop his horse on that knoll, looking out across Calvario. "I don't think they'd trade it for anything."

"That's because they built it with generation after generation of hard work. The only things worth having come from hard work. And once you have them, you have to work to keep 'em."

The rest of the conversation continued along the same lines through the remaining meal.

After dinner we had apple pie and decaf coffee. Mr. Thompson and I talked about the construction business and Mrs. Thompson told me about the ladies' quilting association she belonged to through their church.

Around eleven o'clock I caught Mr. Thompson suppressing a yawn and I decided it was time to go. I thanked them for the dinner and wished them a Merry Christmas. Mrs. Thompson wrote down their address and phone number in Omaha. She gave me a hug and a kiss on the cheek and Mr. Thompson and I shook hands.

"You be sure to look us up if you're ever in Nebraska," she said.

"I'll do that," I said and folded the paper and put it in my pocket. "We're going to have a big party in El Acuario for New Year's. If you're still in town, maybe you'd like to come."

"Maybe for a little while," Mr. Thompson said, "New Year's is really a young person's holiday. It's a bit like birthdays. The older you get, the less excited you are about seeing the passing of another year."

"Merry Christmas, Mr. Thompson," I said as he levered open the coach door. "Have a great time in Tuxtla tomorrow."

"We will," he said. "Merry Christmas, Henry."

We shook hands a last time through the doorway and then I waded into the darkness. I looked over my shoulder once and he was still standing in the doorway, his body silhouetted in the rectangle of light. I waved, but he couldn't see me in the dark and when I looked back a second time, the door was closed.

IT WAS A LONG walk back into town and by the time I got there I felt low. I was glad when I started to see more cars and even some pedestrians. They helped to shrink the vastness of the world. The Thompsons had been kind to share their Christmas Eve dinner with me, but being with them had made me feel far from the States and people who loved me and because I was feeling sorry for myself I wondered if anyone anywhere really loved me. Maybe Mr. Thompson was right about church giving someone a sense of community. I felt awfully alone in the world. I couldn't shake the idea that instead of walking the streets of San Cristóbal I should be sitting with Jenn by the fire and tree and wrapping Suzy's presents from Santa. Then I thought about our last Christmas Eve together when I came up to bed after putting the red tricycle for Suzy under the tree. Jenn was waiting for me on the bed. She was clad in a "Santa's Helper" negligée. Mistletoe hung from the headboard.

"Now we're going to find out who's been naughty and who's been nice," she said as I stood in the doorway, taking it all in.

"I have been such a good boy this year, Mrs. Claus."

"Well, you'd better not be a good boy tonight," she said, running her hand over her body in a way that made us both giggle.

"No, ma'am."

"I want bad."

My god did we make love that night. There are only so many ways two bodies can fit together and we must have tried most of them. Afterwards, while we were snuggling under the covers, Jenn said, "My feet are cold."

"What?" I asked. She pressed her feet against my calves. "Jesus," I said.

"Will you get me some socks?" She sounded like she was half asleep.

"What are you going to do for me?"

"I just did it."

"That was my gift to you."

She smiled. Her eyes were closed. "Well, if you ever want me to return it, you'd better get me some socks."

I laughed. "You win," I said, jumping out of bed and getting a pair of socks from her dresser. "If all I need is socks to get sex like that, I'm taking the credit card to the sock store."

"There's no such thing as a sock store. Besides, tomorrow is Christmas. The sock store is closed."

I gave her the socks and glanced at the clock. "Today is Christmas."

"It's that late?" she asked, pulling the socks on. "Merry Christmas, lover. Now let's go to sleep. Suzy will be up at the crack of dawn."

I snuggled up next to her and wrapped her in my arms. "Merry Christmas," I said. I smelled her hair and listened to her breath and thought about how I was the luckiest man on earth. "Jenn," I said.

"Mmm?"

"Why do you love me?"

"What?"

"Why do you love me?"

"Don't you know?"

"Tell me."

She turned over and looked at me through the dark. "Because loving you, Henry Graham Singer, is like being alive twice." Then she kissed me and said, "Now go to sleep."

And she was right. That was it exactly. It was like being alive twice.

IN THE ZÓCALO PEOPLE were filing into the cathedral for midnight Christmas mass. I wouldn't have gone in but for my talk with the Thompsons and a woman out front who was selling candles. Suddenly it seemed like the thing to do. I thought maybe lighting candles for the girls might make me feel... I don't know what. I bought two and went in the side entrance. The service was just getting started and I moved along the wall to the back. Several candles burned in front of an altar of three wooden figures. I was fairly sure one was supposed to be the Virgin Mary and another was Mary Magdalene. I don't know who the male figure was supposed to represent. Some saint or another. Probably not Saint Christopher because he didn't look anything like the figure on my medallion.

I lit my candles off one that was already burning and found a place for them. Closing my eyes, I tried to pray, but I didn't know what to pray for or how. The only thing I wanted I couldn't have. I opened my eyes and the candles flickered before me, unchanged. Suddenly I felt very out of place. I hustled out of there and sat on a bench in the zócalo. A gentle wind soughed the leaves in the trees and that sound was the sound of eternity and the absolute certainty that each of us is alone and death comes to everyone of us without interest or distinction. All at once I thought I was going to cry, but the tears didn't come. Then I was filled with a sudden and enormous rage and hatred for everything. But the feeling vanished as quickly as it had come and I just sat listening to the rustling leaves. I was still sitting when the Mass let out and Luz and Maria found me.

"What are you doing?" Luz asked, scrambling onto the bench. She was wearing her helmet and a little girl's dress. Maria wore a black turtleneck sweater and a purple skirt.

"Listening to the wind. What are you doing? Did you go to church?"

"Yes," Luz said.

"I saw you inside," Maria said. "You didn't stay."

"I'm not Catholic. I didn't think I ought to."

"I saw you light candles," Luz said.

"That's right. I did light candles."

"¿Porque?" Luz asked.

"Because I was thinking of some special people and I wanted to wish them a merry Christmas."

"What special people?" she asked. She wrapped her arms around my neck.

"Luz ... ," Maria said. "Sorry. She's gotten to that stage where everything is a question."

"That's okay," I said. Then to Luz: "I was lighting a candle for a special person named Jenn and a special person named Susan who was my little girl just like you're your mom's little girl."

"I'm not a little girl. I'm a big girl."

"You have a daughter?" Maria asked. That I could have a child seemed to take her aback.

Then it was my turn to be surprised because I thought she'd known, although I don't know why she would have. It was easy to forget that even though I felt like I had to tell the whole world over and over, there were lots of people who didn't know. I wondered if I'd ever get to stop accepting condolences. "I did. She and her mother were killed in a boating accident."

Maybe it was the dappled shadows of the leaves on her face, but I thought Maria wore a strange expression, less like pity and more like she was seeing me for the first time.

"I didn't know," she said after a moment.

"Why would you have?"

"You might have told me." She said it almost like she thought I'd been deliberately hiding it from her.

"Was I supposed to?"

"No ... I guess not."

"I'm a big girl," Luz repeated. "I'm a good girl too."

"Yes, you are," I said. Maria was still looking at me as if she might see proof of Jenn and Suzy somewhere in my face. The look was unnerving.

"Santa Claus is going to bring me presents," Luz said.

"Do you have plans tomorrow? I mean today. Do you have plans for Christmas?" Maria asked.

"Nothing special," I replied, trying to sound casually cheerful. "I'll probably catch up on some sleep."

"Do you want to have Christmas with us?"

"With the two of you?"

"No," she said, blushing at the suggestion. "I'm having a small group of friends. Antonio will be there."

Suddenly I understood why Antonio had been so cagey about his plans. He'd been invited and he knew I hadn't.

"Yes. I'd like to come. Thank you."

"Good. At one o'clock?"

"At one. Can I bring anything?"

"Just yourself."

"Then I'll be there at one."

Luz was leaning against my knees and scrunching her face at me. I leaned my face down to hers and scrunched my face in return. In the Frankenstein voice that would send Suzy into hysterics, I said, "It's time for you to go to bed so Santa Claus can come to your house and bring you presents."

Luz didn't break up the way Suzy used to, but she thought it was pretty funny. Maria smiled too.

"She's exhausted," Maria said to me. "Say good night, Luz. You'll see Hank tomorrow."

"Buenas noches, Hank."

"Buenas noches, Luz. I'll see you tomorrow. Buenas noches, Maria, y gracias."

"Buenas noches, Hank."

They held hands as they walked across the zócalo toward their apartment. From behind, I could see their profiles as Luz was looking up, saying something and gesturing with her free hand, and Maria was looking down, nodding and smiling and being patient with Luz's short and distracted steps. I watched to see if Maria would look back, but she didn't. After they'd disappeared around their corner, I stood up and walked home. I felt a lot better than I had. A lot better.

16

IN THE MORNING I showered, dressed, undressed, and dressed again. Clothes I wore all the time suddenly didn't seem to fit quite right. Sleeves were too narrow at the cuff or too loose at the collar. One pair of pants was too tight in the thighs and another was too baggy in the seat. I changed my clothes a third time and I wasn't any happier with the result, but I stopped fooling myself about the clothes. Then I started worrying about what to take. Maria had said not to bring anything, but showing up empty-handed on Christmas couldn't be right. But what if other people didn't bring anything? What if they did? I thought that at least I should take something for Luz. But what did I have for a three-year-old girl? It wasn't like there were going to be any stores open in Chiapas on Christmas. All I had was Suzy's doll. It was on my pillow. Like hell I was going to give her that. And what about Maria? I had the blouse I'd bought her in that moment of insanity. I took it from the purgatory of the drawer and laid it on the bed next to the doll. Swell, I thought.

I went over to the main house and put in a call to my parents. It was your fairly standard Christmas call home. They missed me. I missed them. No one mentioned Jenn or Suzy, but they were present in every pause. I was glad when the conversation was over. I loved my parents, but I couldn't talk to them. I couldn't help the way I felt and they knew it and they couldn't help feeling the way they felt either, so none of us ever knew what to say.

Then I called Jenn's folks. I wanted to talk to them even less, but a phone call on Christmas was the least I owed them. I caught a break and got their machine.

My family responsibilities covered, I took an old, expensive-looking bottle of French wine from César's wine cabinet. Although my compadre would never begrudge me the bottle, I made sure it wasn't the only one of that vintage in the collection.

Then I got back to my bungalow and was faced with the doll and blouse again. Fortunately, just as I was about to go through the whole debate again, I caught my reflection in the mirror and started laughing.

"You're a fool," I said out loud to my reflection.

I don't know if it was the sound of my voice or what I had said or the simple fact I was talking to my own reflection, but suddenly I was disgusted with myself. I wrapped the wine, the doll, and the blouse in the newsprint I took from the old stack of weeklies next to the fireplace.

I didn't have any tape, which wasn't a problem with the wine or much of a problem with the blouse, but the doll ended up looking like a wad of trash, so I found a paper bag, painted a Christmas tree on it, and dropped the doll inside. A three-year-old wasn't going to care about the wrapping. I opened a beer. It was eleven o'clock. By one o'clock I'd had three beers and was feeling loose. I put my presents in a plastic tote bag, brushed my teeth, caught myself checking my hair in the mirror, and left for the party. There weren't many people on the street and the mountain air was fresh and clean and it felt nice to be walking to a Christmas party.

Once I'd knocked on Maria's door, however, I panicked about the blouse and was actually reaching into the bag to ditch the gift in the hall when Salvador opened the door.

"Feliz Navidad," I said. It hadn't occurred to me that Salvador would be there.

"Felicidades," he replied. There wasn't much holiday cheer in his voice. "¿Que quieres?"

"Ahh ..." It wasn't a question I was quite sure how to answer. I was relieved when Maria answered it for me.

"He's here for the party," she said, pushing past him and giving me a kiss on the cheek. "Merry Christmas, Hank. Come in."

"Merry Christmas to you. I brought these," I said, handing over the bag. Maria looked even better than usual. I don't like women to wear a lot of makeup, and Maria never wore any to work. But for the party she'd put on some lip gloss and mascara. Not too much. Just the right amount. For clothes she had on her standard blue jeans and boots, but she wore a sweater I hadn't seen before. It was red and had small white snowflakes and reaffirmed that life can be good.

"There are a couple of things for you and Luz, but the wine is for the party. I know you said not to bring anything, but in my country we can't go to Christmas parties without bearing gifts."

"It's the consumerism of your culture," Salvador said.

Maria shot Salvador a look, but I was already through the door and I wasn't going to let Salvador draw me into a quarrel.

"Probably," I agreed.

"Hank!" Luz yelled from where she was sitting on the floor. She was wearing the same dress she'd worn to church, but no helmet. It occurred to me that she probably didn't wear it unless she was going out of the apartment. She really looked like her mother without it. "Look what I got," she said, holding up a coloring book.

"Is it a cow?" I asked, trying not to listen to Maria tell Salvador in hushed but sharp tones that it was her home and I was her guest.

"No, it's a dinosaur," Luz said as she returned the book to the floor and continued scribbling like mad with her crayon.

Antonio, who had been sitting on the sofa by the balcony, stood up when he saw me. "Merry Christmas, Hank," he said.

"Merry Christmas," I said. I crossed the room to give him the three-grip handshake.

"I didn't know you'd be here."

"Maria invited me after Mass last night," I said. I hoped he understood I wasn't upset about his "Italians only" party. "Merry Christmas, Francesca," I said to Antonio's girlfriend.

"Merry Christmas."

"Hank, this is Paola and José," Maria said, introducing me to the two people sitting at the table full of food. I'd seen them a couple of times in El Acuario. They always came together, they always were quiet, and they always left early. "They're sociologists," she added.

"Merry Christmas."

"Merry Christmas," they replied in unison.

"What kind of wine is it?" Antonio asked as he unwrapped the bottle Maria had placed on the table.

"Red and French," I said.

Antonio arched his eyebrow when he read the label. Apparently he knew more about wines than I did.

"I got it from César's wine cabinet," I confided to him when no one else was paying attention.

"Should we open the presents?" Maria asked.

"If you want," I said, taking the corkscrew Maria had brought and reaching for the bottle.

Luz was pretty excited about the doll. I have to admit that I had to hide a pang of regret as she clutched Suzy's doll and showed it off to her father. Suzy should have been showing it off to me like that.

Then Maria, sitting next to Francesca, began to open her present. I concentrated on pouring the wine. At first she didn't recognize it, and even then she seemed a little uncomfortable receiving clothing from me. I was pouring wine into José's glass while watching Maria from the corner of my eye when she realized. She looked at me across the room. I focused on the wine, but I could feel her looking.

"What a beautiful blouse," Francesca said, touching the fabric.

"Isn't it?" Maria said. There was a tone in her voice I'd not heard before and I wasn't quite sure what it meant.

I suddenly felt like everyone, particularly Salvador, was suspicious of some sort of implication to the gift, like it was too extravagant to be a simple Christmas gift between casual friends. Of course, considering the circumstances in which I'd bought it, that suspicion was fair. I must have been out of my mind to give it to her. She was looking at me with the same expression she'd had that first time I showed up at her house.

"I got a deal when I bought five," I lied. "I thought they'd make nice presents when I get back to the States."

My explanation seemed at least plausible and then Francesca came to my rescue: "I buy all kinds of things and then when I get back to Italy and I need a present for someone I just dig into my bag. It's so much easier to shop for people that way. If I have to buy something for someone in particular, I can never find the right thing. This way they just get whatever I have. And somehow I always have the right present."

With Francesca bolstering my lie, I could see a tinge of doubt grow in Maria's face, like she was beginning to believe that it was purely coincidental I'd given the blouse she'd admired. "I don't know if you like that style or if it's the right size," I said, pretending I'd completely forgotten our trip to the mercado. "But I thought I remembered seeing you in one kind of like it and, to be honest, because everything is closed today, I didn't have anything else. I hope it's okay."

"It's very nice," she said. "Thank you."

She seemed to have accepted the story and I swore to myself that first thing in the morning I'd go to Santo Domingo and buy four more blouses so I'd have the evidence to back up my lie just on the off chance she might one day show up at my house.

The rest of the afternoon was quiet and friendly. It turned out that Salvador, José, and Paola didn't drink, so the rest of us drank the wine and then Antonio and I switched to beer while Maria and Francesca sipped at caballitos of tequila. Maria had cooked a gargantuan meal of turkey and beans and guacamole and flautas and squash and several other dishes that we somehow managed to polish off. It was after most of the food was gone and we were lounging around in our food comas that Paola suggested Maria should play something on the piano and Antonio and Francesca immediately started cajoling her in their Italian way.

"No." Maria laughed, waving them off. "I ate and drank too much." But Francesca wasn't going to take no for an answer and Maria finally agreed. "But only one song," she said, and everyone cheered as she moved to the piano bench.

I looked at Antonio as if to ask what all the hoopla was about, but he just grinned and nodded toward Maria.

She was good. She played Beethoven's "Moonlight Sonata"—I know this because I read the title on the sheet music, not because I know Beethoven's songs by name—and while I'm no music critic, I was impressed. I looked at Antonio and he smiled and nodded as if to say, "I told you so."

José was watching her hands move across the keys and Paola stood smiling. Francesca moved her hand like a conductor who can't keep time and Salvador gently nodded his head. I looked at them and then I turned back to Maria at the piano. Then I listened. The music took me away and I closed my eyes on the river and the water was winding its way through the narrow valley and then the music started moving faster and the rapids began to rise and they grew and the music flowed and the water went faster and the music became darker and the whitewater grew and the water rushed the music rolled one note into the next and it kept going and it kept going and it kept going. And then it was over. I opened my eyes.

There was a moment or two when everyone was silent and she sat at rest at the keyboard. The world seemed wobbly. The others started clapping and whistling and I applauded with the rest, but it felt odd to be there in that room in Mexico.

Maria blushed and told us to stop.

"That was great," Francesca said.

"I told you I had too much to eat and drink, but thanks."

Then there was a lull, as if none of us knew what we could talk about after that. I had nothing to say—I was still slipping back from the river, still thinking about Jenn and Suzy. Maria got up and stacked plates on the table. Francesca and Paola helped her while Salvador, José, and Antonio started a discussion about politics.

Luz sat at the table and was coloring a picture of fish in her coloring book. "It's like the fish at Mamá's work. Do you want to help?" she asked me.

"Sure."

"You can color the starfish," she said, handing me a red crayon.

I sat down and started shading in my assigned sea creature. The guys had shifted their conversation from local politics to NAFTA. It was interesting to hear them talk because their view of the trade agreement couldn't have been more opposite to the opinions I'd heard César and his father express. Salvador wondered about how the continued privatization of Mexico's public resources—something César and his father said would stimulate the economy—would further the gap between rich and poor. They talked about losing national sovereignty to foreign corporations. José described what he called "an eradication of culture" that would result from internal migration as people moved to industrial centers.

"But doesn't that mean there will be better jobs for the poor?" I asked. It seemed to me they were being overly dismissive of the benefits the trade agreement would provide.

They looked at me. "What a gringo," Salvador said.

"No," José said. "Hank's right. Some people will move because they will see better opportunity. But Hank, I'm concerned about the people who will move because they have no choice."

"People always have a choice."

"No," José said, "they don't. Look, the US subsidizes corn production. With NAFTA, the US agricultural corporations will be able to dump cheap corn on the Mexican market. For our subsistence farmers, the primary crop is corn. It's part of the lives of the people, particularly the indigenous people in Chiapas. They even call themselves the People of Corn. How are they going to compete against US subsidies? They'll lose an entire way of life and then they'll have to move to these new industrial centers. But they won't have the education or skills for the factory jobs and there won't be enough factory jobs for everyone who's displaced. They'll be refugees in their own land and that won't have been their choice."

The three of them looked at me. "I hadn't thought about it that way," I said.

"Of course you hadn't," Salvador said.

"There're lots of problems with free markets," Antonio said, "but the biggest problem is that they aren't really free. Everything is skewed to favor the corporations and the rich."

I nodded my head in agreement, but I mostly wanted the conversation to move away from me. They clearly had thought about the topic a lot more than I had and I didn't want to argue about a subject that I didn't particularly care about. They seemed satisfied with my deference to their opinion and went back to their discussion. I went back to coloring with Luz.

It had been a good party, but I wasn't unhappy when the women came out of the kitchen and José stood up, stretched, and said, "We should be going."

Antonio took that as his cue as well and stood and stretched. "Come on, Francesca. Let's go home and reenact the making of baby Jesus."

"That was virginal conception by God," she replied.

"Trust me baby, you'll be calling God's name," he said and grinned and we all laughed. "Merry Christmas," Antonio said to everyone and gave Maria a hug. "It was a nice party. Hank, I'll see you at work."

"Sounds good," I said as we went through our ritual handshake.

"It was nice to meet you, Hank," José said after he'd thanked Maria. "I hope you'll think more about NAFTA and what it means to people in my country and in yours."

"Sure. It was nice to meet you, José. It was nice to meet you too, Paola."

Paola smiled and followed José out the door.

"Can you drop me?" Salvador asked José.

"Let's go," José said.

Salvador kissed Maria. It was impossible not to notice he'd tried to kiss her lips and she'd turned to give him her cheek. "Ciao," he said to Antonio and Francesca. "Gringo," he said, that word as much acknowledgment as he was willing to grant me. Then he went out the door and he, José, and Paola started down the stairs.

I said good-bye and thanks to Maria and started to follow the others, but then Maria said, "Your jacket."

"Oh, right."

I stood in the doorway while Maria went to the bedroom for my coat and the plastic tote bag I'd brought with me.

"Thanks," I said, sliding my arms into the sleeves. "Thanks again for the invitation."

Maria smiled. "Merry Christmas. Thank you for the gifts."

"Sure."

She looked at me. "You really don't remember?"

I knew she was talking about the two of us looking at the blouse in Santo Domingo. "Remember what?"

"Never mind," she said after a moment. "Feliz Navidad, Hank."

"Feliz Navidad, Maria. I'll see you at work."

She stood in the doorway until I started down the stairs. I waved and she smiled and closed the door. Out on the street I looked back up her apartment and then started walking home. And that was Christmas in Mexico.

17

WHEN I GOT BACK from buying four more of the blouses from the Indian woman at Santo Domingo, I spent most of the day after Christmas channel-surfing on César's satellite television and playing pinball. I showed up at work at nine, but Antonio said it had been so slow all day that he didn't need me. He'd already sent Maria home and Félix was closing up the kitchen. I sat at the bar and nursed a bottle of Victoria.

"It was a nice fiesta," I said.

"Sí," Antonio agreed, polishing the wineglasses with a damp towel.

"Do you want to go to the go-carts this week?" I asked.

"Sure, if it stays like this."

I nodded. He cleaned a wineglass and slid it onto the rack above the bar. I picked at the label of my beer bottle and watched the fish swim in the tank. One yellow tang seemed to lead two others back and forth in front of their miniature coral reef. A school of three. The mated pair of clown fish stuck close to their sea anemone. They'd wander out a couple of inches and then dart back to the protection of the undulating anemone.

"What's Salvador's problem?"

Antonio lit a cigarette, left it in the ashtray, and resumed cleaning. "He doesn't like you very much. I'll grant you that."

"But why? What did I ever do to him?"

"Nothing. He doesn't like gringos, that's all."

"What's wrong with gringos?"

"Nothing, but that's why Salvador doesn't like you."

"Why are you friends with him?"

"I'm not a gringo."

"Seriously?"

Antonio draped the towel over his shoulder, took a drag from his cigarette, and looked at me. "Why are you friends with César?"

"What does that have to do with anything?"

"I assume you know about what he did to Víctor."

"What are you taking about?"

Antonio moved the ashtray with his smoking cigarette, leaned across the bar, and lowered his voice as if there was someone in the empty restaurant who might be listening.

"Don't get me wrong. Víctor is an A-number-one asshole. He probably deserves whatever he gets, but what I heard is that César sent Ramón and an off-duty federale to deliver a message to stay clear of you."

"Give me a break. It sounds like you were talking to the same people who told you I dropped Víctor on his head."

Antonio did that little splurting-air-through-pursed-lips thing and shrugged. "Well, that's what I heard," he said.

"From whom?"

"I'm not saying, but that's what I heard."

"I bet it was Salvador," I said. "That sounds like a Salvador story to make the gringo and his friend look bad."

"I'm not saying who. I'm just telling you what I heard. But of course you know the bad blood between Salvador and Maria and César, so I can see why you would think he told me."

I watched the school of tangs shuffle themselves and swim another lap. Of course I knew about the problems between

César's family and Maria's family, but César had never mentioned whether or how Salvador fit into those problems. Antonio went back to polishing the glasses. I decided whatever issues Salvador had with César were between the two of them. If César wanted my backup, he knew all he had to do was ask.

"In any case," Antonio said, "I'm only saying everyone has their good and bad qualities. Yes Salvador can be a jerk sometimes, but his heart is in the right place about the stuff that matters and he'll stick his neck out for his friends and what he believes."

"If you say so."

Félix came out of the kitchen with his coat on.

"How much fish do you want me to order?" he asked. Fresh fish was delivered from the coast twice a week, and when the delivery came, we placed our order for the following week.

"How much tilapia is left?"

"Pues ... almost all of it."

Antonio drummed his fingers on the bar.

"Freeze the tilapia."

"I already did."

"Good. We can use it for soup stock. Order five kilos of snapper and let's do something with shrimp."

"Okay. Six kilos?"

"Make it five."

"Esta bien," Félix said. We said good night and Félix went home.

"I still don't understand Salvador's problem with me," I said.

Antonio laughed. "You mean besides that you're a gringo who is best friends with His Majesty Don César Lobos de Madrid?"

"Yeah. Besides that."

"I think he feels threatened."

"Threatened?"

Antonio put down the glass he was polishing and gave me one

of those give-me-a-break looks.

"What?" I asked.

"Maria."

"Maria, what?"

He looked at me. "Okay," he said, finally. "You don't have a thing for Maria and she doesn't have a thing for you."

"What the hell are you talking about?"

"Anyway, you wanted to know why Salvador doesn't like you. I'd say the main reason is Maria."

We didn't say anything else on the subject. He finished the wineglasses and I tried to digest what he'd said. Maria didn't have a thing for me. I mean, what the hell do Italians know about women?

I slid the empty bottle across the bar and climbed off my stool. "Hasta mañana," I said.

"Bueno," Antonio said. We did the handshake and I went out to the street.

When I got back to the compound, I realized I couldn't remember anything from the walk home. A cavalcade of nudists could have marched past me for all the attention I'd paid because I'd been too preoccupied thinking about the way Maria looked at me when she opened the gift and about how her hip brushed against me when she crossed behind in the narrow space of the bar and about the timbre of her voice when she spoke my name and about the contours of her body when she crouched down to speak to Luz and about the way she tucked a loose strand of hair behind her ear and about how she stifled her laughter when I accidentally dropped a whole tray full of glasses and about the faint vanilla and sage scent of her when she welcomed me into her apartment and about a dozen other things. Images of her still were flashing through my mind when I sat on the edge of my bed and saw Jenn in the photo on the dresser.

I sat there a long time. How could that beautiful woman beaming at me from the swing in our backyard be in the cold dark of the earth? It seemed I'd never be able to stop asking that question and there would never be an answer, at least not one I'd comprehend. Probably I'd never even comprehend the question.

"Jenn," I heard myself say. I didn't speak the rest.

18

I TOSSED AND TURNED until late, but when sleep came, it was no relief. The same old nightmare. That I'd had it dozens and dozens of times before never made it less terrifying. That I knew what came next and was powerless to stop it always made it seem worse. But that night, when I came to the worst part, the one moment in the dream that always remained the same, that terrible moment just before I'd wake gasping for breath, the dream changed. Instead of being trapped underwater, I broke the surface. Jenn and Suzy stood on the far shore. They waved and called something.

The numbers of the digital clock read 5:07. I went to the bathroom and splashed water on my face. When the coffee was ready, I poured a cup, sat at the table by the window, lit a cigarette, and let the morning come.

The coffee and cigarettes were gone by seven. I wasn't hungry, but I went out for breakfast anyway. I bought the morning paper and sat on the terrace of the Kiosco Café.

A small boy asked to shine my shoes and I tried to remember if he was the same child who had shined them that first week I'd been in the city. He seemed even smaller than I remembered. I agreed and watched him get started. How many shoes, I wondered, had this young child shined in his short life? Was this what he was destined for? While I was thinking about that, I saw

Maria come out onto one of the balconies of her apartment and drape a throw rug over the rail to air in the sun. I watched her until the boy tapped my instep with the handle of his brush and I looked down and switched one booted foot atop the shine box for the other. The boy set to brushing and I looked up and Maria had gone inside. The front page had an article about preparations for the implementation of NAFTA and the New Year's Eve celebrations planned in the capital. I thought about César and his family and how stupid I had been not to join them. In the Styles & Celebrities section I saw that Bibi Gaytán, the actress who played one of the women in *Dos Mujeres, Un Camino*, was in Chiapas. Apparently she was a native of the city of Tapachula and a parade had been held in her honor. Eduardo Gallegos had another piece on the opinion page. I liked his stuff and had taken to reading his articles when they appeared. He mostly wrote about state politics, so I never fully understood the context of his arguments, but he had this fatalistic wit that was acerbic, funny, and distinctly Mexican. In this article he accused several members of the state legislature of blatant corruption and the illegal sale of indigenous lands to certain ranchers who were identified as friends and associates of the legislators. Then I turned to the sports page. I started reading about the most recent Tecos game and the waiter brought my omelet.

A tour bus pulled into the zócalo as the waiter cleared my plate and refilled my coffee. The tourists filed off the bus, snapped some pictures, and descended on the café.

"Now you're going to work," I said to the waiter.

He watched the groups arrange themselves at various tables.

"French," was all he said before he went for the menus.

He was right. The group that sat at the table next to mine chattered away. Between the distraction of their voices and the breeze that was just strong enough to threaten blowing the paper out of my hands, I couldn't concentrate on the article about the scandal surrounding a Cruz Azul player. I must have read the same paragraph five times, so I folded the paper and called for the bill. While the waiter made change, Maria came back out onto the balcony and hung laundry on a line.

"Buenos dias," I called up to her after I'd crossed the park.

"Buenos dias."

"I missed you at work yesterday," I said. I couldn't think of anything else to say.

"Did it get busy?"

"No."

She nodded.

"It will be slow until New Year's Eve."

"That's what Antonio said."

Some of the French tourists pushed past me on the sidewalk.

"Have you eaten breakfast?" Maria asked.

"I just finished."

Her hair blew across her face and she gathered it and held it against the wind. Some more pedestrians jostled past me. Maria said something I didn't hear.

"What?"

"I said, 'Do you want a cup of coffee?'"

"That would be good," I said. After all, I'd only had like ten cups.

"Come up, then," she said when I hadn't moved.

"Okay."

I tried to think of something engaging to say while I climbed the stairs, but "Hola," was all I could muster when she opened the door.

"Hola," she said and smiled. She tucked a stray curl behind her ear like I'd seen her do many times. "Come in. Luz, can you say hello?"

"Hola," Luz said, her helmetless head bent to the page, too preoccupied with whatever she was coloring to look up from the table.

Maria rolled her eyes as parents will when they are amused by their child's total absorption. "Have a seat. Do you want cream or sugar?"

"No thanks."

Maria went into the kitchen while I sat at the table next to Luz.

"What are you drawing?" I asked, looking at the colorful scribbles on her paper.

"The fish at Mamá's work. This is the big fish," she said, pointing at a purple scribble in the middle of the page. The kid had a thing for fish.

"I can see that."

"Are you sure you don't want something to eat?" Maria called from the kitchen.

"No, gracias." Through the doorway I could see Maria in profile, standing on barefoot tiptoes as she reached up for a mug on the top shelf. As she stretched, her T-shirt rose and exposed the taut caramel skin of her midriff.

"I want to thank you for inviting me to Christmas," I said when she brought in the cups of coffee and a box of juice for Luz. "I had a nice time."

"I'm glad you came," she said, tucking her legs under herself as she curled up on the chair across from me. "And I want to thank you again for the presents. Luz hasn't let the doll out of her sight, have you?" she said, turning her attention to Luz. "Can you tell Hank your doll's name?"

"Reyna," Luz said.

"Reyna. That's a pretty name."

Talking about the doll apparently made Luz want to play with it because she climbed down from her chair, half skipping and half bouncing to her room, and came back with the doll.

"See Reyna," she said, holding the doll up for me to see.

"I see her," I said.

Luz took Reyna over to the couch and began to play quietly.

"It's a very nice doll," Maria said. "Where did you find it?"

"I made it."

"You made it? ¿De verdad?"

"Sí."

"Do you make lots of dolls?"

"No." I laughed, picturing myself making dolls as a hobby. "Reyna is the only one."

"It must have taken you a long time."

"It did," I said. "I'm not much of a craftsman." And then suddenly I realized from the uncomfortable expression on Maria's face that she thought I'd spent a long time making the doll specifically for Luz. "I was making it for my daughter before the accident."

"Oh," she said. Maria stared into her coffee cup and then looked back up at me and smiled softly. "Do you have a picture of her?"

"Sí," I said and took out my wallet. When they were alive I'd never carried pictures, but after the funeral I started to. I didn't carry it to show people. I just had this inexplicable fear I might forget what they looked like.

"She's beautiful."

"Yes, she was."

"And your wife was very handsome."

"Thank you," I said, taking the photo back and looking at it myself. "It's a good picture of her."

"What were their names?"

"Jennifer and Susan." I paused and then said, "Jenn and Suzy."

"Hank, Jenn, and Suzy Singer," she said and smiled. "It sounds good."

I nodded and we watched Luz play with her doll. The conversation having run its course, we sat in silence, drinking our coffee and wondering what to say next.

"So how did you learn to play the piano?"

She smiled. "Lots of practice."

"Well, it paid off. You're really good."

She blushed slightly and shook her head. "I'm not terrible," she conceded, "but with music, the better you are the more you know your limitations."

"I suppose that's true with everything."

She seemed to consider this. "I suppose it is. I hadn't thought about that before."

"It's certainly true with fútbol."

"Is it? Do you play fútbol?"

"I do … or I did. I played in college."

"I didn't know gringos played fútbol."

I laughed. "We don't, at least not very well."

"But well enough to know your limitations."

"Exactly. But it wasn't very hard to see my limitations when I played with César," I said. Then I added, "That's how I know him. We played on the same team in college."

"Ah, yes," she said, "César, the great fútbolista and Chiapas's favorite son." She had a strange expression on her face. Suddenly there was an awkwardness between us.

"Anyway," I said. "I thought your piano performance was great. Did you ever think to try to be a concert pianist?"

She laughed, the awkwardness gone as quickly as it had come. "Now you're making fun of me."

"No, I'm serious."

"No. Pues … I may have dreamed about it as a little girl. But I never seriously thought about it."

"Why not?"

"To start with, I don't think I ever thought I was good enough, but more importantly, no women in my family would ever have been allowed to perform outside the house."

"No?"

"No. My father valued fine art and culture and he expected young women to know a musical instrument so they could bring music into the home. He had a European sensibility like that. Also, it might have been acceptable to teach children, but he never would have permitted me to perform onstage. It just never would have happened."

"That's too bad."

"I didn't mind. I still don't. I like playing for friends, but I prefer to play for myself."

"Why?"

"I challenge myself more when I play for myself. It's hard and I like that it's hard, but I take bigger risks when I'm the only audience. Also my emotions come out more in the music when I play for myself. They're more honest somehow."

"I guess I can understand that. Of course, I'm never quite sure I honestly know what I'm feeling."

She looked at me. It was mildly unnerving.

"What?" I asked.

"You might be a pianist."

"Now you're making fun of me."

"No, really. What you just said took me years and years of playing to understand."

"What's that?"

"Just that all the technical skill in the world doesn't matter if you can't feel the music."

"That's pretty deep," I said.

183

She laughed again. "Sure it is."

Again the conversation stalled and I found myself searching for something more to say. All I could come up with was this: "I like your apartment."

"Gracias."

I admired the high ceilings. "It's spacious," I said.

"I like it because there is lots of space for Luz to play, which is good since there's no garden. If I don't get her outside at least once a day, the apartment gets small quickly."

"Can I get a tour?"

"You've seen everything but the bedrooms."

"So ... ," I said, standing up. I assumed she would lead the way.

"So ... ," she repeated after a moment. "I don't think I know you well enough to show you my bedroom."

I couldn't tell if she was being coy or serious or what, but she didn't get up from her chair, so I sat down, suddenly embarrassed. I hadn't meant anything by suggesting I wanted to see her bedroom, but clearly she thought I had. "What do you need to know?" I asked, trying to joke my way out. "Blood type? Date of birth? Astrological sign?"

She smiled. "That might be a start."

"What else?"

"You know what I want to know?"

"Am I right-handed or left-handed?"

"What does 'Hank' mean?"

"What do you mean, what does it mean? It's my name."

"I know that, but what is it in Spanish?"

"Hank isn't my real name, it's what people call me. My real name is Henry."

"Henry?"

"Enrique in Spanish. Hank is a derivative of Henry. Hank is the equivalent of Kiko or Quique."

Maria smiled, apparently amused.

"What?" I asked.

"You don't look like a Kiko."

"How about Quique? Do I look like a Quique?"

"Definitely not."

"How about Henry?"

"Yes," she said and smiled. "Henry is a nice name. You look like a Henry."

"My parents will be happy to hear it."

"Do they call you Henry or Hank?"

"It depends on how much trouble I'm in."

Maria laughed. "So they call you Henry quite a bit."

"You know me. I'm one of those gringos who likes to get drunk and start fights."

"I'm sorry I said that."

"That's okay. It didn't bother me," I said, remembering how worked up I had been when she'd said it.

"I'm still sorry. I know better than to take everything Salvador says at face value."

The mention of Salvador's name brought another pause.

"Actually, my parents were the ones who started calling me Hank. My mother was afraid people might call me Harry."

"Harry?"

"It's another pet name for Henry."

"Oh. But Harry sounds nice, no?"

"Harry is pronounced the same as hairy," I said, and explained the meaning of *hairy*. It sounded even more absurd in Spanish.

"Hank is better," Maria agreed. "But I like Henry the best. Can I call you Henry?"

"Sure. It's my name."

"Are you close to your parents, Henry?"

"I guess. I don't talk to them all that much, but they're always happy to hear from me."

"You should call them more. You're lucky to have parents you can talk to."

"We don't have a lot to talk about, but my mother would agree with you."

"She's right."

"I know. It's just that since Jenn and Suzy died, every conversation is about how I'm coping."

"That means they care."

"I know," I said. "Can we talk about something else?"

"If you want," she said. There was another moment of silence. Then: "Do you have any brothers or sisters?"

"No. How about you?"

"A brother, but he died when we were children."

"I'm sorry."

"That's okay. It was a long time ago. I was very young."

"Was he older or younger?"

"Older."

I nodded and Maria smiled and we sat there wondering what to talk about next.

"Do you want some more coffee?" she asked.

"No, thank you. I'm over my limit," I said, rising from my chair. "I need to go."

"Oh. Okay," she said. "Did I say something wrong?"

"No, not at all. Antonio and I talked about going to the go-carts. That's all." I hadn't meant for my departure to sound so abrupt, but the truth was the talk of my parents took me back to thinking about Jenn and Suzy and suddenly I just needed to leave.

"Are you sure?"

"I'm positive. Thanks for the coffee."

"You're welcome."

I said good-bye to Luz and Reyna and Maria opened the door.

"So I'll see you tonight," I said.

"Yes. Tonight."

I nodded and started toward the stairs.

"Henry ..."

"Yes?" I asked. The way she'd said my name, I thought for a split second that I'd forgotten my jacket again.

"Nada," she said after a moment. Then she smiled. "It's a good name."

"Thanks," I said and I gave a wave and continued down the stairs.

19

As it turned out, I didn't see Maria that night at work. After I left her place, I tracked down Antonio and we went to the go-carts. Then I went home and took a nap. When I got to El Acuario, Antonio told me I'd be working the bar by myself for the next few days. Maria's aunt had died and Maria had gone to Guatemala for the services.

"But she'll be back for the party, right?" I asked. Antonio had been advertising the party for weeks and Francesca had spent hours on decorations, including dozens of colorful piñata fish to hang from the ceiling. Félix had bought ingredients for twenty-five trays of lasagna. Los Reyes were contracted to play extra sets. Everything was set for a big fiesta and I wasn't thrilled with the idea of working the bar by myself.

"Yes. She'll be back that afternoon."

"Good," I said.

Antonio made his eyebrows go up and down.

"Knock it off," I said and Antonio laughed.

While New Year's Eve promised to be a real wingding, the days leading up to it were deader than dead. We closed early every night. Antonio and I did go to the go-cart track one other time, but otherwise I spent most of my mornings reading the newspaper on the patio of the Kiosco and my afternoons watching TV in the game room. Although I caught myself pausing on the home shopping network more than once, the plotline for *Dos Mujeres, Un Camino* had taken a totally outrageous turn, so TV wasn't all bad. The day's episode had just concluded and I was about to head to work when the phone rang.

"Bueno," I said.

"¿Compadre, como estás?" It was César's voice.

"I'm good. How are you? Where are you?"

"El Distrito Federal. We got here this morning."

"How was Cancún?"

"Amazing. Your compatriots were all over the place. It should be a crime to put that many bikini-clad gringas in one place."

"It should be a crime to let you near them."

"This whole sorority was down from the University of Miami. Remind me again why we went to college in Vermont?"

"Fun, huh?"

"My god!"

"What else did you do when you weren't corrupting the innocents of my country?"

"They corrupted me. There was this one chick, nineteen years old. She did things I didn't even know could be done. She—"

"Easy there, Valentino. I don't need details. So what else did you do?"

"Played tennis, went scuba diving, fished, lounged on the beach, went clubbing, drank too much. You should have been there."

"Sounds like a good time."

"Too good, and the real party hasn't even started. I'm going to need a vacation after this vacation."

"When do you get back?"

"The fourth or fifth. I don't remember. It'll depend. There are some people my father wants to meet with about trucking versus freight rail to the US. NAFTA is going to be a gold mine." He sounded excited.

"Good."

"Is everything all right there?"

"Everything is fine."

"You sure? I shouldn't have let you stay by yourself."

Part of me thought he was right. "That's okay, Mom. I'm fine."

"You could still come up here. I could send the jet to Tuxtla right now and you'd be here in three or four hours."

It was tempting, but Antonio was counting on me. More importantly, I knew I'd feel like a jackass in front of César's family if I changed my mind and had them send the plane for me, particularly after his father had made the point of honoring your commitments. "No can do, compadre. I promised."

He sighed into the phone. "You sure?"

"Yep. Have a good time."

"Well, if you're sure, then I'll see you soon."

"Okay. Oh," I said, the idea just coming to me. "Do you think you could find some sheet music for the piano while you're there?"

"¿Como?"

"I mean is there a music store in Mexico City where you could buy some classical piano sheet music for me?" It was a stupid question. Why would I give Maria sheet music? I didn't even know what she needed and I'd already gone too far with the blouse and doll.

"You mean like Bach and Beethoven and that kind of stuff? I'm sure there is, but I'd have to find it. Why? You don't play piano."

"No," I said, now realizing what I was asking would mean César probably would have to stomp all over Mexico City looking for a music shop. It also occurred to me that he probably wouldn't appreciate knowing he'd bought it for Maria and that would not be a connection difficult for him to make. So I told a little white lie. "This American woman came into the restaurant."

"A woman?"

"No, no. She's old."

"An older woman?"

"Older than that. Like grandma old."

"Oh, compadre. This sounds serious." He was laughing.

"No, really," I said. "She lives here. She told me it's hard to get sheet music in Chiapas." I tried to think of a reason I would have César get sheet music for some old lady. "She kind of reminds me of Jenn's grandmother," I said. And what else, I wondered. "She gave me a really big tip for Christmas. I just thought since you are there maybe you could pick some up for me to give as a way to say thank you, but never mind. It was a dumb idea."

"No, compadre, I'll look."

"No, don't bother, really. You've got better things to do."

"Are you sure? Anything to support your chances with a grandmother."

"Yeah, forget it. Seriously, just forget it." I felt bad for lying.

"Okay. Hey, compadre?"

"Yeah?"

"Happy New Year."

"Same to you, César. Same to you."

That was the last time I spoke to César before everything changed.

As promised, Maria was back in time for the party and helping with the last-minute preparations when I arrived at El Acuario that night. She was wearing the blouse I'd given her and looked as good as ever.

"I'm sorry about your aunt," I said.

She looked at me and smiled her gratitude. "Thanks, Henry. She was sick for a long time. It was for the best."

I put my hand on her shoulder. It was the first time I'd intentionally touched her outside of the customary greetings and the like and I half expected her to pull away. Hell, I half expected that I would turn into a pillar of salt. She didn't. I didn't.

"Are you okay to work tonight?" I asked.

She smiled and I thought she might cry. "Sí," she said. "I'm just sad. She did a lot for me. She's the one who first taught me piano."

Francesca came through the front door carrying a pole with a variety of sea-creature piñatas dangling from it that she planned to use as decorations for the party

"I can cover you if you don't feel up to it," I said to Maria.

"Thanks for offering, but to tell you the truth," she said, her mood suddenly lifting, "I've had enough sadness for one week. I'm ready to dance."

"Amen to that," Francesca said and she did a pirouette with one of the papier-mâché fish. "Vamos a festejar."

When Los Reyes took the stage at nine thirty, we already had a full house. I worked the door until ten o'clock, when despite several uneaten trays of lasagna, Antonio closed the kitchen. No one was interested in food and there were too many bodies to effectively wait on the tables. With the kitchen closed, Félix and Francesca took my place collecting the cover charge. Antonio and I started moving tables and stacking them against a wall. Because it was so crowded, we had to lift them over the heads of everyone bouncing around. The moment we moved a table, people flooded into the vacant space without breaking step with the music, and after we'd moved a couple of tables, the crowd got in on the act and all the tables were hoisted up and buoyed across the room on a sea of hands.

Maria and I hustled to open beers and pour shots and collect money as fast as people ordered, but it didn't feel like work. The festive atmosphere was contagious. Maria danced, working to the rhythm of the music. I had a hard time not watching her move. And I wasn't the only one. Whenever she turned her back to the crowd to reach for a bottle or glass, all the men at the bar would stare as she swung her hips with the music.

Antonio was in rare form. He was everywhere. He danced on top of the bar and poured rows and rows of free tequila shots for whoever wanted them. He put a shot glass in my hand and raised his own.

"Salud, Hank."

"Salud, Antonio."

We clinked our glasses, downed the shots, and sucked on wedges of lime. Then he refilled the glasses two more times, and each time we'd clink the shot glasses together before slamming them. The warmth of the liquor made me flush.

"You want to do some coke?" he asked, speaking into my ear.

"I think I'll stick with beer and tequila."

"Okay. Let me know if you change your mind."

He slapped me on the back, slipped around the bar, and waded through the rocking crowd, closing the door of his office behind himself. A few minutes later he bounced back out, shaking hands, slapping high fives, kissing women on their cheeks, and generally acting the life of the party.

"Five minutes to midnight," the lead singer yelled into his microphone. "Make sure you get your drinks."

There was a rush at the bar on top of the rush that had been going all evening and at a minute to midnight, when Los Reyes started the countdown, Maria and I were madly serving drinks to people waving their money and standing three deep at the bar. With ten seconds to go everyone was standing still and counting down with the band. Like everyone else, Maria and I raised our beers in the air and shouted.

"Diez, nueve, ocho, siete, seis, cinco, cuatro, tres, dos, uno, Feliz Año Nuevo!"

There was cheering and I don't know where the confetti came from, but people were throwing fistfuls in the air. It seemed like everyone was kissing and Maria and I, stuck next to each other behind the bar, exchanged an awkward moment. "What the hell?" I heard myself say through the din and I leaned over and kissed her. To my relief, she kissed back. It wasn't a sexy kiss, only one in the spirit of ringing in the New Year, but when we parted she bit her lower lip. Everyone around us was whooping and cheering.

"Happy New Year, Maria."

"What?" she shouted, unable to hear me over the roar of the crowd as Los Reyes launched into a Jimi Hendrix–style "Auld Lang Syne."

"Happy New Year," I shouted into her ear.

She smiled. "Happy New Year, Henry."

The party rocked until around three when the band, after several encores, called it a night. Forty-five minutes later Antonio was kicking the last of the revelers out. Maria, Francesca, and I stood on the street while Antonio locked up.

"Some party, huh?" Antonio said. He swayed on his feet.

"Hank," Francesca said as Antonio put his arm around her. "You should walk Maria home. This," she said, nodding at Antonio, "isn't the only boracho out tonight."

"I might be drunk," Antonio said.

"Might be?"

"But I'm not too drunk to make salsa in your molcajete," he said, slapping her on the rear.

Francesca's eyes widened in mock shock and we all laughed.

"Can I walk you home?" I asked Maria.

"That'd be nice. Gracias."

"Come on, baby," Antonio said. "I want some of that New Year loving."

"We'll see if you're still conscious when we get home, assuming we ever find a taxi to get you there."

Not a single cab had passed since we'd been standing there.

"What taxi? What home? Let's use the bar inside."

"Hey," Maria said, laughing, "I clean that bar."

We all said good night and Maria and I started down the street.

"Hank," Antonio called after me. "Hold on." He and Francesca whispered something to one another and then Antonio stumbled toward me. Afraid he'd fall on his face, I met him halfway. "Here," he said and pressed something into my hand. It was a condom. "Happy New Year," he said and then turned back to Francesca.

"Take me now or lose me forever," he called to her. The old country line sounded funny in Spanish.

Now I can't say that on some level I hadn't been thinking about trying to get another kiss from Maria, but the possibility something more might happen hadn't even occurred to me. It wasn't that I was nervous about the prospect. It was more like I'd been awakened all at once to the notion that such a thing might be possible. I was still trying to reckon it all when Maria and I came to the zócalo and two soldiers told us we'd have to go around.

"The zócalo is closed," one said.

"What do you mean, closed?" Maria asked.

"The zócalo is closed," he repeated. "You'll have to go around."

"But I live in the apartments above the bank," Maria said.

"I'm sorry. You'll have to go around."

"Pinche militares," Maria began to protest.

"It's a nice night," I interrupted. Antagonizing Mexican

soldiers in the wee hours of the morning didn't seem like the best idea in the world. Besides, I needed more time to wrap my head around the possibilities of the next few minutes. "I can use the fresh air after all that tequila and cigarette smoke."

"Pendejos," Maria called as we backtracked to Calle Cuautémoc. Thankfully, the soldiers let the comment slide.

Just beyond the entrance to Maria's apartments several other soldiers stood in the intersection of Utrilla and Real de Guadalupe. I could feel them watching us when we paused on her doorstep. Her eyes and lips were moist in the moonlight. The way Maria looked at me, I was fairly sure I was reading the signals right, but I hadn't had to read signals for a long time.

"Good night," I said, stuffing my hands in my pockets. I wasn't ready.

"Good night," she said.

I smiled and turned to go.

"Hank ... ," she said, catching me by the sleeve.

Her hand was cool against my cheek while we kissed. It was not a kiss like the one at midnight.

"Do you want to come up?" she asked, huddled against my chest.

"Do you want me to?"

"I wouldn't have asked if I didn't."

"What about Luz?"

"It's all right. I knew I'd be late, so she's spending the night with my neighbor."

I nodded and she led me by the hand. As I stepped into the building, I glanced at our audience over my shoulder. They didn't seem the least bit interested in us.

In the dark of her room, we undressed. I think we were both a little shy. I know I was. And then we slid under the sheets.

"Do you have protection?" she asked.

"Yes."

"You do?"

She sounded hurt, like I'd planned for us to hook up.

"That's what Antonio called me back for in the street."

"Really?"

"Really."

"Oh," she said.

That it wasn't a secret somehow reduced whatever nervousness we both felt and we reached for each other. I had forgotten how extraordinary the body of a naked woman feels and I cupped her breast and kissed her open mouth. I could taste the faint perfume of tequila and it was warm and good. I kissed her neck, her delicate collar bone, and listened to her breath. My hand slid down the curve of her side. Her skin was soft and firm and smooth. I held her hip and her leg wrapped around me and I pressed against her and our bodies moved together and, after a second or two of fumbling with the condom, I was inside. What a blessed thing. It was slow and gentle and long and I lost myself in the contours of her body and in the rhythm of our movements and I was nowhere but there and I learned that there is astonishing beauty in hearing a woman whisper your name as she quietly climaxes in another language.

20

DIFFUSE MORNING LIGHT FILTERED through the opaque glass of the balcony doors and cast the white walls and comforter in a bluish hue. The room was cold and the color of quiet and Maria felt warm next to me. I watched her breathe gently in sleep, her hair spilled across the white pillow. She looked peaceful. I looked at the curve of her ear and traced the line of her jaw. I silhouetted her profile: the slope of her brow, the angle of her nose, the shape of her lips—what is it that makes one form more beautiful than another? Then I thought about Jenn and I felt guilty, like I had betrayed her somehow, like I had thrown away something held between us, something just the two of us shared, and by my throwing it away, we would never get it back. It seemed I had pushed my wife even farther away, farther from our memory of us together, farther into her grave. What would she think about me lying here next to this woman I barely knew while she lay in the cold ground? In that moment, I'd have given anything for it to have been Jenn who was next to me. Absolutely anything. But it wasn't Jenn and it never would be again.

Then a faint boom echoed up from the zócalo and I remembered the soldiers.

I slipped out from underneath the sheets and into my jeans, the tiles cold under my feet. I opened the balcony door as quietly as I could. There were many more soldiers than I'd realized in the night, perhaps as many as two or three hundred. It was hard to tell because most of them were across the square and hidden by the trees. Several others milled around or stood guarding the intersections into the zócalo. Many wore ski masks or hid their faces behind red bandanas. The banging noise was coming from the municipal building. A filing cabinet was pushed from the second-story balcony down to the zócalo. It boomed. Two narrow columns of smoke rose from fires burning in trash cans in front of the building.

These weren't government soldiers. I suppose I should have been afraid, but I wasn't. There were a couple dozen tourists and locals talking with the soldiers and the soldiers didn't seem to be bothering anyone, only keeping people away from the municipal building.

Maria, wrapped in the comforter, came up beside me and we looked on together.

"What do you think is happening?" I asked.

"I don't know."

"Do you think we should go down?"

"Do you?"

"They don't seem to be hassling anyone."

While we tried to decide what to do, I noticed Antonio and Francesca. They were wearing the same clothes they'd had on at the party and were talking to some of the soldiers. I pointed them out.

"Let's go down," Maria said.

"Okay."

We dressed quickly and headed for the door, but before I opened it, Maria stopped me.

"Henry..."

"¿Mande?" I asked, taking my hand from the knob and

thinking I'd forgotten something.

She looked at me as though she had something important to say. "Nada."

"Are you sure?"

"It's nothing. Let's go down," she said and smiled at me. There was something a little sad in her expression. Then she reached for the knob and we went out.

On the way down we stopped at her neighbor's apartment so Maria could check on Luz. Doña Asunta, a large and ugly woman of an indeterminate age, was visibly distraught by all the armed men in the street.

"¡Que barbaridad!" she said.

Luz was still sleeping and Doña Asunta said she would be happy to keep her as long as Maria liked.

"I'm not going to set one foot outside while those guerrillas are in the city. ¡Que barbaridad!"

Down on the street the guards at the intersection didn't give us any trouble and we walked over to Antonio and Francesca.

"What's going on?" Maria asked when we reached them.

"It's some sort of peasant revolt. They're burning the land records," Francesca explained. Antonio looked frazzled and for the first time since I'd awakened I realized I was still drunk from the night before. In fact, for a moment I thought it was because I was buzzed that I was having difficulty following the conversation between Antonio and one of the soldiers, but then I realized the soldier was Indian and spoke Spanish with a thick accent. As they talked, I began to notice that all the soldiers were Indians, many of them women and young teenagers. A few had AK-47s and other automatic weapons and some had rifles or shotguns, but others carried toy guns cut from pieces of lumber. A handful simply carried sticks or machetes. A group of civilians had gathered around a rebel who was quite a bit taller than the others. I pointed him out to Maria and she and I went to see what he had to say.

His Spanish was clear, articulate, and educated and it was obvious, despite the ski mask that he wore, that he was fair-skinned and not Indian like the rest of the guerrillas. He explained that they were called El Ejército Zapatista de Liberación Nacional, the EZLN, and that they were comprised primarily of Totzil, Tzeltal, and Chol Indians. He talked about how peoples across the world had been fighting against dictators, but in Mexico a dictatorship had been able to take hold step by step without opposition. He described the living conditions of the indigenous people in Chiapas and said fifteen thousand died from poverty each year. He said their primary demands were liberty and democracy.

Someone asked him who he was and he identified himself as Subcomandante Marcos. Someone else asked him why his title was "Subcomandante" and the corner of his eyes wrinkled so that it was clear he was smiling. "Because I take orders," he said. Then he excused himself and said he had to get back to the war.

Antonio and Francesca came up to us. "They're declaring war against the government and military," Antonio said.

"We heard," Maria said.

"With sticks?" I asked. I was dumbfounded by the whole scene.

The four of us stood there looking at the soldiers and each other and trying to get our minds around what it all meant.

"Well … ," Francesca said, her voice distant and ponderous, as if she was thinking out loud rather than talking to us, "let's feed them."

"That's a good idea," Antonio said.

"What?" I asked. "This is a revolution. You don't want to get mixed up in this."

Antonio gave me a peculiar look. "Look, Hank," he said and turned and gestured. "They're just poor Indians. They're probably hungry. Besides, what am I going to do with all of the leftover lasagna?"

He was right. Almost half of them were women and they were young. A thirteen- or fourteen-year-old girl was sitting on a park bench next to us. She had a red bandana masking her face and held a fake rifle. There was something pathetic about her. There was something pathetic about all of them.

I turned to Maria to see what she thought.

"Let's feed them," she said. "What can be the harm in feeding hungry women and children?"

I looked at the guerrillas again. I thought about all the poverty I'd seen across Chiapas. "Okay," I said. She was right. Revolution or not, there could be no harm in feeding women and children.

We walked over to El Acuario and Antonio let us in. The muchacha hadn't been in to clean and the restaurant looked a bit like I imagined the inside of the municipal building looked about then. There were eight trays of lasagna left from the night before and together we carried those trays and drinks back to the guards at the intersection. They took a couple of bottles of agua mineral from the case in Antonio's arms. Francesca handed them forks and baguettes. They thanked us profusely and started right in on the food. We took the rest of the stuff over toward the municipal building. The rebels would only let us get so close to the building, but they politely accepted the gifts. Their gratitude made me realize giving them the food had been the right thing to do. In a broken Spanish one of them promised to return the forks, trays, and empty bottles if we would wait.

We didn't have to wait long. They returned everything, down to the last fork. The trays were wiped clean, every morsel of food having been eaten.

"Now what?" I asked, the four of us just standing there. I think we all felt we should be doing something, but exactly what, none of us was sure. At least handing out the food had given us something to do. I looked at Maria. Had I really slept with her?

"They told me their commanders would make some sort of public declaration in the afternoon," Antonio said. "I'm going to take this stuff back to the restaurant and then go home and take a shower." He stacked the empty trays.

"We couldn't find a taxi last night so we slept in the restaurant," Francesca explained.

"Let's all meet at Maria's in the afternoon," Antonio continued. "We can watch whatever happens from the balcony. Is that okay?"

Maria nodded that it was and we all agreed to meet at her place around three o'clock. I thought she might give me some sort of signal to indicate that I should go home with her, but either there was no signal or I missed it. I was a little disappointed that she and I wouldn't have a chance to be alone, particularly since I wasn't sure how I was supposed to act toward her around other people. I wasn't even sure of how I was supposed to act toward her if we were alone.

We split up and I was almost out of the zócalo when I ran into Mr. Thompson. He was with a small group of tourists from the US whom I guessed were members of his RV caravan. They were trying to get information from some of the rebels, but there was a serious language gap. The Indians they were talking with spoke little Spanish and Mr. Thompson and the tourists spoke even less. One woman, who seemed particularly upset, was speaking loudly, slowly and with an English affected by an invented Spanish accent: "How-o can we leave the city-o? Are the road-os open-o?"

"Mr. Thompson," I said.

"Henry," he said, clearly relieved to see me. "We're trying to find out if the roads are open. Do you know how you're going to get out of the city?"

His question surprised me. Up until that moment it hadn't

even occurred to me to leave. "I haven't thought about it," I said. I looked back over the rebels. They were as pathetic as before. "No. I think I'm going to stay."

"Stay? Son, if I understand correctly, these people mean to overthrow the government. This is a war zone. You can bet any moment now the Mexican military is going to be rolling in here."

Naturally, he was right. I hadn't considered the government's response. Still, the moment I heard myself say the words, I knew I wouldn't leave. There was no reason that I could easily articulate other than this city and this life I'd found myself living seemed like they belonged to me in a way the rest of the world did not. That might not have made sense, but I wasn't leaving. I didn't really have anywhere else to go.

The tourist woman with the absurd dialect had started adding pantomime to her questions. It was painful to watch.

"Let me see if I can find out anything," I offered, interrupting the woman. I asked the rebels about the roads, but because their Spanish was nominal and spoken with such a strange dialect it took me a good ten minutes to be sure I understood them correctly.

"Okay," I said to Mr. Thompson and his group. "I don't think you want to go toward Palenque or south toward Comitán. The road to Tuxtla is being guarded and mined, but they are letting civilian traffic through. You shouldn't have any problems getting out through Tuxtla."

"You're sure that's the best way?"

"That's what they say."

"But I have reservations in Palenque," the tourist woman said.

"Sorry," I said, shrugging apologetically. "It's a revolution."

"Henry, do you want to ride with us?" Mr. Thompson asked. "Mrs. Thompson and I have plenty of room for you."

"Thanks, Mr. Thompson. I appreciate the offer. I really do, but I'm going to see how it goes here."

"Are you sure?" His voice was filled with genuine concern.

"I'm sure," I said and smiled.

"Well then," he said, "you keep your head down, you hear?"

"Yes, sir."

"I admire your gumption, son. Heck, if I was your age I might even stay myself. Might be one heck of a show."

"Let's hope not."

He looked at me and offered his hand. "Good luck, Henry."

"Good luck, Mr. Thompson."

As I walked home I thought about what Mr. Thompson had said about the Mexican military and I couldn't help but wonder if I wasn't making a huge mistake by not taking him up on his offer. If the military did come, and it seemed naive to think they wouldn't, there might be street-to-street fighting. I envisioned several horrific scenarios and knew there would be worse ones I couldn't imagine.

Back at the house, I took a long shower and was still running through worst-case scenarios when I stretched out on the bed. Despite the images flashing through my mind, it wasn't long before exhaustion overwhelmed me and my anxiety gave way to the fantastic terror of dreams.

When I woke, it was one thirty in the afternoon. I showered again to wash off the tequila I'd sweated out in bed, dressed, and went through the kitchen cabinets and fridge to make a mental note of what food I had. Then I went over to the main house to try to call César and my folks. An automated voice said long distance service was currently unavailable. The Zapatistas must have cut the phone lines. I rummaged through the food supplies in César's kitchen and pantry. There were three ten-kilo bags of beans and two ten-kilo bags of rice in the pantry. Between the two houses, I had seven unopened jugs of drinking water. And the extra tank of propane meant I could always boil water. I felt fairly confident that I wouldn't starve or die of thirst if we couldn't buy anything for a few weeks. The only things I was really afraid I might run out of were cigarettes, so I bought two cartons at the pharmacy on my way to Maria's. The cashier was ringing up the smokes when I noticed the packages of Trojans beneath the glass of the counter.

"Dame una caja de condones," I said.

"¿Cuales?"

"Umm …" I hadn't bought condoms in several years. I didn't know the differences between the various colored packages.

"¿Los rojos?" he asked.

"Está bien. Los rojos."

When I got to the apartment, Maria, Luz, and Francesca were making pizza. Antonio came in from the balcony off Maria's room. He told me he'd heard the rebels had taken Ocosingo and I relayed what the rebels had told me about the roads to Palenque and Tuxtla.

We ate the pizza and then Maria made a big pot of coffee. The thing I remember most from the lunch was how quiet we were. I don't know why, but we practically whispered when we spoke and all of us jumped when Luz accidentally knocked her plate onto the floor.

Every once in a while one of us would go to Maria's bedroom to look down from her balcony to see if there were any new developments in the zócalo. It was midafternoon when Antonio went to check what was going on. He ducked back in to tell us something was happening. The rest of us hurried through Maria's room and crowded onto the small balcony. A large crowd had massed in the zócalo. People filled the balconies of the other apartments in the building as well as the apartments above the pharmacy, kitty-corner from the square. I wouldn't call it festive, but there was an energy to the event. Then the crowd grew quiet as several ski-masked members of the EZLN came out onto the second-story balcony of the municipal building and stood in front of microphones that had been placed there.

One of them began to speak and the crowd became silent. The sound system wasn't very good or very loud. There was a constant hiss of static and an occasional crackle of reverberation. Everyone strained to hear. Also, whoever was speaking had a thick indigenous accent that made things that much harder to understand. The speaker was reading from a text and there were some words he had difficulty with. I couldn't see them very clearly through the trees of the zócalo and couldn't even tell if there was more than one reader. But I could hear and follow enough to understand that this was a declaration of war and that they, the EZLN, the Zapatistas, fully intended to overthrow the federal government of Mexico and that they felt constitutionally justified in doing so because they saw the president as an illegitimate dictator. The speaker listed specific objectives of their armed uprising, objectives that included marching on the capital and respecting prisoners' rights and issuing summary judgments and demanding unconditional surrender. The speaker asked the people of Mexico to join their cause and then it was over and the Zapatista commanders calmly filed back into the municipal building. It hadn't taken more than ten minutes, but it was ten minutes in which everything would change, not just for me, but for all the people I'd come to know and care about in Chiapas.

21

WHEN SEVERAL HUNDRED GUERILLAS appear out of nowhere and take control of several cities, including the one you're living in, it's not hard to figure out life is about to take a serious turn. But it wasn't until we heard the actual declaration of war that the full significance of what was happening struck home. This was a real revolution. Even if they were malnourished and ill equipped, the Zapatistas meant business. History was in the making, history with a capital *H*. And we had front-row balcony seats.

"Dios mio," Maria said and crossed herself.

We looked at her and at each other.

"You're not kidding," I said.

"Do you think they're serious?" Francesca asked.

"They sound serious to me," I said.

"They're serious," said Antonio.

"Where did they come from? I mean, just in the zócalo there must be two or three hundred soldiers. If they've taken Ocosingo and Las Margaritas and who knows where else, there must be thousands of them. Where did they come from?" I couldn't believe a whole army had seemingly risen right out of the ground.

"They're Indians and campesinos. They came from the campo," Antonio said.

"That's not what I mean. Has anyone ever heard of Zapatistas?"

"Not me," Maria said.

Francesca shook her head.

"So how do you build an army without anyone finding out about it? Look at them. They're organized. That doesn't happen overnight."

"Probably they were hiding in the jungle," Maria said. "There are lots of places in Chiapas where the government doesn't go."

"Okay, but how about their supplies? Granted, they're not exactly outfitted like the US Marines, but they are outfitted. Someone had to supply them. I mean, that's a lot of guns. Where'd they get all those guns?"

Antonio gave me a funny look and it suddenly dawned on me that if César could get guns, then revolutionaries probably could too.

"I just can't believe nobody knew about them," I said.

"Oh, somebody knew. This was a long time coming. Anyone who opened his eyes and looked around Chiapas could see it was only a matter of time," Antonio replied.

There was a knock at the front door and Maria went to answer it. Salvador came in. He was grinning from ear to ear.

"Isn't it great?" he asked. He scooped Luz into his arms and swung her around.

"Careful," Maria said.

"Careful? It's not a day to be careful," he said and burrowed his face into Luz's tummy as his daughter squealed with delight. "It's a day to celebrate."

It was when he put Luz down that he first noticed me. His face clouded, but only for a moment. Apparently even my presence couldn't ruin his good mood.

"What do you think, gringo? I guess you'll be going back to the States now."

Maria looked at me quickly, like it hadn't occurred to her that

I might leave along with the rest of the tourists.

"Not me," I said. "I like a good show."

"A good show, huh?" Salvador said. "Believe me, gringo. This is no show."

"I don't know what it is, but I'm not going anywhere."

"I'll tell you what it is. It's the end of the Mexican oligarchy. Say good-bye to NAFTA."

"It's not the end of anything yet," Antonio said.

"Fair enough," Salvador said. "It's the beginning of the end. What do you say, gringo?"

"I say you better wait and see what the Mexican army has to say."

"You think so, but you're wrong. People all over the country are going to rise up just like they did with Morelos and Zapata. The soldiers are the people too. You'll see. They'll join us."

"Us?" Maria asked.

Salvador looked at her.

"Us," he said after a moment. "The people. The cause. Salinas and his gang of criminals will be dead or in jail by next week. Don't you think so, Antonio?"

Antonio looked at him but didn't say anything.

"You'll see," Salvador said. "Maria, what do you have to eat? Revolution gives me an appetite."

We made tacos and talked about the Zapatistas. Salvador did most of the talking. He took a couple jabs at me, but for the most part he talked about what the change would mean for Mexico. He brought up various sociological theories and economic principals. He quoted Marx and Jung and someone named Gramsci. Actually, as much as I disliked him, I have to admit, Salvador seemed to know what he was talking about. I'd never given any thought to the IMF or the World Bank, but Salvador clearly thought they were bad for Mexico and that this insurrection was a direct challenge to economic policies associated with those institutions. Some of what he said made sense. Some of what he said I didn't fully understand.

After dinner, we convinced Maria to play something on the piano. "What do you want to hear?" she asked, shuffling through the small box of sheet music that she kept by the piano.

"Play that one about the revolution," Salvador said.

"Which?"

"The one about the Poles and the Russians. You know ... the one by what's-his-name. Chopin."

"'The *Revolutionary Étude?*' No, it's too hard. I need to practice it first."

"Come on."

"Let's hear it," Antonio said.

And then Francesca began clapping and started a chant: "Chopin, Chopin, Chopin." The rest of us joined in.

Maria shook her head in good-natured defiance, but she saw it was a hopeless cause and, after a few moments, finally sighed. "Okay. Ya basta."

We cheered.

"But it's not going to be any good."

"Enough excuses. Just play," Antonio said.

"But tell the story behind it," Salvador said.

She looked at him and then nodded. "Okay. So in 1830," she said as she found the folder she was looking for, "a number of Polish officers in Warsaw started a rebellion against Russian rule in what is sometimes called the November Uprising. Chopin was too sick to participate, but he wrote this to express his support for the rebels." She spread out the pages on the piano's shelf and massaged her hands as she studied the music. When she was ready, she took a deep breath. Her whole posture shifted and everything was still for a moment. Then she began.

It was a cascade of descending notes, her left hand racing down the length of the keyboard over and over, her right playing a delicate counterpoint. My fingers ached just watching. We all sat in rapt attention. Even Luz, who was tired and had been fussing some, sat unmoving on the floor with her doll in her lap while her mother played.

When she had finished, we all just looked at one another. Maria looked at the keys.

"That was beautiful," Francesca said finally.

"Thank you," she said. "But I made a lot of mistakes."

"I didn't hear any mistakes," Francesca said.

"They were there," Maria said.

"It was lovely," I said.

"What happened with the revolt?" Antonio asked.

Maria frowned. "It was crushed by the Russian army."

We all sort of looked at each other.

"It devastated Chopin," Maria added. "Luz," she said, rising from the piano bench, "say good night to everyone. Papa is going to put you to bed."

Salvador put Luz to bed while the rest of us cleaned up the kitchen. Antonio and Francesca cleared the table and put leftovers in the refrigerator. Maria washed and I dried. We were on the last of the dishes and I put my hand in the small of her back as I reached across her to hang the saucepan from a hook above the stove. The gesture was innocent, but I held my hand there just long enough to give the moment resonance. When I took my hand away and turned to find a place to hang the towel I'd been using, I saw Salvador standing in the doorway and looking at me. It was not a pleasant look.

"She's asleep," he said. He didn't stop looking at me.

"Good," Maria said. She took the towel from me and dried her own hands.

Antonio and Francesca put on their jackets. "We're going to go," he said. "It's been a long day."

Francesca hugged each of us and Antonio kissed Maria on the cheeks and added a hug to the ritual handshake with Salvador and me.

"Are you going to open the restaurant tomorrow?" I asked.

"I don't know. We'll see how things go."

When they were gone, Maria, Salvador, and I sat back down at the kitchen table. From the way Salvador was looking at me, I could see he didn't plan on leaving until he saw me go. I had hoped for a chance to talk to Maria alone, but I wasn't going to ignite that powder keg with Salvador. As it turned out, Maria lit the match.

"Salvador, you should go too."

"And the gringo?" he asked, as if daring her to admit what he already suspected.

She looked him straight in the eye and her voice was matter of fact. "I need to talk to Henry alone."

"Yo lo sabía," he said slowly, pushing back his chair and rising to his feet. "Estás jodiendo este gringo." He hadn't taken his eyes off me. I hadn't moved, but I was ready in case he came at me.

"That's none of your business," she said, her tone calm but firm.

"None of my business?" he asked. He turned to her. "Of course it's my business. You're my woman. You think I'm going to let you run around with this gringo?"

"Cuidado," I said, feeling a surge of adrenaline.

"No! *You* be careful, cabrón!" he said, pointing at me across the table. "I'm not afraid of your friends."

"What the hell do my friends have to do with anything?" I knew he was referring to the story Antonio had told me about César sending Ramón to confront Víctor. It made me mad and I rose half out my chair and leaned forward, my palms on the table.

But Maria put her hand on my shoulder and stood. "There's not going to be any fighting in my house. Luz is asleep. Sit down, Hank. Please ... Henry."

Salvador was glaring at me, his fists clenched.

"I'll stand," I said.

She must have realized I wasn't going to change my mind because she turned to Salvador.

"Listen to me, Salvador," she said, enunciating each syllable. Her anger was controlled, but just barely. "I'm not your woman. I'll never be your woman. So don't you dare think I belong to you or that I owe you anything. It's you who owe me and the only thing I want from you is for you to leave. This is my apartment, and I want you to leave. Now."

Salvador stood there, eyes still bulging and fists clenched, but it was clear she'd beaten him down more than I could have if I'd punched him half a dozen times.

"That's perfect," he said, "just perfect." And then he left.

Maria sat down in her chair. I had an urge to hold her, but I could see she didn't want to be touched.

"Can I have a cigarette?" she asked after a moment.

I lit two and handed her one. She inhaled deeply, held the smoke in, and then exhaled it with a long sigh. I sat down as well, still shaking, the cigarette slowly easing the rush of adrenaline shooting through my body.

"Henry," she said, "last night was a mistake."

"What?"

"We never should have slept together."

I just looked at her. I hadn't seen that coming.

"I drank too much tequila and it was New Year's and we'd had so much fun that I just sort of pretended like it didn't matter. I haven't been with a man since Salvador."

"And you thought a one-night stand with me would be a good

215

way to fix that?"

"No, it's just that I have Luz to think about."

I didn't say anything.

"I care about you, but it's complicated."

"Complicated how?"

"Complicated because of Salvador."

"You just told Salvador that it's over."

"And it is."

"Then what?"

She looked at me as though the answer were obvious, like the answer, whatever it was, was something not meant to be spoken.

"Complicated because of what?" I asked again.

"Because of César, Henry," she said, finally. "Because of César."

I was suddenly confused. That had not been the answer I'd been expecting. "What does César have to do with anything?"

The expression on her face grew stranger. "Because of what happened."

"What happened?"

She looked at me.

"What?" I said.

"You don't know?"

"Know what?"

"You really don't know?"

"I know your father and César and his father had a screwed-up business deal. So what?"

"That's all he told you?"

"All he told me about what?"

She studied me, as if gauging how to answer. "Okay," she said after a time. "I'll tell you, but you have to listen to the whole story."

There's a whole story, I thought. F-fucking fantastic. Of course there is. "Okay," I said.

She took a big drag on her cigarette and blew a column of

216

smoke into the air. "I met Salvador when I was seventeen. He came from UNAM to work with the Indians. Do you know UNAM?" She looked at me.

"The university in Mexico City?"

She nodded slightly and continued. "I'd never met anyone like him. He was smart and passionate and he was the first person who ever treated me like I wasn't just a pretty girl. He listened to me like what I thought mattered. Well, maybe not to what I thought exactly, but as if I was entitled to an opinion. You have to understand, Henry, that in the world I came from, the men are all machos and the women are just supposed to be quiet and do what the men say. Salvador didn't treat me that way."

"He just did."

She smiled. "Believe me, that's nothing compared to what I'm talking about. He is so different from the men I knew before him and I was young and I really thought I loved him. But when my father found out I was seeing Salvador ..." Her voice trailed off at the memory. Then she looked at me and said, "My father became very angry. He forbade me to see him. I was his only daughter and I was supposed to marry a boy from the right kind of family, a boy he chose." She looked at me and I had a sinking feeling. "My father planned for me to marry César."

"César? Are you serious?"

"Our fathers had arranged it. César was playing with Cruz Azul and we were going to be married in the off season. I didn't want to and I doubt that's what César wanted either. We barely knew each other. But it didn't really matter what we wanted." She seemed to think about this. "Well, I was young and stupid and didn't stop seeing Salvador and I got pregnant. When my father found out, he beat me and threw me out of the house. He disowned me." The way she said it was as if she still could not believe the truth of it.

217

"It wasn't just that I had disgraced myself and him. It caused a big problem with some business he had with César's family too. No one in my family would talk to me. None of my friends would talk to me. All I had was Salvador and he ran off because my father was going to kill him. I didn't have any money. I slept on the street. I didn't know what to do. All my life I'd been taken care of. Whatever I asked for, I was given. Then, all at once, I was on my own with nothing. After a few days, I saw Paola—you know, from the Christmas party. I'd met her a couple of times. She and José were Salvador's friends and they brought me from Tuxtla to San Cristóbal and let me stay with them. Then my father died from a heart attack. My mother says I killed him, that I broke his heart." She paused. "She's probably right."

I could see her thinking about that, but all I could think about was that she'd been engaged to César.

"I did," she said after a moment. And then again: "I did. I killed my father." The fact hung there. She took another drag from her cigarette. "That's when Salvador came back, but he said he didn't believe in marriage, that marriage was bourgeois. We fought a lot and he left again. That was the worst. My father was dead. My mother said I was dead to her. I was pregnant. I didn't have a job. My aunt, the one who just died, was the only person in my family who would talk to me. The rest of my family and friends shunned me. I thought Salvador was gone for good. I knew I couldn't stay with Paola and José forever. I was intruding.

"Then José introduced me to Antonio and Francesca. Antonio gave me a job. He and my aunt helped me rent this apartment. Things started to get better. I became self-sufficient and for the first time in my life I began to feel like my life was actually mine. Then Luz was born. It was hard, but I wasn't alone anymore. I had Luz and she had me."

She wiped her eyes and smiled at the thought of her daughter.

"Luz had her first seizure when she was three months old. I was so scared. I thought God was punishing my baby for what I had done. Sometimes I still think so. I know that's not true, but sometimes I can't help thinking that it is." She meant it too. It was written in her face. I knew that look, or one similar to it. I'd seen it in the mirror. I still see it.

She took another hit from her cigarette. "After a while, Salvador returned and said he wanted me back. He said he'd even marry me. He made it sound like he'd be doing me a favor and I realized I didn't love him anymore. I don't know if I ever loved him. For a long time I think I thought of him as this mature man with all these profound ideas and it was like I suddenly saw him as a boy. Now he is a part of my life because of Luz and he's good with her and I respect him for a lot of the same reasons I first liked him. He's a friend and he's my daughter's father, but that's all."

When she finished, we sat in silence for a long time. I stared at the foot of the table, but I could feel her studying my reaction.

"Aren't you going to say anything?" she asked.

"I don't know what to say."

"Say whatever you're feeling."

"I'm feeling a lot of things."

"Like what?"

"I don't know. What is there to say?" And what was there to say about anything? Jenn in the grave. An arranged marriage to César. This beautiful woman sitting across from me for whom I suddenly realized I genuinely ached despite the guilt such aching made me feel. What was it all about?

"At least you understand now why last night was a mistake."

I looked at her. Her eyes were wet. There was a chasm between us. There was a chasm between me and myself, too. "I'm going to go," I said and stood.

She nodded but didn't move from her chair. I put my jacket on and let myself out. She was still sitting, cigarette filter smoldering between her fingers, when I closed the door behind me.

22

OUT ON THE STREET, the night air was brisk. The Zapatistas were still there, milling about. They weren't doing anything and I walked past three men with ski masks and automatic rifles without giving them a second thought.

How was it possible César had never told me about Maria? Not a word. She'd said the marriage had been arranged when he'd been with Cruz Azul. He'd not had a shortage of female companionship when he'd been playing. I knew that for a fact. He'd told me about all the groupies who trolled the hotel lobbies during away games. But he'd never said anything to indicate something serious about any of them. Then I remembered that he had said something about a girl waiting for him back home. When had that been? Could he have meant Maria? He definitely hadn't said anything about being engaged. He hadn't even mentioned her name. I thought about what he'd said about the dealings between the families and wondered if César had simply seen the arranged marriage as part of that deal, a single clause in a larger business contract. An arranged marriage—what did such a thing even mean? What did it mean that César had never said anything? What did it mean that he'd said nothing even when I'd taken the job at El Acuario? But he had. He'd told me in no uncertain terms to stay away from Maria and he'd tried to convince me not to work there. He hadn't tried very hard, but he definitely hadn't encouraged me to take the job. Why hadn't he just told me not to work there because of Maria? Of course, the answer was Johnny Gilbride. Johnny Gilbride and the fact I'd said the job might help me keep my mind off Jenn and Suzy. That was the real reason. He'd intended to lighten my burden no matter what it meant to his own. But had he been burdened? He was angry about the business deal, but what about the rest of it? I mulled it over the whole walk home and then at the kitchen table in the guesthouse over several cigarettes and a couple bottles of beer.

The next morning I must have awakened around ten. I rolled out of bed and was making coffee when it occurred to me that maybe it didn't matter that César hadn't told me about Maria. The light of day can do that.

As far as I know, English has no specific word for the hours between midnight and sunrise, but in Spanish those hours are called *la madrugada*. If ever the sound of a word matched its meaning, it's *la madrugada*. At three in the morning, when I'd been tossing in bed, trying to unravel the equation of Jenn and Suzy being dead and in the darkness of the earth and my compadre's secrets and Maria sleeping with me and turning me away and my feeling small and alone in the universe and personal redemption for our failings always seeming more complicated and impossible with each passing hour and eternal oblivion waiting with its yawning jaws agape, *la madrugada* is as close as a word can get to what I was feeling.

But I finally fell asleep with the day's first light and sleep was a restful blankness and then I woke and, as I drank my first cup of coffee that morning, I simply didn't see any reason to worry about my friendship with César. There's no law that friends have to tell each other everything. The Maria thing was a little screwed up, but he couldn't blame me for sleeping with her if he hadn't told me what they'd had between them. And if he hadn't told me, there was no reason I had to tell him I'd slept with her. Maria was right. What had happened between us had been a mistake, but it wasn't a mistake I had to tell César about or feel bad about or make again. It wasn't like I was in love with the woman. I'd already been in love. I doubted anyone got lucky enough to feel that way twice.

So I felt good. Better than good. In fact, I decided that after I made myself breakfast—frying bacon and eggs and feeling good—I'd go to Maria's to tell her that everything was okay and we'd just remain friends and coworkers.

The Zapatistas were gone when I got to the zócalo. I was so involved in conversations with myself about what I was going to say to Maria that I might not have noticed but for all the trash and wreckage outside the municipal building and Viva Los Zapatistas! spray-painted on the wall.

"I wasn't sure you were coming back," Maria said after she opened the door.

"I wasn't sure either."

"Do you want to come in?"

"Yeah."

"Coffee?" she asked as I took off my jacket.

"No. Thanks, though."

"De nada. Have a seat."

We sat at the table. A bottle of nail polish was on the table. That was what I had been smelling. She was barefoot, cotton balls between her toes, her toenails red. A silver ring was on the middle toe of one foot. Even her feet were attractive.

"New nail polish?"

"Sometimes a woman needs to pamper herself."

I nodded. "I've been thinking about what you said …"

Luz came out from her room.

"Mamá," she asked, "where's Reyna?"

"No sé, mi amor. Did you leave her in my bedroom?"

"I don't know."

"Why don't you check?"

Luz half bounced, half pirouetted to her mother's bedroom.

"I'm sorry," Maria said. "You were saying?"

"I was saying I thought about what you said."

"Henry, I didn't mean it was a mistake. I really like you. It's just …"

"I get it."

"Mamá," Luz called, "I can't find her."

"Did you look next to the bed?" Maria called back.

"She's not there."

Maria sighed. "If she doesn't find the doll, she won't give us a minute's peace."

I nodded.

Maria got up from her chair. "She really does love that doll," she said to me.

I tilted my chair back onto two legs and studied the shape of the room. I heard Maria tell her daughter that the doll was right next to the bed where she'd said to look. Then I heard her tell Luz that she wasn't supposed to go on the balcony without her, that it was dangerous. I wondered if Luz was big enough to open the door or if Maria had left it open.

"Henry … Come here," Maria called from her room. There was urgency in her voice.

"What?" I asked as I came into the room. Maria and Luz were standing on the balcony and Maria gave me a worried look over her shoulder. I could hear the engines before I got to the balcony. Two columns of armored vehicles were rumbling into the zócalo, one from Calle Insurgentes and the other from Diego de Mazariegos. Then came the tanks. Loudspeakers mounted on top of two vehicles told people to stay in their homes and the few pedestrians in the zócalo scattered and vanished. Foot soldiers wearing helmets and carrying automatic rifles dashed through the square and down the various streets, taking up defensive positions in doorways and along the sides of buildings as they went. Several soldiers, clearly officers, barked orders and directed the vehicles. A tank idled right beneath us. Its turret cranked around until its barrel faced directly up Calle de Guadalupe. Several canvas-covered trucks rolled into the zócalo, plumes of diesel smoke belching from their vertical exhausts. The trucks stopped. On command, they simultaneously dropped their gates and dozens and dozens of soldiers hit the ground running, fanning out across the square and following the lead detachments up the streets in force. There were lots of soldiers, and after the casualness of the Zapatistas, the military precision of the Mexican army in motion was awesome and more than a little scary. I was impressed enough by the spectacle that I probably would have stayed out on the balcony if Maria, wide-eyed and ashen-faced, hadn't pulled me inside and slammed the doors shut.

"Jesus!" I said, the two of us standing in the room staring at one another in shock. Then we heard rifle fire, just a single round of a large-caliber weapon echoing up from the street. It didn't sound like gunfire in the movies.

"Mamá, what's that noise?" Luz asked.

Maria snatched Luz up into her arms and held her tightly, looking at me over Luz's shoulder. She looked as freaked out as I felt.

"What's that noise, Mamá?"

"Those are trucks," I said.

"Not the trucks," Luz said.

"It was just a noise," I said more sharply than I'd intended. I took Maria by the elbow and steered her toward the door. "Why don't we take Reyna to play in the other room?" I said, forcing myself to sound as upbeat and relaxed as possible.

I released Maria's elbow only after she was sitting at the table with Luz in her lap. I didn't notice it at the time, but I'd gripped her so tightly that I'd left a bruise. Maria and I kept glancing at one another while we tried to pay attention as Luz told us about Reyna's favorite flavor of ice cream, chocolate. Luz said it was her favorite too. There were more gunshots. It was then that we heard the soldiers storming up the stairs of the building, yelling to residents to stay in their apartments.

"Help me barricade the door," Maria said, putting Luz down and moving to push the couch. If I was scared, she was visibly terrified. I helped her with the couch because I didn't have the heart to tell her a sofa probably wasn't going to keep the Mexican army out of her apartment if they wanted to come in.

Apparently they didn't want to because when they were in the hallway outside our door they called "All clear" and again shouted for everyone to remain inside and continued up the stairs to the roof.

With the sofa blocking the front door and a half dozen or so soldiers no longer stomping through the hallways and stairwell, Maria seemed to calm.

"Let's go into Luz's room," she said. Although it had one wall facing the street, it was the most interior room in the apartment. The three of us sat on the bed.

"It will be okay," I said, trying to reassure myself as much as I was Maria. "They're just making sure the city is secure. The Zapatistas are gone. I don't think they'll be back."

We spent the rest of the day in Luz's room, mostly trying to keep her quietly entertained. I made ham sandwiches for lunch and then again for dinner. Maria didn't have much else on hand. Antonio never showed up—not that we expected him to—and like lots of Mexican households, Maria didn't have a phone, so we didn't hear from anyone.

Once things had quieted down enough, I made regular trips into Maria's room to peek out the balcony door and see what was going on. The zócalo and municipal building were firmly and unquestionably back under the Mexican government's control. I suppose more for symbolic and psychological reasons than tactical ones, the army was using the zócalo as a base of operations and they had fortified it accordingly. The tanks and armored vehicles that had first moved in remained at the four corners of the square. Sandbag bunkers and machine gun emplacements had been added as well, including one right below our balcony. Trucks kept rolling in, unloading soldiers, and then rolling out with other soldiers who had arrived only a few hours before. I could hear the occasional faint concussion of an explosion from somewhere in the distance. The military installation at Rancho Nuevo was pretty far away from the city, but a layer of smoke hazed the sky in that direction and I assumed there was a battle going on around the base and that the soldiers were being advanced to the fighting.

That night we all slept in Luz's room. I'd thought about trying to go back to the compound but decided that if the Mexican military tells you to stay inside, you should probably do as they say. Maria and Luz lay on the bed we'd pushed to the wall away from her balcony door and I sat on the hard tile floor with my back against the wall. I didn't really sleep and by one in the morning I was stiff and sore and got up to stretch.

"Where are you going?" Maria whispered in the dark. I wondered if I'd awakened her or if she'd been awake.

"Nowhere. The floor is too hard. I'm going to lie down on the sofa."

"There's room here," she said. It was a child's twin bed.

"It's okay. I'll just be in the other room."

"Don't go anywhere."

"I'm not going anywhere. I'll just be in the next room."

"Leave the door open," she said as I started to close the door.

"Okay," I said, pushing it back open. "Try to get some sleep." I flopped down on the sofa and it was heavenly soft after the floor, but I didn't sleep any better. Trucks kept coming and going in the square below and a group of soldiers went up or down the stairs a few times and the occasional rifle shot barked from someplace in the city and the simple fact is I was scared.

23

As was true with almost all the buildings in the old part of the city, there was no central heater in Maria's building and it was the damp cold that got me up just before dawn. Shivering, I rubbed my hands over my arms and regretted having left the house without my jacket. I went into Maria's room to check on the developments from the balcony. There weren't any. The soldiers were as before. Not another soul was anywhere to be seen. The whole city seemed to be on lockdown.

I went to the kitchen and found the coffee and brewed a pot. I had just lit a cigarette and sat down with my first cup when Maria came out.

"Coffee smells good." She spoke in a near whisper.

"Did you sleep?" I whispered back.

"Not really. Did you?"

"Sort of."

She went into the kitchen and came back with a cup and sat at the table, pulling her feet up to the seat of the chair, her knees tucked under her chin. "The warm cup feels good."

"It's cold," I agreed.

She asked me for a drag of my cigarette and I passed it over. She was handing it back when we heard the tromp of boots coming up the stairs. Maria looked at me. She was biting her lip.

"I think they're just doing a changing of the guard on the roof," I said. "I heard them go up and down a few times last night." Sure enough, a few moments later more boots clomped by.

"What are we going to do?" Maria asked.

"I've been thinking about that. We can't stay here."

"Pues, we can't leave."

"There's nothing to eat in this apartment and it's not like any markets are open."

"We still have leftovers from the tacos."

"Not really. We can't stay. It's as simple as that. Besides, do you want to wait to see if they decide to come into your apartment?"

"You don't think they will, do you?"

"I don't know, but we won't be able to stop them if they want to."

By her expression I could see that Mexican stormtroopers in her home was not a difficult image for her to conjure. "Where can we go?"

"My house. I've got plenty of food."

"Your house? You mean César's house? Henry—"

"I know, but look, César isn't there. He's with his family and the army has this city so buttoned down that he probably couldn't get in even if he wanted to."

"I can't go to César's house."

"Well, you could stay here and I could try to get some food and bring it back."

"You mean split up? What if they won't let you come back?"

"That's why you should come with me."

"What about a hotel?"

I hadn't thought about a hotel. "Do you think any will be open?"

"If we can get to one and someone is inside, I'm sure they'll rent us a room."

I took out my wallet and counted my cash. It wasn't enough. I thought about my credit card. It was back at the compound. I'd put it in a drawer as a precaution, figuring that on the off chance I lost my wallet in Mexico, it would be a colossal pain in the ass to replace both my debit and Visa cards at the same time. "Do you have any pesos?"

"In the bank."

"Well, the bank sure isn't open."

"What about the ATM?"

"Do you use Banamex?" I asked.

"Yes, right downstairs."

She meant the bank that was literally under her apartment two floors below. It was the same ATM machine I always used because Banamex was the only bank I'd found that would let me draw from my Bank of America account back in the States and, as far as I knew, it was the only Banamex in the city. At the moment, there was a sandbagged machine gun emplacement right in front of the door to the small glass room that housed the ATM. "I don't think we'll be getting money from the bank today."

"I can't stay at César's house."

"I have a credit card and food at my place. We can get both and either come back here or go to a hotel."

Maria pursed her lips. "Do you think they'll let us leave?"

"They either will or they won't, but they're not likely to confuse us with Zapatistas. I've got my passport."

"I don't know."

There was a burst of automatic gunfire, closer than any of the other shots had been, and Luz started crying from her bedroom. Maria hurried to comfort her and I wondered what they could still be shooting at here in the city. It didn't sound like fighting. It sounded like random shots.

Maria carried Luz in and sat at the table with the girl on her lap. Luz was sniffling and looked like she wasn't quite awake yet. "So we'll just go to your place and then try to go to a hotel?"

"That's it. I think things might be better if we get away from the zócalo."

"Okay, then we'll go. When?"

"Let's finish this coffee and you can pack a bag for the two of you."

"Está bien."

We drank our coffee and I had a second cup while Maria got Luz dressed and filled a backpack with their things. Maria strapped on Luz's helmet and then she said, "We're ready."

I pushed the sofa out of the way and made Maria and Luz stand off to the side while I opened the door an inch to look into the landing. It was empty. "Stay here and keep the door locked. I'll be back in a minute," I said. Maria nodded and I heard the bolt turn when I was in the hall.

I went down the stairs with my arms raised, passport in my hand. My biggest fear was first contact. I didn't want to accidentally surprise a soldier and get shot for it. The second-floor landing and first-floor foyer were empty, but the front door to the street was wide open. I paused at the doorway and tried to decide the best way to step out onto the sidewalk. There didn't seem to be a best way, so with my arms up and my passport in plain view, I took one long stride though the doorway and out as far away from the building as I could.

"Halt," a voice barked. You can believe I did.

"Soy estadounidense," I tried to yell, but the words caught in my throat. All the soldiers behind the sandbagged machine gun emplacement beneath our balcony had their weapons pointed at me. The tank was behind them, its barrel pointed up the street and in my general direction.

"Yo soy estadounidense," I repeated, the words getting out this time. "Don't shoot."

"¿Estadounidense?"

"Sí, estadounidense."

"Come forward five steps. Keep your hands up."

I did as instructed.

"Turn around."

I turned around until my back was toward them. Soldiers were along the walls of the buildings farther up the street. They were watching, weapons ready but not pointed at me. I suppose they didn't want to miss me and shoot one of their pals by accident. A soldier from the emplacement came up from behind, took my passport from my hand, and reviewed it while standing off to the side. Out of my peripheral vision I could see two soldiers, one on either side, standing behind me, their automatic rifles aimed at my back.

"This doesn't look like you."

"It's me. It's an old passport. Look at the date."

"What are you doing in San Cristóbal?"

"I live here."

"What are you doing on the street."

"I want to go back to my house."

"Where's your house?"

I gave him César's address.

"Why were you in this building?"

"My girlfriend lives here." I used the word *novia* instead of *amiga* for girlfriend. Don't ask me if it was simply a second-language error in a moment of stress or what. It doesn't matter. It sure didn't matter as I was standing there in the street. "I was visiting when you guys got here."

"And now you want to go to your house?"

"Sí."

"What's the address?" he asked again.

I gave him the address again.

"Okay," he said, handing back my passport. "You can go, but not through the zócalo."

"I understand. My girlfriend wants to come with me."

"Where is she?"

"Upstairs in her apartment."

"Why didn't she come down?"

"We were afraid."

"She has a passport?"

"I don't know if she has a passport."

"No passport?" he asked suspiciously.

"She has identification. She's Mexican."

"Your novia is Mexican?" He sounded surprised.

"Sí."

"What floor is she on?"

"The third."

"Okay. Go get her. We will need to see her identification."

I went back upstairs for Maria and Luz. The three soldiers were waiting for us just outside the door when we crossed the foyer.

"Identification," the soldier said to Maria when we'd stepped outside.

She handed it to him and he studied it and then studied her before handing it back.

"¿Es tu novio?" he asked.

She glanced at me and then looked back at the soldier. "He is," she said matter-of-factly.

"¿Y la niña?" he asked. He was looking at her pink helmet.

"My daughter."

The soldier nodded as if to say he saw the resemblance.

"And what is in the bag?"

"Clothes. Personal items."

"Open it, please."

Maria passed Luz to me and unzipped the backpack. The soldier examined the inside of the bag, removing a hair dryer and a package of crayons from among the items on top and feeling through the rest of the bag with his hand. He put the items he'd taken out back in the pack and zipped it closed.

"You may go." He stepped aside and directed us with his arm up Calle de Guadalupe and away from the zócalo.

We headed up the middle of the street, me carrying the backpack, Maria walking close beside me and holding Luz. We were stopped three more times on the way to the house, but we didn't have any problems. Besides the soldiers, no one was to be seen. Not a single person. We were half a block from the front gate and I already had my keys out when we heard several short bursts of a machine gun from the street from which we'd just turned, so we sprinted the rest of the distance. I opened the door and let Maria and Luz inside. In the doorway I stopped to listen to the gunfire. There were several more short bursts and then a long, deeper-sounding clatter from a larger-caliber weapon. As the larger gun went quiet, a truck filled with soldiers turned the corner and rolled past. It stopped at the corner of the street where the gunfire had been and the soldiers jumped down and fanned out and took up positions. A Mexican Jeep came onto the street and the driver stopped right alongside my doorway. He wore aviator glasses with reflective lenses. I could see myself in them. He pointed his finger at me. "Go back inside and shut your door and don't open it again or you'll be shot."

I nodded and shut the door and looked at Maria. She'd heard him as well.

"What'd that man say, Mamá?" Luz asked.

"I don't know," Maria said. She was looking at me.

"Luz, do you see the fountain?" I asked, kneeling down and

pointing the fountain out to her.

"Sí."

"Hay peces dentro."

"Fish?" she asked, wide-eyed with excitement.

"Go look."

Maria and I watched Luz run over to the fountain.

"What are we going to do?" Maria asked.

"I don't know."

"I can't stay here."

"Do we have a choice?"

She looked at me and then at the courtyard and then at the door and then back at me. "But it's César's house."

"I know."

She looked at the door again and then again at me. There was nothing to suggest.

"I know," I repeated. "But here we are."

"Mira, Mamá," Luz called, pointing into the fountain. "Pescaditos."

"¿De verdad?" Maria called back, pretending to share her daughter's enthusiasm. She looked at me once more. It was not a happy expression, but I could see the resignation in her face. "Okay," she said finally.

"Good. I'm going to see if the phones are working. Then I'll make us something to eat. Okay?"

She tucked a curl behind her ear and nodded. "Okay, novio." There was no irony or sarcasm in her voice.

"I just thought it would be easier to let us all come together if they thought we were novios."

"It was a good idea," she said. She looked at me and gave my hand a squeeze and then walked over to the fountain where Luz was up to her elbows in the water. I watched the two of them together for a moment, Luz splashing the water and Maria sitting on the edge of the fountain, and then I went into César's house to try the phones. They were still down. I got the same automated voice as before.

The maid hadn't been in since I'd last been home, so after I'd washed and dressed, I made the bed and picked up a pile of dirty laundry from a chair and put it in the hamper. I turned on the radio and tuned it to the BBC and washed some cups and plates I'd left in the sink. I took a whole chicken out of the freezer and put it in the sink to thaw. Maria and Luz came in and I gave them the threepenny tour. Then we listened to the radio while Luz used her crayons. Around noon, the girls went back out to the courtyard to play with a ball while I made lunch, my specialty, tuna fish sandwiches. I was cutting the sandwiches in half when Maria and Luz came inside. Luz was dripping wet from her hair right down to her sneakers. She was shivering and her lips were purple with the cold.

"She jumped in the fountain," Maria said, unclasping the helmet and then tugging off her daughter's shoes. "Do you have a towel?"

"I'll get you one."

Maria had stripped Luz and was rubbing her down with the towel while she gently chastised her. I carried Luz's clothes outside, wrung them out, and draped them over the patio chairs on my little terrace. Then I got some logs and kindling from the woodpile next to the house and brought them inside to build a fire.

Maria redressed Luz in dry clothes while I wadded up some of the leftover newspaper and got the fire going in the fireplace, gradually adding larger and larger pieces of kindling and finally putting in a log. We ate our sandwiches in front of the fire and Maria and I sipped coffee laced with the Jack Daniel's I'd borrowed from César's liquor cabinet one night after the trip to Calvario. That's when we heard the helicopters. They were far off,

237

but by the time we got outside they sounded much closer and then three military-green gunships, flying low, thundered over the courtyard and out of view.

"¡Que horror!" Maria said, holding Luz and looking up in the direction in which they'd gone.

"Come on. We might be able to see something from the main house."

"I can't go in César's house."

"Come on."

"No. I wouldn't feel right. I feel strange enough just being here at all."

"It's not that big a deal."

"Yes it is."

"Look, given the circumstances, he'll understand."

She gave me a strange look, like maybe we were talking about two different people. "I don't think so. You go ahead and tell me if you see anything. I'm not sure I want to see anything anyway."

So I crossed the courtyard and went into the main house by myself. The compound wall was too high to see anything from César's second-story bedroom, so I went up the stairs to the roof. There was a small rooftop patio and from there I could see far out across the city. The fog had thinned some, but the buildings remained shrouded in mist. Beyond the city I could just make out the dark line of the mountains. The three gunships had loosened their formation and were circling the city, flying cover. When the first helicopter flew back over the house, despite the fog, I could clearly see the pilot wearing his helmet. He was right there. His visor was up and he looked right at me as that gunship swung past. It was when the second helicopter went by, at a slightly more comfortable distance, that I saw off in the direction of the military base at Rancho Nuevo three bright flashes that rose up through the mist and mushroomed into giant balls of fire, the red and orange flames clearly visible despite the fog. A few seconds later came the muffled concussion of the blasts. I couldn't tell if they were planes or helicopters over Rancho Nuevo, but they were dropping bombs or shooting rockets, and once the explosions started, they kept coming at irregular but constant intervals.

"My god!" I heard myself say under my breath as the balls of flame rolled up from the earth and I thought of the young Zapatista girl who'd been carrying the fake gun. "It's a massacre."

I watched the bombing until one of the circling helicopters swung so close to the house that I instinctually ducked and dashed back inside.

"What's going on?" Maria asked when I got back to my bungalow. She had Luz on her lap and looked scared.

"The military is bombing the Zapatista positions around Rancho Nuevo." As if to punctuate what I'd said, we heard several more muffled explosions and a while later a reporter on the BBC confirmed that was exactly what was happening. I wondered how close to the action he was. I didn't envy him his job.

All that afternoon the bombing continued and the helicopters circled over the city. Maria and I sat in front of the fire and listened to the war both live and on the radio. We wondered aloud about Antonio, Francesca, and Salvador. Were they safe? What were they doing? I wondered where César and his family were. We speculated about how long the bombing might last and tried not to think about how things might get worse. But really we spoke very little. When bombs are falling and gunships are passing overhead and there are tanks parked on your street corner, there's not a whole lot to talk about. You're kind of just waiting for the next shoe to drop.

Fortunately Luz was too young to understand what was really going on. The helicopters excited her and she stood by the window to watch them when they passed overhead. At least her enthusiasm gave us something else to concentrate on. When Luz asked about the sound of the bombing, Maria told her it was thunder, an explanation Luz accepted without further questions.

At five I marinated the chicken and some fingerling potatoes with lemon, honey, rosemary, and garlic, popped the dish in the oven, tossed a salad, and went over to the main house for a bottle of sauvignon blanc that I took from the refrigerator in the bar. The food and wine were good, but only Luz ate much.

"Do you hear that?" Maria asked as I scraped our leftovers onto one plate.

I stopped what I was doing and listened. It took me a moment to realize that what I was straining to hear was the silence. We hadn't heard a bomb in the last twenty minutes and the helicopters were gone.

"Do you think that's all?" she asked.

"I hope so," I said, still listening to the quiet, half expecting another explosion. "They may have just stopped for the night."

"¡Ojala que no! I don't want to listen to another day of that."

"I'm sure that's all," I said.

"¡Ojala!"

"Ojala," I agreed. "I hope so too," I repeated to myself in English as I carried the dirty dishes into the kitchen.

I gave Maria and Luz my bed and put some sheets and a pillow and a blanket on the sofa for me. While I did the dishes, Maria dressed Luz in her pajamas and sang her to sleep. The song was about a mother hen and her chicks. Listening to the gentle lull of her voice, I was reminded of Jenn singing "Twinkle, Twinkle, Little Star" and "Itsy Bitsy Spider" to Susan. There is no sound on earth more comforting than a woman singing her child to sleep. After a time, the singing stopped and I thought Maria would come back out, but she didn't. I poked my head into the bedroom and they were face to face, breathing gently, both fast asleep.

...

THE NEXT MORNING THERE was no sound of bombs or helicopters. I got up and listened to the BBC as I made breakfast. They reported heavy fighting continuing in and around Ocosingo and toward Las Margaritas but that the Zapatistas around Rancho Nuevo had vanished in the night. No one knew how many people had been killed. One report said dozens. Another estimated the number to be in the hundreds. There were additional reports of Indians sympathetic to the Zapatista cause rising up and taking over large ranches. Other reports said ranchers were killing Indians. I wondered what, if anything, was happening at Calvario. I went over to the main house to try the phones again. No luck.

When I got back to the guest house, Maria asked if it was okay if she took a shower. "I never got around to it yesterday."

"Of course," I said and got her a towel.

"Thank you," she said.

"Sure."

"No," she said. "Not for the shower. For getting us out of the apartment."

"You're welcome."

"I don't know what I would have done if you'd left us there."

"I wasn't going to leave you." We looked at each other. She held the towel. "I wouldn't have left you," I said.

"I know," she said. "It means a lot to me." She looked at me the same way she'd looked at me on her doorstep on New Year's Eve.

"You're welcome," I said.

"I mean it."

I nodded. "Luz," I said, "let's go see the fish." I took a stale slice of bread from the kitchen and Luz and I went out to the fountain. "No getting wet," I said to Luz when we neared the water.

"Okay," she said. We watched the fish for a few minutes and then Luz asked, "What kind of pescaditos are they?"

"Minnows," I said in English, which was simply the translation of *pescaditos*.

"Minnows," Luz repeated. We fed the fish bread crumbs and after a while Luz asked me if they had names.

"No, but you can name them."

She gave them some silly names that can't really be translated, but they were along the lines of "Fishy-wishy" and "Bubbly-wubbly." Then she said, "What's that smell?"

"What smell?" I didn't smell anything, but I had a smoker's nose.

"That funny smell."

"I don't smell it."

"It's giving me a funny feeling in my tummy."

"A smell is giving you a funny feeling in your tummy? What kind of funny feeling?"

Luz looked at me. She had a confused expression on her face.

"What kind of funny feeling?" I asked again.

She looked around the courtyard like she wasn't quite sure where she was.

"Luz," I said.

She looked at me. It was like she didn't recognize me. Then her eyes rolled back in her head and she started convulsing.

"Luz!" I lunged, but her head bounced off the side of the fountain before I could catch her. Thank God for that helmet. Her back arched. It bowed. Her legs kicked and bucked. She gurgled and foamed at the mouth. "Luz!" I called. "Luz!" And then shouting: "Maria! Jesus Christ, Maria!" I didn't know if it was the right thing to do, but I pressed her to my chest. She was as rigid as wood, yet seizing and convulsing. Her head snapped back, the tendons like steel rods bulging from her tiny neck. I tried to corral her arms to keep them from slamming against the cobblestones.

I don't know how long it lasted, but almost as quickly as the attack had come on, it subsided. It was as though her body wilted. She wasn't exactly conscious and her eyes weren't actually open, but at least her irises weren't turned into her skull. I lifted her in my arms and headed for the house. "It's okay, Luz. It's okay, baby. Maria!"

The bathroom door was closed and the hair dryer was blowing. "Maria!" I shouted and the dryer stopped and the door opened. She was dressed, but her hair was still wet. She had a brush in her hand. She took one look at us and the expression on her face changed instantly and the brush was on the floor and she was taking Luz from me.

"What happened?"

"She had a seizure."

Maria's eyes flashed. Luz had started crying softly, and Maria shushed her and patted her on the bottom. "Shhh, mi amor, shhh." She carried Luz into the bedroom and put her on the bed. I watched from the doorway. She cuddled with her daughter and whispered to her.

"Can I do anything?" I asked. Maria didn't break her murmuring to Luz, but she waved her hand to say, "No." I sat down. I stood up. I poked my head back into the bedroom. I sat down again. I didn't know what else to do, so I got up and went into the kitchen and brewed a fresh pot of coffee. I'd just poured myself a cup when Maria came out and closed the door to the bedroom.

"She'll sleep for several hours."

"I didn't know what to do."

"It's like that. It's always like that."

"I was scared."

"Me too. I am every time. You'd think I'd be used to it by now, but I'm not."

"I don't know how someone gets used to something like that."

She looked at me and I didn't know what else to say.

"Do you want a cup of coffee?" I asked.

She made no gesture, so I gave her mine and went back for another. She was sitting on the sofa when I came back, her face in her hands.

"It will be okay," I said for lack of something else.

Maria didn't take her hands from her face. "Goddamnit."

"Hey," I said, sitting next to her and putting my hand on her knee, "Luz will be okay." Maria looked at me. Her face was a mask of contradictions. I put my arm around her shoulder. "Everything will be okay." And we looked at each other and in that moment something passed between us. A mistake or not, we didn't care.

And then we were upon each other, kissing and tugging at belts and pulling at zippers. I peeled off her shirt and her elbow caught me in the chest. My foot knocked over one of the coffee cups. I squeezed one of her breasts and she bit my lip. Her hand was on my cock and I flipped her onto her stomach so she was bent over the arm of the sofa, yanked down her white cotton panties, and entered her from behind. She was grinding back on me with her hips and I had a handful of her hair and yanked her head back and we fucked and with each thrust I tried to impale her, tried to cleave her in half, and with each thrust she cried out, louder and louder, and I clamped my hand over her mouth like I wanted to suffocate her and she bit the heel of my hand and kept biting and we fucked and fucked and fucked like we were fucking away the war and fucking away Luz's sickness and fucking away the stress and fucking away the death of my girls and fucking away our fucked-up situation. I wanted to destroy her. It wasn't love. It wasn't sex, either. It wasn't even fucking. It was rage. It was defiance. It was revenge for being alive.

And then it was over.

I was panting and gradually released her and rolled off and sank back into the sofa. She was slow to lever herself from the position I'd bent her to and slow to pull her panties up and then her jeans. I thought for certain she would never look at me again, but she turned and faced me, her expression inscrutable.

"I've never done that before," she said.

"Are you all right?"

She looked at me like she was trying to discern the meaning of the question. "I don't know," she said, "but that was exactly what I needed."

"It wasn't another mistake?"

"Probably, but I don't care."

"Are you sure?"

"Yes. I'm sure." She stood up. "I'm going to wash."

"I'll go after you."

She smiled and I thought to myself: Our lives are about to get really complicated. And I thought to myself: So what? Let them.

We didn't talk about what had happened, but whatever was between us had changed and there was no going back. We listened to the radio. The fighting was bad. Maria checked on Luz, but she was sleeping peacefully. It was midafternoon and Maria and I were playing a game of backgammon when Luz woke up. She fussed and was lethargic, but she seemed to be better. To help improve her mood, we abandoned the rules and let Luz roll the dice and move the pieces as she wanted. Then we sat out on the patio and Luz played with a ball while Maria told me about the different composers she liked and why. She mostly talked about their music, but she mentioned lots of biographical tidbits too, like Schubert likely having died from mercury poisoning, a common treatment for syphilis at the time, or Mozart being so manic that he was unable to sit still for his barber without taking breaks to compose. Maria said her aunt had gossiped about the private lives of composers as though they were people in the neighborhood. Then we had dinner and Maria put Luz down while I washed the dishes. I hadn't finished them when Maria came up behind me in the kitchen and said, "I put Luz on the sofa."

"Why?"

"Because, novio," she said, slipping her arms around my waist, "I want you to come to bed."

"¿Novio?" I asked, turning around.

"I'm testing it."

"And?"

"I think I like it."

"Me too," I said and took her into my arms.

For the first time we made love openly and without the shyness of the first time or the anger and emotional desperation of the morning. There was only the wonder of new lovers and we gave ourselves over to one another and we were the only two people in the world and when we lay quietly in the dark afterwards, it took us a long time to return from that place we had been.

"¿Novio?"

"Yes?"

She said nothing more and suddenly I realized she was crying. She wasn't making any noise, so in the dark I don't know how I knew she was crying, but she was. "Hold me," she said.

"I am."

A while later she stopped crying and her breathing became regular and I thought she was asleep.

"Henry," she said. "Can I ask you something?"

"Uh-huh."

I waited for the question, but it took her a moment to ask it. She lay still, her head resting on my chest.

"How did your wife and daughter die?"

I stared into the blackness of the room. I had the sense I was seeing into the dark, like it was a thing, an expanse unfolding before me.

"You don't have to tell me," she said.

"It's okay," I said. And then: "They drowned." And in the darkness I could see the river as I had seen it in my mind, as I had seen it and seen it and probably would see it for the rest of my life.

"We were camping and we went canoeing." It was like I was listening to someone else tell the story. "We'd canoed there before, but the spring runoff was high." What I didn't say was that we'd argued about whether Suzy should be in the canoe at all and that I'd insisted there was nothing to worry about. "There was a bend in the river with little rapids, but at that time of year they weren't so little. Jenn said we should pull out, but I told her we'd be fine." What I didn't say was that Jenn had practically begged me to go to the riverbank and I hadn't because I'd been trying to make some macho and idiotic point. I thought about that and I remembered the rushing water. I could hear it rushing. I saw Jenn holding on to Suzy and the final look she gave me as she glanced over her shoulder. It was only for a millisecond, but the terror on her face was frozen in my memory.

"When I realized we weren't going to be fine, it was too late. We got sideways and hit a boulder. We hit hard and all three of us were thrown into the rapids where the water curled back on itself. It sucked us under."

I remembered the pressure of the water, my powerlessness against it.

"Even with life jackets, we got pinned under. I got my hand on one of them. Jenn's arm or Suzy's leg. I don't know. I think it was Jenn's arm. Then the current shot me out."

I remembered my grip wrenching loose.

"I couldn't hold on. The water was too strong. I don't know

why they weren't thrown clear like me. They just weren't."

I remembered thrashing in the water as the water carried me farther and farther away.

"I tried to swim back, but I couldn't. The current was just too strong, too fast. I couldn't go back. I let go and that was all."

And suddenly I was crying. I mean really crying, crying like I had never cried before, crying harder than I had at the funeral or even when the paramedics loaded their sheet-draped bodies into the back of the coroner's ambulance. It just poured out and Maria held me and I curled into her and wept and it kept coming and coming and coming.

"I made it to shore about a quarter mile downriver," I said finally. The tears had stopped. "We found their bodies eleven days later on a sandbar three miles below where I came out. They washed up together. They weren't more than twenty-five yards apart."

Maria held me and stroked my head, but she didn't say anything.

"A hiker found them," I said. I thought about how they were already being loaded into the ambulance by the time I got there, how no one would let me see them, how Jenn's bare foot stuck out from beneath the sheet. I remembered how I just wanted to cover her foot, but they wouldn't let me. Then they closed the ambulance door. I never saw either of them after that. Jenn's uncle identified their remains. Given the condition of the bodies, everyone told me I should spare myself from seeing them, so I did. I thought about that. In the dark I saw Jenn's foot and the closing ambulance door. I thought about the girls. I thought about the river and I thought about the darkness and I thought about Maria. I thought about the girls. "I should have found them," I said finally. "It shouldn't have been a stranger." Then we didn't say anything more and Maria stroked my head. Sometime later, I fell asleep.

24

WHEN I AWOKE IN the morning, Maria was looking at me. She kissed me on the forehead and smiled gently when I turned my face fully to her.

"Did you sleep?" I asked.

"Yes. Did you?"

"Yes."

"Good."

All that day and the next two were spent inside the compound. We cooked food and drank wine and read books and kicked a ball in the courtyard with Luz. Luz had fully recovered from her attack. She colored and I taped the crayon drawings on the refrigerator until it was covered. When I taught Maria how to play blackjack, she took me for twenty-five pesos. I showed Luz how to throw coins into the fountain for luck and all Maria's winnings ended up in the water with the fish. From the phone in the main house, I kept trying to reach my folks and César at the number he'd given me for the house in Mexico City, but the phone service remained down.

Because Maria wouldn't go into César's house, I washed and dried the girls' clothes in the machines in the main house and sat in the game room and drank a beer by myself while I watched the second half of a Jazz and Nuggets game. At night I listened to

Maria sing Luz to sleep and then we made love. The compound became our own private world, like a country unto itself, and it was odd to think that outside the walls there was a war going on. I think I almost would have been able to forget that there was any war at all if we hadn't kept the radio on, murmuring in the background.

While I was perfectly content to let the whole outside world fall away, on the morning of the eighth, Luz began to ask for Salvador.

"Do you think we should go out?" Maria asked, sipping her coffee.

"Do you?"

"I'm kind of curious to see what's going on and I wouldn't mind seeing my piano. I haven't gone this long without playing since I left my parents' home. I'm going to be rusty."

"I doubt that."

"You'll hear," she said and laughed. "It'll be terrible. Besides, Salvador will be wondering about Luz."

"Sure," I said.

Maria smiled at me. "You're not jealous, are you? He is her father."

"It's not that. I was just kind of enjoying having it just be us."

Maria got up from her chair, slid into my lap, and kissed me. "Me too, but we've already been here too long."

"I know."

"Don't you want to see what's going on?"

I hadn't, but now that I knew we were at least going to try to go out, I realized I was curious to see what was happening. "Yeah, I guess I do. Maybe we can find Antonio and Francesca."

"Maybe the soldiers are gone," Maria said, brightening at the possibility.

"Maybe," I agreed, but I doubted it. The fighting might

have moved a lot farther south and east, but if the BBC could be believed, there was still a pitched battle raging. Since the Zapatistas had started the war from the zócalo, I didn't think it was likely that the Mexican army would abandon it, if only to remind the population who was in charge.

"So, should we go?"

"Let me take a look."

When I opened the door to the street, I was surprised at the number of people walking around and the number of cars driving by. I'd had a fleeting fear I'd be confronted by the soldier who'd told me to stay inside or be shot, but people seemed to be going about their business as usual.

"What do you see?" Maria asked from behind me.

"It looks okay. It looks normal."

Maria poked her head out the door and then looked at me. She seemed as surprised as I was.

I shrugged. "Vámonos."

The tortilleria on the corner was open, as was the farmacia and several other stores on the next block. While there were quite a few pedestrians on the street, everyone appeared to be moving with particular purpose. Maybe it was my imagination, but no one seemed to be just hanging out. We saw the first soldiers when we turned onto Calle 20 de Noviembre, but they didn't seem to be doing anything except making their presence felt. They weren't asking anyone for identification. We walked right on by.

Though the city was open, the zócalo remained closed. The tanks, armored vehicles, and sandbagged machine gun emplacements still guarded the intersections at the four corners of the square and there were lots of soldiers around the municipal building. We explained to a group of soldiers that we were trying to reach Maria's building across the square and they told us we'd have to go around the cathedral to get there.

Three notes were taped to Maria's door, one from Antonio and the other two from Salvador. Once inside, Luz ran to her room and Maria read the three notes.

"Antonio is opening El Acuario today," she said, passing the note over.

Maria didn't share them with me, but I could see from their length that the notes from Salvador were really one note and one letter. As she read the letter, I tried to resist the urge to study her reaction to it. All the same, I did notice a flicker of a smile at one point, a frustrated sigh at another, and a small laugh and frown at a third. So much for resisting.

"So, do you want to go to El Acuario?"

"Bueno," she said. "Let me leave a note so Salvador knows where we are and we'll go to the restaurant."

"Good."

There were quite a few foreigners standing at the bar and Antonio was in the middle of taking a lunch order from two people at a table when we came in. The moment he saw us, he bailed on the customers mid-order.

"Hey!" he shouted, dashing over to give us all hugs. He and I did our secret handshake as Francesca ran out from behind the bar and Félix came out from the kitchen. We were all laughing and jumping around and babbling on about the tanks and helicopters and bombs and everything for four or five minutes until the people at the table Antonio had abandoned started to make some noise. Antonio went back to apologize and complete the order.

"¡Aye, la Bolognese!" Félix said before dashing back into the kitchen.

"I'm glad you two showed up," Francesca said. "We've been busy since we opened and I don't know what I'm doing behind the bar. I've charged the wrong price three times."

"Who are all these people? I thought the tourists left."

"They did," Francesca said. "This is the press."

It turned out the journalists had started arriving in force on January 5, and their numbers had been growing ever since. We had pretty regular business all afternoon until four, when all the journalists cleared out for some press conference. That's when Francesca cornered Maria and me behind the bar. "So where were the two of you?"

Maria blushed and she and I glanced at one another, embarrassed but pleased with ourselves all the same.

"Then it's true," Francesca squealed like a schoolgirl, clapping her hands together. "Que bueno. Que bueno. I'm so happy for you," she said, mostly speaking to Maria.

"Salvador is taking it hard," Antonio said, lighting a cigarette.

"It's true." Francesca nodded somberly.

Maria frowned.

"Where's Papa?" Luz asked, having heard her father's name.

"Estoy aqui, hija," Salvador said, walking through the door.

"Papa!" Luz yelled and jumped off her stool to run as fast as her little legs would carry her across the room and into Salvador's outstretched arms.

"Where have you been?" Salvador asked as he carried Luz back to the bar and shook hands with Antonio. Although he asked Luz, the question was clearly directed at Maria.

"I didn't want to keep Luz downtown," Maria said.

"So where were you?"

She glanced at me. "Henry let us stay with him."

I washed glasses, determined to stay out of their discussion, but I could feel Salvador give me a hard look.

"Who told you you could take Luz to his house?"

"¿Que?"

"I always knew you'd go back to your coleto roots, but I never imagined you'd let a gringo raise our child."

Maria looked quickly at Luz and then back at Salvador. "Don't make a scene," she said.

"I'm not making a scene. I just want to know why you think you can disappear with my daughter without telling me where you're going. Did you think about how worried I might have been?"

"I'm sorry. You're right. But we didn't have a choice."

"What do you mean you didn't have a choice?" he said, putting Luz on a stool. "You could have left a note."

"We didn't have a choice," I interjected.

"Please, Henry ... ," Maria said.

"Yeah, Henry," Salvador said. "Why don't you mind your own damn business."

"Salvador ... ," Maria said.

"No, really, who does this gringo think he is?"

"Back off," I said.

"Back off?" he said. And then more loudly: "Back off? You back off."

I put both of my hands on the bar and looked at him.

"What?" he shouted. "What are you going to do?"

The patrons at the tables were looking at us.

"I think you need to leave," Maria said after a moment, her voice very quiet.

"Salvador ... ," Antonio said.

"I'm not leaving. The goddamned gringo can leave."

"Enough," Antonio snapped. We all looked at him. Everyone in the room did. "Either lower your voice or leave the restaurant."

Salvador looked at him. Then he looked at Maria and me. "Fine," he said. Then he turned and strode out without another word.

"Papa!" Luz cried. "Papa! I want Papa!"

III

25

WE WORKED FOR A while that afternoon, but Maria was distant and distracted. I knew she was upset about Salvador, like she was worried that she might have permanently driven Luz's father away, but in retrospect I realize that she saw the scene with Salvador as a symptom of a larger issue, one I didn't yet recognize. The intimacy and emotional intensity of those days when we'd hidden ourselves away from the war and the world had now run into the reality of our lives. I hadn't understood just how weird it was going to be until Luz got restless and Antonio told Maria to take her home. Francesca suggested that I walk with them. Maria said it was unnecessary, but Francesca gave a look to Antonio and he said, "Have Hank go with you. Let's give Salvador a little more time to cool off."

So I walked them home, and as we walked down the street, I pointed to soldiers whitewashing over Zapatista graffiti. Maria nodded but didn't say anything. We came to the door of her building and she lifted Luz into her arms and turned to me.

"Did you want to come up?" she asked.

I had assumed I would, but with the two of them facing me and blocking the doorway, what had been us was now strangely them and me. I didn't understand what had happened, but something had.

"I think I'll go back and help at the restaurant."

"Then I'll see you tomorrow," she said.

"Sure," I said. "I'll see you tomorrow."

The three of us stood there for a moment. I wanted to ask what was going on, but instead I leaned across the invisible barrier between us and gave her a kiss on the cheek. "Hasta mañana," I said to them.

"Hasta mañana," Luz said and they went in.

I worked into the night, but business was dead and Antonio let me go early. Back at the house, I smoked cigarettes and drank a beer and thought about the day. Then I thought about Jenn and I remembered our early days together when we were just getting to know each other. On our second date we went to one of those retro burger joints where the waitress is on roller skates and she brings the food out to the car and attaches a tray to the car door. When the food came, I passed a soda over to her and, as I did, I accidentally spilled some of the drink on the console between us, a small amount splashing on Jenn. There was a small towel in the back, so I apologized, got out, opened the hatchback, gave Jenn a chance to dab the spots on her overcoat and dress, and wiped up the spill. Then I returned the towel to the back, closed the hatchback, climbed back into my seat, and pulled the door closed. My milkshake, both hamburgers with special sauce, two orders of chili cheese fries, two sides of ketchup, and the plastic tray all came flying through the window and right onto our laps. Frozen in simple shock, we both took a moment. Then we turned to each other. Her face held a look of wide-eyed disbelief. I felt nothing but mortified horror, but whatever my feelings were, my expression suddenly caused Jenn to burst into howls of laughter. It took me a moment to appreciate the humor of the situation, but then my humiliation vanished and I was laughing too, just a chuckle at first, but then full-throated and uncontrollably. I don't think I ever laughed that hard before. My sides hurt and we both were crying and just when it would begin to subside, we'd look at each other and it would start all over again. We probably sat there in hysterics and covered in milkshake and chili cheese fries for ten minutes before I extracted myself from the mess to retrieve the towel from the back and get another from the waitress.

Anyway, instead of going to a club to hear some bands as we'd planned, I took Jenn back to her place and she changed and let me clean up a bit. Her roommate had gone out, so she opened a bottle of wine and we sat on the sofa and talked into the night.

And as I thought about Jenn and that night and the easygoing nature of our early days together, I realized how relatively low the stakes had been. Maria and I had gone from friendly coworkers to live-in lovers in the span of one night and things were a lot more complicated than they had been with Jenn. The stress of war had thrown us together and created an emotional intensity unlike anything I'd ever felt before, but we didn't even really know each other. Now that Maria and I were no longer in the cloistered realm of the compound, we would have to figure things out, and there were a lot of variables to consider. Even though Jenn and I had felt an instantaneous connection, we'd taken things relatively slowly. We hadn't slept together until we'd been dating for almost a month. Maria and I had skipped that in-between time.

Then it occurred to me that Maria and I could never have a courtship like I'd had with Jenn. I didn't even want one. Somehow at that moment life seemed simultaneously too complex and too frivolous for such a romance. Even the thought of such a relationship seemed exhausting. And with that thought, whatever anger or hurt I'd felt about Maria's rejection vanished. There was something between us and we both felt it. It wasn't love like I'd had with Jenn, but it was something. Whatever it was, I was going to pursue that and not let the rest of the bullshit get in the way. The rest of the bullshit didn't matter. At least, it didn't matter then.

THE NEXT MORNING I returned to Maria's apartment. A group of soldiers standing by the tank on her street corner watched me. I nodded to them, but they made no gesture in response and just kept watching as I entered Maria's building.

"Hola," I said when she answered the door. She was wearing the red sweater with snowflakes. "Can I take you two for breakfast?"

She looked at me for a moment. Then she smiled and brushed a strand of hair behind her ear. "Okay," she said. She smiled again. "I mean thanks. That would be nice."

I waited in the doorway while she put Luz's shoes on.

"Is it cold outside?"

"It's not too bad in the sun."

She got jackets for both of them, strapped on Luz's pink helmet, and grabbed her handbag and we headed out.

The soldiers were still there and they were still watching, but it was Maria they were looking at now. She knew it too, because when we got out of earshot of them, she said, "I hate the way they look at people." I didn't tell her that they didn't look at everybody the same way that they looked at her.

With the Kiosco closed, we went to a courtyard café on Utrilla.

"Let's sit in the sun."

I ordered a coffee and Maria ordered an espresso for herself and a hot chocolate for Luz. We looked at the menus and Luz chased pigeons in the courtyard and we ordered food when the waiter brought the hot drinks. Steam rose from the cups in the cold morning air. We watched the steam and Luz at play.

"The thing with Salvador upset me," she said finally.

"I know."

"Henry, how is this going to work?"

"I don't know, but I've been thinking about it." I told her that everything had unfolded very fast. I told her I didn't regret anything that had happened between us, that in fact I was glad for it, but I also said that what we had gone through had set us up for unreal expectations and that I thought we needed to reduce the pressure we both felt and just get to know one another. I almost told her about Jenn and the burger fiasco, but I decided that memory was just for Jenn and me. Instead, I told her I just wanted us to do things without all the heavy implications. "So what do you think?" I asked when I had finished my little speech.

She smiled at me. "Does this mean you're going to invite me to dinner and a movie?"

"I don't know," I said. "It depends on what kind of films you like."

"Monster movies."

"What?"

She smiled more broadly. "And anything with Pedro Infante."

And that's how Maria and I started dating. Under the new arrangement, we met at a restaurant for breakfast a couple of times and on Monday afternoon I took Maria to the movies and to dinner. And there really is a difference between meeting for a date and simply going out with someone with whom you live. There's a certain effort implied in getting ready and meeting someone for a date that doesn't exist when you live together. I'd walk her home after work and sometimes we'd say good night on the doorstep and sometimes she'd invite me up and I'd listen to her play music or we'd snuggle on the sofa to talk or we'd slip into her room and make love, but always I'd leave before morning so she could wake up alone with her daughter. It may sound odd, but we did drop all the expectations and we just enjoyed spending time together. We learned things about each other too. For instance, she really did like monster movies, the old classics like Boris Karloff's

Frankenstein and Béla Lugosi's *Dracula*. And her crush on Pedro Infante was serious. I learned she was fascinated by insects but terrified of spiders. Also, she had zero sense of direction and was a serious chocolate aficionado. According to Maria, the best chocolate in the world came from Tabasco. I didn't tell her that her passion for chocolate reminded me of Jenn's ice cream addiction. For her part, Maria was impressed with the traveling I'd done. In truth, I'd only been to most of the states in the lower forty-eight and on two summer trips to Europe, but to Maria that was a lot. She'd been to Mexico City once and to the states that bordered Chiapas a few times and to Guatemala some to visit her aunt, but those had all been brief trips and she'd not otherwise left Chiapas. She'd always lived there and she couldn't quite comprehend that I'd resided in so many different places. Also, she confessed that she thought my accent was sexy. It hadn't dawned on me that my gringo accent could be attractive, but she assured me it was.

Our new arrangement also gave Maria a chance to smooth things over some with Salvador and he resumed his regularly scheduled visits with Luz. Salvador and I never were going to be friends, but apparently he felt less threatened by me when he learned I wasn't going to be living under the same roof as Maria and his daughter.

We'd been dating like this for almost two weeks when, under extreme pressure from the Mexican people, President Salinas called a ceasefire that the Zapatistas agreed to honor. The fighting that had been raging in the various corners of Chiapas suddenly stopped. No one knew for certain how many people had been killed, but most people believed it was many more than the dozens the government claimed. No matter how many actual casualties there were, the ceasefire brought a genuine sense of relief to the streets. Antonio gave Maria the night off so she could celebrate the peace with a girls' night out with Francesca and Paola. Probably because all the journalists were working on stories regarding the cease-fire, business was slow. We decided to close early. There was one couple still lingering over dinner, but Antonio told Félix to shut the kitchen down. Félix was putting on his jacket when Antonio called him over and poured three shots of tequila.

"Por la paz," Antonio said.

"To the peace," Félix and I repeated and we drank the shots in a slow, somber silence.

I HAD JUST GOTTEN back to the compound after a late lunch date with Maria the following day when I found César's black pickup truck parked in its usual garage bay. Two white pickups were also in the courtyard. A stranger wearing a cowboy hat stood in the shadow of the terrace. He watched me approach and then called something through the door to the kitchen. César emerged from the kitchen to stand on the terrace, hands on his hips, that famous smile spreading across his face. I felt myself smile too.

"Dude," I said, "your country is fucked up."

"It's good to see you, compadre." César stepped off the terrace and we embraced like the brothers we were in all but blood. "Are you all right? I've been worried about you. You have no idea."

"I'm good. How are you?"

He looked tired. His eyes were sunken and ringed with dark circles. He had a bandage wrapped around his left forearm. "I'm okay," he said. "Oh, that," he shrugged when I nodded at the bandage. "That's nothing. A small cut. Nada."

"¿Y tu familia?"

"Mi familia … pues … they're okay."

"That's a relief. So what the hell is going on in Mexico, compadre?"

"The hell if I know. Can you believe it? They're traitors. They've betrayed everything the country stands for, everything we have been trying to build."

"It's totally screwed up is what it is," I said. "When did you get in?"

"About an hour ago."

"From Mexico City?"

"No. Calvario."

I nodded. "I see we have company."

The man with the cowboy hat had been joined by another man with a bad complexion. Both of them were about our age.

"Yeah, I brought some friends along. We didn't know what to expect and I wanted to have some help if I needed it. Caballeros," he said, turning to the men, "este es mi compadre, Señor Henry Singer. Hank, meet Octavio and Luis."

"Mucho gusto," I said.

The two men smiled and nodded. Luis, the one with the bad complexion, had a mouth full of silver.

"Come on, compadre," César said, slapping me on the back. "Let's have a drink."

He led me through the kitchen, pausing to introduce me to a third man, Miguel, who was sitting at the table reading a glossy tabloid that was something like the Mexican equivalent of *People* magazine. With his shoulder-length hair, fine features, and smooth skin, Miguel struck me as something of a pretty boy.

César poured himself a large scotch and I opted for a Coke. We sat on the sofa in the game room.

"So where's Ramón?"

"He's around here somewhere."

As if having heard his name, Ramón walked into the room. "Hank," he said, lumbering over to shake my hand. "We're glad you're okay. El padrón was worried."

I wondered if he meant César or Señor Lobos de Madrid.

"Are we going to go see the general now?" Ramón asked César.

"Do you have the money?"

"Claro."

"Let me just finih this," César said, holding up his glass. "Cinco minutos."

"Bueno. Hank, nos vemos."

"Hasta luego," I said as he went out. "Who's the general?" I asked César when Ramón had left.

"A family friend. He's going to give us some military passes so we don't have to stop at checkpoints. The army has roadblocks set up all over the place. It took us five hours just to get here from Calvario. So how are you, Hank? I've been worried about you, compadre. I half expected you to have left with the rest of the turistas. I tried calling you a couple of times, but the lines were down. Was it bad?"

"It wasn't good. The Zapatistas didn't really do anything besides tear up the municipal building, but when the army arrived it got scary."

"An army that isn't scary isn't much of an army."

"No, I guess not. They didn't do much here besides make their presence felt, but it must have been ugly down by Rancho Nuevo. They bombed the hell out of the rebels."

"Good."

"I think it was probably a massacre."

"They had it coming."

"I don't know, man. From what I saw they were mostly a bunch of kids with sticks."

"Kids with sticks, huh?" César studied me for a moment while he unconsciously stirred the ice in his glass with his finger. "Well, they weren't kids with sticks at Calvario."

"There were Zapatistas at Calvario?"

"Yeah. Well, maybe not Zapatistas exactly, but a bunch of

campesinos who seemed to think we were going to let them have Calvario just because a couple of terrorists with ski masks came out of the jungle and said they could have it. Some of those cockroaches even worked for us. Can you believe that? Our own employees betrayed us." He looked dumbfounded by the very idea. "My father," he said, "they betrayed my father."

"So what happened?"

"They hauled off most of the coffee harvest. We still don't know how many cattle are missing."

"Ah, man," I said.

"That's not even the worst of it." He looked at me. "They were living in the house." The way he said it made it sound like he couldn't believe it himself. His eyes grew wider, an anger and disbelief in them I hadn't seen before. "They were in my sister's bed." He leaned slightly forward, biting off each word. "They were in my mother's bed."

"Damn! But they're gone now, right?"

"Gone?" he asked, as if he was trying to remember the meaning of the word. "Yeah," he said after a moment. "You better believe they're gone. We took back what's ours."

"Is that how you got that?" I asked, pointing at the bandage on his arm.

"Yeah. This cabrón tried to take my arm off with a machete."

"Shit, Compadre! You were in the fighting?"

"It's my house, my family's home. Yeah, I was in the fighting. So was my dad and Ramón and those guys you just met, among others."

"It was that bad?"

"It was that bad," he said. "They killed Ramón's cousin."

"What?"

But before César could say more, Ramón stuck his head through the doorway.

"Oye, César. The general is not going to wait."

"Voy," César said and downed the rest of his scotch. "I've got to take care of this."

"I'll go with you," I said.

César seemed to consider this. "I don't know if that's such a good idea."

"Why?"

"You know I'd love to have you come, but the military is pretty twitchy right now and this general is sort of stretching the rules by giving me the pass, so he'd probably rather not have a foreigner present."

"Oh," I said. "Okay."

"Don't be pissed."

"I'm not. I just thought we'd catch up."

"We will. Don't worry. Are you going to hang out?"

"Maybe I'll see if there are any games on."

"Will you be around when I get back?"

"I don't know. I have to go to work."

César let out a contemptuous snort. "Are you still working that stupid job?"

"What? I like it."

He shook his head. "Okay, compadre. I'll see you later then."

"Okay. Later. And César," I said just as he was about to leave the room. "I'm glad your family is all right."

He looked at me. "Gracias, compadre. Oh, before I forget, that sheet music you asked for is on the bar." He pointed at a cardboard box.

"What?"

"The stuff for the piano for your friend. I had to go to three different stores to find someone who knew what he was talking about, but I think I got some good stuff. They had a big selection anyway."

"Really?"

"Sure," he said. "You said you wanted it, right?"

"Well ... yeah, but I didn't want you to go to any trouble."

"No trouble. It's in the box. I didn't really know what you wanted, so I got a selection."

"Thanks," I said. I was dumbfounded.

"No worries," he said. "Hasta luego." He waved and went out.

I went over to the bar and looked in the box. It held twenty-five or thirty booklets of sheet music for the piano from various composers, everyone from Bach and Beethoven and Brahms to Mozart and Mendelssohn to Liszt and Schubert and Chopin. Maria was going to be blown away. I knew she already had some of what he'd gotten, but he definitely had found compositions she didn't have. I couldn't believe he'd actually brought the box. That was César. On a whim, a friend asks him to do a favor and César doesn't just go out of his way. He goes to three different shops, probably on opposite ends of one of the world's biggest and most chaotic cities, buys half the store, and then, even though he and his family have been busy fighting for their lives and their home, he still remembers to bring it to the friend. Yeah, that was César exactly.

I went over to the window to call to him, but he'd climbed into the passenger seat of the black truck before I could get the window open. He said something to the three guys getting into one of the white pickups and then closed his door. Luis jumped out and immediately opened the gate. I don't know if it was his hand gesture or the tilt of his head or what exactly, but something about César reminded me of his father. There was a forcefulness in his demeanor, like he wasn't asking. He was telling.

...

I CHANNEL-SURFED FOR an hour, hoping César would return. He didn't, so I took the box César had brought me over to the guesthouse before heading to El Acuario. I was excited to tell Maria about the sheet music, but it occurred to me there was going to be more than a little awkwardness about explaining where all the music booklets had come from. I needed to think of a way to handle it. Our shift at El Acuario was uneventful and when Antonio let us go, I walked Maria back to her apartment.

"Do you want to come up?" she asked after we'd kissed on the doorstep. "Luz is spending the night with Salvador."

"Okay."

We made love. It was slow and gentle. Then we held each other in the dark.

"Will you spend the night?" she asked.

"Do you want me to? I thought we'd decided about this."

"Just one night."

"Okay. One night," I said and she squeezed my hand.

The next morning Maria went to pick up Luz and I went back to my place. There were no trucks in the courtyard, but César must have seen me come in the gate because he came out the kitchen door and called me over.

"I didn't think anyone was home," I said, climbing onto the terrace and following him into the kitchen.

"I sent the guys on an errand. You want one?" He was fixing himself a turkey sandwich for breakfast.

"Sure."

"Get a plate," he said, nodding toward the cabinet.

I did and he put half his sandwich on it.

"What happened to you last night?" he asked, his mouth full of food.

"What do you mean?"

"I mean you didn't come home."

I took a big bite of sandwich and made a minor theatrical performance of chewing. Knowing his past history with Maria, I'd been wondering how I was going to explain our relationship. It was a conversation I'd known we'd have to have, but I hadn't been looking forward to it.

"You want a glass of water? This thing is dry," I said.

He nodded. I got up and poured two glasses.

"So what errand did you send them on?" I asked him, setting his glass in front of him and hoping I could leapfrog over the subject of where I'd been.

"The general mentioned the names of some people who are saying some things that aren't particularly productive right now. Because of the ceasefire and politics, the military can't really get directly involved. I sent Ramón and the guys to sort of pass along the general's message. So where were you?"

"Well," I said, putting my sandwich down. "It's like this—I met a girl."

César stopped chewing and the corners of his eyes began to wrinkle as he smiled. "You met a girl?"

"Yeah. A woman, I guess I should say."

César's smile grew and suddenly he burst into laughter. As always, his laughter was contagious and I felt myself start to grin and blush, which only made him laugh harder.

"Pinche Hank," he said once he'd gotten his laugh under control enough to take a swallow of water and wash down the bite of sandwich he'd been chewing. "The whole country is falling apart and you're out getting laid."

"It's worse than that. I think I'm falling for her."

This set him off on a whole new wave of hysterics. I let him laugh. It was good to see him. "In love, huh? When did all this start?" he asked when he'd wiped the tears from his eyes.

"Well, I don't know if I'd call it love, but it's kind of serious. We hooked up on New Year's Eve."

"At El Acuario?" He laughed again. "I stand corrected. The job wasn't such a waste of time."

"I told you."

"Well, compadre," he said, beaming. "That's great. I'm really happy for you." And I could tell he was. He never looked more sincere. "So where is she from? When do I get to meet her?"

"She's from here."

"She's from Mexico?"

"She's from Chiapas."

"You're kidding."

"Nope."

"Damn, Hank. I'm impressed."

"Thanks."

"Seriously. Chiapanecas don't usually mix with outsiders. Hell, they don't even go to places like El Acuario. You must have found a wild one."

"She's nice."

"I'll bet. What's her name? God, I probably know her family," he said, laughing. "I'm not protecting you from some crazy father or brother. You're screwed if she has brothers." He thought it was all very funny. "So what's her name?"

"Maria," I said cautiously, waiting to see if he'd make the connection.

"Maria what?" The laughter wasn't gone from his voice, but it was going. He'd made the connection. He just didn't want to believe it.

"Look, César—"

"Ahh, compadre." He sighed and held his head in his hands. "You stupid, stupid fuck. I told you to stay away from her."

"César, I know all about what happened between you and her. She told me."

He didn't move or say anything for a long time.

"She told you," he said finally. The tone of his voice was totally flat.

"Yeah."

He lifted his head and looked at me. His eyes narrowed. "And you still slept with her? Are you fucking with me? This is exactly the kind of betrayal I'm talking about."

"She didn't tell me until after we'd started seeing one another."

"I told you to stay away from that bitch."

"Easy, man."

"Easy? Fuck easy!"

"Compadre—"

"You tell that bitch it's over."

"I'm sorry that's how you feel, but—"

"She's a fucking puta, Hank." César studied me, his cold eyes tumbling over and over on themselves. Finally he leaned back in his chair and nodded, more to himself than to me, as if he'd reached some conclusion with himself. "Okay, compadre," he said. "You made your choice. Now take your shit and get out."

"César—"

"I mean it," he snapped. "Get the fuck out of my house."

"Compadre—"

"Now!"

I got up from the table and went across the courtyard to the guesthouse. It took me about fifteen minutes to jam my stuff in my bags. I looked at the box with sheet music. It made me feel worse. Then I thought, fuck him. He didn't have to react that way. So I put the sheet music in my daypack with the extra Indian blouses I'd bought after Christmas, hefted up my duffel bag with the rest of my stuff, and left.

272

Once out on the street, I wasn't sure where to go. I didn't really have a place, so I decided I'd rent a room at a hotel and figure out my next move. But before I went to a hotel, I decided to stop at Maria's apartment to tell her I was moving. The fact he'd kicked me out pissed me off and I kind of wanted Maria to share in my indignation.

I was going up the stairs of Maria's apartment building when I remembered I'd kept my keys to César's place. So what, I thought. That's his problem.

"So," I said when Maria opened the door, "I'm moving to a hotel."

"What? Why? What happened?"

"César and I had a fight."

"He's back?"

"Yeah."

"What did you fight about?"

I looked at her.

"Oh," she said after a moment. She understood. Then she said, "What are you going to do?"

"I don't know. Get a hotel room, I guess."

We stood there. Luz appeared between Maria's legs.

"Hola Hank," she said.

"Hola Luz."

"Don't go to a hotel," Maria said.

"What?"

"You can stay with us."

"That's okay," I said. "I'll go to a hotel." I suddenly wondered if I'd gone to Maria's with the subconscious hope she'd invite me to stay.

"Don't be silly."

"Well ..."

"Well what?"

"Are you sure?"

Maria looked down at Luz. "Is it okay if Henry stays with us for a while?"

Luz didn't respond. She was too busy wrapping herself around her mother's leg.

Maria looked back at me. "We're sure," she said and opened the door wide to let me through.

I stepped into the apartment and she closed the door. "Where do you want me to put my stuff?" I asked.

Maria looked at me and then around the room. She put her hands in her hip pockets and looked at me again. She gave a reluctant smile. "If you are going to move in, you might as well move in."

I was pretty sure I knew what she meant, but I didn't want to presume.

"Come on," she said and started to head toward her bedroom. "I'll give you some space in the closet."

I carried the bags into Maria's room, our room, and put them on the bed.

"Are three drawers enough?" Maria asked as she started to remove things from her bureau.

"Plenty," I said.

I started unloading my duffel and Luz wanted to help, so without really thinking about it I suggested that she unpack my backpack. Luz unzipped the pack and that's when Maria noticed the sheet music. "What's that?" she asked, pointing to the stack of folders in my backpack. From the look on her face I could tell she was trying to keep herself from hoping it was what she thought it was.

"Those are for you," I said, taking the stack from the bag and handing them over.

She held them for a moment and then looked at me in disbelief.

Then she sat on the bed and started turning through the folders. "How ...," she said. "Where ... Handel's Suite in B flat major ..." She looked at me. "Where did you get all this?"

I hesitated for a moment, but there didn't seem to be an alternative to the truth. "I asked César to get them for me when he was in El Distrito Federal."

The joy in her face darkened.

"I asked him before I knew about the two of you."

She looked at the music in her hands. Then she held it out to me. "You should give it back to him."

"I can't."

"Well, I can't take it."

"Yes, you can. It's from me, not from him."

She looked at me doubtfully. "I don't want it," she said.

"Look," I said, putting the folders atop the bureau. "Play them or don't. That's up to you, but they're from me. It doesn't matter how I got it." Of course that last part was a lie. It mattered. It would have mattered to César, but there wasn't any point in trying to return the sheet music to him.

I deliberately turned away from Maria and the music and took the remaining shirts from my duffel and hung them in the closet space she'd provided. From the corner of my eye I could see that she was looking at the pile of folders on the bureau. I was pretty sure that at some point she would convince herself it was okay to keep the music.

I put the empty duffel bag on the floor of the closet, slid the door closed, and took three hundred pesos from my wallet. "Here," I said to Maria.

"What's that for?"

"My share of the rent. Is that enough?"

"You don't have to pay rent."

I had wondered about this moment. Maria took such pride

in her economic and personal independence that I'd wondered if she'd fully thought through what it would mean to share on equal terms the space she'd worked so hard to provide for herself and Luz. I knew she could use the money, but I also knew she'd feel like she was giving something up if she took it.

"Maria, you don't think I'm going to live here without paying my share of the rent, do you?"

"I guess I hadn't thought about it."

"Well, if I'm going to stay here, I'm going to need to pay my share. Is that going to be okay?"

She looked at the money and back at the stack of sheet music. She was beginning to understand just what a change this would be for her. Then she looked at me and smiled. "You're not going to hang any pictures of naked women or leave the toilet seat up in the bathroom, are you?"

"I'll put the toilet seat down, I promise. The pictures of naked women we might have to negotiate."

And that's how I started living with Maria.

26

I was surprised at how easily we fell into a domestic routine. It had taken Jenn and me a good three months to adapt to living with one another. We'd had quarrels about which cupboards the dishes went in or how the bed should be made or whether we should leave the outside lights on when we went to sleep. Stupid things that didn't matter, but things that took us a while to work out nonetheless. With Maria there was none of that. None of her habits bothered me and none of mine seemed to bother her. That said, there was a certain distance between us. At the time I thought there was something of a cultural gap that couldn't be crossed, but I realize now we both were carrying around our personal sense of grief and we were incapable of sharing that part of ourselves.

Most days Maria would wake early to give Luz breakfast and make coffee and then the three of us would lounge until eight thirty or nine o'clock when Maria would start household chores while I played with Luz or took her for a walk in the zócalo. Because Maria had to work the lunch shift at El Acuario, she'd leave a little before noon. Either she'd drop Luz with Doña Asunta or Salvador would come to pick up his daughter.

Salvador had thrown another tantrum when he'd found out I'd moved in, but this time we didn't let it affect us. When he threatened to stop coming to see Luz unless I left, Maria told him flat out that if he was the kind of man who would abandon his daughter as a means of emotional blackmail, Luz would be better off without him. That got his attention and after a week of pouting by himself somewhere, he resumed their regular afternoons together. I stayed clear of Salvador as much as possible and I think he grew to begrudgingly accept the situation.

Sometimes I'd go with Maria to El Acuario for lunch before her shift, but usually I ate in the apartment. Then I'd go out to do the grocery shopping or sit on the terrace of the Kiosco to drink coffee and read the paper.

The ceasefire was holding and the military had withdrawn to positions outside the city, but there were increasing reports of white guard paramilitary groups terrorizing Zapatista supporters. One group, ironically calling itself Paz y Justicia, was said to be making death threats against outspoken activists and Zapatista sympathizers. But overwhelmingly the news focused on the articulate and charismatic, non-Indian man who wore a ski mask and went by the nom de guerre "Subcomandante Marcos" and who was thought to be the real leader of the Zapatista movement. It was the same man we'd spoken to in the zócalo that first day. Everyone wanted to know who he was and where he'd come from. His flamboyant style and mysterious identity and communiqués about serving the poor and defending justice made him something of a contemporary Robin Hood or Zorro. Lots of female television personalities started talking about how sexy he was. The man had started a civil war and wore a terrorist's balaclava and women were talking about his voice and his eyes and his hands. He was a total rock star and the traditional dolls that the Chamulan women and girls sold suddenly started appearing with ski masks and Indians were calling them Marcos. I started a collection. The newspapers made it fairly clear that the government was desperate to unmask the man. The Mexican army would win the ground war if fighting resumed, but Marcos was winning the war for public opinion. The media was falling-over-themselves in love with him. But you could hardly blame them. It's hard not to like a guy who, in response to a government effort to undermine his romantic appeal by claiming he's homosexual, writes something about being gay in San Francisco, black in South Africa, an Asian in Europe, a Chicano in San Ysidro, a housewife alone on Saturday night in any neighborhood in any city in Mexico, an unemployed worker, a dissident, a human being, any exploited and oppressed minority who resists and says, "¡Ya Basta!"

During the work week, Maria would leave work after the lunch rush and we'd take Luz to get an ice cream cone or we'd go to the mercado to shop or we'd simply go for a long walk through the city, the winter air crisp but not cold in the sunny afternoons and the pleasant scent of wood smoke from people's chimneys drifting on the light breeze. Around six we'd go to El Acuario for an early dinner before we started tending bar. On Sundays, Maria and Luz would attend morning mass, usually at the cathedral but sometimes walking up Real de Guadalupe to the Iglesia de Guadalupe. Maria went to the confessional three times a week as well. At one point it occurred to me that our living and sleeping together might have been one of the things causing her Catholic guilt, so I asked. She looked at me and the fact of it was written in the expression on her face. But then she said, "There's no point in confessing the sins you're not going to repent." At the time, I didn't know what to think of that. I have a much better understanding now.

Work had changed some. With the tourists gone, most of our clients were the hardcore expatriates and journalists. The festive atmosphere had died down and Antonio decided that once Félix closed the kitchen, he could leave Maria or me to close the bar, so

279

he gave us each a set of keys and would usually head home early.

Having finally cooled off and hoping César had done the same, I went by his place a few times to see if we could patch things up, but nobody was ever around. I figured he must have gone out of town. Then one day during the week Antonio was out of town, I was just about to ring the bell on César's front gate when Ramón came out the door on his way somewhere.

"Hey, Ramón."

"What do you want?"

"Is César in?"

"Sí."

"Gracias," I said, but when I started to step past him he put that baseball mitt hand of his on my chest to stop me.

"He doesn't want to see you."

"Yeah, well, I want to hear it from him, so do you want to let me by, or what?"

"You don't understand," he said, stepping in front of me to block my path. "I have my orders. You're not going in."

"Orders? Get your goddamned hand off me."

Just as I said it, the door opened behind Ramón, and Miguel and Octavio stepped out.

"¿Que pasa?" Miguel asked.

"Señor Singer was just leaving," Ramón said.

I looked from Ramón to Miguel and Octavio. They each looked at me with the same indifferent expression. It was like they weren't looking at me at all, like I wasn't even there.

"Adios, señor," Miguel said flatly.

"Tell César I came by."

"Adios, señor," Octavio added, just to make sure I understood they were a unified front.

"Just tell him," I said to Ramón and I turned and walked back up the sidewalk. I was so angry that when I turned the corner and was out of sight of Ramón and the other two goons, I leaned my back against the wall of a building until the adrenaline rushing through my body subsided enough that my hands were no longer shaking. I decided that if that was the way César wanted to be, then so be it. I'd tried. Now if he still wanted to be friends, he'd have to make the effort. I sure as hell wasn't going to deal with those three idiots again.

I didn't mention my little standoff with Ramón to Maria or anyone else. In fact, I didn't mention César's name again at all. I just went on living with Maria and Luz and working off and on at El Acuario. Because there wasn't enough for me to do at El Acuario and because he no longer could afford to pay me, Antonio cut my hours to the weekends only. He felt bad, but there was nothing he could do. The journalists just didn't make up for the lost tourist business. He and I hung out a couple of times outside of work, but his friendship with Salvador made things somewhat awkward. I knew Salvador bitched about me to Antonio on a fairly regular basis and the downturn in Antonio's business gave him enough to worry about without playing the middleman to Salvador and me, so mostly I spent my free time with Maria or by myself.

In February, the Mexican government and the Zapatistas agreed to hold a formal dialogue in the San Cristóbal Cathedral. Bishop Samuel Ruíz Garcia, a man much trusted by the indigenous of Chiapas, was to be the moderator. The talks were scheduled to begin on February 21, and the city was abuzz with expectations. Even though I'd known the talks were going to happen, I hadn't really thought about what that might involve. I certainly wasn't prepared to find Mexican military police standing virtually shoulder to shoulder in a ring that extended around the entire zócalo and cathedral. Each soldier stood in a rock-solid, eyes-forward pose and held a two-foot truncheon in front of him. I hadn't seen any soldiers, at least not any doing their soldiering thing, since the military had pulled back to the outskirts of the city. Even though there were all kinds of civilians stepping past the soldiers and walking through the zócalo unhindered, just seeing all those soldiers standing erect like that brought back all the fear I'd felt during those first days of the conflict when I'd come to understand on a visceral level that no matter what rights you think you're entitled to, the truth is the people with the guns decide. I hurried back to the apartment and was relieved when Maria came home that night.

As it had with the war, the balcony off our bedroom gave us front-row seats to the peace talks. The soldiers had stood in their positions all night long and now that it was the morning, the zócalo and cathedral were totally sealed off. The soldiers stood outside a white line that had been painted on the ground. Behind the first line was a second line. Between these lines stood civilian volunteers wearing white jerseys with "Ciudadanos por la Paz" printed on them. Citizens for the Peace were there to make sure the military didn't storm the cathedral during the talks and kill the Zapatista leadership. Inside the second line, the Mexican and International Red Cross kept their vigil. All three groups—the Mexican army, the Citizens for the Peace, and the Red Cross — were to remain in place twenty-four hours a day for the duration of the negotiations.

Maria, Antonio, Francesca, and I stood on the balcony, huddled together against the cold morning air. The sidewalks were crowded with people waiting to get a look at the Zapatistas, particularly at Marcos. The last time the Zapatistas had been in the zócalo, nobody had truly understood the implications of what was going on. Now everyone knew we were witnessing history, and everyone wanted to catch a glimpse of the man who was the personification of that history, if not the actual architect. I wondered if César was somewhere in the crowd. I wondered if he was as curious as everyone else.

The crowd lining the sidewalk down Calle Insurgentes began to make noise and jostle for better views as a motorcade turned onto that street and slowly approached the square. Two federal police cruisers, lights flashing, led the way. Three white Suburbans with red crosses painted on their doors and roofs followed closely behind. Two more federal cruisers completed the column. When the motorcade reached the zócalo, the line of military police parted just enough to let the vehicles pass through and then resealed the park. The federal cruisers swung off to the side and Red Cross Suburbans, flanked by Red Cross workers already in the park, pulled up in front of the cathedral entrance. The doors of the Suburbans remained closed for several minutes, but the passenger-side windows were down and every so often a Red Cross worker would lean into the vehicles, apparently to converse with the passengers. Finally the doors opened and several Zapatistas, wearing black ski masks and traditional Indian clothing, including round sombreros with colorful streamers dangling from the brims, climbed out. A cheer rose up from the crowd, but Marcos was not among these first arrivals. The Zapatistas waved briefly in response to the calls from the crowd and then they filed into the cathedral.

This same process was repeated several times through the morning and into the early afternoon as Zapatista leadership arrived from various undisclosed rendezvous locations. Each time the doors of the Suburbans would open, the crowd would cheer and each time Marcos failed to appear, there would be a collective sigh from the crowd. And then, around midafternoon, Marcos arrived. He was wearing his ski mask, military fatigues, and shotgun bandoliers. He shouldered his pack and carried his pistol-grip sawed-off shotgun. The crowd, which had lost some of its enthusiasm as the afternoon had worn on, roared back to life at the sight of him, but unlike other Zapatista leaders, Marcos made no gesture to the crowd. He simply crossed the short space between the Red Cross vehicles and the cathedral and disappeared through the doorway.

"I guess that's that."

"I wish he'd waved," Francesca said.

"He didn't need to be any more exposed than he was," Antonio said.

"Still," Francesca said and gave a little sigh, "I wish he'd waved."

Antonio grinned and looked at Maria.

"Well, you have to admit," Maria said. "He's quite the man."

We hung out for another hour and then dropped Luz with Doña Asunta before going on to the restaurant. I had decided to work that night just to hear what people would be saying about the day's events. As it turned out, all of the press must have been writing up their stories because we only had a few customers and the few we did have didn't have much to say. For the most part people seemed to think it had been overwhelmingly anticlimactic. What we'd all been expecting, no one could say.

After we got back from work and carried a sleeping Luz up from Doña Asunta's apartment and tucked the girl into bed, Maria and I lit candles and curled against one another in bed. The fact of her naked body never ceased to amaze me. As we lay there, the sound of a guitar rose up from the street below our bedroom and a woman began to sing. It was a love song. I'd heard it before. "Despierta Dulce Amor de Mi Vida." The woman had a fine voice, strong and clear and filled with longing.

"What's that?" I asked as we listened.

"A serenade. She's serenading Marcos."

We wrapped ourselves in the comforter and went out onto the balcony. There in the street, standing just a few feet from the immovable wall of military police, a solitary woman played guitar and sang, her face awash in moonlight as she tilted it skyward so her voice would carry over the cathedral walls to the rooms where Marcos slept.

"Do you think he's listening?"

"He must be."

"It's like she's serenading us."

"It's beautiful, isn't it?"

"Yes. It is."

I stood behind Maria and held her and we listened. The woman sang for half an hour and then, without fanfare, turned and walked up Real de Guadalupe, disappearing into the night. Maria and I closed the doors and climbed back into bed.

"Do you want me to blow out the candles?" I asked.

"Not yet."

"All right."

I thought about the woman singing to Marcos and about Jenn and about Maria and about how wrong my college postmodern literature professor had been when he said romantic love doesn't exist. The thought made me smile. Maria saw me smiling and propped herself up on an elbow.

"What are you smiling about?"

"About you. About us." I looked at her.

Maria smiled. "That's nice," she said and kissed me lightly.

I slid my arm under the small of her back and laid my head against her belly. She gently stroked my hair.

"Henry ..."

"Mmm?"

"Nada."

"Tell me."

"I was wondering if you'd seen César."

"Why?"

"No reason," she said. "But he's your friend. I don't want to be responsible for you not seeing your friends."

"You're not responsible."

"¿Estás seguro?"

"I'm sure."

"Okay," she said after a minute. "If you're sure. You can blow the candles out now."

I stretched out in the sudden darkness and Maria put her head against my chest and I began to wonder if I should try to see César again. I knew if I could get past Ramón, if I could just see César, I could make him understand. It seemed stupid for our friendship to end just because Ramón wouldn't let me by. We were Batman and Batman and to hell with Ramón. Maybe Maria and César would never be friends, but Ramón and I were never going to be friends either. Maria was right. Who says your girlfriend and your best friend or you and your best friend's jackass have to like each other?

"Mi amor," Maria said softly.

"¿Sí?"

"Sleep well."

WHEN MARIA LEFT TO work the lunch shift the next morning, I walked up Calle Utrilla past the line of soldiers outside the cathedral walls to a liquor shop. While the cashier rang up the six-pack of Sol, I couldn't help but think how odd it was that on one side of the street I was buying beer and on the other side of the street a war was being negotiated. The cashier gave me my change and put the beer in a bag and I went back onto the street and walked to César's house.

I didn't know how I was going to get past the door if César wasn't the one to answer and the thought of having another scene

286

with Ramón or the other guys so disgusted me that I almost turned around and went back to the apartment, but as it happened, the front gate to the compound was open.

Ramón and Octavio were under the hood of Ramón's pickup. César was reading at the table on the terrace outside the kitchen. Apparently the three of them were engrossed in what they were doing because I'd crossed half the courtyard before Octavio looked up from under the hood and called out.

Octavio's voice caused César and Ramón to look up at the same time. César's face was expressionless as I approached, but when Octavio and Ramón took a couple of steps in my direction, he made a small gesture for them to stop.

"Did you forget something?" César asked, closing the folder from which he'd been reading.

"No."

"Then what do you want?"

"A game of foosball."

César's face remained expressionless.

"How about a cigarette then?" I asked, nodding toward the pack on the table.

"Help yourself. What's mine is yours, apparently."

I stepped up onto the terrace, set my bag of beer on the table, lit a cigarette from the pack, and resisted the impulse to tell him Maria had never been his. Cigarette dangling from the corner of my mouth, I slid a bottle of beer from the bag and popped the cap off with the bottom of the Bic lighter.

"You want a cold one?" I asked, pointing the bottle at him.

He took it and I opened another as I sat in one of the empty chairs. We sat for a few minutes, drinking our beers and smoking our cigarettes in silence. Ramón and Octavio, who seemed to be waiting for further instructions, eventually turned back to their work on the truck.

"How's your girlfriend?" César finally asked after half a beer.

"Fine. What's wrong with the truck?"

"Nada, but you know how Ramón is about the truck."

"Yeah."

We sat quietly through the rest of our beers and I opened two more. Miguel and Luis came out the kitchen door and stopped short when they saw me at the table. César glanced at them and they shrugged and stepped off the terrace to join Ramón and Octavio at the truck. One of them must have made some sort of joke because they all looked briefly in my direction and laughed. After a few more minutes, Ramón shut the hood of the truck and, tapping his fingers to the back of his wrist, called to César.

"Ahorita," César replied. Then to me he said, "I have to go out of town for a few days."

"Where are you going?"

"Tuxtla. I've got some business to handle."

"Okay. You want one for the road?"

"That's all right. You drink it," he said, rising to his feet. "Do you still have the keys to the house?"

"Yeah. Do you want them back?"

"No," he said, crushing his butt in the ashtray.

"So we're okay?"

He looked at me hard, his blue eyes doing their kaleidoscoping thing. It was a long look. "It doesn't matter if we're okay. We're compadres," he said. "But," he added, pointing at me, "I don't want to see your girlfriend. I don't even want to hear about that bitch."

"Fair enough, so long as you don't call her that."

"I mean it."

"Me too."

He kept staring at me like he was trying to decide if this was a reasonable deal. Then he exhaled and a hint of a grin appeared on his face. "Okay, compadre." To Ramón and the others he called, "Let me grab my bag."

César disappeared into the house and I finished the last of my beer. I was cracking another when I noticed the two manila folders César had left on the table. Out of idle curiosity, I opened one.

There were five or six photographs of the same man in different locations. There were several news clippings as well. They all were articles written by Eduardo Gallegos, that editorialist I'd taken to reading. I'd seen his picture alongside his column and Gallegos was clearly the man in the other photographs. I'd already read most of them, including his series on electoral reform in the state assembly. In one article in the folder, he articulated several reasons for supporting Zapatista objectives, particularly those regarding land reform, which he claimed were guaranteed under the Mexican constitution. In a more recent editorial, he accused the government and military of calling for a ceasefire while providing clandestine material support for various anti-Zapatista paramilitary groups. He made a compelling case.

In the second manila folder there were photos of another man and one newspaper article with a photograph of several people who apparently were members of a civil rights group. The face of one of the members had been circled with a red felt-tip, and the caption below the photo identified him as Rodolfo Muñoz. Muñoz was the same man in the other photographs in the folder.

I didn't think too much about what I saw. César had always been interested in politics and it made sense to me that he'd be following what various people had to say about the current situation. I suppose if I'd been thinking in any sort of critical way rather than simply satiating a dull curiosity, I'd have been conscious that the two men in the photographs didn't seem to be aware that their pictures were being taken. But I didn't notice in a conscious way.

Instead, I closed the folder and drank my beer.

César came back out with a gym bag in his hand. "So you'll lock up when you leave?" he asked.

"Sure. See you when you get back," I said.

"Okay, compadre," he said, taking the folders from the table. "Hasta luego."

The engines rumbled to life and César climbed into the passenger seat of the black pickup before Octavio's pickup pulled out and Ramón and Miguel swung in behind. Something about the three trucks, each in turn pulling out the gate, reminded me of the Red Cross motorcades of the day before.

I finished my beer before taking the one remaining beer inside and leaving it in the refrigerator. Back on the patio I dumped the ashtray into the bag of empties and took the bag over to the trash can by the garage.

I looked around the courtyard one last time to make sure I wasn't forgetting something and then stepped onto the sidewalk, locking the door behind me. I felt good. I had a pretty good beer buzz and César and I were back on track. Or at least we were on the mend. I felt good.

27

FOUR OR FIVE DAYS had passed since César and I had patched things up and he'd left town. The peace talks were still going on and Subcomandante Marcos had become an absolute media darling. As a result, fresh journalists were arriving every day and business picked up in the evenings. At one point I was serving beer to a producer of *60 Minutes* and a writer for *Time* magazine. The guy with *60 Minutes* was trying to line up an interview with Marcos for Ed Bradley.

The journalists didn't stay very late or drink much, but some of them tipped fairly well and by eleven o'clock, when El Acuario was all but empty, Maria had made just over three hundred pesos. She was pleased. She was recounting her tips and straightening out some of the more crumpled bills when Salvador came into the restaurant and he and Antonio went into the office and shut the door. When they finally emerged and Salvador left, Antonio locked the front door and then poked his head into the kitchen.

"Hank, can I talk to you for a minute?"

"Sure," I said and followed him to the office.

"¿Que pasa?" I asked after he told me to shut the door.

He ran his hand through his hair a couple of times. He seemed to be searching for a way to start. "Do you know about my business with César?" he asked. He ran his finger along the edge of his desk and then checked it for dust. The gesture was so contrived I almost laughed.

"You mean the guns and cocaine?"

"Sí."

"That's what I know. He gave you some guns and you gave him some coke."

"Do you know where he gets the guns?"

"Why?"

"I'm just curious."

I looked at him. I wasn't sure how much César would want me to say.

"Do you think he gets them from the police?"

"I don't really know much about it. But yeah, he told me he gets them from friends in the police. As I understand it, the police confiscate them from smugglers."

"So the serial numbers would be registered?"

"How would I know?"

"But they might be?"

"I really don't have the slightest idea. What's this about?"

Antonio readjusted himself in his chair. "I just want to know if the guns could get traced back to me."

"I don't know. Sorry. What, did Rinaldo and Silvestro get busted?"

"Rinaldo and Silvestro?"

"Yeah. Didn't you give the guns to them?"

"What makes you think that?"

"Forget it. It's none of my business. It was just something César said."

"César thinks I gave them to Rinaldo and Silvestro?"

"He said he didn't know, but that he thought you were fronting for one of your paisanos who was smuggling cocaine. He thought it was either Rinaldo or Silvestro."

Antonio seemed to consider this. And then as much to himself as to me, he said, "I guess that's better than the alternative." And then to me: "The guns and the coke have nothing to do with each other."

"If you say so."

"They don't. I have a friend who gives me the coke because we're friends. I'm not saying it's Rinaldo or Silvestro. César wanted to deal directly with my friend with the coke, but I told him my friend didn't want to work that way. But the truth is the guns are for another friend. They're not the same deal. I trade the coke for the guns and that way I get to keep the money meant for the guns. The guy with the coke doesn't know I'm trading it to César and the guys who want the guns wouldn't approve if they knew, particularly since I'm keeping their money."

"That sounds complicated."

"It is."

"Sorry, man. Is there anything I can do?"

He looked at me for what seemed like a long time. "Hank, what do you think about the Zapatistas?"

It was not a question I'd expected. "I don't know. I guess I'm glad they're talking instead of shooting."

"But you can see the Zapatistas are only looking for justice."

"I'm not so sure they're going to get it by trying to overthrow the Mexican government, but it's not hard to see they have some legitimate complaints."

"What does César think about the conflict?"

"He was pretty upset about what happened at his family's ranch."

"What did happen?"

"From what I understand, some Zapatistas tried to take the ranch and César and his family decided they couldn't have it."

"What do you think about that?"

The truth was I hadn't really thought about it beyond what it had meant to César's family. Poverty was rampant. That was obvious. And I understood that given the circumstances some people would blame people like the Lobos de Madrid family for that poverty. But that didn't mean they were responsible. It was a systematic problem. "Well," I said. "I guess I can't blame anyone for defending their home."

Antonio seemed to consider this. "No. Maybe not."

"Anything else?"

"No. Thanks."

"I don't know what for, but you're welcome."

I opened the office door and Maria was sitting at one of the tables. She got up when I came out and we put our coats on, said good night to Antonio and Félix, and left.

We walked back to the apartment and I listened to Maria talk about the conversation she'd had with one of the reporters who'd left her a big tip. Or I half listened. I was trying to make sense of the conversation I'd had with Antonio.

Luz was sleeping when we picked her up from Doña Asunta's apartment, so Maria carried her upstairs. I was smoking a cigarette at the table when she came out of Luz's room after putting her down.

"What did Antonio want?" she asked, sitting in the chair across from me and reaching for the cigarette in my hand.

"I don't know. It was a weird conversation."

"Weird how?" she asked, taking a drag.

Normally I wouldn't have said anything. Whatever business Antonio and César had together was between them, but the Zapatista talk had raised some flags.

"Well, you know about the guns, right?"

"What guns?"

"The ones Antonio gets from César."

"Antonio gets guns from César?"

"I thought you knew. I figured you and Antonio were so tight he would have told you."

"What? No."

"Well, you know Antonio uses cocaine, right?"

"Unfortunately."

"So Antonio traded some cocaine for some guns."

"Antonio traded guns for coke with César? Are you joking?"

"I'm not. César said he thought Antonio was getting them for whoever he gets his coke from, but Antonio says that's not the case."

"It's not. Silvestro gives Antonio the coke and Silvestro wouldn't touch a gun. He's a total pacifist."

"Well, I don't know. Like I said, it was kind of a weird conversation." I couldn't decide if I should tell her any more. Then I said, "He asked me some questions about what I thought about the Zapatistas and justice."

"I don't ..." Maria's voice trailed off. She seemed to be thinking about something and then she took a deep drag on the cigarette.

"What?"

"Pendejos," Maria said, more to herself than to me.

"What?"

She blew a long column of smoke into the air and looked at me. "I think he might be fronting for Salvador," she said finally.

"What?" That didn't make sense. "Why the hell would Salvador want guns?"

"Henry," Maria said, handing the cigarette back across the table. "Why do you think Salvador came to Chiapas?"

"I don't know. I thought you told me he'd come to work with the Indians."

"That's right."

"So? What's that got to do with guns?"

Maria raised her eyebrows as if waiting for me to make some grand connection. I didn't.

"So what do you think a liberal student organizer from UNAM is doing with Indians in Chiapas? Teaching them to read?" She wasn't smiling.

Suddenly it dawned on me as to what she was suggesting. "Wait. Are you serious?"

"I don't know. Salvador hasn't always told me exactly what he does in the communities. I mean, he's told me some, but not everything. In fact, he used to say he couldn't tell me everything because it wasn't safe." She seemed to think about this. "I thought he meant not safe for me because of who my family was. It's not like the conflict between the campesinos and people like my father is new."

"But that doesn't make him a Zapatista."

"What is a Zapatista? Is there only one kind? They can't all wear ski masks and live in the jungle."

"Come on, though. Salvador? I just don't see it."

"Let me ask you this: Where do you think the Zapatistas got their guns?"

She had a point. It wasn't like they'd used Visa cards at Revolutionaries "R" Us. Still, it seemed a big stretch to believe Salvador could be a Zapatista. That Antonio could be involved seemed like an even bigger stretch. Yet the fact remained that Antonio had been getting guns for someone. "But why wouldn't Antonio want Salvador to know that he was trading the guns for cocaine? It doesn't make any sense."

"That's why it makes sense. Salvador doesn't know Antonio does cocaine. He'd be furious if he knew. Salvador hates drugs. He doesn't even drink. Alcoholism is a real problem in the indigenous communities so Salvador has always said that anyone going into the communities and trying to help has to set an example.

Think about it. Subcomandante Marcos has said the same thing in interviews. It's even a rule for the Zapatista soldiers."

That was true. I'd read an interview with Marcos about that very thing. Zapatistas were not allowed to drink. "But why the hell would Antonio be involved with this? He drinks and we know he does cocaine." Of course, the money he was pocketing was the obvious answer.

"I'm not saying Antonio's a Zapatista, but he's a leftist. Has he ever told you why he left Italy?"

I remembered back to Antonio telling me he wouldn't live in Italy so long as the fascists were in power and suddenly what Maria was saying seemed plausible. I thought about Salvador's political diatribe at Christmas. I thought about what Antonio had said about the Zapatistas. But most of all I thought about the fact that Salvador had visited Antonio right before Antonio had called me into his office. What had Salvador said that had prompted Antonio to speak to me?

"Are you sure?" I asked Maria.

"No," she said, but I could tell she was.

28

WHEN I WENT TO El Acuario the next night, I hadn't decided whether or not I'd confront Antonio about Salvador and the guns. I didn't know what such a confrontation could possibly yield, but just suspecting that Antonio and Salvador were mixed up with the Zapatistas made me feel like I was somehow more involved in the conflict than I had realized or wanted to be. That made me want to confront them.

But when I walked into the restaurant, it turned out Antonio had taken the night off and left Maria in charge. She hadn't found out anything because I had gotten her reluctantly to agree not to say anything to Antonio or Salvador about the guns. They'd deliberately kept her out of the loop and I'd convinced Maria that since they hadn't intended for her to know it was just as well that she stay out of it until we decided whether there was something we should do.

It was a slow night, and when Félix closed the kitchen, I told Maria to go home. We hadn't had a single customer in the last forty-five minutes and she hadn't slept well the night before, partly because Luz had been up several times in the night and partly because she was worried about Salvador's possible involvement with gunrunning.

"Are you sure you don't want me to stay?" she asked.

"I'm sure. I'll close up in a half hour if no one comes in."

"All right. I'll see you at home," she said and kissed me on the cheek before slipping into her jacket.

I listened to some music for twenty minutes and then decided to close shop, but as I flicked off the stereo, Bern came in, his ever-present Confederate cavalry hat on his head, his riding gloves tucked in his belt.

"How is business?" he asked. He sat on the same stool he'd been sitting on the first time I'd met him.

"Booming. How are you, Bern?"

He took off his hat, ran his hand through his hair, and repositioned the hat. He had dark bags under his eyes.

"Like I watched Sherman march to the sea. May I have a Dos Equis?"

"How's that?" I asked, setting the beer and a glass in front of him.

Ignoring the glass, he took a long drink from his beer and then looked at the bottle, slightly dissatisfied.

"Not cold enough?" I asked.

"It is fine, but what I wouldn't give for a genuine Spaten."

"So what's this about Sherman?"

"The army is in my pueblo. They say we're all Zapatistas. They took my father-in-law off to jail and kicked me out. My house is being used as a barrack." He shook his head at the thought of it and drank from his beer again.

"They can do that?"

"They did it."

"Shit, Bern. I'm sorry. Why'd they take your father-in-law?"

"They say he's a leader."

"Is he?"

"Of the community, yes. He's an old man," he said.

"How's your wife? She okay?"

He shrugged and drank his beer. "She stays in the hotel room. They almost wouldn't let her leave with me. I'm waiting for money from Germany and then we'll go down to Tuxtla to try to buy her father out of jail. We're told he's being held in Cerro Hueco."

"I don't know what to say. I'm sorry."

"Danke. Between you and me, I'm not so optimistic they'll let him out."

"Why? What did he do?"

Bern removed his wire-rimmed glasses and cleaned them with a handkerchief he took from his shirt pocket. He looked at me and then finished cleaning his glasses before putting them back on. They were round and small for his face.

"I don't know if I should speak to you of these things."

It was an odd comment.

"No? Why is that?"

"Didn't you tell me you are friends with the Lobos de Madrid family?"

"Good friends."

Bern nodded and drank from his beer.

"So?"

"So you heard about their ranch?"

"I did. But you can't blame them for defending their property. His family has been working that land for generations."

"You mean his family has been forcing other families to work that land for them for generations."

"Look, Bern. You can't blame César or his parents for everything that happened in the past. That would be like me blaming you for the Nazis."

He winced at the reference and said something to himself in German that I understood to be at my expense. Then in English: "You Americans and the Nazis. Always the Nazis."

He had a point. It was a cheap and overused card to play. "I

301

just mean you can't blame people for things others did before them. That'd be like me blaming someone from the Georgia of today for the Civil War." But as I said it, I reminded myself that the current Georgia state flag was a Confederate battle flag and I reminded myself that no one really escapes their history—not the South and not the Germans and not the Lobos de Madrid family. Not even me.

"I don't blame them for what happened in the past. What I blame them for is what they did at Calvario."

"What, taking back their house? You would have done the same thing."

"I might have taken back my house, but once I had it I wouldn't have executed two people on their knees with their hands tied behind their backs."

"And you think that's what César and his family did?"

"There were three campesinos who were captured. Your friend shot one in the back of the head and his father shot another. They let the third man go so he could tell what happened."

Bern was so matter-of-fact about it that I almost believed him, but only for a second.

"You're telling me that César Lobos de Madrid and his father murdered two people in cold blood and then let an eyewitness go. Why would they do that? César is a national fútbol star, for Christ's sake. His dad is one of the most well-respected business men in Mexico. That's the stupidest thing I ever heard, and if there is one thing I know about César and his father, it's that they're not stupid."

"No, they're not. That's why they let the third man go."

"Whatever."

"I know the third man."

"Yeah?" I asked, starting to lose my temper. "Well, I know César. Your third man is full of shit."

"Maybe," Bern said, standing up and pulling some money from his pocket. "Why not ask him about it?"

"I'll do that," I said. Of course I didn't mean it. César wasn't a killer. But something about Bern's earnestness, like a challenge, was pissing me off. My response was more of an answer to his challenge than anything else.

"Anyway," Bern said, laying his pesos on the bar, "that's why I don't know if I should speak to you of these things."

"Bern, that's up to you. In any case, good luck getting your father-in-law out of jail."

"Danke."

"And good luck getting your ranch back. Hopefully you won't have to shoot anyone."

I'd meant the last part as a joke, as if to dismiss all the absurd talk about César with something equally absurd, but it came out sounding wrong and it caused Bern to snap his eyes at me. He pursed his lips as if he was going to say something, but he didn't. Instead, he shook his head and walked out. That was the last time I ever saw him.

After Bern left, I locked up and went to Maria's. The lights in the sitting room were on, but Maria lay asleep, cuddled up against Luz in Luz's bed. Maria's boots stood at the foot of the bed, but otherwise she was fully dressed. Illuminated by the light of the hallway, she looked so peaceful snuggled against her daughter that I watched the two of them sleep for a few moments before turning off the lights in the hall and going into our bedroom. In the dark, I shucked off my clothes, piling them on my desk chair before groping my way under the covers. The sheets were cold. I don't know how long I lay in the dark thinking about what Bern had said, but the bed was already warm when Maria padded into the room and spooned up against me.

Before Maria left to work the lunch shift the next day, we

agreed to meet at El Acuario for dinner. When she left, Luz and I played dolls for an hour or so. Then I dropped her with Doña Asunta and walked over to César's house to see if he was back from Tuxtla. He was.

I'd thought to tell César what Bern had said, thinking we might have a laugh about it, but when I got to his place he seemed preoccupied. Even though we'd started to patch things up, I still felt like I had to watch what I said or I'd set him off. So instead, we drank coffee and smoked cigarettes at the table in front of the kitchen. César read the paper and I watched Ramón and the other guys kick a soccer ball around the courtyard. I felt like we should be talking about something, but I couldn't think of anything besides Bern's story. "Did Tecos win?" I asked finally.

"Take a look," César said, folding the paper and handing it to me. He pushed back his chair and went into the kitchen. I opened the paper to the sports page and scanned through it.

César came back out with the pot of coffee and filled his cup. "You want a top-off?"

"I'm good. Did you see how much Toluca is paying their new goalkeeper?"

"Yeah. They make it sound like he's got four hands," César said, lighting a cigarette.

"He ought to for that kind of money."

César nodded as he exhaled a stream of smoke. I sipped my coffee and turned to the front page. I glanced over two articles about the results of the peace talks. That's when I noticed the headline below the fold. "Reporter Found Murdered." There was a photograph of police with the body. My stomach knotted as I read the article.

The body of Eduardo Gallegos, longtime editorialist, was found early this morning along a roadside outside Tuxtla. Kidnapped from his house by armed assailants five days before, he appeared to have been tortured and then shot, execution style, at the base of his skull. His body was found by a passing motorist.

The article went on to say a number of his friends and associates claimed Gallegos had been receiving death threats for several weeks, and while the government claimed there was no evidence to indicate who might be responsible, few people doubted it was the work of anti-Zapatista paramilitaries. Gallegos was survived by his wife and three children.

I looked at César sitting there smoking his cigarette and watching the guys kick the ball. It had been six days since César had gone to Tuxtla with Ramón and his friends. Six days since I'd seen the manila folder with the photographs of Gallegos. I tried to tell myself it was a coincidence. I looked at Ramón and the others. I looked at César.

"Did you read this article about the journalist who was murdered?"

César locked eyes with me for a moment, took another drag on his cigarette, and then turned his gaze back to the guys in the courtyard. "Gallegos? Yeah," he said. "Chinga su madre. If you write the lies he wrote, somebody is going to do something. He got what he deserved."

I knew César could feel me staring at him. The three feet of distance between us seemed to visibly grow. The ball was kicked. It skittered across the courtyard and was kicked again. The sound echoed off the walls. It was distinct. Acute.

"César," I said, my voice slow and steady, "what happened at Calvario?"

He leaned back in his chair, but he didn't look at me. He clenched and unclenched his jaw. "I told you. Some campesinos thought the uprising gave them the right to move into my father's home. There was a fight and we threw them out," he said. He glanced at me and then turned his attention back to the courtyard.

"I heard a story," I said.

"Oh yeah?" He pretended to watch the ball. "What kind of story?"

"I heard you killed a man."

He looked at me and then looked back at the courtyard. Two of the guys were yelling at each other about something. I could hear them clearly, but it was almost as if I couldn't hear them at all. Everything seemed to speed up and slow down simultaneously.

"Only one?"

I looked at him. "I heard you executed him."

"Where'd you hear a story like that?"

"Does it matter?"

"No," he said after a moment. "I guess not."

"So is it true?"

"I don't know," he said, stubbing his cigarette out in the ashtray. "You're the one who heard it. You tell me." Now he was looking right at me. It was almost as if he was looking through me. His face was expressionless. Totally blank. Suddenly his cold facade cracked and the famous César smile spread across his face.

"God! Compadre," he said, bursting into laughter. "Where do you hear this stuff? Come on!"

As always, César's smile won me over and I instantly felt stupid for listening to Bern and giving any credence to his impossible story. "Yeah," I said, smiling sheepishly, "I thought you'd get a kick out of that."

"Hey, Ramón," he called.

Ramón trapped the ball and looked over. The game paused. The other guys looked over as well.

"You should hear what Hank just told me." And then to me, César said, "Go on. Tell them."

They were all staring, waiting for me to speak.

"It was nothing," I said.

César looked at me. "Are you sure? It's pretty funny."

I said nothing.

Ramón looked puzzled.

"Never mind," César said after a moment.

Ramón shook his head and resumed the game, kicking the ball to Miguel.

And like that, the subject was closed, dismissed outright as being too absurd to acknowledge with anything more than a laugh and a shake of the head.

"Compadre," César said, "I have to go out of town again for a few days."

"Are you going to Calvario?"

"No. I've got some more business in Tuxtla."

"What kind of business?"

César smiled over his cup as he brought it to his lips. "Don't you know? I've got to execute someone."

When I left later that afternoon, César had me fairly convinced of his innocence. He'd explained that because of his Lobos de Madrid political connections, there were always people out to slander his family, his father in particular. For generations they'd contended with rumors of unfair dealings and mistreatment of people at Calvario. Stories of abuse, he assured me, were either grossly exaggerated or patently false. Powerful people have powerful enemies. That's reality. And in a time when tensions are running high and everyone is unsettled, it was only natural that the propaganda machine would switch into overdrive.

While everything César said made sense, I was more convinced by César's attitude than his arguments. The way he simply laughed off the whole idea that he might be involved with something as insidious as summary executions made me ashamed for doubting him.

But when I was out on the street, halfway to El Acuario to meet

Maria for dinner, out of the direct brilliance of César's charisma, two aspects of the afternoon started gnawing on me. The first was the fact, printed in black and white, that somebody had kidnapped and executed Eduardo Gallegos with a bullet to the back of the skull. It was a fact that hadn't bothered César in the least. But the second thing, the thing that really began to gnaw on me, was César's reaction to my suggestion about events at Calvario.

It was perfectly believable that César would be cavalier in his dismissal of wild rumors. That was his nature. It wasn't that he didn't care what people thought. He did. He cared a lot. His name and reputation were a point of honor with him. They were a part of his old-world values. I think that was why he hated Maria. Although I didn't fully appreciate it at the time, I think he saw her relationship with Salvador as a blow to his reputation and he was afraid everyone was laughing at him as a result. But César only ever cared about things that were true. I knew from his fútbol days he'd always laughed off the critics who didn't know anything, even though they always seemed to scream the loudest. If people were making up stories about him, he couldn't be bothered. He knew who he was and there was no end to his self-confidence. I was sure that what he'd said about his family always having to deal with some crazy story or another was true. But what I didn't believe was that César could be so casual toward me, toward my lack of faith in him.

Of all the qualities César looked for in himself and in others, the one he valued most was loyalty. He had complete faith in the people he cared about and he expected complete faith in return. He could forgive a friend for almost anything but betrayal. His response to my relationship with Maria was proof of that. But in so many words I had just told César that I believed a story about him killing someone at Calvario and he had made a joke of it. The more I thought about it, the more I began to think that was not the response I should have expected. I'd shown a brief but serious lack of trust and he'd laughed. There was something wrong about that. Why hadn't he flown off the handle?

As I walked, I decided I had to know why. I didn't want to know and I definitely didn't want to have my suspicions confirmed, but I had to know. Of course, I didn't have any idea of how I could find out, or at least I didn't until I'd walked into El Acuario and found Salvador sitting at a table with Antonio.

Maria was behind the bar.

"What do you want to have for dinner?" she asked after I'd leaned over the bar to give her a quick kiss.

"I don't care. I'll have whatever you have."

I glanced over at Antonio and Salvador. Antonio gave a little wave that I returned. Salvador made no gesture.

"You haven't said anything to them about what we talked about, have you?" I asked Maria.

"No. I've been aching to smack both of them for being so stupid, but I haven't said anything."

"Good. Listen, I'm going to talk to them for a minute."

"About that?"

"No. Something else."

She gave me a curious look. "Are you all right?"

"I'm fine."

Maria stepped into the doorway of the kitchen and told Félix what we wanted and I went over to Antonio and Salvador. Antonio and I did our three-grip handshake. Salvador and I simply nodded to one another. I got the distinct impression I'd interrupted their conversation.

"Can I speak to you guys for a minute?"

"Have a seat," Antonio said.

"No. In the office."

Antonio looked at Salvador and Salvador shrugged. "Claro.

Let's go."

Antonio sat behind his desk while Salvador, arms folded across his chest, remained standing, leaning against the closed door. "¿Que paso?" asked Antonio.

"That thing we were talking about the other day," I said, looking at Antonio.

"What about it?" Antonio asked, glancing quickly at Salvador before returning his attention to me.

"Do you know who Rodolfo Muñoz is?"

Antonio shook his head, but Salvador said, "Yes, I know him."

"I'm not sure, but I think there might be an attempt on his life in the next few days."

"What makes you think that?"

"It's just something I overheard."

"Overheard where?"

"At a café. I heard two men talking at the next table. They seemed to assume I didn't speak Spanish. I don't have any specifics. It might not happen at all, but from the way they spoke, I think it might."

"And why are you telling us?" Salvador asked. He still hadn't moved.

I looked at Salvador in a way that I hoped told him that I thought I knew who he was. What I said was, "I don't know. I thought maybe if you knew him, you could warn him or something."

"Is that all?"

"Más o menos."

"You're sure there's nothing else?"

"Yeah," I said. "I'm sure."

Salvador opened the door and stepped aside. "Thanks then," he said. The way he said it and the way he stood holding the door open made me feel like I was being dismissed, which I obviously was.

I nodded and walked out, the office door closing behind me.

I don't know what response I had expected from the two of them, but something about the way Salvador had opened the door for me—I mean literally the crook in his elbow and the configuration of his fingers on the door—made me realize just how sick I was of being in Chiapas. It was an odd realization because it had come out of nowhere and yet I now saw that it had been building since my first falling-out with César.

I walked over to our table and sat down.

"What was that about?"

"I'll tell you later."

Félix brought a pizza to the table and we thanked him.

"Buen provecho," he said and returned to the kitchen.

Maria put a slice on her plate and I watched her lick the tomato sauce from her fingers while I took a drink from my bottle of mineral water. She caught me watching her and she made a face that only half feigned embarrassment before she reached for a napkin.

"Do you want to leave?"

"The pizza just got here and I have to work," she said, sprinkling chili onto her slices.

"No. I mean if I left Chiapas, would you leave with me?"

"Like on a vacation? I'd have to see if Antonio would give me the time off."

"Maybe. Maybe more permanent than that."

Maria put her slice of pizza back on her plate.

"We could go to Denver or Arizona or Texas or wherever. We could go to San Francisco. You'd like San Francisco. Do you have a passport?"

"Yes. To visit my aunt in Guatemala. What did they say to you in there?"

"Nada. It has nothing to do with them."

"Then why do you want to leave?"

"I don't know. I guess I'm just tired of the scene."

"This isn't a scene. This is my life. This is home."

"We could find a new home."

"And what about Luz? This is her home. This is where her father lives. What am I supposed to tell her? 'Luz, baby, say good-bye to your daddy because Henry is tired of the scene and wants us to uproot our whole lives and move someplace where we don't speak the language?'"

I hadn't considered the Luz issue. I drank my water and nodded. "Just a vacation then. We don't have to leave Mexico. We could go to the beach or something." I must have sighed or sounded defeated or something because Maria reached across the table and took my hand.

"Do you really want to leave?"

"I don't know. I need a break. But not without you." But I wondered if that was even true. Who was this woman? Who were any of these people? What the hell was I doing here?

She smiled and gave my hand a squeeze. "I'll think about it. Okay? I don't promise anything, but I'll think about it."

"Thanks."

The door to the office opened and Salvador came out. He saw us holding hands and leaning across the table toward one another and he left the restaurant without speaking a word to either of us. A little while later Antonio came out of the office and told me that he was going to work that night so I wasn't needed. I told him that was fine by me and Maria and I finished dinner. It was good pizza, but I didn't have much of an appetite, and when Maria went back to work, I left with half the pie wrapped in aluminum foil.

29

FOR THE NEXT FEW days I stayed away from El Acuario. I told Maria to tell Antonio I was sick. I didn't want to deal with him or Salvador. I stayed clear of César too.

I'd given Maria a slightly different version of my conversation in Antonio's office, concentrating on my belief that Antonio and Salvador had been buying guns for the Zapatistas. She was angry with both of them and she'd finally confronted Antonio head-on, yelling at him for being so stupid as to get mixed up in something so dangerous. I wasn't very happy with her since Antonio had told me about the guns in confidence, but she was too angry to care. I think she was partly afraid that if something happened to Antonio, she'd be out of a job, which for a single mother, given the circumstances, was no small thing, but on a deeper level she was genuinely afraid for the two of them. I think she was angry about my talk of leaving and not going to work as well. She seemed to sense there was more at stake than I'd let on. Of course Antonio denied everything, but Maria told him she didn't believe him and said she was going to talk to Salvador. Antonio told her Salvador was out of town.

It was in the morning a few days later, the peace talks having concluded, that I next saw Salvador. Maria had taken Luz to see her pediatrician for a nasty cough. I was drinking coffee and eating toast on the balcony, watching the first elements of the Zapatista negotiators climb into their Red Cross vehicles and exit the city to less fanfare than when they'd arrived, when there was a knock at the door. I went to answer and it was Salvador and José. Salvador had a newspaper folded in his hand. I hadn't seen José since Maria's Christmas party.

"Hola, José," I said.

"Hank," he said. He was not smiling.

"Maria's not home," I said to Salvador. "She had to take Luz to the doctor."

"¿Que tiene?"

"Just a cough. Nothing serious."

"Good. But we didn't come to talk to Maria or Luz."

We sat at the table in the sitting room and Salvador laid the paper in front of me. José didn't take his eyes off me. I had an urge to ask him what the hell he was staring at.

"Have you seen today's paper?" Salvador asked.

"No."

He placed his index finger on a headline below the fold of the front page. "Read that," he said.

The headline read, "Assailant Killed in Gunfight."

> Noted civil rights activist Rodolfo Muñoz Valdez survived an apparent assassination attempt late Thursday night.
>
> Residents in northern Tuxtla were awakened to gunfire shortly after midnight when a number of heavily armed masked men broke into the Muñoz Valdez family home and opened fire.
>
> One of the alleged assailants, identified as Octavio Cienfuegos Obregon, was shot and killed in a gunfight with bodyguards of Muñoz Valdez. Muñoz Valdez, his

family, and bodyguards all escaped with minor injuries.

An outspoken supporter of the Zapatista National Liberation Army, Muñoz Valdez has claimed to have received death threats for several weeks. A written statement issued by a spokesperson for the family claimed that "the threats were not taken seriously until specific information suggested an attempt might be made against the family of Muñoz Valdez. At that time the family felt it prudent to employ assistance." The spokesperson said the family was certain anti-Zapatista paramilitary groups were responsible for the attack.

Captain Victor Sanchez of the Tuxtla Police Department suggested that the attack on Muñoz Valdez might have been staged by the EZLN. "As far as our agency is aware, the only armed militant group in Chiapas at this time is the EZLN," Sanchez told reporters. "This may have been a staged ploy by the EZLN to undermine the government's position in the peace talks under way in San Cristóbal de Las Casas."

Sanchez also stated that there was no apparent connection between this attack and the recent kidnapping and murder of journalist Eduardo Gallegos.

It is unknown if any of the other assailants were injured in the gunfight.

"I assure you," Sanchez told reporters, "the perpetrators of this crime will be brought to justice."

No one has been apprehended at the time of this writing.

So Octavio was dead. It didn't seem real. César and his friends had tried to kill Muñoz, and Octavio was dead. They'd killed Gallegos and now I knew they'd murdered those people at

Calvario. It just didn't seem real.

"How did you know?" Salvador asked when I looked up from the paper. Neither he nor José had stopped boring their eyes into me.

"I told you. I overheard some men talking about it?"

"What men? What café?"

"Look, I'm not getting involved in this."

"You are involved," José said quietly.

"No, I'm not."

"You don't think so? Well, let me ask you, was your friend César Lobos de Madrid one of the men in the café?" Salvador asked.

"What? No. It has nothing to do with him," I said. César and I were finished. The moment I'd read the article I knew that I was leaving Chiapas and that I wouldn't speak to César before I left. I didn't plan to speak to him ever again. Our friendship was over. Still, I'd be damned if I'd turn him over to Salvador.

"No?" Salvador asked.

"No."

"Hank," José said, "The Lobos de Madrid family is connected all through the government and military. As much as anyone, they are the symbol of what the revolution is fighting against. And you're telling me they are not involved. I think you knew about Muñoz because César told you."

"Wait a minute. What's your story?" I asked José.

"What do you think it is, Hank?"

I looked at him. Then I looked at Salvador. I probably outweighed each of them by fifty pounds. "You know what?" I said, standing up. "Who do you think you are coming around asking a bunch of questions like you're the goddamned FBI or something? Fuck you. Get the fuck out of my home."

Salvador had risen to his feet and his fists were clenched, but

José didn't move. He didn't even bat an eye. He just looked at me as though trying to read something in my posture or expression. Then he nodded almost imperceptibly and stood up.

"Do I need to tell you that you shouldn't tell anyone about this conversation or what you've told us?" José asked.

"Get the fuck out."

José studied me a moment more while Salvador seemed to be waiting for instructions. Then José said, "I'm sorry to have bothered you."

"Whatever."

He didn't stop looking at me, but to Salvador he said, "Vámonos," and then they left.

Once they were gone, I sat at the table, shaking and staring at the paper. I wasn't reading. I just stared at the words because what the words said and what they actually meant to me were two different things. The article had nothing to do with me, yet it so clearly said I had come to the end of something.

I don't know how long I sat there, but I was still sitting when Maria got home with Luz in tow.

"She has a sinus infection," Maria said, putting her purse on the table and carrying the pharmacy bag into the kitchen. Luz climbed onto one of the chairs. "The pediatrician told me to give her amoxicillin. I don't know why I bother to take her to the doctor. It's just an extra expense. They always prescribe the same thing." She opened the refrigerator and put the antibiotics on the shelf in the door before pouring herself a cup of coffee and coming out of the kitchen. "I should just go to the pharmacy and buy the medicine. We'd save sixty pesos," she said, sitting in the chair where Salvador had been sitting. The coffee cup was halfway to her lips when she really looked at me for the first time since she'd come in. "What is it?"

"Salvador and José came by."

"What did they want?" she asked, sensing it had not been a pleasant visit.

"To show me this." I turned the newspaper around and slid it across the table to her.

She gave me a puzzled look, put her coffee down, and began reading. I watched her read.

"I don't know how the government can say there aren't any paramilitaries in Chiapas," she said when she had finished. "Do they really think anyone is going to believe the Zapatistas did this? How stupid do they think the public is?" She shook her head. "But I don't understand. Why did Salvador and José want to show it to you?"

Looking at Maria, I tilted my head at Luz.

"Luz," Maria said, "why don't you go find your doll?"

Luz slid off her chair and went to her room.

"Salvador is the one who warned Muñoz," I said when Luz was gone.

"Really? He told you that? Why?"

"Because I warned Salvador. He came by because he wanted to know how I knew about the plot."

"How did you?"

"Octavio, the guy who was killed, worked for César. That was César and his friends who tried to kill Muñoz. They killed that journalist, Eduardo Gallegos."

"César did?"

"Yeah. I didn't tell Salvador that, though, because I think Salvador and his Zapatista friends mean to go after the people responsible."

That got her attention.

"Maria," I said, "I'm done with this. I'm leaving."

She looked at me. "You're leaving?" Her voice was hollow. She was still trying to comprehend the possibility of violence between

Salvador and César.

"I want you and Luz to come with me."

"You want us to come with you?"

"Look," I said, formulating a plan as I spoke. "It doesn't have to be permanent. Let's just get out of Chiapas for a while until all this blows over." I didn't tell her I had no intention of ever coming back to San Cristóbal.

"You mean like a vacation?"

"Yeah, a vacation like we talked about. Sort of. Let's say a long vacation."

"Where would we go?"

My thought was back to the States. "San Miguel de Allende or Guadalajara or Mérida or wherever," I said, simply rattling off names of Mexican cities I'd heard of. "It doesn't matter. Just away from here."

"What about my job?"

"Antonio is smuggling guns for Salvador and José, guns that he bought from César. César is the goddamned white guard. If César ever finds out, Antonio will be lucky to get out of the country. Forget about the job. We'll find new jobs."

"What about my apartment?"

"What about it? We'll give it up."

"I can't give up my apartment. What about my things, my piano?"

I understood what she meant. The stove, the refrigerator—all of her possessions—were symbols of her independence. Her piano was like a piece of her. In a place where so many people live in houses with dirt floors and walls made of sticks or planks, where they die in droves from exposure or hunger or cholera or dozens of other lesser diseases that are easily preventable, Maria had made a life for herself all on her own. And I was being cavalier about that.

"Okay," I said. "We don't have to give it up. I'll pay six months of rent in advance."

"Six months? You want to be gone six months? I can't take Luz away for six months. What about Salvador? He's her father."

"We don't have to be gone six months. I'll just pay six months of rent."

"But you think we might be gone that long. I can't take Luz from her father for six months."

"Maria, Salvador is doing dangerous stuff. These people are killing each other. Do you really want Luz mixed up in that? When all this blows over, we'll come back." I'm never coming back here, I thought to myself again.

She looked around the apartment and then at me, her eyes bright with tears. "When?"

"Mañana."

"¿Mañana?"

"Or the next day at the latest. There's no reason to wait."

"You're really going to leave."

"I am. And you're going to come with me."

She lifted her chin and looked at the ceiling. Then she wiped her eyes and looked at me. "Okay. We'll go."

I leaned across the table and took her head in my hands and pressed my forehead against hers.

"Te quiero," she said.

I kissed her. "It will be okay."

To be honest, I was surprised she'd agreed to go.

30

I WAS READY TO go that same day before Maria changed her mind, but she insisted she had to tell Salvador. I was afraid of how Salvador would react at hearing that Maria and Luz were leaving with me, so I wanted to be there in case he tried something. But Maria wanted to tell him by herself. It was the one condition she had if she was going to go with me. She did realize, however, that Salvador probably wasn't going to take the news lightly and that Luz didn't need to be around for his initial reaction. So the plan was for me to take Luz out before Salvador arrived. We'd give them two hours to themselves and then I'd bring Luz back to the apartment to say good-bye. Maria figured two hours would be enough for Salvador to digest the news and accept it. I didn't think two days or two weeks would be enough, but it was what Maria wanted, so I went along with it.

We started packing that afternoon and that night Maria went to work and when Salvador came in she told him she had something she wanted to say and asked him to come over the following afternoon. The next day I took Luz for a walk while Maria played Beethoven's *Pathétique* and waited for Salvador. I could still hear her piano as Luz and I started down the steps of the building and I thought that was damn near the saddest song I had ever heard.

Luz and I went up to the Plaza de Guadalupe where a little

feria had been set up to celebrate some saint or another. Luz rode the carousel. She liked it. Suzy had too. Then we listened to music and watched the dancers. I wondered how things were going between Maria and Salvador. After about an hour and a half, I'd had enough of the *feria*, so I hoisted Luz onto my shoulders and we went for ice cream. Much to the amusement of the girl behind the counter and my diminishing patience, Luz changed her mind five or six times before deciding on her initial selection, chocolate on a waffle cone.

We stopped on the second-floor landing because the ice cream was running down her hand. I wiped her face with a napkin and after a brief negotiation Luz let me have her cone so I could lick up the dripping chocolate and clean her hands. Once we had the ice cream situation under control, we started back up the stairs. The closer we got to the apartment, the more I began to dread facing Salvador. I knew he'd make a scene. In fact, I was surprised that we hadn't heard him shouting since we'd entered the building.

We hadn't climbed more than four or five steps when the door to Doña Asunta's apartment opened just enough for old woman to peer into the landing. She'd kept the chain on the door.

"Hola, Doña Asunta," I said, giving her a neighborly wave. Since the conflict had started, the poor woman had been a nervous wreck. I don't think she'd left her apartment a single time. Maria and another neighbor had done all her shopping.

"Shhh," she hushed sharply and frantically waved me over.

"¿Que paso?" I asked when she'd undone the chain and hurried Luz and me into her apartment, quickly checking the landing and hallway to make sure no one had seen us before she shut the door. She seemed even more distraught than usual.

"I don't like to get involved," she said, wringing the fabric of her housedress with one hand.

"Involved?"

"What my neighbors do is their business, but such yelling."

"Yelling?" I asked, becoming more concerned.

"You all are always so quiet and Maria is such a nice girl. I was worried."

"What yelling?"

"I don't like to get involved. What my neighbors do is their business."

"Doña Asunta, tell me what happened?"

"There were loud voices upstairs. Then I heard Maria screaming and men shouting. I could hear them breaking furniture."

There was no noise coming from upstairs now.

"Men shouting? When did this happen?"

"Thirty minutes ago."

I crouched down and grabbed Luz by the arm to get her attention. "Luz, you stay here with Doña Asunta." To the señora I said, "I'll be right back."

I ran up the stairs, taking them three at a time. Our front door was wide open and two of the living room chairs had been upended and Maria's piano bench was splintered across the floor, sheet music scattered everywhere.

"Maria!" I shouted, looking into the kitchen and then running to the bedrooms. "Maria!" The apartment was empty. I shut the door on my way out and ran back downstairs.

"What happened?" I shouted once Doña Asunta had opened her door.

The old woman stepped back and covered her face with her hands. She was absolutely terrified.

"What happened?" I repeated, trying to speak more soothingly. "Doña Asunta, you have to tell me what happened. Did you see the men?"

"I don't like to get involved, but I was afraid for Maria."

"Did you see them?"

"Just for a moment. They came down the stairs and they were shouting and I opened my door to see—"

"What did they look like?"

"I only saw for a second and then one of them told me to mind my own business."

"Did you see Salvador? Was Salvador with them?"

"Yes."

Salvador and his damn friends, I thought. I am going to beat that prick to a pulp.

"They had Salvador and Maria."

"Wait … what?"

"Some of them were shoving Salvador and another was dragging Maria by the hair. ¡Que barbaridad!"

"Who did? Who were they?"

"¡No se! I don't know them!"

"The one who told you to shut the door, what did he look like?"

"No se."

"Try to remember. Was he tall? Short? Fat? Thin?"

"He was big, a very big man. And he had a scar."

"A scar?" I suddenly had a sinking feeling. "What scar?"

"Here," she said, drawing her finger across her eye and down her face.

Ramón.

"I'm going to leave Luz here for a little while."

"No, no, no!" she said, waving her hands. "I can't get involved. No puedo."

"I'm going to leave her here," I repeated. "I'll be back for her soon."

"No."

"Sí," I said. It wasn't open for discussion. "Luz," I said, picking the child up and putting her in a chair. "You stay with Doña Asunta, okay?"

"Where's Mamá?" she asked.

"I'm going to get your mom right now," I said and kissed her on her forehead. "Okay?"

"Okay."

I grabbed a taxi in the zócalo to travel the eight or nine blocks to César's house. I didn't know what I was going to do when I got there. I didn't even know if they'd be there or if the old woman had seen what she'd said she'd seen. It didn't seem possible. But of course it did. Our open apartment and the broken furniture were proof enough.

There was no one outside the compound and everything looked normal. I didn't wait for the driver to make change. I slid my key into the lock, turned it, and stepped into the courtyard. They were all in front of the steps of the main house and I came in just as César smashed the butt of his pistol into Salvador's nose, blood instantly gushing as Salvador collapsed to the ground.

"César!" I roared, storming across the courtyard.

They all turned and spread out a step or two. For all the blood, I barely recognized Antonio on the ground next to Salvador. On her knees, Maria was being held by Miguel. He had a clump of her hair in his hand. One side of her face was purple and swollen.

"What the fuck are you doing?"

"Get out, compadre!" César shouted. He pointed at me as I stomped toward him. "This is none of your business."

"Like hell!" I was so enraged I went right over Luis, but then Ramón slammed the barrel of his shotgun across my midsection and I was on the ground.

"Henry!" I heard Maria scream as someone kicked me on the side of the head.

"Shut up," César barked.

The blow left me gasping for breath and the kick knocked clear my blinding rage. Suddenly it began to dawn on me how real and how dangerous the situation was.

"Why?" I gasped.

"I told you this is none of your business," César said as Ramón and Luis dragged me to my feet.

Salvador was holding his hands to his bloody face. Antonio rasped in a fetal position. Maria was now facedown on the ground with a boot on the back of her neck.

César stepped right up to me so I could feel his breath on my face. "Now get out of here."

"I'm not going anywhere. Look at what you're doing. Why are you doing this?"

He looked at me. "You want to know why I'm doing this? I'll tell you why. Those guns I traded to this sack of shit," he said, stepping over to Antonio and kicking him, "the army took two of them off dead Zapatistas. He didn't sell them to a drug smuggler like he said. He sold them to"—he kicked Salvador—"this sack of shit."

"Can you imagine how that makes me look? I buy guns from the police and they end up in the hands of those hijos de su puta madre. Can you imagine how that makes me look? Can you? It makes me look like a Zapatista. Me, a fucking Zapatista."

Then he hauled Salvador up by the hair, bent his head back, and growled into his ear. "I want a name. You're going to tell me who you gave them to, aren't you, you Zapatista faggot?"

Salvador's body was so limp and his face so void of expression that I thought he might be unconscious, but then in a faint but clear voice he said, "Chinga tu puta madre."

"¿Que? ¿Que me dijiste?" César said, shaking with rage. He shoved Salvador back to the ground and snapped his fingers at Luis. "Dame la gasolina."

"César," I said as Luis took a can of gasoline from the back of one of the pickups. "You can't do this."

"Shut up, compadre."

"Let me take Maria and we'll leave."

"No, compadre. You wanted to stay, so you stay."

"Then let Maria go."

"No."

"Why? What does she have to do with this? She didn't do anything."

"No? She has everything to do with this. I told you that she was no good. She betrayed me for this maricón," he said and kicked Salvador again. Then he crouched down and grabbed a fistful of Maria's hair and jerked her head up. "And you made Hank betray me too, didn't you?"

"Compadre," I pleaded. "Just let her go. César, you can't do this."

But he wasn't listening to me anymore. He was listening only to his own madness. He stuffed his pistol in his waistband, took the can of gasoline, unscrewed the cap, and began dumping the fuel on Antonio.

Antonio's collapsed body convulsed to life and he began to scream and writhe around, trying to get away. Ramón started laughing and then so did all the others.

"'¿Chinga mi madre?' No, chinga tu madre," César said to Salvador as he splashed Antonio. "You see what I'm doing to your friend here? Do you see? I'm going to do worse to you until you give me a name. Then if you still won't tell me I'm going to start in on that mother of your bastard child."

Because it was only Ramón holding me now and because he was laughing like the others, his grip loosened just enough that I shrugged him off and tackled César. I got three or four good shots in before Ramón and the others were on me and they hauled me back to my feet.

César touched his finger to his lip where I'd punched him

and looked at the blood. He stepped toward me and I blinked instinctively as he moved to hit me. But he didn't hit me. He simply patted my cheek and smiled.

"I'm sorry you have to see this, compadre, but Mexico isn't the States. We make our own rules. When people break those rules, they get burned," he said and turned to Salvador. "Don't they, you pinche communist?"

Now I don't know why I said what I said next. It was a stupid thing to say. He was going to do it and nothing I could say would stop him. I guess that's why I said it. I wanted to hurt him and the only thing available was the truth.

"It was me, César."

He turned and looked at me. "It was you what?"

"Why do you think they were waiting for you when you went for Muñoz? I told them. It was me. I told them, César. I told them."

He blinked and took a step back. I could see his mind trying to make adjustments and for a moment I thought the shock of what I'd said might make him give the whole thing up.

"It was you?" It was a question, but not one meant for me. It was meant for himself, like he was trying to comprehend how this new variable affected some larger equation he held in his mind. He drew his pistol from his waistband and pressed the muzzle against my head. "Get out of Mexico or you're dead. You understand, compadre? Muerto." He practically whispered it. Then, all at once, César pivoted and smashed the gun against the side of my face.

I was on the ground and couldn't hear anything. The world seemed distorted and elongated, like I was watching everything on television and someone was playing with the color contrast and horizontal picture. Everything went very far away, then came very close, then went very far away again. I saw flames. Then I blacked out.

Then I was in Ramón's truck. We were going somewhere. Ramón was driving. César was next to me. The world was bright. It rolled by. I felt sick. There was a buzzing. Where were we going? How long had we been in the truck? Had we just gotten in? I couldn't figure it out. I wanted to ask César something, but I couldn't remember what. Everything kept tilting. Did we stop? César hit me again. A detonation of stars.

IV

31

CÉSAR SHOUTING SOMETHING. Shouting and shoving me out of the truck. The black truck. Screeching tires. Shower of gravel. Sunlight. Bright sunlight. A pulsing. Dirt. Weeds. Something black in the weeds. Then a tilting. A chain link fence. A tilting. A tilting and a darkening. Maria. A darkening. Nothing.

SOMETHING BLACK IN THE weeds. Something black trembling into focus. The carcass of cat. Desiccated. Decomposing. Ants. Ants on a carcass. Ants crawling in and out of the eye sockets. My head pulsed. A buzzing. I lay there. Dirt and gravel. Dry grass and a chain link fence. The canopy of sky. The sunlight was bright. Bright and hot. A car. It went by. I lay there in the ditch. The weeds. The cat. The ants crawling. I lay there. A buzzing. I reached for the fence. Buzzing and pulsing. I staggered up out of the dirt.

Everything tilted and was tilting. A rush grew over the buzzing. I held on to the fence and closed my eyes. Sunspots. Buzzing. I opened them. An airplane roared down the runway on the other side of the fence. It lifted into the sky. The sky was blue. The sunlight was bright. So bright. My hands on the fence. Dried blood on my hands. The mountains in the near distance. Another

333

car went by. I watched it go down the road. The road to the airport terminal. The terminal shimmered in the heat. How far? Maybe three-quarters of a mile away. Maybe closer. Maybe farther. My mouth tasted of copper. I stood there. I held the fence. The world kept tilting. The smell of gasoline. My legs seemed far away. I was looking down at them from a great height. They were someone else's legs. Someone else was controlling them. Move, I told myself. A leg moved. I took another step. Then another. Another car went by. I stumbled along the fence and road. I concentrated on walking. I concentrated on my boots and the gravel and the dry weeds. I concentrated on the buzzing. I looked up and the terminal moved farther away. The sunlight was bright. Bright and hot. More cars went by. I kept walking. The buzzing continued. I concentrated on my boots. The terminal moved farther away. It kept moving farther away. Then it got closer. I stepped onto the sidewalk.

Vehicles were coming and going from the terminal, being loaded and unloaded. Sunlight reflected off bumpers and wind-shields and pavement. It was bright. Bright and loud. Loud but muted. Buzzing. A traffic officer blew his whistle and waved people along. A man argued with a baggage handler. The traffic officer blew his whistle. The whistle was a wire through my eye. A voice came over the loudspeaker and said something. The man arguing with the baggage handler gestured some more. He was yelling, but I could barely hear him over the buzzing. The man's wife was watching me. It was a look of disapproval. She tracked my progress down the sidewalk. I stared back and she looked away. The glass doors slid open and I went in. I went past the lines at the ticket counter. I passed the newsstand. I passed a seating area and the souvenir shop. I found the men's room.

The restroom was cool and dim and quiet. The dimness was a relief. So was the coolness, the quiet. In the mirror, a welted purple abrasion ran from my ear and across my cheekbone and the whole left side of my face was swollen and turning green and blue. I could barely see out of my left eye. Dried blood was caked around my nostrils. The buzzing was still there. The pulsing had changed to a throb. I had the perpetual sensation that I didn't know the answer to a question I couldn't remember. How long did I stand there? A minute? Two? Five? I ran the faucet and splashed water on my face. The water was cold and good. A toilet flushed. A man in a suit came out of one of the stalls and washed at the next sink. I could sense him looking at me, but then he dried his hands and exited. I gradually slipped back into my body, like everything in the room was shrinking back to normal, untilting, settling back into place. I splashed more water and things grew less disjointed. The decibel level dialed down. The chain with my wedding ring and St. Christopher medal had come out of my shirt front. I looked at them. I washed the remaining dried blood from my face. I thought of César. I thought of Maria. I saw Maria's face as he struck me with the gun. I thought of Jenn and what she would expect of me. I thought of Maria and I felt, all at once, a calm, focused, and deliberate purpose. It was a feeling I hadn't felt in a long, long time and I tucked the chain back inside the collar of my shirt and went out.

As I made my way back through the terminal, I checked that my passport was still in my buttoned shirt pocket and pulled out my billfold and counted my pesos. I stopped at the newsstand and bought a pair of sunglasses. The attendant handed over my change and looked at me. I thought he would say something, but he simply took the sunglasses from my hand, clipped the tag with a small pair of scissors, and offered them back. I put them on, nodded, and walked out. The electric doors slid closed behind me. Cars were still coming and going and people were still loading and unloading and the traffic officer had been joined by another and they were blowing their whistles and waving. The disapproving woman and her angry husband had vanished and the baggage handler was dollying someone else's bags down the sidewalk. I climbed into the backseat of a taxi and told the driver to take me to San Cristóbal. Besides the staring of the woman at the curb and a couple of sidelong glances from the businessman at the next sink in the bathroom and the unasked question from the newsstand guy, no one seemed to think twice about some gringo with a punched-up face who'd wandered through the Tuxtla airport. The cabbie gave a couple of curious looks in his rearview mirror, but even he didn't say a word after he'd made sure I had my passport to get through the military roadblocks. He just adjusted the rearview mirror, put the car in drive, and pulled out.

From Tuxtla, the road to San Cristóbal de Las Casas rises 2,300 meters in eighty-two steep kilometers, and as the taxi traversed up the narrow switchbacks, the valley floor fell away so that I could see far out across the plain. I watched the arid landscape through my own battered reflection in the window and tried to calculate how much of a head start César and Ramón had in getting back to the house and Maria. It was hard to gauge how long I had been unconscious in that ditch, but I didn't think it had been more than a few minutes. It just didn't seem like the afternoon had progressed very much. The stumble to the airport probably had taken fifteen minutes, maybe twenty, and I guessed I'd spent another fifteen minutes or so at the airport. They probably had a forty-five minute jump on me. Maybe an hour. I hoped it wasn't more than that. Of course, he'd left those other two assholes with her when he and Ramón hauled me to the airport. But even if those guys had done nothing in César's absence, an hour was plenty of time for César to do something terrible. I tried not to think what those various terrible things might be. I even tried to convince myself that César would come to his senses and let her go, but I didn't believe it, so I thought about what I was going to do, what I would do, and what I might have to do, and whether I'd have the nerve. Suddenly I realized that I actually was going to do something. I didn't know what that was, but I was going to do something and all at once I wondered if I'd ever really made a choice that mattered in my entire life. My college had been the only one to offer a scholarship. I hadn't chosen Jenn so much as found her and, really, she'd found me. I'd been the one who hadn't known where he was going in life. I'd been the one who needed finding. Her father gave me the job. I hadn't earned it. It wasn't something I'd worked for or particularly wanted. Even Suzy had been unplanned. My god. Suzy. My little girl in that water. There's no denying I'd chosen to go down the rapids, but I hadn't understood the choice. I should have, but I hadn't. Coming to Mexico hadn't been a choice either. It had just been me flailing around. And Maria? I didn't choose Maria. The conflict and those few days when we'd been sequestered in the compound had done that. And I sure as hell hadn't chosen to take a side in the Zapatista conflict. And right then, sitting in the taxi, it seemed so obvious which side was right and which was wrong. How had I failed to choose?

People chose sides about something important, something that was meant to shape the whole world and how people live in it, and what did I do? I poured drinks in a bar. Men and women and children were being pushed right up against the edge and they rose up, some of them with nothing more than sticks, some of them with nothing more than their voices. "Ya Basta!" they said. "Ya Basta!" What did I do? I fed them a few pans of leftover lasagna. And I had to be talked into doing that.

The taxi continued to climb into the mountains and the view changed from the dry plain to narrow valleys, from scrublands to leafier tropical vegetation. We climbed and rose from one deciduous zone to the next, and the vines and lush foliage gave way to a pine forest. The driver turned off the air conditioner and rolled down his window. The air was cool. We climbed and passed into a fog. The world became ethereal, the forest shrouded, dripping with mist. The fog thickened and the taxi slowed. Everything disappeared in the whiteness, only the yellow lines rising up from the vanished road to delineate direction. My reflection in the window grew ghostlike. I looked at my image and at the white nothingness that masked it. Who was the person I saw there?

The rumor was that Subcomandante Marcos first arrived in Chiapas in 1983. The man I'd seen in the zócalo definitely wasn't Indian and he couldn't have been older than thirty-five or forty, which meant he was about my age when he hiked into the jungle from wherever he'd come from and started organizing. He had chosen. He had come to Chiapas and he'd seen what was going on and he put on a mask and he did something. Salvador had done something too. So had Antonio. And me? I'd seen it too. But I was a tourist. I was like the Thompsons. I was like that woman in the zócalo worried about her reservations in Palenque. Christ! Reservations in Palenque! I'd been so wrapped up in my own private pity party, my self-indulgent grief, my personal Palenque, that I hadn't seen what was right in front of my face or tried to do anything about it. I could have done something. What had I done? Nothing. And by doing nothing I had aligned myself with César and his family and what they stood for—wealth and power and commerce over people. Maybe that's oversimplifying it. Not maybe. But maybe we have to simplify things sometimes just so we can choose and act. In any case, I was choosing. I just wish I could have chosen sooner. I should have. Things would have turned out very differently.

We rose out of the fog and a few minutes later came upon the first checkpoint. The taxi rolled to a stop behind a third-class bus and two cars. Dozens of soldiers, automatic weapons at the ready, flanked the column of vehicles or manned machine guns behind sandbag installations. While several soldiers opened the baggage bays and searched the luggage, others had the male passengers climb down and circle the bus in single file as their identifications were checked one man at a time. The women were kept on board. Once the soldiers were satisfied, the bus was reloaded and groaned through the checkpoint, leaving a cloud of black exhaust in its wake.

They reviewed the two cars ahead of us. Then it was our turn. The soldiers interviewed the driver and then me and reviewed our identifications. We didn't have to get out of the taxi.

A soldier looked at my passport.

"¿Americano?" he asked.

"Sí."

He nodded and then leaned his face closer. "What happened to your face?"

"I fell off a friend's motorcycle."

The soldier studied my expression. "You speak a lot of Spanish for an American."

"I studied in school."

He nodded again. "And where are you going?

"San Cristóbal."

"For what purpose?"

"I've been living there."

He reviewed my visa form tucked in the passport. "Your immigration form expires next month."

"I know."

He folded the form back in the passport and handed them over. "Muy bien," he said. "Do you have anything in the trunk?" he asked the driver.

"No."

"Open it, please."

The driver got out and opened the trunk for inspection. There was nothing. They closed the trunk, and once the driver was back in his seat, the soldiers raised the red bar and waved us through. There were two more checkpoints before we reached San Cristóbal. They were stopping traffic in both directions and I wondered how César and Ramón had managed to get through all three with their guns and an unconscious gringo bleeding in the cab of their truck. Then I remembered the vehicle pass César had gotten from the general. The soldiers probably hadn't even stopped them.

"What address?" the cabbie asked as we rolled into San Cristóbal.

I gave him the address of El Acuario. I'd been trying to formulate a plan ever since we'd left the airport, but I hadn't come up with much beyond arming myself.

I told the driver to wait. The door of El Acuario was locked, but I had my key. I had half expected to find Félix working, but I knew he didn't have a key, so when none of the rest of us showed up, he probably figured Antonio had decided to give everyone a day off. It was a weird thought to have at that moment, but it occurred to me Félix didn't know he was out of a job. That thought combined with the hum of the fish tank filter and the empty stillness of El Acuario brought home the full reality that Antonio was dead. I forced myself to believe Maria was not.

A pang of dread went through me the moment I touched the handle of the desk drawer in Antonio's office. What if Antonio had gotten rid of the pistol or had taken it home when the conflict started? I didn't know what I was going to do if he had. But he hadn't. The revolver was right where I'd last seen it the day he'd given me the shopping list to take to Maria. God, that day seemed like years ago, not months.

I picked it up and the weight of the gun made me realize I

didn't know how to use it, not really. Despite having seen thousands of gunfights in movies and on TV, I'd only fired a .22-caliber rifle at camp one summer when I was fifteen. Other than that, the only guns I'd ever touched were those César and Ramón had shown me.

I remembered how César had shown me to check to see if the gun was loaded. It was. I removed the bullets, put them on the desk, and snapped the cylinder back into place. Even unloaded, the gun made me nervous.

With two hands, I raised it at arm's length, sighted the barrel at the middle of a fish painting on the wall, and squeezed the trigger. It took more force than I'd imagined, but I watched the hammer draw slowly back. I blinked when it snapped forward. I went through the exercise seven or eight more times and then practiced manually cocking the gun and firing. I tried holding the gun in one hand but decided on using two.

Then I reloaded it, put the revolver on the desk, and tossed the other drawers for any extra money that I could find. Antonio wouldn't need it. I found a thousand pesos in the cash box. I stuffed the money in my pocket and reached for the pistol. I hesitated. Could I really do what I was about to do? I picked it up. This was the choice. I was choosing. I wrapped it in a dish towel that I took from behind the bar and went out to the taxi.

I gave the cabbie directions to César's house and had him drop me at the corner down the street from the gate to the compound. The taxi pulled away and I made my way down the sidewalk. At the gate I strained to hear any sound coming from the other side. There weren't any sounds, but that didn't mean anything.

I waited until a woman walked past me before I unwrapped the towel from the revolver. I took my sunglasses off and put them in my pocket. The key slid into the lock. The quiet turning of the bolt was the loudest noise I'd ever heard. I opened the door

341

a fraction of an inch, almost sure César and company would be waiting on the other side.

Ramón's pickup was parked in its usual spot next to one of the white trucks. The third truck was missing. The courtyard was empty and quiet. Then I heard occasional muffled shouts coming from the main house. Running in a crouch, I crossed to the pickups. As always, Ramón had left his keys on the seat. I grabbed the keys and crept toward the front door and the rough cheers and occasional shouts coming from within. They sounded like drunk crowds at a fútbol game. Then I saw the remains of Antonio and Salvador. I didn't look twice. I didn't need to. I will remember what I saw there as long as I live.

I went through the kitchen door. The noise was coming from the game room. I slipped past the staircase and the dining room and through living room and den. Someone shouted something, and they laughed, and I heard the familiar crack of a ball against wood. How could someone be playing foosball? I peeked through the gap where the open door was hinged to the doorframe. César and Ramón were there, bent to a game. It seemed so weird to see them doing such an ordinary thing, something I had done with César so many times, that for a brief instant I almost thought I might call next game like nothing had happened. It had happened, though, and there they were playing a game of fucking table soccer. Where was Maria? Suddenly I wondered if maybe they had let her go.

Then César, without turning his focus from the game, said, "Don't worry, mamacita, just two more goals and I'll give you some more attention."

That's when I saw her. She was huddled in the corner across the room, her bare knees pulled to her chest, my view partly obscured by the billiard table. I couldn't see her face, but she didn't move when he spoke to her.

I didn't see Miguel or Luis. Ramón's shotgun was on the bar. So were some other guns. I couldn't tell if they had any weapons on them, but I wasn't going to let Ramón get to that shotgun. They were so involved in the game that neither of them noticed I was in the room until I stood between them and the bar, the revolver cocked and held at arm's length. It was Ramón who saw me first and César, not realizing Ramón had stopped playing, scored. "Goooooooooal!" he cheered and then broke off his celebration in the next moment as he looked at Ramón's face and then followed his gaze.

"Compadre." César sighed, shaking his head as he turned to face me. "What did I tell you would happen—"

"Shut up," I snapped and pointed the gun at him. "Where are Miguel and Luis?"

"Right behind you," César said and I startled and glanced over my shoulder. There was no one there, but I had just shown César how jumpy I was. He laughed. In the brief moment César had distracted me, Ramón had taken a step around the table, but he was frozen again now that my concentration and pistol were directly on them. "Relax. I sent Miguel and Luis to see the general to get some body bags for your friends outside. But don't worry. They'll be back any time now."

"Maria," I said, "come over here." I didn't take my eyes off them, but I didn't see Maria moving. "Maria," I said again. "Can you hear me? Get up, baby."

Then Maria did get up, but slowly. Her blouse was torn. She was naked below the waist. Ramón took a step as if to block her path. "No te muevas," I said and turned the revolver directly on him. He paused, as if calculating my commitment, and then stepped back. "Maria, come here," I said. She walked slowly, unsteadily, like she was drunk. I didn't lose focus on César or Ramón.

"What are you doing, compadre? Put the gun down. We'll

play some foosball," César said. He sounded so casual. "Come on, compadre. What do you want to point a gun at me for?" I could see César's calmness was giving Ramón confidence.

"No tiene los cojones," Ramón said.

"I don't know," César said. He tilted his head to one side as if to evaluate my resolve from another angle. "Do you have the cojones, compadre?"

"There's one way to find out." My voice didn't sound as confident as I'd intended.

As Maria passed Ramón, he shoved her in my direction and both he and César rushed me and everything unfolded in one fluid motion and I pushed her behind me toward the bar and pulled the trigger twice before Ramón tackled me. We tumbled across the floor, grabbing at one another and wrestling. He got the upper hand and was on top of me and punching me in the face. I don't know how many times he'd hit me when his body was thrown off as if by some invisible hand. I scrambled for the revolver before my mind had registered what had happened. Ramón was dead on the floor, the top half of his head simply gone, sprayed across the room and the green felt of the pool table. Maria held the shotgun that Ramón had left on the bar. César lay propped against the foosball table where he'd fallen when I'd shot him. He was trying to catch his breath like he'd had the wind knocked out of him. His hands clutched at his abdomen. There was blood.

"Jesus, compadre," César said, practically laughing in disbelief until he was overcome with a fit of coughing that brought blood to his lips. "Jesus!"

I didn't know what to say. I just stood there, my gun aimed at César. Then Maria was standing next to me, Ramón's shotgun pointed at César. I thought she might speak, but she said nothing and pulled the trigger. Nothing happened. She'd unloaded both barrels on Ramón.

"Maria," I said, putting my hand on the barrel. That's when I saw her face, her eyes. They were black and blue and swollen, but it was what I saw in them that scared me. I don't have the vocabulary for what I saw there. There aren't words for that. "It's okay," I said, and something deflated in her. She seemed to shrink, to literally grow smaller, and she loosened her grip and let me take it.

"That's right, mamacita," César said to her, a grin on his face unlike any other I'd ever seen. "You can't kill me. You know you liked it too much."

I looked at him and stepped forward and cocked the hammer of the revolver and pointed it at César's forehead. He didn't flinch or blink. He stared right back at me. And I knew I couldn't do it. He knew it too. After a moment, I backed away and set the shotgun down just long enough to take the three other pistols from the bar and tuck them into my waistband.

"Don't you dare leave me here," César said.

I said nothing and picked up the shotgun and moved toward the sofa and took the blanket and wrapped Maria in it and then moved her toward the door, careful not to step in the ever-expanding pool of blood around Ramón.

"That's right, compadre," César said before breaking into another coughing fit. He wiped the blood from his lips with the back of his hand. He hadn't stopped looking at me. I could see the anger building in his eyes. "You'd better run because I'm going to scour the earth for you and that bitch."

I put the blanket over Maria's shoulders. "Let's go," I said to her. She seemed to be elsewhere, oblivious, but she moved when I gave her a gentle nudge with my forearm.

"Compadre," César called when we had reached the door. I looked at him one last time.

"Fuck you," he said. I turned to go and he said, "I hate you and I'm glad Jenn died."

I looked at him. He was smiling.

"That's right. I'm glad that cunt is dead." He was smiling and smiling. "Your little girl too."

Then something like lightning jolted through me, like everything inside me flashed electric white. I took three or four deliberate strides toward him, levered back the hammer, and, without another thought or hesitation, shot my best friend in the face.

32

I DON'T EVEN REMEMBER moving through the house. It was like we were in the room with César and then we were outside, but in the courtyard everything seemed to slow down. I dumped the shotgun and extra pistols into the bed of Ramón's pickup and helped get Maria into the cab. I crossed the courtyard to open the gate. The damn thing wouldn't open and Miguel and Luis were going to show up and we were going to be dead. But then the gate was open and I ran back across the courtyard and got in the truck and we weren't dead. I fired it up and hauled ass. Just as we careened onto the street, I thought for sure we'd run straight into Miguel's truck. We didn't. I thought the same thing at each intersection. It didn't seem possible we wouldn't run into them. I drove to our apartment.

We pulled up to the curb and I jumped out. I didn't want to leave Maria in the truck, but one look at her and it was clear she wasn't getting out. I left her there with the engine idling and ran upstairs and grabbed the bags we'd packed the day before, double-checking to make sure I had the bag with Maria and Luz's passports. I stopped at Doña Asunta's apartment. She finally opened the door and I burst past her, grabbed Luz, and dashed back down the stairs, calling thanks over my shoulder as I went. I shoved Luz into the cab with Maria and tossed the bags into the bed of the pickup and we were off. Luz looked at her mother and I thought she might cry. I told her to keep her mouth shut. I don't know if it was the tone of my voice or what, but she fell silent.

It wasn't until we were outside the city limits that I began to believe we'd actually escape without running into César's friends. I pulled over and threw all the guns into a gully off the side of the road. I hesitated when I went to toss the last pistol, but I finally pitched it. We didn't need to be stopped with a truckload of weapons when we went through the military checkpoints and a single pistol wasn't going to do me much good. As it turned out, I didn't need to worry. Thanks to the pass that César had gotten from his friend the general, we didn't have any problems. The soldiers saw it hanging from the rearview mirror and just waved us through, no stopping, no questions asked.

Except for the checkpoints, the ride to Tuxtla was a blur. I remember concentrating on driving because now that we were out of immediate danger I was afraid I'd crash the truck. Maria didn't say anything. She stared blankly straight out the windshield the whole way. I talked a lot. I don't remember exactly what I said. I think I just kept telling Maria and Luz that everything would be okay. I don't know if I was saying it for their benefit or mine.

The sun was going down by the time we reached the airport. In the parking lot, I had to help Maria put on panties and a pair of jeans that I took from her luggage. I made her wrap her head in a scarf and put on my airport sunglasses to hide her black eyes. My head was killing me. The pounding had been there the whole time, but now it had moved to the front and it felt like someone was hammering on the inside of my skull. I slipped Maria's feet into a pair of sneakers and tied the laces. Luz was wide-eyed, but she didn't say anything and she got out of the truck when I told her to and stood by the tailgate. I checked my own reflection in the side mirror on the door. We were quite a threesome, Luz with her helmet and Maria and I looking in need of helmets. César had left his Cruz Azul baseball cap on the dash and I put it on and pulled the bill down as far as I could before marshaling the girls into the terminal.

It felt strange to be back in the airport. I went back to the same stall where I'd bought the sunglasses and bought another pair. It was the same clerk and he gave me a look like he was having a *Groundhog Day* kind of moment. Still, he didn't say anything. The woman at the ticket counter seemed to take forever to process the sale and check us in. She took so long that I began to think she was keeping us waiting so one of César's police connections could grab us, but then she was done and smiled and wished us a pleasant trip.

At the security gate, one cop seemed to take a particular interest in us, so I made a point of asking him in English if he could direct us to our gate. The difficulties with the language barrier flummoxed him enough that he forgot his suspicions. When he finally understood what I was asking, he pointed us to the gate, happy to be of help and relieved to be rid of us. Thirty-five minutes later, our Aero Mexico jet took off for Mexico City.

Because Maria and Luz didn't have visas, we took a taxi to a hotel on the Plaza Grande. Our hotel window looked directly across to the Palacio Nacional. César had been in one of the rooms in that building the night the Zapatistas appeared in San Cristóbal, the night that changed our friendship. I don't know why exactly, but it was an unsettling thought.

By the time we'd arrived at the hotel, Maria still hadn't said anything besides simple yes or no responses to the few questions I'd asked, and when we got into the room, she went into the bathroom and shut the door and took a long, long shower while I put Luz to bed. Luz didn't give me any trouble. She had clearly sensed something was really wrong because she'd been remarkably quiet through the whole trip, but she'd eaten food on the plane and was tired, so she went to sleep without any fuss or questions. I ordered room service, chain-smoked a couple of cigarettes, and stared at the paisley bedspread. Maria was still in the shower when the food arrived. I tipped the guy and then went into the bathroom to check on her. She'd rubbed her skin raw and was curled up on the shower floor, rocking herself in her arms. I turned off the water, climbed into the shower, and held her. We were like that for a long time.

The following morning we went to the US embassy to get visas. The embassy wouldn't issue them. Because of all the illegal immigrants, INS won't issue tourist visas to Mexicans unless you can show evidence that you don't intend to stay in the United States. Immigration wants to see proof of property and employment. Of course we lied and said she had a house and a job, but without paperwork to back up the lie, our claims didn't mean much. I cussed and swore and harangued and pleaded and got nowhere. Then one of the embassy officials asked me about our bruises. It was the way he asked, the investigative tone of his voice, that suddenly made me realize we didn't need visas. Visas weren't going to solve our problems. We were on the run and we always would be. "We were in a motorcycle accident," I said. "We'll come back with the proper documentation." He looked at me. He was memorizing my face. So were all the cameras. "Thanks for your help," I said and hustled us out of there.

There was nowhere for us to go where Señor Lobos de Madrid couldn't use his political connections and wealth to have us arrested. We were fugitives whether it was on this side of the border or the other and I began to wonder if it wouldn't be easier to hide in Mexico than in the US, where law enforcement is so plugged in. If we were caught in the States, we'd be extradited. We needed to disappear, to change our identities and drop off the grid. So that's what we did.

We stayed in Mexico City for a couple of days while I worked to get the remaining money from the sale of our house wired from my bank in Colorado. It took some time to process, but everything went more smoothly than I had hoped it might. Each time I went back into the bank to see if the transaction had gone through, I expected to find the police waiting, but the powers that be evidently hadn't set the bloodhounds on us yet. The Banamex bank manager was a little upset when the wire went through and I promptly said I wanted to close the account to which I'd had the money deposited.

And that was it. I sent a letter to my parents that said I was sorry and good-bye, and then we went underground. Maybe we stayed in Mexico City, or maybe we didn't. I won't even promise we stayed in Mexico. It is plenty easy to enter the United States illegally from Mexico, so maybe that is what we did. It's even easier crossing into Guatemala and El Salvador. Argentina and Venezuela and Chile, I'm told, have lots of places where a family of three can be inconspicuous too. Disappearing wasn't the hard part. We're always looking over our shoulders and probably always will be, but no, disappearing wasn't the hard part. Maria and I changed our looks. Nothing drastic, but enough. We bought new identities. We found a place to be and we like where we live—the house we rent, the park nearby with the playsets, the neighborhood stores. The weather is good and people are pleasant, pleasant but not inquisitive. Maria has made some friends at her church. There's a river not far from the house where I like to walk to be alone, something I never wanted or needed before.

Tomorrow will mark eight months since I killed César and as I walk beside the river now, watching the riffles of water and feeling the sun on my shoulders, I'm not sure how that's possible. I replay that moment in my mind over and over and it feels like it was yesterday. I didn't just kill him. I murdered him. It doesn't seem real, but I did. I murdered him. He was defenseless and I shot him in the face. Maria and I don't talk about it much, but we did once and she told me he deserved it. Maybe he did. Not maybe. He did. But not from me.

Often I wake up at night and pace the house. It's not like I'm angry. I mean, I'm plenty angry—angry at myself, angry about what I did, angry at César for making me do it—but that's not what gets me up. It's confusion about what I'm supposed to do now. It's like there's no way to atone for what I've done, no way to restart my life, no way to do something for the greater good. That's not it, not exactly. I pace the house.

Maria understands. In fact, that's probably the basis of our love now, that understanding. Love. Can we even call it that? It's so different from what I had with Jenn. Jenn and I were always laughing and doing things and having fun. We shared joy, the joy of each other, of Suzy, of ordinary and day-to-day things. We shared adventures, but the kind where there's no real danger. Well, no danger until that day on the river. But up to that day we shared the joy that comes with the promise of tomorrow. We were so in love that I don't think we believed anything could touch it. We believed it was forever. Maria and I don't have that. What we share isn't joy.

I bought her a piano, but she doesn't play it. She's never played a single note that I've heard. I caught her sitting at it one time though, just staring blankly at the keys. There was so much sadness and remorse on her face that I felt like I was looking at the reflection of my soul, the loss and sorrow inside me. That's what we have, that sharing of loss and sorrow—the loss of the people we loved, the loss of the lives we might have lived and the people we might have been, the sorrow for what we have done or have failed to do, the sorrow of who we've become. Actually, there are times when I kind of wish I could ask César what he thinks I should do. But what could he tell me? What advice could anyone give? What's done is done and I can't take it back. I'm not even sure I would if I could. So I just try to be present for Maria and Luz.

Speaking of Luz—she saw a specialist about six months ago. I met this gringo doctor who had spent his entire career working with epileptics before he lost his medical license for selling prescriptions for painkillers. He offered to take a look at Luz and recommended putting her on a new medication. She hasn't had a single episode since then, but she still wears her helmet outside the home. He said, "She'll probably continue to experience the epileptic aura and it may even seem that they're happening more frequently as she get older, but she'll just be recognizing it more as she matures and is able to differentiate between what's normal and what's not." I asked him what he meant by aura and he explained that auras are seizures as well, but not with all the convulsing. He listed different symptoms like dizziness or a headache or a queasy stomach and I thought about Luz saying something about a funny smell just before her attack. He said she might have a profound sense of déjà vu or jamais vu.

"I know what déjà vu is," I said, "but what's jamais vu?"

"In jamais vu, an experience feels like it's happening for the first time even though the experience is a familiar one."

"I don't understand."

"Like in that Talking Heads song, you know, the one where he sings, 'This is not my beautiful house. This is not my beautiful wife.' It's like that."

"Oh," I said. The ceiling light glinted off the ballpoint pen clipped to the pocket of his Hawaiian shirt. What I didn't say was my whole life feels like jamais vu. What I didn't say was every hour of every day I ask myself, "My god, what have I done?"

At least Luz has made a quick adjustment. Little kids are like that, I guess. Already she has lots of friends at her preschool. Sometimes she asks about her father and we just say he's on a trip. We don't know what else to say and she's still too young to understand. One of these days we'll have to tell her. But Luz likes where we live. She likes her room in our house. She likes school. She likes her friends. What she likes most right now is that she's going to have a new baby brother.

That's the big news. It happened that day. You know the one. I wasn't positive until I brought up the option of abortion. Maria became hysterical, absolutely flipped out, screaming that I was a horrible person for even doubting the baby was ours. She screamed and cried and smashed a bunch of plates and for a moment when she picked up a knife from the kitchen counter and had this look in her eye, I thought she might do something really crazy, but then she suddenly calmed down and put the knife in the sink and said it was our baby. She said she didn't believe in abortion, called it a sin, said she'd sinned enough and whatever happened it wasn't the baby's fault. And that was the moment I knew it wasn't ours. I'd known before because I'd known the due date and how much time had passed between the attack and the next time she and I had been together and I could do the math, but it was in that moment in the kitchen when I really knew. That also was the moment I realized that she knew and had known all along it wasn't ours and that she was going to carry it to term out of some irrational and deep-seated guilt that this is what she deserved. I recognized the feeling. I still do.

I find myself wondering what the baby will look like and hoping it gets more of Maria's traits than César's, but I'm not fooling myself. Even if the child gets all of Maria's looks, it'll still get those trademark Lobos de Madrid eyes. I'll see my friend every time the kid turns to me. I know it the same way I knew it was a boy before the ultrasound. Call it intuition. Call it fate. Call it justice. It doesn't matter what you call it. I'll see my friend's eyes and in them I'll see what I've done. For some actions, there is no atonement, not in this life or in any other. But if I can raise César's son, if I can do that one decent thing, maybe I can get back some small piece of who I was, of who I thought I was and who I wanted to be. I don't know if I can do it, but I'm going to try. I don't mean try. I'll do more than try. That's what I tell myself. I tell myself: I can love this boy. We were compadres, César and I, and that's what compadres do. That's what I tell myself.

And that's what I think about when I come down here through the reeds to this river. It's what I think about when I walk along its muddy banks and climb the slopes of its levies. It's what I think about when I walk out onto the abandoned railroad trestle and look down into the water. The river is swollen now, swollen but clear. Its waters are deep and rush over a bed of smooth, dark stones. The current is strong. The water rushes. Upon its calm surface the river reflects the sky. The sky is clouded, shrouded, gunmetal gray. The water holds the reflection of the sky and the shadow of the trestle. It holds the shadow of the trestle and the man upon it. The water rushes. There are no features in the shadow it holds, no features save the clear darkness of the smooth stones. The water holds his shadow and the stones and the rushing. The water holds the darkness and it holds the man. The water.

ACKNOWLEDGMENTS

THIS BOOK HAS BEEN a long time in the making and many people who helped shape it along the way to its present form deserve mention. First, I'd like to thank my parents for their early and uncompromising encouragement to follow my dreams, even when those dreams were not as practical as parents might sometimes hope. The value of your support has been immeasurable. I'd also like to thank Jonathan Selwood, who was the catalyst for our adventure into Mexico and who was with me the first time I arrived in San Cristóbal de Las Casas in 1993, a trip that changed the course of my life and planted the seed for this book.

A todos mis amigos en México, a aquellos que estuvieron a mi alrededor en el tiempo en que la historia se desarrolla y aquellos que estuvieron junto a mi durante la creación del primer manuscrito, merecen mi reconocimiento. Ellos son demasiados para nombrarlos uno a uno, pero les doy gracias a cada uno de ustedes. Desde luego quiero darle gracias a la familia de mi esposa por todo lo que me han enseñado acerca de su cultura y por todo lo compartido, por aceptarme como uno más y hacerme sentir que México es mi segundo país. Gracias a todos ustedes.

I'd like to give a hug and big thanks to my brother, Stephen Spurgeon, who was my daily sounding board during the writing of the first draft and who is the best brother a man could hope for.

357

Many people read various versions of the book and offered comments. In particular I'd like to thank Erik Beckett, Barbara Braun, David Dominguez, Karen Haas, Pam Houston, Jonathan Morken, Jefferson Pitcher, Daniel Rounds, and Eric Sohn. Your feedback was useful and is much appreciated. Thanks to everyone at Ad Lumen, particularly the Editorial Committee: Lois Ann Abraham, Michael Angelone, Karen Burchett, and Tammy Montgomery. Your comments helped a great deal in shaping the final form. Thanks to Tim Michels for his design efforts and Don Reid for his beautiful typesetting. Thanks also to Claire Davis, Betsy Harper, and Miranda Ottewell for their careful eyes and copyediting skills.

I'd like to thank Holden and Catherine Spurgeon for their opinions about the title and cover design and for their understanding when my attention sometimes went to the book and not to them.

Elizabeth, who knows where the lines of truth and fiction are drawn in this book and who gave me advice about characters and plot and who double-checked my Spanish, thank you my love. I also thank you for putting up with all my manic behavior during the writing of this novel. I was not always easy to live with, so your patience and your willingness to give me the space I needed to practice my art makes me truly grateful.

Finally, I'd like to thank my good friend and editor, Christian Kiefer, who fought for and believed in this book and my abilities even when it seemed beyond all reason to do so. Without you as its champion, this story would still be a stack of manuscript pages in the back of some drawer. Thank you for all you have done to bring it to the light of day and into the hands of whoever now is reading these words. Thank you.

About the Author

Michael Spurgeon was residing in San Cristóbal de las Casas at the time of the Zapatista uprising. He and his wife and their two children currently live in Sacramento, California, where he is a tenured professor of English at American River College. Visit him at www.michaelspurgeon.com.

AD LUMEN PRESS
American River College

Housed at American River College, Ad Lumen is a small press devoted to publishing works of high artistic and/or literary value that reflect the diverse nature of our college's faculty, staff, students, district, community, and region.

On the Typeface

This book is set in Adobe Caslon Pro, a typeface based on the work of William Caslon, who developed his first typefaces in 1722. Caslon based his types on seventeenth-century Dutch type styles, which were popular in English typesetting at the time. Caslon's designs were immediately popular throughout Europe and America and were used extensively by printer Benjamin Franklin. The first printings of the United States Declaration of Independence and the Constitution were set in Caslon. Type designer Carol Twombly has updated this typeface for modern usage.